Clive Egleton brings years of experience in the Intelligence and Counter Espionage fields to his enthralling novels of suspense. Widely regarded as one of Britain's leading thriller writers, he is the author of twenty-eight highly acclaimed novels, most recently *The Honey Trap*. He lives in the Isle of Wight.

ONE MAN RUNNING

Trying to live as a civilian with his wife and young children in hiding, former SIS agent Peter Ashton finds himself once again thrown into the front line when his old home is blown up. Threatened by his past, Ashton determines that the safest guard for his family is himself. Meanwhile, an assassination in Russia leaves an old friend running from the Mafiozniki. With a price on her head and nowhere to go, she is desperate for Ashton's help. With no protection from SIS and all his contacts denying they've ever heard of him, Ashton is only one step ahead of the IRA terrorists who are out to retire him for good.

A Peter Ashton thriller.

Books by Clive Egleton
Published by The House of Ulverscroft:

CLIVE EGLETON

ONE MAN RUNNING

Complete and Unabridged

CHARNWOOD
Leicester

First published in Great Britain in 2001 by
Hodder and Stoughton
London

First Charnwood Edition
published 2002
by arrangement with
Hodder and Stoughton
a division of
Hodder Headline
London

British Library CIP Data

Egleton, Clive, 1927 –
One man running.—Large print ed.—
Charnwood library series
1. Ashton, Peter (Fictitious character)—Fiction
2. Spy stories
3. Large type books
I. Title
823.9'14 [F]

ISBN 0–7089–9383–4

Published by
F. A. Thorpe (Publishing)
Anstey, Leicestershire

Set by Words & Graphics Ltd.
Anstey, Leicestershire
Printed and bound in Great Britain by
T. J. International Ltd., Padstow, Cornwall

This book is printed on acid-free paper

This book is for
Peter and Margaret Ashman

1

Harvey Littlewood had joined Mitchell and Webb after leaving school at sixteen without any academic qualifications. Twenty-two years later he was still without any qualifications but there wasn't much he didn't know about the real estate business. Along the way he had also become something of a psychologist and was particularly adept at sizing people up. It was his proud boast that within minutes he could tell whether a prospective buyer was really interested in the property on offer or was merely going through the motions — like Mrs Julie Carmichael was now. Although she hadn't expressed any reservations about the property as yet, she had gone out of her way to give the impression that the asking price would not be a problem, which was invariably a bad sign.

According to Julie Carmichael, husband Simon was a hotshot insurance broker who had been making 60K a year up in Newcastle. Now that he had been moved south to head up the London office his basic salary was set to double. As for herself, she had been the personal assistant to the MD of Northern Rock Promotions and was confident she would have little difficulty in finding a similar well-paid job in London.

'We haven't got to wait for a prospective buyer either,' Julie smiled. 'As it happens we've already exchanged contracts on our four-bedroom house in Newcastle.'

'That will speed things up, should you decide to buy.'

'The garden is a bit of a jungle.'

Here we go, Littlewood thought. 'We can get a contractor in to tidy things up,' he said. 'Shouldn't cost more than two hundred and I think we can prevail upon the vendor to reduce the asking price accordingly.'

'There's no garage.'

'The vendor never had any trouble parking outside the house. Of course, he hardly ever used his car. Still, you could always root up the front garden and concrete it over to make a hard standing.'

'How far did you say the station was from here?' Julie asked.

'No more than a ten-minute walk,' Littlewood told her. 'You take the alleyway past the Royal Masonic Hospital and cut through Ravenscourt Park.'

'Oh, right.' Julie Carmichael glanced at her wristwatch, wondered out loud what could be keeping her husband, then dipped into her shoulder bag and took out a mobile phone. 'Simon was supposed to ring me if he couldn't get away from the office,' she added.

There was no way Littlewood could listen to what her husband would say to her, but it wasn't necessary to overhear both sides of their conversation. The estate agent was prepared to bet his shirt she would inform him that regrettably hubby had been detained and they would therefore have to arrange another date to view the property, and that would be the last he saw of the Carmichaels.

'Simon reckons he will be with us in five minutes.' Julie switched off the phone and tucked it away in her shoulder bag. 'Seems there has been some sort of hold-up on the District Line.'

The phone call didn't change Littlewood's opinion; he was still convinced the Carmichaels weren't really interested in acquiring the semi-detached in Rylett Close. Nevertheless he was quite happy to wait for the other half to put in an appearance. After all, it wasn't as if there was a mountain of work to deal with back at the office, and it pleased him to spend time in the company of a very attractive young woman. Julie Carmichael was definitely easy on the eye — petite, slender, dark shoulder-length hair framing a pert-looking face with the bluest eyes he'd ever encountered. Although he was the first to admit he was no good at judging a woman's age, he couldn't see how she could be much older than her mid-twenties.

'Who said let the train take the strain?' she asked with a lopsided smile.

'Probably some politician who goes to work in a chauffeur-driven car.'

'Tell me something, Mr Littlewood, why did the Durkins leave their furniture behind when they moved house?'

'Actually the name is Durban. Their idea was to let the property fully furnished on a six-month lease in the absence of a firm offer by the end of July.'

'In other words a fortnight from now?'

'Yes. Needless to say, should you decide to buy, the furniture will, of course, be removed the moment the contracts are exchanged. We'll also get somebody in to clean the place from top to bottom.' Littlewood smiled. 'At no expense to you,' he added.

'Fair dos.'

Julie didn't like the house but lacked the nerve to tell him so. She was counting the minutes until Simon arrived to rescue her from a situation she couldn't handle. Fortunately she didn't have long to wait.

In no way did Simon Carmichael resemble the mental image Littlewood had formed of him. He had presumed the insurance broker would be equally good-looking as his wife but clearly the relationship between the couple had been founded on the attraction of opposites. Simon Carmichael was an inch or so taller and at least twenty pounds the heavier of the two. Dark hair, clipped short enough to reveal the scalp, crowned a narrow face with slate-grey eyes and thin lips. Blessed with a brusque manner and lacking any kind of charisma, he was not the sort of man Littlewood could warm to. Leaving his executive briefcase on the hall table, Carmichael gave him a limp handshake and immediately asked his wife what she thought of the house.

'I think it will do us,' Julie told him.

'The question is, do you like it?'

'Yes. It's certainly nicer than other places we've looked at.'

'I think I'd better see it for myself. That OK with you, Mr Littlewood?'

'Yes, of course.'

'Right, let's start with the rooms upstairs.'

Carmichael began with the bathroom and the lavatory, then moved on to the double bedroom overlooking the back garden. Aware of its unkempt appearance Littlewood felt compelled to draw his attention to the fact that the house had been kept in a good state of repair by the present owners.

'When was it built?'

'Almost eighty-four years ago. Back in 1912 the first owner paid three hundred and fifty pounds for the property; in 1988 it changed hands at a cool two hundred thousand.'

'And now it's on offer at a hundred and eighty K. Why is that?'

'The bottom dropped out of the housing market in '91, interest rates rose to record levels and the economy went from boom to bust. This place was repossessed by the building society when the young couple who'd purchased it on a hundred per cent mortgage fell seriously into arrears with their repayments. I understand both of them had been made redundant. Anyway, the Durbans purchased the house for a mere sixty-five thousand a few months later.'

'And now they're looking to make a quick buck,' Carmichael said scathingly.

'The housing market is on the way up again. Mark my words, this time next year 84 Rylett

5

Close will change hands at a cool three hundred thou.'

'Offer them one sixty.'

'What?' Completely taken aback, Littlewood felt his jaw drop and closed it hurriedly. 'Are you serious?' he asked.

'You want proof of my intention?' Carmichael reached inside his jacket and produced a cheque book. 'How about a deposit of two thousand? Would that convince you?'

'Absolutely.'

'Good. Let's go downstairs and sign up.'

The cheque for two thousand was made payable to Mitchell and Webb and was drawn on the Grey Street branch of Lloyds Bank, Newcastle upon Tyne. Carmichael wanted it clearly understood that the deal was entirely dependent on a favourable report by the surveyor he proposed to engage. He also asked for the name and address of the solicitor who would be representing the Durbans.

'I'm in a hurry to move into a place of our own,' Carmichael said by way of an explanation. 'I'm tired of living out of a suitcase.'

'So long as you don't cut any corners,' Julie said.

'What's that supposed to mean?'

'This is an old house, Simon. When I was in the kitchen just now I thought I could smell gas.'

'I didn't notice it earlier on,' Littlewood said, and was immediately conscious of sounding defensive.

'I'm not surprised, my wife has a vivid imagination.'

'And you have no sense of smell,' Julie countered. 'I remember the time I had to tell you your jacket was on fire after you'd shoved a lighted pipe into one of the pockets.'

Husband and wife at each other's throats and an unexpected sale about to go down the toilet. That was just dandy. Littlewood coughed politely.

'Why don't we satisfy ourselves there isn't a gas leak?' he suggested diplomatically.

'Yeah, why don't we?' Carmichael said tersely.

There was no smell of gas in the kitchen or elsewhere in the house, which was enough for Julie to concede that she had been mistaken.

At eighteen minutes past three, some two hours after Littlewood and the Carmichaels had departed, an explosion ripped through 84 Rylett Close, demolishing all the rooms at the back of the house and starting a fire which rapidly spread to the rest of the semi-detached.

★   ★   ★

Had they been asked, few of the desk officers and support staff at Vauxhall Cross would have had a good word to say for Roy Kelso, the Assistant Director in charge of the Administrative Wing. As such, he was responsible for courses, internal audits, expenses, departmental budgets, control of expenditure and Boards of Inquiry. His empire included the Financial Branch, the Motor Transport and General Stores Section plus the Security Vetting and Technical Services Division. To run such a diverse and

7

compartmentalised department required a sense of humour, an attribute which Kelso sadly lacked. He was fifty-five, tired, disappointed, embittered and small-minded, qualities which were not calculated to endear him to his subordinates.

Kelso had been promoted to Assistant Director a week after his thirty-ninth birthday. Despite the fact that he had always been in the Admin Wing of the Secret Intelligence Service and had never held an operational appointment, he had convinced himself that he was destined to go right to the top of the tree. It had taken him all of ten years to realise that he had reached his ceiling and wasn't going anywhere. The passage of time hadn't made it any easier for him to accept this fact of life, especially when he was obliged to consult Jill Sheridan, the Deputy Director General of the SIS. He could not forget that she was seventeen years his junior and had been a probationary grade III intelligence officer when he had already been a head of department for eighteen months. Worse still, following an internal reorganisation, she was now his immediate superior officer.

Leaving the cubbyhole he'd just acquired on the top floor, Kelso walked down the corridor towards Jill's office, which enjoyed a commanding view of the Houses of Parliament across the river. Anyone who wanted to see the Deputy DG customarily went through the PA, a convention which Kelso habitually ignored in order to bolster his self-esteem. He simply walked straight into her office, though out of politeness he did

8

tap on the door first.

'Can you spare me a few minutes?' he asked.

'Provided it is important, Roy,' Jill said, without looking up from the file she was reading.

'I've just heard that 84 Rylett Close has been gutted by fire.'

He had her complete attention now and with good reason. Four years ago he had purchased the semi-detached for the SIS for use as a safe house. Barely eleven months later the Treasury had instructed the SIS and other government ministries to reduce their housing and office stock by fifty per cent as part of an ongoing so-called peace dividend. In order to comply with the directive, Victor Hazelwood, the Director General, had authorised the in-house sale of Rylett Close to Peter Ashton at a knockdown price.

'When did this happen, Roy?'

'Shortly after three-fifteen this afternoon. Some two hours after Littlewood left the house with a Mr and Mrs Carmichael who were thinking of buying the place. There was a loud explosion — '

'Explosion?' Jill's voice rose half an octave.

'Yes, didn't I mention it?' There were, Kelso thought, few things in life to equal the pleasure of putting the wind up Ms Sheridan.

'Any chance this explosion could have been an accident?' Jill asked, gritting her teeth.

'You mean a gas leak? It's too early to say yet. However, Mrs Carmichael thought she had smelled gas in the kitchen. Naturally both

Littlewood and the woman's husband checked for a leak; in fact they went over the entire house. As it happened, they couldn't smell anything and, in the end, Mrs Carmichael agreed she must have imagined it.'

'Where was the epicentre of the blast?'

'Some room at the back of the house,' Kelso told her. 'Probably the kitchen.'

'So it could have been a gas leak?'

'Maybe. Question is, can you afford to believe it?'

Seven weeks ago Ashton had been compelled to give evidence at a coroner's inquest to ascertain the circumstance in which Kevin Hayes of Sandrock Road, Lewisham, had sustained fatal injuries. He had not been granted anonymity and the barrister representing the deceased's family had made the most of it. The coroner had been particularly lenient in allowing him to question Ashton closely about his claim to be a civil servant to the point where there hadn't been a person in court who hadn't concluded he was a spy of some sort. In one brutal afternoon the lawyer had destroyed Ashton's career and forced him and his family to go into hiding.

'If it wasn't an accident, why did they wait so long, Roy?'

'I haven't the foggiest notion.'

'They must have known the Ashtons had moved away from the area. There has been a 'For Sale' sign outside the house for several weeks now.'

'If that's the way you want to play it, Jill, I'll

10

merely send you a brief memorandum and mark the file NFA.'

NFA stood for No Further Action. While Kelso had no time for Ashton, he was damned if he was going to be left holding the baby should anything happen to the man. Unlike Ms Sheridan he didn't have any friends in high places who would bale him out if there was any unpleasantness.

'On second thoughts, I think you had better get on to our police liaison officer at Scotland Yard, Roy. Tell him what has happened and then ask the man to have a word with the Staffordshire Constabulary. It would be helpful if one of their officers from Special Branch called on Peter and warned him to be on his guard. Emphasise that we don't expect them to provide close protection for Ashton. All Peter needs to do is observe the usual precautions, like checking the underside of his car before he uses it.'

'I'll make sure he gets the message.'

'And keep me informed,' Jill said as he was about to leave.

'Concerning what?' Kelso asked, and immediately wished he'd kept his mouth shut.

'Isn't it obvious? I mean surely it must have occurred to you that the police and fire service will try to discover what caused the explosion?'

It was, Kelso reflected, typical of Ms Sheridan that she should be determined to have the last word. Tight-lipped with anger, he turned about and stalked out of the office.

★ ★ ★

11

Hazelwood skimmed through the catalogue produced by the Property Services Agency and then transferred it to the out-tray. It had been suggested that he might like to change the paintings in his office but those pictures which did appeal to him were already out on loan, according to the addendum clipped to the back page. The early L. S. Lowry, the Jackson Pollock and Andy Warhol which Jill Sheridan had chosen when she had been appointed Deputy DG were not to his taste, and he suspected it had been the price they would fetch if auctioned at Christie's which had proved the major attraction for her.

Whatever her reasons for choosing them, Hazelwood had no time for paintings which required you to look for some hidden meaning; he preferred something which was instantly recognisable. Art critics might dismiss him as an admirer of the chocolate-box school of painting but there was nothing sentimental about Terence Cuneo's *The Bridge at Arnhem*. The truth was he'd always had a soft spot for the armed forces and the other two services were represented by pictures showing a battered-looking Corvette on a storm-tossed Atlantic entitled *Convoy Escort*, and *Enemy Coast Ahead*, which depicted a vic of three Wellington bombers on a moonlit night approaching a smudge of land on the horizon.

Hazelwood's identification with the armed forces stemmed from his father, a wartime officer in the Queens who had been killed in action at Salerno in 1943 when Hazelwood had been six years old. He had been a toddler when Arthur had joined the army in 1940 and any memories

12

he had of the sleek, dark-haired subaltern in the photograph which his mother had kept on the bedside table had been planted in his mind by her.

Hazelwood himself had been called up for National Service in 1955 and had joined the Parachute Regiment after completing basic infantry training at the Depot of the Royal West Kents. Less than twelve months after joining, he had been commissioned into his father's old regiment, having been awarded the Sword of Honour at his passing-out parade from the Officer Cadet Training Unit, Eaton Hall. By a dint of wangling, he'd managed to join the 2nd Battalion of the Paras and had seen active service in Cyprus. He would have taken part in the Suez Operation had he not broken his right ankle and leg in a practice jump. Medically downgraded, Hazelwood was sent on the long intelligence course simply because Airborne Forces Depot had been allocated a vacancy which had to be filled and nobody else had been available.

The course had been a turning point for Hazelwood. He had gone to the School of Military Intelligence expecting to hate every minute but had come away completely enthralled and knowing what he was going to do in life. All thought of becoming a regular officer had evaporated; on demobilisation he'd studied Russian at London University and in due course had applied to join the Foreign Office.

A faint tap on the communicating door between his office and the PA's prompted Hazelwood to reach for the topmost file in the in-tray. Before he could open it Jill Sheridan appeared.

'I'm not disturbing you, am I, Victor?' she asked as if she had caught him catnapping.

'Of course you aren't,' he said irritably.

'Only both lights are extinguished.'

Two 60-watt bulbs, one coloured red, the other green, were mounted on the transom above the communicating door in the PA's office. They were operated by a two-way switch under Hazelwood's desk; a red light meant he didn't want to be disturbed, the green signified he was free.

'The green one must have blown,' he said.

'Quite. A short time ago Roy Kelso informed me that 84 Rylett Close had been gutted by a fire following an explosion.'

Hazelwood paused in the act of taking a Burma cheroot from the ornate cigar box which he'd purchased on a field trip to India years ago.

'What caused the explosion?'

'We don't know yet. However, action is being taken to warn Ashton.'

'Let's assume it wasn't an accident. How safe is Ashton? I mean, can he be traced?'

'Anything is possible, Victor, if you are prepared to invest the time, money and resources. But if Peter is found it will be due to his carelessness, not some mistake on our part. We gave him and his family a new identity which is fail-safe. Furthermore, their present where-abouts is known only to Roy Kelso, you and me.'

'I don't think we should be too complacent.'

'Nobody wants to be accused of that, least of

all me. What do you suggest we do, Victor?'

'Well, first of all we are not going to wait for the police and fire service to finish sifting through the rubble before taking action. I want you to re-examine the legend we constructed for the Ashtons and see if there are any weaknesses a terrorist might pick up on. Then you'd better start working out a contingency plan in case it's necessary to relocate the family.'

'I doubt if Peter will take kindly to that. You know what he's like; he will start looking for people who want to kill him.'

Hazelwood took a Burma cheroot from the box and lit it. Jill was right, of course; it was the sort of thing Peter would do instinctively. He had entered the SIS by the back door; while reading German and Russian at Nottingham Ashton had joined the University Officers Training Corps, which must have given him a taste for the army. When he was taken on by British Aerospace as a translator-cum-technical author, he had joined 23 Special Air Service Regiment in the Territorial Army. Bored to tears by the work he was doing, Ashton had volunteered for a nine-month tour of duty with the regular army's Special Patrol Unit in Northern Ireland, a move which had cost him his job.

Back in civilian life again, he had found temporary employment teaching Russian to mature students at a night school funded by the London Borough of Camden. Six months into the course the student body had sunk from fifteen men and women to just two. Four weeks later the Argentinians had invaded and captured the Falkland Islands. Still a part-time soldier with 23 SAS, he had volunteered for active duty and travelled south with the task force. As a supernumerary officer with D Squadron of 22 SAS, Ashton had taken part in the raid on Pebble Island when eleven Pucara ground attack aircraft and a fuel dump had been destroyed.

The war over, Ashton had been attracted by the idea of a career in the regular army but there was no permanent officer cadre in the SAS and had he joined an infantry regiment, contemporaries in his age group would have had a minimum of five years seniority over him. The problem of what to do for the rest of his working life had been solved for Ashton by Headquarters Special Forces. A word in the right ear had led to a covert approach by the SIS soon after he returned from the South Atlantic and the rest was history.

'Perhaps you don't agree with me, Victor?'

Hazelwood looked up. 'What did you say?'

'That Ashton will start looking for the people who want to kill him.'

'I've no quarrel with that assumption but Peter can't do it on his own. He will need help.'

'He had friends in Vauxhall Cross,' Jill said meaningfully.

'Like who?'

'Brian Thomas, Head of Security Vetting and Technical Services; he would do anything for Peter. Our ex-detective chief superintendent practically has an open line to the Met. Then there is Terry Hicks, the electronic whiz-kid.'

'So what do you recommend we do, Jill?'

16

'First we should send them two copies of a formal letter warning them to have nothing to do with Ashton under any circumstances. To avoid any possible misunderstanding, they will be required to sign and return the duplicate copy. Secondly, we change their extension numbers because you can bet Peter knows them by heart and it will stop him bypassing the switchboard to come straight through.'

'I don't like it,' Hazelwood growled.

'Neither do I, but we have to isolate Peter for his own good. If we don't there is no way we can protect him, Victor.'

He thought Jill always had a good reason for doing something unpleasant, especially where Ashton was concerned.

'All right, let's do it,' he said reluctantly.

'Will you sign the formal letter to Thomas and Hicks?' she asked. 'I think the warning would carry more weight coming from you.'

And that was another thing about Jill. She was adept at getting other people to do her dirty work.

2

The six-bedroom house was on the south side of Gaia Lane. From the attic room, which was supposedly his office, Ashton enjoyed an unobstructed view of Lichfield Cathedral, The Close, Stowe Pool and St Chad's Cathedral School. Below him in the long rectangular walled garden, two-year-old Edward was busy with a bucket and spade in the sandpit Ashton had made, while Harriet was resting on a sun bed, legs outstretched, her back to the dining room. To her right, fast asleep in the pram was Carolyn, the newest addition to the family, born twelve weeks early and weighing a fraction over three pounds.

Harriet had gone into labour the day after they had arrived in Lichfield and had been rushed to Victoria Hospital in an ambulance. Nobody was taking any chances after Ashton had told the 999 operator that his wife had suffered a miscarriage a little over a year ago when she had been four months pregnant. The first time Ashton had seen his daughter her tiny face had looked like a wrinkled prune and the gynaecologist who'd delivered Carolyn had told him her chances of survival were not good. Minimal had been the word he'd used when Ashton pressed him to be more specific, but Carolyn had proved a lot tougher than the specialist and nursing staff had thought possible. Harriet had been allowed

18

home forty-eight hours after giving birth, while Carolyn had remained in intensive care until she had regained her birth weight and put on a couple of additional pounds. They had collected her last Friday, having already purchased the pram a good fortnight beforehand.

The gynaecologist had wanted to know Harriet's medical history for which he needed the name and address of the GP who had looked after the family before they'd moved to Lichfield.

'I'm worried about Mrs Durban,' he'd told Ashton. 'She's a young woman who seems fit and healthy and yet she has this tendency to miscarry.'

There was, of course, no way the gynaecologist could be permitted to see Harriet's medical records before a duplicate set bearing their new name had been produced by the Admin Wing. It had, however, been safe to tell him that the first miscarriage in June '95 had been the result of a domestic accident where Harriet had fallen downstairs after treading on a drumstick which Edward had left on the landing. As for the premature birth of their baby daughter, Ashton believed it had a lot to do with the inquest and the sudden realisation that the whole family would be at risk unless they moved house.

Not so very long ago, when Harriet had been the bright young officer from MI5, the Security Service, on secondment to the SIS, she would have taken the necessary countermeasures in her stride. Her sangfroid had begun to melt away after she had been caught up in a race riot in the Kreuzberg district of Berlin where the

Gastarbeiters lived. A Turkish worker, believing she was one of the neo-Nazi demonstrators who had been making life hell for the community, had thrown a rock at Harriet which had smashed into her head and fractured the skull. It was, however, the last eighteen months which had really done for her. In that short space of time her mother had committed suicide, she had suffered a miscarriage and her father had succumbed to Alzheimer's.

The phone ringing on the desk to his left dragged Ashton away from the window. A man whose mellifluous voice suggested he had enjoyed an extended lunch several hours ago asked him if he could speak to Mr Durban.

'And who shall I say is calling?' Ashton enquired.

'My name is Caswell, I'm an assistant chief constable.'

'Oh, yes?'

'I can well understand your scepticism, Mr Durban. What I'd like you to do is to look up the number of the constabulary headquarters in your telephone directory and call me back. Will you do that?'

'I don't see why not.' Ashton put the phone down, looked up Police in the business section, then lifted the receiver again and punched out 01785 257717. When the switchboard operator responded he asked for the Assistant Chief Constable.

'My name is Durban,' he added. 'Mr Caswell is expecting my call.'

The Assistant Chief Constable was nothing if

20

not business-like. In a few brief sentences he informed Ashton that a Detective Sergeant Milburn from the Cannock Division would be calling at his house in half an hour's time. He then described his appearance.

'What does he want to see me about?' Ashton asked.

'It's in the nature of a liaison visit,' Caswell told him cheerfully and hung up before he had a chance to question him further.

* * *

The detective sergeant arrived ten minutes earlier than Ashton had been led to expect. Milburn was about five feet eight, had light brown hair parted on the left side and appeared to be in his early thirties. His one notable feature, which Caswell had told Ashton to look out for, was the right eye, which was a shade higher than the left.

'I'm DS Milburn, sir,' he said, and produced his warrant card to prove it. 'I believe Mr Caswell has spoken to you?'

'That he has. You'd best come in.' Ashton stepped aside. 'The sitting room is down the hall, second door on your right.'

Milburn was the polite sort; he waited until Ashton entered the room and waved a hand in the direction of an armchair before he sat down.

'Mr Caswell said this was a liaison visit but I don't believe it. You're Special Branch. Right?'

'Yes, sir.'

'So what's happened in London?'

21

'Your old house in Rylett Close was virtually destroyed this afternoon. Evidently there was some sort of explosion which set the place on fire.'

'Are we talking about a bomb?'

'A gas leak is favourite at the moment.'

'But my firm doesn't think it was. Why else would you be here?'

He wasn't looking to Milburn for confirmation. Of course there hadn't been a bloody gas leak. What was the point of acquiring a safe house which was in danger of blowing up? Before Roy Kelso bought 84 Rylett Close he had had the semi-detached inspected from top to bottom. He had also called in the gas board on the spurious claim that, because the house had been built in 1912, the surveyor had recommended the mains should be looked at.

'The thing is, Mr Durban, we've been told you are in the high-risk category and what I'm saying is you should be on your guard.'

Milburn wanted him to observe all the usual security measures — like checking the underside of the car before turning the key in the ignition and varying his daily routine wherever possible. He should report anyone he saw behaving suspiciously to the police and was to treat every caller at the house with caution.

'We don't have the manpower to give you protection round the clock,' Milburn continued. 'However, if more positive indications of a threat materialise we can look to the West Midlands Force for support.'

'That's comforting to know,' Ashton said drily.

22

'We haven't been told who you are running from, Mr Durban. The betting is that it's some splinter group which has broken away from the Provisional IRA, such as the Irish National Liberation Army.' Milburn reached inside his jacket and produced what at first appeared to be several strips of Polyfotos glued to a sheet of paper. 'This is our rogues gallery,' he said, and passed the snapshots to Ashton.

In all there were five men whose ages probably ranged from mid-twenties to late forties. The one woman looked decidedly masculine.

'Who are these people?' Ashton asked.

'Staunch Republicans, IRA sympathisers; most of the faces are in the building trade or connected with it. According to the National Identification Bureau, none of them has blotted his or her copybook. To our knowledge all they have done is a little fund-raising. They're not your ruthless gunman or bomber, but they would happily assist the IRA any way they could. If it is the Provos who are after you, Mr Durban, they would be willing to spend time tracking you down.'

'Thanks for the tip. I'll be sure to keep my eyes open.'

'Well, if you do spot somebody who even remotely resembles one of those faces phone us straight away.' Milburn got to his feet and moved slowly out into the hall. 'Doesn't matter if it turns out to be a wild-goose chase. Better to be safe than sorry, Mr Durban.'

'My feelings exactly,' Ashton said. 'So how about giving me a firearms certificate?

'You are joking, sir?'

'Actually I was just testing the water.'

Milburn let himself out of the house, then turned about to give Ashton a word of advice. 'About the firearms certificate,' he said, 'at the moment you don't have a strong enough case.'

Ashton watched him drive away, then closed the door and returned to his office in the attic. Milburn had told him very little about the explosion, possibly because he hadn't been given all the facts. However, Brian Thomas, Head of the Security Vetting and Technical Services Division, would have all that at his fingertips. The ex-detective chief superintendent still had a lot of clout with the Met and would have made it his business to find out exactly what had happened when he heard about the incident in Rylett Close.

No time like the present, Ashton thought; lifting the receiver he called Brian Thomas. The number rang out just three times before a familiar voice came on the line. As soon as he had said hello and identified himself, the switchboard operator cut in to inform Ashton he had the wrong number. A loud oscillating screech then made any conversation impossible. Ashton hung up, waited a couple of minutes and tried again, only to have the call intercepted a second time.

'Somebody doesn't like me,' he murmured.

Ashton went downstairs and walked out into the garden. Harriet was still lying on the sunbed, long tanned legs outstretched, eyes hidden behind dark glasses. She looked to be catnapping, which was all to the good because it gave him more time to decide what, if anything, he was going to tell her.

'Who was that on the phone a while back?' Harriet said. 'And don't make out it was a wrong number because you had a visitor shortly afterwards. I heard the doorbell.'

'That was Detective Sergeant Milburn.'

'From Special Branch?'

'Yes.'

Harriet removed her sunglasses the better to see him. 'What's happened?'

'Our old house has been gutted by fire. There was some sort of explosion which set the place ablaze.'

'Are we being targeted, Peter?' she asked quietly.

'It could have been an accident. You know — a gas leak. I mean, we moved out seven weeks ago and the estate agents would have planted a 'For Sale' notice outside the house. Why would somebody try to blow the place up when it's obvious we're no longer there?'

'I don't know, Peter, but clearly somebody at Vauxhall Cross was sufficiently alarmed to have the local Special Branch look you up.'

'They are just covering their backs.'

'Can the Provisionals trace us to Lichfield?'

'I don't see how they could.'

Once it became obvious that the Home Office was not prepared to give Ashton anonymity at the Coroner's inquest into the death of Kevin Hayes, Harriet and Edward had been whisked

25

off to Amberley Lodge, the SIS training centre outside Petersfield. This had happened two days before Ashton had gone into the witness box and they had never returned to Rylett Close. The Ford Mondeo had been disposed of and replaced by a two-year-old Volvo 850. The old vehicle registration document had been doctored to show a different name and address under subsection A, and in addition the Ashtons had been given completely new identities. Everything had been taken care of — driving licences, National Insurance numbers, passports and bank accounts. Mail addressed to 84 Rylett Close had been intercepted at the sorting office and redirected to 'The Secretary, Box 850' where it had fetched up on Roy Kelso's desk. The financial branch had then settled all the household bills. Finally, their medical records were in the process of being reconstructed to conform with their new identities. In Harriet's case this had also meant that her maiden name had to be changed as well.

'Well, if you are sure we can't be traced we've nothing to worry about.' Harriet swung her feet off the sunbed and stood up. 'Or have we?' she added.

'There are friends and relatives . . . '

'You mean they could betray us?' Harriet snapped.

'Unintentionally.'

'I have no friends, only acquaintances, the kind whom you hear from once a year when you exchange Christmas cards and pop a brief note inside. You should know that.'

'Your brother, Richard, and Lucy, his wife?' Ashton ventured.

'And let's not forget my father, who's wandering around with Alzheimer's.'

There was no mistaking the venom in her voice as they stood there, toe to toe, face to face, eyeballing each other like two boxers called together for a pep talk by the referee before the bell went for round one. He had never seen her in such a rage but even though the perfect symmetry of her face was distorted she was still the most beautiful woman he'd ever met. He wrapped his arms around Harriet and held her close.

'Let go of me,' she hissed, and tried unsuccessfully to push him away.

'You're jumping to conclusions. I'm not accusing them of anything.'

'You hadn't better,' she said, and tried to pummel his chest with a clenched fist.

'Listen to me,' he said calmly. 'If what happened this afternoon was for real the Provos are already looking for me. When the trail goes cold for them, they will latch on to your family.'

'And just how the hell are these hit men going to discover my maiden name?' Harriet demanded.

'From Mrs Davies, the daily woman who cleaned the house for us. She certainly knows your father's name and address, the number of times you've had to drive up to Lincoln for one reason or another.'

Suddenly Harriet was no longer struggling to break away from him. 'Oh my God,' she whispered, 'you're right. What are we going to do?'

'I'm going to phone Richard from a callbox and tell him how to play it. Don't worry, love, it's me they're after, not your family.'

'You are my family,' she said, and kissed him.

Harriet pressed against him, lips parting, her tongue seeking his. She was wearing a none-too-fashionable pair of cotton shorts and all he had to do was unfasten a button to get at the zip.

'What do you think you are up to?' she asked in a slightly strangled voice.

'I think it's called having a bit of a nooky.'

'Look 'ere,' she said in a passable cockney accent, 'I'm a good gel, I am.'

★　★　★

Jill Sheridan paid off the cab outside the National Liberal Club in Whitehall Place and went inside. The man she was going to meet was Robin Urquhart, the senior of four deputy under secretaries at the Foreign and Commonwealth Office. Although unaware of it at the time, he was the man who had rescued her from oblivion almost six years ago when she had requested to be relieved of her appointment in Bahrain. Undoubtedly it had been an admission of failure but Urquhart had considered it was largely the fault of the then DG of the SIS. Although on paper Jill Sheridan had appeared to be exceptionally well qualified to co-ordinate intelligence operations in the Arab Emirates, the

DG should have known that in the Arab world a woman was definitely a second-class citizen. She had found herself in an impossible position and to function at all she had been forced to pose as the secretary to her own grade III assistant intelligence Officer.

Jill had met Robin Urquhart for the first time over three years ago when she had been promoted to head the Mid East Department. Within a few weeks it had become evident to Jill that he was completely besotted with her, a factor which she had frequently used to her advantage. With Urquhart in her corner, Jill was practically unassailable.

They had become lovers nine months ago; more recently Robin had talked of divorcing his wife, Rosalind, something many of his friends thought he should have done ages ago. Rosalind was a first-class bitch; she was county, had money of her own, and in her crueller moments she delighted to remind Robin that he was the archetypal grammar school boy of working-class parents who'd made good.

After sixteen years of married life, Rosalind had suddenly left him and moved in with a junior but well-heeled partner in the biggest firm of commercial lawyers in the City. From childhood she had ridden to hounds with the Belvoir Hunt in Leicestershire. Thanks to her lover's influence, Rosalind had subsequently joined the Witherspoon Hunt. One frosty morning in November 1989 she had put her horse at a tall hedgerow by a ditch and the animal had baulked. Rosalind had been thrown and, landing awkwardly, had broken two vertebrae, leaving her paralysed from the waist down. The lover had disappeared while she was still in Stoke Mandeville Hospital and Urquhart had taken her back. He had moved Rosalind into a specially adapted house in Islington and had hired a live-in nurse to see to her every need for which she was not the least bit grateful. As Rosalind never tired of pointing out, it was her money anyway. The miracle was that he had tolerated her abuse for almost seven years before deciding to do something about it. The one positive thing he had done so far was to move out of the family home into a flat in Finchley.

Jill climbed the marble, spiral staircase past the busts of famous Whigs and Liberals of yesteryear displayed in alcoves on the inner wall. Robin was waiting for her at the top of the staircase, looking every inch the senior Foreign Office diplomat in a beautifully laundered white shirt, discreet club tie, black jacket and striped trousers in a slightly lighter shade. His welcoming smile was more polite than affectionate, his kiss on her cheek was circumspect. The somewhat diffident reception was strictly for public consumption; she knew that when he told her he had booked a private room.

'Oh, good,' Jill said in a wholly neutral voice.

'Well, I didn't want us to be disturbed by the other members. We've a lot to talk about and very little time.'

'When does your plane leave for Belfast?'

'We're not travelling on a scheduled flight. The Minister has a BAe Jetstream on standby from 19.45 hours but I need to drop by the flat and change into something less formal.'

The private room which Urquhart had booked was used for committee meetings and the furniture consisted of an oak table and eight upright chairs with leather seats. There was also a drinks tray and two glasses which Robin had obviously requested.

'Gin and tonic?' he asked.

'Please.'

Urquhart poured a generous tot into her glass from a bottle of Gordon's, added a slice of lemon and topped it up with Schweppes Indian Tonic Water.

'I'm afraid there's no ice.'

'That's OK.'

Urquhart fixed himself a small whisky, diluted it with soda, then raised his glass to Jill before sitting next to her, his left leg gently pressed against her right.

'Have you anything further to tell me about the incident in Rylett Close?' he asked.

'It's beginning to look less and less like an accident. However, the police and fire service are still reluctant to commit themselves.'

'Anything else?'

Jill nodded. 'Peter tried to contact Brian Thomas, Head of the Security Vetting and Technical Services Division at approximately half past four this afternoon. Acting on my instructions, our telecom supervisor was monitoring his number and blocked out the call. She did it a second time when he tried again a few minutes later. I think Peter has got the message by now.'

'You hope.'

'By lunchtime tomorrow both Thomas and Hicks will have different phone numbers.'

'But will that deter him? Ashton is a resourceful man; he is also very headstrong and dangerous.' A hand came to rest on Jill's thigh. 'You should know that better than anyone else, my dear.'

One of the less endearing things about Robin was his habit of gently reminding her that she and Peter had once shared the same bed. Occasionally he would bring up the subject of her ex-husband, the detestable Henry Clayburn whom she had divorced within eighteen months. Sometimes she thought Robin derived a vicarious thrill from talking about her old love affairs.

'We have to keep Ashton isolated for his own good,' Urquhart continued. 'I'm flying to Belfast tonight in order to have exploratory talks with Sinn Fein and the IRA and keep the ceasefire alive. I'm sure you appreciate the political situation is very delicately poised. Outwardly the Government has been very strong about not dealing with the terrorists. They can get away with this provided nothing happens to disturb the delicate balance.'

'What are you actually saying, Robin?'

'Ever since he was in charge of the Eastern Bloc Department Victor Hazelwood has had a soft spot for Ashton. He has fought his corner many a time and might do so again.'

'He can't reach Victor at the office because all incoming calls are routed through his PA.' Jill frowned. 'I think I can persuade Victor to change the number of his secure phone at home.'

'And his private number?'

'It's ex-directory — '

'So what?' Urquhart said, interrupting her. 'Ashton probably knows it by heart.'

'I was about to say that changing the subscriber's number will involve a lot of work for his wife, Alice. She has a large circle of friends and acquaintances. Even if BT gave her enough cards she would still be writing an awful lot of notes. I don't think Victor will entertain the idea.'

'So how do we secure his co-operation?' Urquhart shifted his hand and gave her thigh an encouraging pat. In fact several pats.

'A knighthood might do it,' Jill said eventually.

'What?'

'Sir Victor and Lady Hazelwood — I think he would definitely like that, especially as a knighthood doesn't necessarily go with the job these days.'

She didn't have to dot every i and cross every t for Robin. The New Year Honours List was only five months off and a recipient was always sounded out beforehand to see if he or she would accept the award. The offer was, of course, conditional on the recipient doing nothing to blot his or her copybook in the meantime.

'You're a genius,' Urquhart told her. 'I'll get our honours and awards man to phone Victor at home tonight.'

★ ★ ★

The public callbox was in St John Street, just up the road from the prep school. Ashton gazed at the telephone, willing it to ring. Approximately fifteen minutes ago he had tried to catch his brother-in-law, Richard Egan, a former RAF Tornado pilot who had left the service ostensibly to read Law only to finish up as a second officer with British Midland Airways. From the outset Ashton had known the chances of catching Richard at home were pretty slim but that hadn't made the farcical conversation he'd had with Lucy any less frustrating.

He would have got her husband out of the house and into the nearest callbox with little or no trouble. Lucy, however, was slower to catch on.

'I can't hear you,' he'd told her. 'There's something wrong with your phone,' and she had said, 'That's funny you sound as if you are in the next room.'

He had insisted her line was malfunctioning and Lucy wouldn't have it and had said she would get the operator to check it out. After a good deal of yelling, Ashton had finally managed to get her to write down the number he was calling from. She had also grudgingly agreed to call him from a pay phone.

Just when he was beginning to think Lucy was going to let him down the phone suddenly jangled and he snatched the receiver from the hook.

'All right, Peter, I'm here,' she snapped. 'Now tell me what all this nonsense is about. There is nothing wrong with our telephone.'

'I know there isn't,' Ashton told her. 'And there is nothing wrong with Harriet either.'

'Then why did you dragoon me out of my own home on the pretext that she was ill?'

'Because our house in Rylett Close was virtually destroyed by fire this afternoon and I'm not sure it was an accident.'

Before Ashton could get another word in, Lucy told him it was a matter he should discuss with Richard who had a free day tomorrow. Right now he was somewhere between Malaga and East Midlands airport.

'There's nothing I need to discuss with Richard,' Ashton said when Lucy paused for breath. 'I think your house may be bugged.'

'Bugged?' Her voice rose an octave. 'Don't be ridiculous, who would want to eavesdrop on us?' Lucy paused as if expecting him to answer her question, then suddenly the penny dropped. 'Has this got anything to do with you?' she asked.

'Yeah, but don't worry about it. I'm going to have your place spring-cleaned for bugs. All you've got to do is to be there tomorrow or the next day. OK?'

'I suppose so.'

'Thanks, Lucy. We'll be in touch. Bye for now.'
Ashton broke the connection, then rang directory enquiries and asked for the phone number of Mr T. Hicks of Sunleigh Road, Alperton.

3

The daily briefing chaired by the DG usually started at eight-thirty and lasted approximately forty-five minutes. Universally known as morning prayers, it was attended by the Deputy DG, heads of departments, and Victor Hazelwood's PA, who recorded the minutes. Although senior to the other four assistant directors, Roy Kelso was something of a Johnny-come-lately to morning prayers. In the days when the Admin Wing operated from Benbow House in Southwark his presence was never required on the grounds that his department was not in the intelligence-gathering business. He had only joined the top table, as it were, after the SIS had moved from Century House to Vauxhall Cross and the whole organisation was housed under the one roof.

Ordinarily Kelso had little or nothing to contribute. Even when the budget was being prepared for the next financial year Hazelwood would not allow any discussion on the subject at morning prayers, maintaining this was best dealt with by the estimates committee. Today, however, was different; today he most definitely had something to impart and everybody round the table was going to sit up and take notice. Meantime, he was quite happy to sit there listening to Rowan Garfield, the Head of the European Department, wittering on about the worsening situation in Bosnia and what might well happen should Macedonia go sour. Roger Benton had already indicated that the Pacific Basin and Rest of the World Department had nothing fresh to report, so also had Henry Orchard, who ran the Asian show.

That left Winston Reid, the Assistant Director in charge of the Mid East, who was pretty much of an unknown quantity. He was Ms Sheridan's replacement now that her appointment as Deputy DG had been confirmed. A Foreign Office man with no previous experience of the intelligence world, he was still finding his feet and was unlikely to have much to say for himself if the previous five weeks were anything to go by.

The Head of the European Department finally dried up and everybody round the table gazed expectantly at Winston Reid, which Kelso thought was a big mistake in the light of what happened. Contrary to his appraisal Reid was sufficiently encouraged to give a lucid analysis of the talks between Netanyahu and Arafat. He was, moreover, commendably brief, which was a definite plus.

Kelso glanced at his notes and automatically cleared his throat, then before he had a chance to say anything Jill Sheridan was apprising them of yesterday's incident in Rylett Close. He did not interrupt her, merely sat there trying not to look like the cat that had eaten all the cream because her information had been overtaken by events.

'I'm afraid that's old hat, Jill,' he said when she had finished speaking. 'Scene of crime officers are now satisfied the explosion was caused by a bomb.'

'When did you hear this, Roy?' Jill asked through gritted teeth.

'This morning, shortly before we assembled for the daily briefing,' Kelso smiled. 'Sorry, Jill, but you were otherwise engaged with Victor at the time and I didn't get a chance to see you.'

'What sort of bomb was it?' Hazelwood growled.

'A very sophisticated device roughly the size of two boxes of Swan Vestas taped one on top of the other. It was placed in the kitchen cupboard where the gas and electricity meters are. The charge was shaped like a miniature beehive so that the blast would go downwards, smashing through the floorboards to rupture the gas main itself. The Semtex explosive was command-detonated, as were a number of incendiary bombs placed elsewhere in the kitchen. At the moment they are unable to say just how many there were but the remains of two miniature transceivers were found in the rubble.'

'Anything else, Roy?'

'Well, yes, there is. Soon as the estate agents heard about the fire they decided to investigate the last couple to view the property.'

Littlewood had telephoned Northern Rock Promotions in Newcastle upon Tyne and had spoken to the Managing Director who had never heard of Julie Carmichael. The Grey Street branch of Lloyds Bank did have an account for Mr S. Carmichael but it had only been opened three weeks ago and there were insufficient funds to meet the cheque which Littlewood had collected from him.

'Finally, Littlewood looked up the address of the hotel Mrs Carmichael had given him when she had first called at the estate agents and, surprise, surprise, there is no Belmont in Golders Green.'

'Has Ashton been informed of this latest development?'

'If he doesn't already know he soon will, Victor. Our liaison officer at Scotland Yard has passed the word to the Staffordshire Constabulary.'

Hazelwood asked Kelso if he had finished, then went round the table to see if there were any last-minute points. At eight thirty-six, nine minutes earlier than usual, the meeting broke up. The thing which amazed Kelso was the fact that Victor had reacted in such a low-key fashion. A couple of years back he would have demanded to know what the police were doing to protect Ashton.

'A word in your ear,' Jill said, tapping him on the shoulder as they filed out of the conference room.

'Look, I know what you're thinking — ' he began.

'I very much doubt it, Roy.'

'What I said just now was true. I only heard the news — '

'That's all water under the bridge,' Jill told him.

'It is?'

'Yes. How far along are we with providing new

40

identities for the Ashtons? Do they have passports, for instance?'

'Yes.'

'Credit cards?'

'It's not our job to provide him with credit facilities. Ashton can apply for his own card; obtaining a piece of gold plastic is the easiest job in the world.'

'Provided you have a reasonable income.'

'We gave him twenty thousand as a start-up. He also remains on full pay plus London weighting allowance for the next eighteen months.'

'I'm aware of that, Roy. Salaries can be cut off at a moment's notice, which is precisely what we will do at the first sign of trouble from Ashton.'

'What do you mean by trouble?' Kelso asked.

'Any attempt by him to circumvent the lock-out we've imposed. So keep an eye on Brian Thomas.'

'Yes indeed,' Kelso murmured, 'they've always been rather close.'

Ms Sheridan could lay down the law until she was blue in the face but no way was he going to tangle with the ex-detective chief superintendent. Thomas was a real hard-nose and very much his own man. He had already earned one sizeable pension, his family was off his hands and he'd paid off the mortgage on the house. The Firm had no leverage on him; if push came to shove, Thomas would tell all and sundry in no uncertain terms where they could stick their bloody job.

The Administration Wing was located on

41

several floors. Apart from the squash court, the Motor Transport and General Stores Section occupied the whole of the basement area. The pay department nested on the second floor while the Security Vetting and Technical Services Division was on the third. It was this spread that enabled Kelso to justify a lodgement for himself on the top floor among the so-called élite. He had ended up with a view of Vauxhall station instead of the river, and in an office which was not conveniently placed to watch over his bailiwick. However, what counted for him was the fact that he was up there in the eyrie with all the other assistant directors where he belonged.

Kelso stopped by the bank of lifts, summoned one of the cars and went down to the third floor. In keeping with his usual practice Brian Thomas left the door to his office wide open and he wished him a cheerful good morning as he walked past. Terry Hicks was conspicuous by his absence and it was also evident he hadn't been anywhere near the office. The room was neat and tidy, just as the cleaners had left it last night, whereas by now Hicks would have turned the place into a pigsty.

Kelso retraced his steps and tapped on the door of Thomas's office.

'Any idea where the electronic whiz-kid is this morning?' he asked.

Thomas looked up from the file he was reading. 'Terry's got the day off, some problem with his wife's mother up in Northampton.'

'What sort of problem?'

'A mild heart attack,' Thomas said, poker-faced. 'He rang me at home last night to ask if he could run his wife up to Northampton and I told him to take the day off.'

'You gave him leave of absence?' Kelso said in a hollow voice.

'Yeah, any reason why I shouldn't? Damn it, he works for me.'

'I'm aware of that.'

'You're surely not suggesting that I should have consulted you first?'

'Absolutely not. I was merely curious to know where Hicks was.'

'Can I help in any way?'

'No, thanks, it'll keep,' Kelso said, and withdrew with as much dignity as he could muster.

Inwardly seething with anger, Kelso took the lift up to his office on the top floor. There was no illness in the Hicks family; he knew it, so did ex-Detective Chief Superintendent Thomas. If it took him from now until the middle of next week he was going to prove that bloody little oik of a technician was ignoring the warning he had been given under the Official Secrets Act. On entering his office, he opened the combination safe and took out the personal telephone directory which listed the home numbers of everybody in the Administrative Wing. There was no answer when he rang the Hicks household in Alperton.

★ ★ ★

Yesterday the Assistant Chief Constable of Staffordshire Constabulary had telephoned the house to advise Ashton of Milburn's impending visit; today there was no forewarning. Shortly after Harriet had gone shopping, taking Edward with her in the Volvo, the Special Branch officer turned up on the doorstep.

'Don't tell me,' Ashton said, taking him into the morning room at the front, 'it wasn't an accident. Right?'

'You've heard the news already?'

'No. I just assumed you wouldn't have called unless there had been some sort of development. I couldn't see how it could be good news.'

'You're right, of course. Scene of crime officers found evidence which shows the fire was triggered by a high-explosive device. It appears there were also two small incendiary bombs.'

'Have I now got a strong enough case?' Ashton enquired.

Milburn gaped at him. 'What?'

'For a firearms certificate. Remember what you said yesterday afternoon?'

'Ah, yes. Well, the fact is, Mr Durban, you haven't been directly targeted yet.'

'Somebody blows up my house and you say that is not a threat?'

'It was the work of an arsonist.'

'According to who? The Met?'

'Yes, sir.'

'In other words they recognised the handiwork of this fire raiser?'

'So I was told, Mr Durban.'

Milburn sounded as if he didn't believe it

44

either. Although Ashton was no expert on the psychology of an arsonist, he reckoned a fire raiser would derive greater satisfaction from torching a department store than he would gain from igniting a semi-detached in a quiet backwater of London.

'It has to be a cover-up,' Ashton said, voicing his thoughts. 'The politicians are determined, so far as the great British public is concerned, that the IRA ceasefire is still holding up. Nobody is allowed to voice an opinion to the contrary.'

'I wouldn't know about that,' Milburn said.

'Neither do I, Sergeant.' Ashton paused, then asked if he had anything else for him.

'No, just more of the same, sir — be alert and report anyone seen behaving suspiciously to us.'

Ashton saw him out, then looked in on Carolyn on his way up to the attic to make sure she was still fast asleep in her cot.

Kelso had been reluctant to disclose the name of the estate agents who would be handling the sale of the semi-detached in Ravenscourt Park but in the end he had been overruled by Victor Hazelwood. After verifying the number of Mitchell and Webb, which he'd noted in his pocket diary, Ashton rang their office in Hammersmith. From the office manager he learned that a Mr Harvey Littlewood had been looking after 84 Rylett Close and was put through to his extension.

Although they had never met, never even spoken before, he was able to satisfy the estate agent that he was the unfortunate Mr Patrick Durban whose house had been reduced to a fire-blackened shell.

'A bad business all round,' Littlewood said. 'I have to admit I was completely taken in by Mr and Mrs Carmichael.'

'Who are they?' Ashton asked.

'The couple who said they wanted to buy your house. Practically everything they told me about themselves turned out to be false.'

The fire had started roughly two hours after they had left the house and was the reason why Littlewood had immediately made a few enquiries about the potential clients.

'You see, I remembered Julie Carmichael had thought she could smell gas and that was too much of a coincidence.'

He had discovered there was no such hotel as the Belmont in Golders Green where the Carmichaels had claimed to be staying, and Northern Rock Promotions had never heard of Julie Carmichael. The lady had definitely made an impression on Harvey Littlewood, who had been able to give the police a pretty detailed description of her appearance and the clothes she had been wearing. He hadn't been nearly so forthcoming about Simon Carmichael.

'Any idea what part of the world he came from?' Ashton asked.

'Why do you want to know that?'

'Because the claims inspector of my insurance company isn't going to be happy with the usual 'medium height, medium build' description. Now, did he have an accent you could place?'

'He has a current account with the Grey Street branch of Lloyds Bank in Newcastle upon

46

Tyne. Didn't have much of a Geordie accent, though.'

'Any trace of a brogue?'

'No, he's definitely not Irish.'

'What about his wife?'

'She sounded as if she originally hailed from Canada or maybe America. She's been over here a long time, though; the accent is very toned down. Sorry I can't be more helpful.'

Ashton assured him that on the contrary his information was invaluable and apologised for taking up so much of his time. In return Littlewood informed him it had been a pleasure and then hung up.

Somebody at Vauxhall Cross had taken steps to freeze him out; he wondered if that same person had asked MI5 to follow that lead. There was, of course, only one way to find out. He had a choice of two contacts: after a moment's reflection he decided to put his money on Francesca York, a former lieutenant in the army's Special Counter Intelligence team who had been taken on by MI5 at the end of her five-year short-service commission. He had met Francesca when she had been nominated as the MI5 liaison officer to the Combined Anti-Terrorist Organisation known as CATO, a talking shop which had been the brainchild of Jill Sheridan. He looked up her number in the back of his pocket diary and, lifting the receiver, tapped it out. He did not have to wait very long for her to answer the phone.

She answered in the clipped unnatural voice that owed a lot to an elocution teacher. '5947.'

47

'Hi, Fran,' he said cheerfully, 'how are you doing?'

'Who is this?'

'Peter Ashton.'

'I'm going to hang up.'

'Don't do that.'

'I have to. I'm not supposed to talk to you.'

'Who said so? Richard Neagle?'

One of the best interrogators in the business, Neagle was Francesca's immediate superior. He was also cold, ruthless, highly intelligent and extremely sarcastic. Ashton thought Francesca York was a little afraid of him.

'Was it Neagle?' he repeated.

'Yes, but the request came from your Deputy DG.'

'Just answer two questions and you'll never hear from me again. OK?'

'No, it isn't OK. You have been suspended by the SIS and are not to have access to classified information.'

'Two questions, otherwise I will ring every damned extension and pretend we've been cut off. That should make the high-priced help in Gower Street sit up and take notice.'

'You bastard, you'll get me fired . . . '

'Two questions.'

'All right, let's have them.'

'Barry Hayes — is he back in this country?'

'No.'

'And Kevin's widow, is she still living in Lewisham?'

'Affirmative,' Francesca said, and put the phone down.

Barry Hayes had grown up during the Troubles. Aged nine he had been on the streets of the Bogside, throwing stones at the British soldiers, subsequently graduating to petrol bombs before he was ten. He was nippy on his feet and had proved he had a good eye by scoring a direct hit on a senior RUC officer which had left the man with second-degree burns to the neck and back.

For reasons unknown to the Special Branch of the Royal Ulster Constabulary, the family had moved to West Belfast from Londonderry. The truth was young Barry had never been caught by a foot patrol, the rest of the family had not come to the notice of the police and therefore Special Branch had had no reason to open a file on the Hayes family. They did, however, have cause to open a file on Brian Aherne in 1977.

Brian Aherne had been the commander of the IRA Flying Column of County Mayo from January 1920 to May 1921 when he had been killed in a firefight with a platoon of auxiliaries, a paramilitary force composed of young, unemployed ex-army officers, many of whom had been decorated for bravery during the Great War. To Barry Hayes, Aherne had been a lifelong hero and he had adopted his name in honour of him when he'd joined the Provisional IRA in 1977.

As Brian Aherne, Barry Hayes had killed his first man on his nineteenth birthday. The victim had been an off-duty part-time soldier in the Ulster Defence Regiment. The second had been a stoolie, a forty-six-year-old unemployed father of four who was suspected of spying for the RUC. He had been snatched from his home and taken to a derelict garage where he had been questioned for three days and nights, which had left him with both kneecaps shattered, two broken arms, a fractured pelvis, a broken jaw and five cracked ribs. Hayes had been summoned to dispatch him with a bullet to the head after he had confessed. The third victim had been a court usher who had been shot to death in front of his heavily pregnant wife.

But it was as a bomb maker that Hayes had really enhanced his reputation. For someone with little or no formal education he had shown an absolute genius for designing everything from a massive car bomb to the most highly sophisticated booby trap. In 1989, when things had finally got too hot for him in Northern Ireland, Hayes had slipped over the border and the rumour had been put about that he had fled to America, whereas he had in fact sneaked into England. For the next seven years he had lived in London under his real name while commanding a dormant active service unit of the Provisional IRA. Hayes would still have been living in London had he not been named by a former battalion commander in West Belfast who had turned supergrass, having become sickened by the punishment beatings and kneecappings of petty criminals authorised by the Army Council. Warned by friends in Belfast that his former commanding officer had gone across, Barry Hayes had skipped back to Eire.

Barry Hayes had the technical know-how to build the sophisticated delayed-action high-explosive device and incendiary bombs which had destroyed 84 Rylett Close. He also had a strong motive for revenge because Ashton had killed his younger brother, Kevin.

Ashton just hoped MI5 had got it right and Hayes really was still in Eire.

★   ★   ★

Without looking up from the file she was reading Jill Sheridan knew who was about to ask if she could spare him a few minutes. The rap on her door had been unmistakable — three quick taps followed by a much heavier one, the morse code for the letter V.

'Come in, Roy,' she said before he could ask the usual question.

'This won't take a minute,' Kelso promised her.

'I won't hold you to that but I do have a lot on,' Jill said, and waved a hand over the crowded in- and pending trays.

'Hicks hasn't come into work today. Apparently he phoned Brian Thomas at home last night to inform him his mother-in-law had had a mild heart attack and that he proposed to run his wife up to Northampton.'

'So you decided to find out if his story was genuine?'

'Well, yes, I did. I mean yesterday he received a letter from the DG warning him to have nothing to do with Ashton and then the next day

51

he takes off for Northampton. Wouldn't you have been suspicious?'

'Quite. What exactly did you do, Roy?'

'I phoned his house. I must have tried half a dozen times but eventually Mrs Hicks answered the phone. She had just returned from shopping at the local supermarket and had no idea where her husband was. You can bet Brian Thomas knows.'

'You're right, of course, but he won't admit it, at least not to you.'

'We're not going to let them get away with it, are we?' Kelso demanded indignantly.

'You should know me better than to ask. When is Ashton due to be paid again?'

'This month's salary will be transferred to his account in Lichfield on Friday the twenty-sixth.'

'Freeze it. Tell the Pay Branch no more payments without my authorisation.'

'Right.' Kelso cleared his throat. 'And Thomas?' he asked hesitantly.

'You can leave Brian to me. Incidentally, has his office number been changed yet?'

'Yes and Hicks's.'

'And everybody has been advised of the new numbers?'

'That's in hand.'

'Just make sure it is,' Jill said, and returned to the file she had been reading.

* * *

Harriet stepped out of the lift at level one of the multistorey car park and walked towards the

Volvo 850, wheeling the shopping trolley with one hand while holding on to Edward with the other. The car was parked between a dark blue Honda Accord and a green BMW just short of the bend. Pausing by the boot she left the shopping basket in the upright position, took out her car keys and sent a signal to switch off the alarm and release the central locking. She then lifted the shopping basket into the boot, closed the lid and opened the rear nearside door. It wasn't until she had strapped Edward into the centre seat and had moved round the Volvo to get in behind the wheel that she noticed the message sellotaped to the instrument panel.

The message had been composed with individual letters cut from newspapers and glued to a sheet of A4.

It read: 'tell AshTOn we can Get you AnYtime we WaNT'.

4

Ashton heard the Volvo coming and went downstairs to meet Harriet. By the time he opened the front door she had already parked the car on the cinder patch, which served as a hardstanding, and was busy releasing Edward from his child seat in the back. Harriet was, he noticed, decidedly agitated as if she was late for some appointment she couldn't afford to miss and was trying to make up for lost time.

'Well, just don't stand there, Peter,' she snapped. 'Make yourself useful and get the shopping basket out of the boot.'

Harriet didn't actually run into the house as she swept past him but she came close to it. She was holding on to Edward's left wrist and he started bawling because his feet were only touching the ground now and again. Ashton asked her what the hell their son had done to deserve such treatment and immediately wished he had kept his mouth shut. There had to be a damned good reason for Harriet to behave so out of character.

He lifted the shopping basket out of the boot and slammed it shut, then walked forward on the driver's side of the vehicle. The keys were still in the ignition and the door was not fully closed; nor, as he rapidly discovered was the rear nearside door. He activated the alarm and central locking, then wheeled the shopping basket into the hall and closed the front door. From the sitting room Harriet told him to lock it and hook the security chain into the slot. It was not, he decided, the time or the place to ask her why.

Edward had stopped crying and had his arms around Harriet's neck as she walked up and down the sitting room, bouncing him on her right hip.

'I could use a drink,' she said.

'Sure. What would you like — white wine? Red?'

'Whisky, and make it a strong one.'

'Anything with it?'

'Just a splash of soda.'

Ashton crouched in front of the drinks cabinet, looked out a glass tumbler and poured a more-than-generous double from the bottle of Teacher's, then unscrewed the cap on the soda water. 'Say when,' he said, straightening up and turning to face Harriet, tumbler in one hand, bottle of Schweppes in the other.

'They've found us.'

'Who have?' Ashton topped the whisky with soda, handed the glass to Harriet and set the bottle down.

'The people we are hiding from, the people who burned down our old house. They want you to know they can take me whenever they like. You'll find their message in my handbag.'

Harriet had obviously intended to tear the message to pieces, only to have second thoughts after ripping the sheet of paper in two. She had then crumpled the two halves and stuffed them into her handbag.

Ashton placed both pieces on a low table and smoothed them out the best he could.

'Where did you find this?' he asked.

'Taped to the instrument panel. And before you ask, the car was locked and the alarm had been activated.'

In keeping with her usual practice she had parked the Volvo in the Frog Lane/Birmingham Road multistorey. Since the opposition had obviously had them under surveillance for some time, she thought they would also have known that regular as clockwork the Ashtons shopped on Saturdays and Thursdays.

'They were pretty cool, weren't they?' Harriet said, a nervous edge to her voice. 'I mean the multistorey is almost within hailing distance of the police station.'

'Did you have any difficulty finding a parking space?'

'It's never busy on a Thursday.' Harriet gave the tumbler to Ashton while she put Edward down, then took her whisky back from him and drank some. 'And no,' she continued, 'I didn't see anyone loitering on level one when I parked the car.'

'How long were you gone?'

'An hour, seventy-five minutes at the most. I didn't see anybody when I returned to the car park.' Harriet drank some more of the whisky. 'It scared the hell out of me when I found the note, Peter.'

'I can imagine. Day or night, there's always

something vaguely menacing about a multi-storey.'

'The question is, what are we going to do? Our new identities have been discovered, they know our address, the registration number of our car and they even have a spare set of keys to the damned Volvo.'

'I guess we report the incident to the police,' Ashton said, then placed a finger over his lips, pointed to the garden and signalled Harriet to follow him.

'Well, let's hope they give us something more than a burglar alarm.'

Ashton moved to the French windows and opened them. 'I think you'll find we will have a couple of hairy great policemen living with us.'

'I know who will be feeding them,' Harriet said, and followed him into the garden. She didn't say another word until they were near the sandpit, some fifteen yards from the house. 'Do you think the place has been bugged?' she asked.

'I don't know,' Ashton told her. 'I'm just playing safe.'

'Are you going to inform the police?'

'I ought to. You never can tell, somebody's prints besides yours might be on that sheet of paper.'

'You don't seriously believe that, do you, Peter? These people are far too clever to make such an elementary mistake.'

For a highly intelligent woman like Harriet to advance such a reason for doing nothing had to be a mental aberration.

'What are you really saying?' he asked quietly.

'What will happen if we do inform the police? We will be back to square one: the SIS will move us to a new location, and we will be given yet another legend with every possibility it will be blown just as easily.' Harriet swallowed the rest of the whisky, wiped both lips on the back of her wrist, then pointed the empty tumbler at his chest. 'If you, me and the children are to disappear and leave no trace, we have to do everything ourselves.'

'Do you have any idea what that will entail?'

'Yes. Amongst other things it'll mean we don't exist on paper. Our names do not appear on the electoral roll, we are not registered with a medical practitioner or a dentist. We have no tax reference or employer reference and there is no entry relating to us on the Department of Health and Social Security computer at Newcastle on Tyne. Furthermore, we don't have a bank account.'

'And what do we do for money?'

'We withdraw the whole twenty thousand the SIS gave us and live off that.'

'For how long?'

'Until you think it's safe to stop running,' Harriet told him.

★ ★ ★

Jill Sheridan could count the number of times she had been down to the third floor on the fingers of one hand. On the four previous occasions when she had found it desirable to bypass Kelso and deal directly with the Head of the Security Vetting and Technical Services Division she had always summoned Brian Thomas to her office. That afternoon she had thought it politic to make an exception, a role reversal she accepted with some difficulty.

'If you are busy, Brian, I can come back later,' she said, then told him to please sit down as he started to get up.

'There is nothing here which can't wait, Jill,' Thomas said, sinking back into his chair. 'What can I do for you?'

'Well, Roy tells me that Terry Hicks may have done something stupid. As I understand it, you gave him permission to take the day off because his mother-in-law in Northampton had suffered a mild heart attack, and her daughter was anxious to make sure she was all right?'

'That's correct.'

'I'm afraid he lied to you, Brian. The only journey Mrs Hicks has done today is to the local supermarket and back.'

'I took him at his word,' Thomas said, his voice expressionless.

'Quite. I would have done the same in your position. What do you suppose Hicks is up to?'

'Search me. Perhaps he's got a bit on the side; Terry's always had an eye for the ladies. Then again, maybe he's doing some job for Peter Ashton.'

'Really!'

'Why so surprised, Jill? You must know he tried to phone me yesterday afternoon. My number was being monitored before I ever received a warning letter from the Director.

Ashton could have phoned him at home. If he knows Terry's address all he had to do was ring directory enquiries.'

Jill smiled. 'The same could apply to you, Brian,' she said, almost purring.

'Well, he didn't call me at home.'

'I'm sure he didn't.'

'You don't have to take my word for it,' Thomas said angrily. 'You're one of the few people who know where Ashton is living, the name he's using and his phone number. Get British Telecom to give you a list of the calls he's made.'

Jill looked away, only too aware how badly she had mishandled the situation. Given their mutual dislike, it didn't take a lot of effort on her part to rub the former detective chief superintendent up the wrong way. It was common knowledge that she hadn't wanted him to head the Security Vetting and Technical Services Division when Frank Warren had taken early retirement in December 1995 but he had been Victor Hazelwood's choice and she had been overruled.

'Humour me,' she said presently. 'Let's assume Peter did contact Hicks. Why would he need his services? The appropriate Special Branch is looking after him; they were told to spring-clean the house the day before the Ashtons moved in and install the usual electronic defences.'

There were no electronic defences and none had been requested but Thomas was not to know that.

60

'I'm not a mind reader,' Thomas growled.

Uncooperative and surly with it. Somehow Jill managed to control her anger without making it obvious.

'Maybe Peter suspects there has been a breach of security,' Jill said tentatively. 'He knows his house in Ravenscourt Park was firebombed; perhaps that reminded him of some earlier incident he had previously dismissed.'

'What sort of incident?'

'A chance encounter with a friend or distant relative who shouldn't know where he is now living.' Jill shrugged her shoulders. 'Your guess is as good as mine, Brian.'

'Would it help if you knew who this friend or relative might be?'

'Definitely.'

Thomas summoned the clerical officer who looked after the personal security files and told her to bring him the vetting papers relating to the Ashtons. A few minutes later she returned with both files and handed them to Thomas.

'I'll go through Ashton's,' he said, after the clerical officer had departed. 'You can have Harriet's file.'

The latter had been rescued from the dead sack where it had reposed ever since it had become apparent that Harriet Ashton née Egan had no intention of returning to the fold. Her positive vetting clearance, which had given her constant access to Top Secret material, had automatically been cancelled, as had the special Signal Intelligence access issued by Government Communications Headquarters, Cheltenham.

The file would remain extant until Harriet reached the age of sixty-one some twenty-nine years hence. The same provision would apply even should she die tomorrow.

The security file was like a biography that was constantly being updated. It recorded the most intimate details of her life, her financial status, psychological assessment, drinking habits, sexual proclivities, medical history, and general character traits as seen by friends and superiors. Harriet had made plenty of friends during her three years at Birmingham University but they had gradually fallen by the wayside after she had moved from the Home Office to MI5. In the four years she had spent in Gower Street her one really close friend had been Clifford Peachey, the leading light of K1, the 'Kremlin watchers', who had later become the Deputy DG of the SIS.

Jill mentally crossed Peachey off the list. She had taken over from him when he had retired in January and moved to Helmsley on the edge of the North York Moors where he and his wife, Ann, were still being guarded by Special Branch officers. The close family, however, was a definite possibility.

'I think Hicks has gone to Lincoln,' Jill announced. 'Richard and Lucy Egan live in Church Lane and Harriet's father, Frederick, resides with his housekeeper at 11 Ferris Drive. Frederick Egan suffers from Alzheimer's and could be considered a security risk. I doubt if he could keep a secret to save his life . . . '

Jill closed the file and handed it to Thomas.

'When Hicks returns to work, tell him there will be no witch-hunt but I do need to know exactly what he did at Ashton's request. You should point out that if he withholds this information, he may well put Peter's life in danger. After all, we can't protect the Ashtons if we don't know what is going on.'

★ ★ ★

The man had been photographed at a newspaper and magazine kiosk outside Moscow's Park Kultury Metro station. The subject was out of focus, which was only to be expected since the picture had been taken covertly by a rank amateur. The print and negative had been acquired by George Elphinstone, Head of Station, Moscow, and subsequently computer-enhanced by the Security Vetting and Technical Services Division. It had been studied by intelligence officers of the Russian Desk whose doubts concerning the identity of the subject were shared by Rowan Garfield. Even so, he had wasted no time in bringing it to Victor Hazelwood's attention.

The man at the newspaper kiosk was thought to be Pavel Trilisser, one-time special adviser to President Yeltsin on foreign affairs. A lean, aesthetic-looking man, Trilisser had often been taken for a member of the Academy of Sciences, an academic, a High Court judge or a distinguished physicist by strangers encountering him at a social function. Now aged fifty-seven he had, at one time, been the Deputy Head of the

First Chief Directorate of the KGB, an appointment he had retained under Gorbachev when the old organisation had suddenly been redesignated as the Russian Intelligence Service. In his day Trilisser had been rightly regarded as a brilliant officer. He had received accelerated promotion to lieutenant general and had been the youngest Deputy Head of the First Chief Directorate when he had been appointed to the post in 1987.

'He's not what you call lean and aesthetic now, is he?' Hazelwood growled, looking up from the computer enhancement.

'It could be the passage of time,' Garfield smiled. 'Most of us tend to put on weight the older we get.'

'How much did George Elphinstone pay for the photograph, Rowan?'

'A thousand pounds; he thought it was cheap at the price.'

'And naturally, having shelled out that amount, he is satisfied the man is Pavel Trilisser.'

'I don't think the amount he paid for the photo necessarily clouded his judgement.'

Hazelwood looked at the photograph again. Somebody in Technical Services had marked it with a red arrow which pointed to a copy of the *International Herald Tribune* displayed in a rack behind the counter. The date below the logo was Tuesday, 26 March.

'This photograph is four months old.'

'Yes, I know.'

'According to Elphinstone, Trilisser was under house arrest, allegedly for misappropriating government funds to speculate on the US futures market.'

'He's always been a survivor, Victor.'

In August 1991 Trilisser had sided with the Communist hardliners when they had turned against Gorbachev. Although they hadn't been able to prove it, his detractors had been convinced he had waited until it was evident the coup was going to fail before he arrested his own chief and sent word to the Minister of the Interior, Boris Pugo, that he should surrender himself to the paratroops of the Ryazan Division who were about to surround his apartment.

Two years later he had again demonstrated some fancy footwork when Vice President Aleksander Rutskoi had attempted to overthrow President Yeltsin. He had raised and secretly financed a special task force of three hundred plus men and women drawn from Spetsnaz units, the equivalent of the SAS. It was thought this special task force had been created in order to seize and hold key communication centres which included all major TV stations, but in the event Trilisser had waited to see which way the wind was blowing. When it became clear that forces loyal to Boris Yeltsin were about to storm the parliament buildings, he had decided to remain loyal to the President. In furtherance of this he had used the Spetsnaz teams to arrest the civilian specialists who had been recruited to run the TV stations and communication centres. He had also murdered his second in command.

'Do you know where Trilisser is living these days?'

Garfield fingered the moustache he was cultivating. 'He's certainly lost his *pied-à-terre* in the Kremlin now that he's no longer a special adviser to Yeltsin, and that house he acquired on the Moscow Heights near the Lomonosov Moscow State University has been empty since the beginning of the year.'

'He has a dacha somewhere outside Moscow, hasn't he?'

Garfield nodded. 'At Solnechnogorsk, forty miles out of town on the St Petersburg highway. If he still owns it, I don't see Trilisser commuting to Moscow. It's strictly a weekend retreat.'

'So what do you think, Rowan? Are we looking at Pavel Trilisser in this picture or not?'

'To be honest, I can't make up my mind.'

'Neither can I.' Hazelwood shook his head. 'Do you mind if I keep this photograph for the time being?' he asked.

'Keep it as long as you like,' Garfield told him, and moved towards the door. 'It's a spare copy.'

There was, Hazelwood thought, one man who might give him an unequivocal answer. Moments after the Head of the European Department had left, Hazelwood called Jill Sheridan into the office.

'Who do you think this is?' he asked, and handed the computer enhancement to her.

Jill studied it carefully, her eyes drawn to the arrow, forehead creased in a frown. In that instant he knew that whatever answer she gave would be based on a logical deduction rather than recognition.

'Taken in Moscow,' she murmured, 'over

sixteen weeks ago. Has George Elphinstone been running a surveillance operation?'

'No.'

'Then some Russian entrepreneur sold it to one of his minions.'

'You're getting warmer,' Hazelwood told her.

'Doesn't say much for our security if the entrepreneur knew who to approach. How much did Head of Station pay for it?'

'One thousand pounds.'

'Obviously the man by the kiosk has to be a VIP.' Jill squinted at the photograph again, her eyebrows almost knitted together before a smile suddenly appeared on her mouth. 'It has to be Pavel Trilisser,' she announced triumphantly.

'You're right, but you didn't actually recognise him.'

'Well, he's in profile and what little you can see of his face is out of focus.'

'Don't take it to heart, nobody is criticising you. None of the officers on the Russian Desk recognised him either.'

'Which is hardly surprising, Victor. After all, like me, they have never met him face to face.'

'But Ashton has — many times. He's smelled his breath.'

Jill stared at him, mouth open in naked astonishment. 'What are you suggesting, Victor?'

'I'm going to send this computer enhancement to Mr Durban, 12 Gaia Lane, Lichfield, and seek his opinion.'

Jill had a dozen reasons why he should do no such thing, including the fact that the SIS had dispensed with Ashton's services.

'What on earth gave you that idea?' Hazelwood asked. 'As far as I'm concerned we've simply put him out to grass until things calm down.'

'We've given him twenty thousand pounds . . .'

'Oh, we can recover that easily enough, Jill, over a period of time.'

'And for the next eighteen months he is on full pay and allowances.'

'All the more reason why he should start earning it,' Hazelwood said breezily.

★ ★ ★

Last Christmas Harriet had given Ashton a mobile phone as a slightly jokey present. It had been a reminder that it would be helpful if just once in a while he managed to let her know he was going to be late home. The phone on the grass beside his deck chair was not the one he had found on his plate done up in wrapping paper with a mock holly leaf sellotaped to the ribbon tied in a bow. That had been replaced by Roy Kelso when they had gone into hiding. At ten minutes to six that evening Ashton received his first incoming call on the mobile. Answering it, he rattled off the subscriber's number.

'It's me, Terry,' Hicks said. 'Where are you — indoors?'

'No, outside in the garden. Are you telling me my brother-in-law's place has been tampered with?'

'Yeah. They put a transmitter in the phone on

68

the hall table and another in the sitting room. Neat little jobs, both mains-powered with the maximum range of a mile and a half. I reckon they were installed eight weeks ago.'

'How did you work that out, Terry?'

'Mrs Egan put me on to it. Seems an electrician from East Midlands Electricity called at the house one Monday morning in late May. He told her she was one of the householders in the area who had been chosen for a free inspection. He had a proper ID card and looked the part.'

The electrician had spent over an hour checking the fuse box, wiring power points and the loading on each circuit. At the end of his inspection he had given her a detailed written report and had advised her that, although the present system was safe enough, she should consider replacing the existing fuse box with a Memera 2000.

'Mr Egan rang East Midlands while I was there and they denied all knowledge of a selected household scheme. He wondered about informing the police but I said it might be better to have a word with you first.'

'I'll ring him later this evening.'

'I think you should know I didn't get to see old Mr Egan's house in Ferris Drive. Your brother-in-law was adamant I shouldn't go near the house, said it would only upset the old gentleman and would serve no purpose. He reckons the eavesdroppers have already got all the information they need.'

'He's undoubtedly right,' Ashton said.

'Would you like me to take a look at your place?'

'No, you've done enough. Besides, if the house is contaminated, I can use it to advantage.'

'If you say so.'

'I do. Listen, if you find yourself in trouble with Kelso, go and see the DG and tell him I sent you.'

'With respect, Mr Ashton, what good will that do?'

'Quite a lot. I happen to know where all the bodies are buried.'

5

In the cycle of sleep Ashton was suspended just below the surface of consciousness. No dream had brought him to the edge of wakefulness; he had in fact been disturbed by a faint scratching noise, as if the climbing rose was rubbing against the window because the wind had got up. Except it had been a hot day and Harriet had partially opened one of the sashcord windows to cool the bedroom and there wasn't even a breath of air, never mind a stiff breeze. That was why they were sleeping with only a sheet over them.

Suddenly he was fully alert and listening to catch the slightest noise. Harriet was lying on her back and the way her head was turned away from him towards the bedroom door suggested she too had heard something.

'Are you awake?' he whispered.

'I think somebody's broken into the house,' she murmured.

'So do I.'

It couldn't have been the sound of Carolyn breathing he'd heard over the baby alarm and it certainly hadn't been the noise Edward would have made climbing out of his bed. Besides, he would have invaded theirs by now.

Ashton drew the sheet aside and quietly got out of bed. In the darkness the luminous hands of the alarm clock registered twenty-four minutes after two and he could just make out the

71

shape of the mobile phone on the bedside table. Taking care not to sweep anything on to the floor, he picked up the mobile and passed it to Harriet.

'Get ready to phone the police,' he told her in a low voice.

'Where are you going?'

'Downstairs to see what's happening.'

'Well, for God's sake be careful. There's nothing of value in this house that's worth risking your neck for.'

'I don't think the intruder is after our few bits of silver.'

Ashton looked under the bed and fished out the choke chain for a large dog which the previous owner of the house had left behind when he had moved. When wrapped around the clenched fingers of his right hand, the chain made an effective knuckle-duster. The other weapon he had brought to bed with them was a heavy steel poker, which he gave to Harriet.

'Just in case he gets past me,' he murmured.

He crept round the bed and edged towards the door in bare feet. Because the lock was stiff and tended to grate, he turned the porcelain knob anticlockwise slowly and deliberately, like a cracksman opening a combination safe. He opened the door just wide enough to slip out onto the landing and make his way to the head of the staircase.

It was an old house and a number of the tread boards creaked when any weight was put on them. The trouble was he hadn't lived in the place long enough to know which ones to avoid.

Ashton went down sideways, side-stepping crab-style, the upper half of his body draped over the banisters, the handrail supporting most of his weight. Twelve steps on tiptoe, then a ninety-degree turn to the left followed by a second flight of twelve to the hall below.

Seven tread boards from the bottom Ashton heard a faint thud which had nothing to do with his weight on the staircase. He tried to place where the disturbance had come from and immediately ruled out the parlour directly to his front because the door was ajar and the noise had been too muffled to be that near at hand. The hall cloakroom was round to the right but it had only a porthole window and there was no way even the thinnest of intruders could have wriggled through it. Day or night, old or new, a house was never still. Maybe what he'd heard was one of those inexplicable sounds?

He negotiated the remaining steps without making a sound, crossed the hall and stepped into the parlour. Nothing — sashcord window intact, no sign of a forced entry. He moved silently across the hall again and checked out the cloakroom even though he was ninety-nine per cent sure that no one was there. One thing he had learned during his spells of active service in the army was always to make certain no hostiles were behind you before moving on to the next phase.

Suddenly the telephone started to ring, which set Ashton's pulse racing. He wasn't the only one who had been spooked; as he backed out of the cloakroom he saw a figure run from the sitting

73

room to the kitchen and automatically yelled at him to hold it right there. The intruder spun round to face him and raised a weapon of some kind into his shoulder. Ashton didn't wait to identify what the man was aiming at him; without a second's hesitation he threw himself flat and hugged the floor. Something pretty solid cleaved the air above his head and thumped into the front door.

Crossbow: it was vital to get the intruder before he could reload because the bastard was unlikely to miss him a second time at such close range. Ashton launched himself from the floor, driving forward like a sprinter leaving the blocks in the 100 metres dash. The intruder disappeared into the kitchen, slammed the door in his face and ran out into the walled garden. Ashton went after him, his feet skidding on a patch of ice that had formed on the back doorstep. Ice? Hell, this was July and the sole of his left foot felt wet and was beginning to smart. With the intruder nowhere in sight, it figured he must have turned right to double back past the kitchen and sitting room. Ashton followed suit and was travelling at speed when he literally ran into the second intruder.

The other man was armed with what appeared to be a broom handle which he was holding like a rifle and bayonet in the on guard position. Lunging forward, he caught Ashton just under the breast bone and put him down on hands and knees. The pain was searing, as if a morsel of food had gone down the wrong way and was lodged somewhere in his windpipe. Black spots danced in front of his eyes and the ground beneath him seemed to be revolving. As he fought to regain his breath, the intruder turned his back on him and ran at the garden wall. Slamming one foot against it to give himself the necessary leverage, he got both hands on top of the wall and straightened his arms. By the time Ashton was back on his feet, the intruder was lying flat on top of the wall with only the left leg trailing. Ashton hobbled towards him, nursing his chest and stomach with one arm while somehow unravelling the chain he had wrapped around his right fist. Before the man could swing his trailing leg up and over, Ashton lashed out with the chain and cracked him on the ankle. In his present state he could no more haul himself over the wall than fly to the moon. The yell of pain followed by a string of obscenities from the intruder as he landed heavily on his damaged ankle was therefore music to Ashton's ears.

'Peter.'

Ashton turned round and saw Harriet advancing towards him, flashlight in one hand, steel poker from the sitting-room fireplace in the other.

'Are you OK?' she asked.

'I'll live.'

'There are spots of blood on the path by the back door and a lot of broken glass.' The flashlight dipped, the beam centring on his feet. 'You've cut yourself,' she said accusingly, as if he had deliberately injured himself. 'You'd better lean on me.'

'I can manage.'

'Don't come the hero, we can do without the stoicism.'

Harriet was half an inch under six feet, the same height as himself. She tipped the scales at a hundred and forty-five pounds and there was no way she could lose weight without looking like a poster for War on Want. There was in fact not a pinch of spare flesh on her entire body.

'Here, hold this,' Harriet said, and gave him the poker.

She put his arm over her left shoulder and wrapped her right arm around his waist; then, leaning away, she practically lifted him off the ground so that he was forced to hop along beside her on his one good foot.

Back inside the house, Harriet switched on the lights in the kitchen, filled the washing-up bowl with warm water and told him to soak his injured foot in it while she fetched the first aid box. She returned five minutes later with a wad of Elastoplast, a bottle of TCP antiseptic liquid, a tube of ointment, a roll of lint and a pair of scissors. Some of the liquid antiseptic went into the washing-up bowl, a lot more was applied to the sole of the foot after Harriet had dried it on a clean tea towel.

'The slit is about three inches long,' Harriet told him. 'The wound is not deep and it's very clean. I don't think it needs stitching but I can do it if you like?'

'No, thanks, I think I'll forgo that pleasure.' Ashton grimaced as she pressed a piece of lint smothered in ointment over the wound and began to tape it firmly into position. 'What about

Carolyn and Edward?' he asked. 'Are they awake?'

'No, they've slept right through the disturbance.'

'Long may that continue. Let's hope the police don't rouse the whole neighbourhood with their sirens.'

Harriet got to her feet, went over to the sink and turned both taps full on. If the place had been bugged no eavesdropper was going to overhear their conversation.

'They're not coming,' she told him.

'Why not?'

'I didn't phone them.'

'I don't understand. What the hell were you playing at?'

'Think about it. If I had phoned the police who do you suppose would have turned up on our doorstep later on this morning?'

'DS Milburn. What's wrong with that?'

'Oh, for God's sake, Peter, word would get back to the SIS and they would move us on to a new location. When I showed you that anonymous note yesterday, we agreed that when the time came for us to disappear we could do everything ourselves. It is the only way we can be safe . . .'

He listened to Harriet with only half an ear as she repeated all the familiar arguments. The house was lit up like a gin palace now, and from where he was sitting, Ashton could see right down the hall. What held his gaze was the steel arrow from the crossbow buried deep in the front door.

'I could have been killed,' he muttered.

'I made a hideous mistake, Peter. I used the mobile to ring the telephone in the sitting room. I thought if I could frighten the burglar there was a chance he would panic and run away. It never occured to me he might be armed.'

'There were two of them.' Ashton shrugged. 'I suppose they could have been a couple of tearaways on the lookout for easy pickings.'

'I don't care who or what they were. It's time to move on.'

Harriet had given it a lot of thought. They would pack what they needed today, load the car when it was dark and leave early on Saturday. They would use their PIN numbers to obtain whatever money they needed from cashpoints up and down the country. She would use the mobile phone to call Clifford Peachey and ask him to put them up for a couple of days while they figured out their next move.

'I know he won't refuse to help us, Peter.'

Peachey would certainly do anything for Harriet. He had always regarded her as the daughter he and Ann had never had. Whether the former MI5 officer and erstwhile Deputy DG would do the same for him was another matter. Ashton was only too aware that Peachey was not one of his admirers and thought Harriet was far too good for him.

'And we can trust him not to say anything to Victor Hazelwood.'

Ashton thought he would probably keep shtum if Harriet asked him but she would be wise to leave Victor out of it. She had a thing about the Director and couldn't understand why Ashton had always defended him. In her view, loyalty extended in both directions, down as well as up, but with Hazelwood it was strictly one way. He was, she maintained, a man who used people and gave nothing in return.

'When push came to shove, he didn't stand up for you, Peter.'

'It was the Home Office which refused to give me anonymity.'

'Do you know what bothers me?' Harriet said, changing the subject. 'How did the Hayes family learn where my brother was living? And don't tell me their solicitor got it from Mrs Davies, our daily, because I never told her Richard had moved into our old house in Lincoln. I only ever talked about my father and his problems.'

'So where do you think they got their information?'

'From the Foreign and Commonwealth Office with a little help from somebody in Vauxhall Cross.'

'The FCO?' Ashton shook his head. 'I don't think so.'

Before making the allegation, Harriet had given it a lot of thought. Determined to reach a settlement in Northern Ireland, the Government had deliberately involved Dublin in the talks with the Nationalist community. Whatever responsibilities the Home Office might have for Ulster, Sinn Fein would not sit down at the same table with their officials.

'It seems to me the Government is bending over backwards to accommodate the Provisional

IRA and the various splinter groups. There are no secrets any more; they demand justice for Kevin Hayes, you get fed to the wolves. Be interesting to know if our security files were walked across the river.'

Harriet went over to the sink again and turned off the taps. 'I doubt we'll get to sleep,' she said for the benefit of the eavesdroppers, 'but let's go back to bed.'

★ ★ ★

For all that Brian Thomas had been born in Stanmore, he saw himself as a Londoner through and through. Given any choice, he would have been quite content to spend the rest of his life anywhere within a five-mile radius of Bethnal Green where he had met his wife, Brenda, when both of them had been police constables serving in H District. However, Brenda had always dreamed of retiring to a cottage in the country with roses round the door or a bungalow on the Cornish Riviera. They had settled for a detached four-bedroom house in Chorleywood, approximately twenty-five miles north-west of London and the last but two stops on the good old Metropolitan Line to Amersham.

He had tried to make Brenda see that the house was far too big for them but she had set her heart on it the moment she had laid eyes on the place. Brenda had maintained the spare bedrooms were needed for the children and grandchildren when they came to visit. The truth was they had two daughters, one of whom was definitely gay while the other, though married, was too busy pursuing a career in advertising to think of raising a family.

There was another truth Brenda hadn't faced; they had sold and bought at the wrong time. Contrary to what the estate agent had thought, their flat in Highbury hadn't fetched anything like the amount they had hoped for. Chorley-wood was a much more desirable area than Highbury which, coupled with the fact that they were buying a larger property, meant Thomas had had to take out a sizeable mortgage. As a former chief superintendent he received a fairly substantial pension, and the building society had been happy to lend him the money. However, because of his age, they had stipulated the loan had to be repaid within ten years. He still had five years to go; whenever he felt like throwing the towel in this was the inescapable factor which kept his nose to the grindstone.

Thomas was a highly organised man whose routine never varied except at weekends. Every morning from Monday to Friday he rose at six-fifteen, prepared his own breakfast and left the house at twenty past seven to walk the half-mile to the station. It wasn't the easiest journey in the world — the Metropolitan Line to Baker Street, change on to the Jubilee Line before alighting at Green Park for the final leg to Vauxhall courtesy of the Victoria Line. His well-established routine suffered a hiccup that morning when the telephone rang ten minutes before he was due to leave the house. Although he tried to ignore the strident summons, he had a feeling the caller would hang on until somebody responded. Lifting the receiver, he rattled off the area code and subscriber's number.

'Guess who?' said a familiar voice.

Thomas came close to sighing out loud. Ordinarily he had a lot of time for Ashton but right now he was bad news.

'I've been warned off you,' he said quietly.

'Are you going to hang up on me?'

'Not before I've heard what you want.'

'Terry Hicks will be back at work today.'

'That's nice to know,' Thomas said acidly.

'He found a couple of bugs in my brother-in-law's house. There is reason to suppose they were planted over seven weeks ago.'

'While you were staying at Amberley Lodge?'

'So it would appear. Whoever did it could only have got Richard Egan's address from our security files.'

'Now just a minute,' Thomas said heatedly, 'are you inferring I leaked the information?'

'You're the last person I'd suspect.'

'Didn't sound that way to me.'

'Roy Kelso would have sent for my security file when the high-priced help decided the best thing I could do was disappear. Right?'

'Yes. For the record that decison was taken before the coroner's inquest was convened. Incidentally, he also sent for Harriet's file, which was in the dead sack.'

'What was it doing there?'

'Where else would it have been?' Thomas said, then realised what Ashton was getting at.

Harriet's security file had come across from MI5 when she had been seconded to the SIS. It should have been returned to Gower Street when she had resigned after being seriously injured by rioting Turkish *Gastarbeiters* in Berlin. In the end the oversight hadn't mattered because eighteen months later she had returned to the fold as a standby 'housekeeper'. However, back in March, Harriet had been made redundant in a cost-cutting exercise. Evidently Ashton believed they'd been wrong to keep the file but Thomas disagreed.

'I think we were right to retain the file. After all, we were the last people to employ Harriet and it wasn't as if she was going back to Five.'

'OK, when did Kelso return our files to you?'

'Three weeks ago.'

'So he kept them for a month after we left Amberley Lodge and went to ground.'

In the brief silence which followed Thomas could hear Ashton clucking his tongue.

'Any idea who else might have seen the files during the time they were in Roy's possession?'

'Come on, Peter, you know better than to ask.'

'You're right, it's almost impossible to keep track of a file when it's in the hands of a senior officer. It gets shown to colleagues who are thought to have an interest. Damned thing could even be walked across the river to the FCO and no one would be any the wiser . . . '

'Jill and I looked at your files yesterday. Roy Kelso had discovered Hicks had taken a day off and reported the facts to Ms Sheridan. She figured he was doing something for you and put two and two together when she found your brother-in-law's home address.'

'In whose file?'

'Harriet's.'

'Was the same information contained in mine?'

'No. It should have been and I can't think why it wasn't.' Thomas glanced at his wristwatch and was startled to see it was coming up to seven-thirty.

'Listen, I have to go . . . '

'OK, but let me give you the number of my mobile . . . '

'Forget it, you're *persona non grata*.'

'I need to get in touch with Nancy Wilkins.'

Thomas blinked. What the hell did Ashton want with Nancy Wilkins, the most unconventional clerical officer the SIS had ever recruited? She looked about fourteen years old and, as befitted someone who'd graduated in Media Studies, had been known to appear in trainers, jeans, and a denim jacket over a dark blue cotton shirt. He recalled her turning up in a brown leather suit that creaked with every step she took and it wouldn't surprise him if one day she came to work with a stud in her nose. The betting had been that she wouldn't last a month but five months later she was still working in Central Registry.

Central Registry; that's why Ashton wanted to get in touch with Nancy Wilkins. He was going to ask her to check the Confidential, Secret and Top Secret dispatch registers for the critical four weeks when Kelso was holding on to his and

Harriet's security files.

'OK,' Thomas said, 'let's have the number of your mobile.'

★ ★ ★

His name was George Foley, a tall, handsome-looking thirty-one-year-old from County Monaghan, whose ready smile gave the impression that he wouldn't harm a fly. Operating across the border, he had in fact killed three Brits in the bandit country of South Armagh with a .50/12.7mm calibre RAI long-range sniper rifle. Although employed as a sniper, Foley was not a marksman but then he didn't need to be. All three Brits had been shot from a well-concealed hide at a maximum range of 300 metres. It wasn't necessary to go for a head shot; the body armour which could withstand a hit from the Research Armament Industries rifle had yet to be developed. Furthermore, the damage caused by the .50 calibre round was such that even a shoulder or leg wound could prove fatal if there was any delay in airlifting the casualty to the nearest surgical unit.

Right from the moment it had first been mooted by the army's High Command, Foley had profoundly disagreed with the concept of a ceasefire. In his view a war was fought to be won and a lot of good men hadn't been killed in action so that arseholes like Gerry Adams and Martin McGuinness could sit around a table hobnobbing with the enemy. He had therefore left the Provisional IRA and joined Continuity

85

IRA, a hard-line splinter group which had pledged to carry on the struggle. Cross-border operations were out; Continuity believed in striking at the mainland.

In pursuance of this policy, Foley had been sent to London where on and off for the past four weeks he had been residing with a widow in Lewisham. Alighting from the 3.18 p.m. stopping train from London Bridge, Foley left the station and made his way to 104 Sandrock Road.

The only thing which distinguished number 104 from the other semi-detacheds in the road was its close proximity to the bowling greens, cricket ground and tennis courts of Hilly Fields. Foley pushed the gate open, walked up the front path and rattled the knocker until Sandra Hayes came to the door.

'Couldn't let you spend the weekend alone,' he said, and stepped past her into the hall.

'I have the boys.'

She had three sons: Tyrone aged twelve; Billy, ten; and Sean, eight.

'So where are the boys now?' Foley asked.

'Up the rec.'

'Yeah? Well, let's have a bit of fun while we can.'

He steered Sandra towards the staircase, gave her a friendly pat on the backside and got an appreciative wiggle in return. One thing you could say for widow Hayes, she didn't believe in grieving overlong.

'Where have you been all week?' she asked as she unzipped her dress and pulled it off over her head.

'Up in Lichfield, frightening the life out of Ashton's bint.'

'You should have killed her husband while you had the chance. You could lose track of him.'

'There's no danger of that,' Foley said, and forced her down into a kneeling position on the bed.

* * *

The brown envelope which arrived with the first post was the only item of personal mail amongst the dross pushed through the letter box. The rest were circulars addressed to The Occupant, 12 Gaia Lane, Lichfield, Staffs. Ashton didn't recognise the handwriting, and while the postmark showed that the envelope had been mailed in London yesterday, the actual district was illegible. He held the envelope up to the light and felt all round the flap to satisfy himself it wasn't a letter bomb, then, somewhat gingerly, slit the envelope open and withdrew a large black-and-white photograph.

Attached to the photo was a memo written in green ink, the prerogative of the DG whose hand Ashton immediately recognised. The note from Hazelwood was brief and merely asked him a question he could have answered with ease, but the days when Ashton would have done almost anything for Victor at the drop of a hat were long gone now. So he locked everything away in the centre drawer of his desk up in the attic room, and went about his own business.

Ashton drove into town and drew eight

hundred pounds from his and Harriet's joint account. From a hardware store he purchased a pane of glass, a small trowel and 500 grams of putty. Nobody had ever accused him of being a handyman, and removing the remaining portion of the pane of glass in the kitchen door took him far longer than he cared to think about. It was only after he had chipped out the old putty and cleaned up the frame that he discovered the replacement pane was a shade too small. Sneaking out of the house, he went to a glazier on the outskirts of Lichfield and got him to cut another piece of glass. By the time Ashton finished the job it was gone four.

Brian Thomas rang at six-thirty from his home in Chorleywood and gave Ashton Nancy Wilkins' phone number and address in Burnt Oak. He took the call on his mobile upstairs in the attic room and suddenly, for no good reason, he felt compelled to do something about the photograph. Unlocking the centre drawer he took out the blurred photo and looked at it again. No question: the man standing at the kiosk outside the entrance to the Park Kultury Metro station was Pavel Trilisser. As a former Head of the Russian Desk and subsequently the Eastern Bloc Department, Hazelwood should have known who he was. Ashton wondered if in some convoluted way Victor was throwing him a lifeline. There was, however, no point in trying to second-guess his intentions; switching to transmit, he tapped out the number of the Mozart phone in Victor's study. It was, he knew, the one sure method of reaching him.

'It's me,' he said when Hazelwood answered. 'Don't switch to secure.'

'All right, but be careful and keep it short.'

'You're right, it's him. Is that short enough for you?'

'Indeed it is. Thank you for calling.'

'Is that all you can say? Don't you have anything for me?'

'Well, if there is anything I can do for you please don't hesitate to call me on this number.'

It was not the unequivocal response Ashton had hoped for.

6

They left the house in Gaia Lane at 10.30 a.m. on Saturday morning to follow the route to Helmsley which Ashton had worked out using the *AA Big Road Atlas*. From Lichfield he intended to take the A38, bypassing Derby to join the M1 motorway at South Normanton. At Junction 32, via the M18, they would switch to the A1 and stay with it until they were beyond RAF Dishforth. Thereafter they would make their way eastwards to pick up the A170 at Thirsk, which would lead them on to Helmsley where the Peacheys and their Special Branch minders were living.

Ten-thirty was a good time to depart. The milk, daily newspaper and the post had all been delivered and the Ashtons' absence was unlikely to be noticed by the neighbours until the milk piled up on the doorstep. As a precautionary measure, Ashton had walked round the car giving the bodywork a flick with a duster for the benefit of anybody who might be watching, while using the peeper with his free hand to examine the underside of the Volvo. The peeper was a wooden stave some four feet long with a mirror slotted into the tip at an angle of five degrees; it was the only item of defensive equipment he had been issued with and had, in fact, been in his possession for the past six years. When they finally departed, Ashton made a point of driving in and around Lichfield for a good twenty minutes before heading out of the city on the A38.

'I didn't see anybody following us,' he said presently.

'Neither did I,' Harriet told him.

'All the same, we'd better keep our eyes open. Sing out if you think we've got company.'

Harriet adjusted the door mirror on her side until she had the optimum wide angle view of the road behind them.

'I was going to do that anyway,' she said quietly.

'Yeah, I'll be teaching my grandmother to suck eggs next.'

Surveillance, tracking, evasion, defensive and offensive driving skills had all been part of the syllabus for the induction course Harriet had attended when she had transferred to the Security Service from the Home Office. Ashton remembered Peachey once telling him that Harriet had been head and shoulders above the rest of her entry.

'What did you tell Clifford Peachey when you phoned him yesterday?' he asked.

'The truth. I said we'd had to disappear and had had our new identities disclosed by a person or persons unknown. This had happened so rapidly we'd lost confidence in The Firm's ability to hide us. Hence we were making our own arrangements and would he and Ann be prepared to put us up for a couple of days while we sorted ourselves out?'

'And he was quite happy to do that?'

'Yes.'

'What about Ann — was she equally happy?'

There was a noticeable pause before Harriet said she imagined Ann had had no objection.

'In other words, Clifford didn't bother to ask her.'

'He didn't have to,' Harriet retorted.

'How do you know?'

'Because he told me so when I suggested he ought to have a word with Ann before lumbering her with the Ashton family.'

Ashton imagined it hadn't been all sweetness and light when Ann had learned what Clifford had let her in for. They were a childless couple and they were about to have their whole world turned upside down. Edward was hyperactive and an early riser, sometimes as early as four o'clock in the morning. If he had to share a room with his baby sister it was even money he would wake Carolyn and then the yowling would really begin.

'How many Special Branch officers are living with the Peacheys?'

'None.' Harriet paused, then said, 'Well, that's not strictly correct. There are a couple of nightwatchmen on duty from dusk till dawn.'

'Six months ago the Peacheys were being guarded round the clock.'

'According to Clifford the threat was reassessed in June and it was decided some scaling down on the level of protection would be in order.'

'Yeah? Who takes care of the daylight hours?'

'They have been issued with a number of

panic buttons,' Harriet told him. 'There are two in the house, one in the car and each has a personal bleeper. Press one of the panic buttons and the police guarantee an armed response team will be on the scene within four minutes.'

Ashton didn't like what Harriet was telling him. Last night she had assured him Clifford Peachey would not inform London they were staying with him; now, in the cold light of today, Ashton couldn't see that the former Deputy DG had much choice in the matter. The present security arrangement would prove inadequate when the Ashtons descended on the Peacheys. They would need round-the-clock protection again, and to get it Clifford would have to submit a case.

'A penny for them,' Harriet said.

'They're not worth it.'

Ashton knew that if he so much as hinted that Clifford would have to break his word to her, she would really go off at the deep end. Better to let Harriet work it out for herself.

'Be like that then,' she said, and lapsed into silence.

Time appeared to have a habit of standing still when Harriet wasn't talking to him. The speedometer had been hovering on sixty ever since he had turned on to the A38 and he began to wonder if he hadn't miscalculated the distance to the junction with the motorway at South Normanton. He had been driving automatically and didn't even remember bypassing Derby.

'I think we've got company,' Harriet said, breaking the silence that had existed between them for far too long. 'There's a red Ford Sierra four cars back.'

'When did you first notice it?' Ashton asked.

'Shortly before we reached the outskirts of Derby.'

'OK. Have a look at the road map and tell me where he could have left the A38.'

'I don't need a road map. From Derby onwards there are any number of major interchanges for places like Matlock, Ripley and Chesterfield. You could say he was spoiled for choice.'

'Well, let's see if we can draw him out of his shell.'

Ashton tripped the indicator to show he was going to head north on the M1 and eased into the slip road. After joining the motorway, he stayed in the inside lane until he saw the Ford Sierra was still tagging them. He checked his wing mirror to make sure it was safe to pull over into the centre lane, then dropped into third gear and floored the accelerator. The five-cylinder engine responded with a deep-throated snarl. He went into fourth, then overdrive, moved over into the outside lane and started overtaking everything on the road, the needle flirting with a hundred miles an hour.

'For God's sake,' Harriet exploded, 'slow down before you kill us all.'

Edward caught the anger in Harriet's voice and gave way to tears, which set Carolyn off. Ashton eased his foot marginally and allowed their speed to fall back to ninety. As he did so, Harriet assured Edward that she certainly wasn't cross with him and it was just Mummy being silly because Daddy knew what he was doing. Her narrowed eyes told a different story and she was giving off enough static to light up a house. Nevertheless, Ashton stayed in the outside lane all the way to Junction 31, covering fourteen miles in just nine minutes. Observing a gap in the traffic using the middle lane, Ashton moved across, easing the Volvo between a coach and a Volkswagen Passat. A few seconds later the red Ford Sierra overtook them in the outside lane.

'HDA 908Z,' Ashton said, reading the number plate. 'You want to make a note of it?'

'I already have,' Harriet informed him. 'I logged the number as we joined the motorway.'

The ability to read numbers backwards and upside down was one of the tricks of the trade Harriet had acquired on her induction course.

Ashton checked the rear-view mirror for fast traffic in the outside lane and tripped the indicator. 'Hold on to your hat,' he said, and pulled out.

Conscious that Harriet was watching the speedometer like a hawk, he didn't go above ninety. After covering approximately five miles in the outside lane, he spotted the Ford Sierra on the inside, boxed in by a 38 ton rig and a dumper truck.

'That's what you call a bad move,' Ashton said cheerfully.

'Only if he is on his own,' Harriet said quietly.

'What have you seen?'

'A Mazda 323, pale green, metallic finish, with a West Midlands registration number. LKV 533

95

something — could be a V or a W.'

'When did you first notice the car?'

'Soon after we joined the motorway.'

Ashton glanced at the tripmeter. It had been registering thirty-seven miles when they turned onto the M1, now it was showing fifty-seven. The driver of the Mazda had therefore done exactly twenty miles on the motorway, which didn't seem at all sinister to Ashton.

Ashton stayed in the outside lane. He assumed the Ford Sierra was still boxed in because there was no sign of the car in the rear-view mirror. One mile short of the junction with the M18, he moved into the centre lane, then filtered into the slow track next to the hard shoulder. The Mazda sailed on past them, so did the Ford Sierra, both drivers looking to pass east of Doncaster as he continued on the M1.

'Looks as though we were worrying about nothing,' Ashton said. 'Unless of course you've noticed a third vehicle playing tag with us?'

'We would use three vehicles,' Harriet reminded him. 'If they are doing the same, spotting the tail-end Charlie could be difficult.' Her eyebrows met in a frown. 'I keep thinking about the threatening letter which was left in the Volvo. We thought the IRA was engaging in a bit of psychological warfare but what if the note was meant to create just such an impression? What if they had to get into the Volvo to plant something?'

'Like a miniature homing beacon,' Ashton said thoughtfully. 'It's transmitting a signal we can't hear.'

96

'Exactly.'

He glanced at the facia. 'And it's probably lodged behind the instrument panel.'

'Never mind where the damned thing is located; unless we do something about it we will lead these people straight to the Peacheys.'

'Then we'd better get ourselves some alternative transport. Give me a route to the nearest major town.'

Harriet reached for the *AA Big Road Atlas* which she had tucked between the seat and the nearside door, and opened it at page 55.

'We are approaching Junction 37,' Ashton told her.

'OK. If you take the A628 at the junction then the A6, we'll be on the road to Wakefield. From there, we have a choice of routes into Leeds.'

Ashton nodded. 'There's an airport serving Leeds and Bradford,' he said. 'See if you can find it on the map.'

The Leeds – Bradford airport was likely to be no more than a feeder but Ashton figured there was a reasonable chance of finding an Avis or Hertz rental agency at the terminal building. If he was wrong, there was bound to be somebody who could point him in the right direction. His plan was simple enough; he would send Harriet and the children on to Helmsley in the rented car while he headed south to London in the Volvo. Once there, he intended to shake a few branches and see what fell out of the tree.

★ ★ ★

97

There had been a time when Katya Malinovskaya would not have looked out of place on the front cover of any of Moscow's fashion magazines which had burgeoned with the coming of Perestroika. In the changed circumstances of the former Soviet Union, she had been chosen to represent the more acceptable face of the KGB's Second Chief Directorate. But in those days Katya had been more than just a pretty face. In fact, until a near-fatal knife wound in the back had put paid to her career, she had been one of the rising stars in the Criminal Investigation Division, which had grown out of the former Twelfth Department.

Invalided out of the service, Katya Malinovskaya had established her own security agency at number 124 Gorky Street, a grey, anonymous building near the top of the incline some four hundred yards from what used to be Marx Prospekt. Her clients were the nouveaux riches — the commodity brokers, currency speculators and almost every entrepreneur threatened by the Mafiozniki, because he, or she, had jibbed at the amount of protection money they had demanded. No job was outside the bounds of acceptable behaviour; the only thing which interested Katya Malinovskaya these days was the colour of a client's money. Long ago she had accepted that to maintain her present lifestyle she couldn't afford to be choosy.

Nevertheless, despite living in the lap of luxury, the last three years had not been kind to her. Although not yet an alcoholic, she was drinking far too much, overeating and not taking sufficient exercise. Nowadays there was a spare tyre around her waist, her face had filled out and her complexion was blotchy. She was thirty-two years old but appeared to be nudging forty. However, the odd strand of grey which had begun to appear in the light brown hair was entirely due to her latest client, Vladislav Sergeevich Kochelev, and the enemies he had made.

Kochelev was a government auditor who had been appointed by President Yeltsin to examine the disbursement of monies from the Kremlin's domestic budget. By the time he had completed his investigation, Kochelev had irrefutable evidence that Pavel Trilisser, the President's special advisor on foreign affairs, had misappropriated twelve million dollars which he had used to speculate on the US futures market. Had he deliberately set out to embarrass President Yeltsin, Kochelev could not have done a better job.

The twelve million dollars, along with the rest of the Kremlin's domestic budget, had been siphoned from a multibillion aid package put together by the International Monetary Fund to bale out the Russian economy. The financial sleight of hand had been effected without Yeltsin's knowledge; the fact that it had been perpetrated by one of his closest advisers had angered him beyond measure.

Pavel Trilisser had been charged with twelve counts of embezzlement and had supposedly been under house arrest since the beginning of February. In practice, the police weren't enforcing the order and it seemed the former special advisor was free to wander around Moscow whenever he felt like it. Furthermore, a trial date originally set for Wednesday, 27 March had been postponed twice and was now scheduled for Monday, 22 July.

The trial date could not come soon enough for Katya Malinovskaya, whose agency had been looking after Vladislav Kochelev ever since Pavel Trilisser had been indicted. She had been given the job by Moscow's Chief of Police, Major General Gurov, who had refused to put the lives of his own men at risk. He had also been aware that Kochelev was walking around with a hundred-thousand-dollar price tag on his head and Gurov wasn't too sure some of his officers wouldn't be tempted.

Katya and the government auditor had survived thus far because she had made it a rule never to spend more than four nights in one place. In Moscow, she had stayed in the Olympic village, then moved to the Borisova district where she had joined a community of squatters occupying an old abandoned infantry barracks. A fire-gutted medical centre in Chimki-Chovrino had been her last refuge before leaving Moscow for St Petersburg.

Two days after arriving in St Petersburg, Major General Gurov had sent word that the local Mafiozniki knew she was in their neck of the woods and were looking for her. Thereafter Katya had lived a nomadic existence journeying to Tallinn in Estonia and thence to Tartu, Pskov, Luga and Novgorod. Yesterday, Katya

Malinovskaya, Kochelev and the two body-guards who had been with her since day one, had stayed at Torzhok. Tonight they would stop at Tven', one hundred miles north-west of Moscow.

They had been on the run for twenty weeks and it was almost inevitable that relationships had been strained to breaking point. Everybody hated Kochelev but there had been numerous spats between the two bodyguards, both of whom had had a go at Katya on more than one occasion.

When it came to safeguarding valuables, property and business people, Katya Malinovskaya normally found the manpower she needed from off-duty police officers who were eager to supplement their income. Kochelev was an abnormal case because there was a huge bounty on his head and the police officer or militiaman who wouldn't cut his grandmother's throat for the money on offer hadn't yet been born. The only two people Katya could trust implicitly were Sasha Vasilyev, her long-serving bodyguard, and his girlfriend, Raya Oskinova.

They stopped for lunch at a small village called Novo Osery, which was so insignificant that, even though it was on the main Moscow-to-St Petersburg line, only one train a day in each direction stopped at the wayside station. The village did, however, boast a log cabin which served as a beer hall and restaurant. Much to Katya's surprise the food was good, especially the cold vegetable soup of dill, cucumber, onion and garlic with small pieces of beef and a dash of kvas. They were just finishing their meal when Katya's battered-looking Skoda saloon attracted the unwelcome attention of a militiaman.

'This is bad,' Kochelev said nervously. 'Why is he so interested in the car?'

'Perhaps he hasn't seen a Skoda before,' Sasha said, and laughed.

'You're a mentally retarded fool.'

'Apart from being a complete prick, you know what your trouble is, Vladislav Kochelev? You don't have a sense of humour.'

Katya slapped the table with her palm. 'That's enough everybody,' she said angrily. 'No more sniping at each other. Drink your beers and cool it.'

'It's all very well for you to say cool it,' Kochelev whined, 'but you're not likely to be assassinated by the Mafiozniki.'

That's all you know, Katya thought. She had fallen foul of the Mafiozniki once before, in March 1995, when they had called at her villa five miles out of town on the road to Sergiyev Posad. The gang, who came from the notorious Babuskin district of Moscow, had used a 6 × 4 Zil truck to smash down the railings and wrought-iron gates which surrounded the property. Then they had broken into the house, dragged Katya out of bed and had frogmarched her out of the house. It had been a bitterly cold night and she had been forced to stand there in her pyjamas and bare feet while two gunmen armed with Kalashnikov AK-47 assault rifles had riddled her Mercedes Benz SL600 with automatic fire until it had resembled a sieve. 'Next time we do this to you,' one of them had told her.

Six months later the Babuskin Mafiozniki had ceased to exist. Every last man had been gunned down in a vicious gangland war with the more powerful organisation in the neighbouring Medvedkovo district. One of the reasons why Katya had agreed to look after Kochelev was the mistaken belief that following the demise of the Babuskin gang, she had nothing to fear from the other Mafiozniki groups.

'I wish I had never reported the discrepancies in the Kremlin domestic budget,' Kochelev said plaintively.

'You're not the only one,' Raya Oskinova told him.

'What choice did I have?' Kochelev asked her. 'The President was convinced the budget was being milked and I was told what he expected me to find.'

Sasha rested both forearms on the wooden table separating him from Katya Malinovskaya and leaned forward. 'That militiaman is taking a good hard look at the Moscow plates on the Skoda,' he said quietly. 'It could be he is just plain nosy but I think we ought to move on.'

'You're right.' Katya raised her voice. 'Drink up everybody — let's go.'

When they went outside, the militiaman was walking round the Skoda as though appraising its condition and market value.

'Thinking of buying it?' Sasha asked cheekily.

'Are you the owner then?'

'No, I am,' Katya Malinovskaya informed him.
'I have four hundred American dollars,' the militiaman said.

'That's enough for the spare wheel. Try again when you've got some real money,' Katya said, and got into the car.

The temperature was up in the high seventies and even though she had left the window partially open on her side, the interior of the Skoda was still like an oven. She felt hot, breathless and was perspiring freely, which was only to be expected. The stomach cramps were, however, attributable to pure fear.

* * *

It was the best day of the week and the best time of the day in the best season of the year. Six-thirty on a beautiful Saturday evening after a hot summer's day. Hazelwood was lying on a sun lounger, a contented man smoking a Burma cheroot, with a large gin and tonic, instead of the usual whisky soda, within easy reach. Having just mowed the lawn, it was, he thought, no more than he deserved. Then the resident bodyguard, a former SAS NCO, had to go and spoil it all by suddenly appearing on the scene with the news that Mr Peachey was on the phone and would like to have a word with him.

'Which telephone?' Hazelwood asked.

'The residential one, sir.'

There were three linked phones in the house, one in the hall, another in the kitchen, the third in the sitting room. The fact was, the study was the only room where smoking was permitted. It also happened to be where the Mozart secure-speech facility was installed, which Peachey was now unable to access.

'No peace for the wicked,' Hazelwood grumbled, then got to his feet and made for the nearest telephone. Before going indoors he buried the cheroot in one of the large terracotta pots of geraniums either side of the front door.

It was the first time he had heard from his former deputy and he guessed Peachey hadn't called him for purely social reasons.

'This is a pleasant surprise,' Hazelwood said casually. 'How has life been treating you, Clifford?'

'Pretty good,' Peachey told him. 'We've got Harriet and the children staying with us. She arrived this afternoon.'

'How is she?'

'A little worried.'

'And Peter?'

'He's not with them.'

'Never mind the veiled speech,' Hazelwood told him. 'Just give it to me in plain English.'

Peachey did exactly that, beginning with the threatening letter which had been left inside the Volvo before moving on to the crossbow incident. Harriet had also told him they had been tagged by a three-vehicle surveillance team and was convinced a homing device had been attached to their car, but he had his reservations about that.

'I think Ashton planted the idea in her head,' Peachey said.

'Why would he do that, Clifford?'

'You shouldn't have to ask me, Victor. You've known him a hell of a sight longer than I have. Running from trouble has never been his style; he goes looking for it but Harriet is a restraining influence. So he has to make her see it his way. Naturally, once Harriet has got it into her head that a homing device has been attached to their Volvo, she agrees something has to be done about it otherwise they will lead the IRA to us. As a result she comes on with the children in a rented car while Ashton heads south in the Volvo, drawing them off.'

'You make him sound positively Machiavellian.'

'Well, I happen to think he is,' Peachey said quietly. 'For the record, Ashton hasn't reported any of the incidents I've just related to their Special Branch liaison officer. But I will have to because we're going to need round-the-clock protection again. And by 'we' I mean Harriet and the children.'

'Right. How can I help?'

'You could try bringing Ashton to heel,' Peachey said, and hung up.

★   ★   ★

Katya had counted on reaching Tver' before nightfall but the fates had conspired against them. The radiator on the Skoda had sprung a leak and had boiled over twice, which meant they'd had to stop and wait for the engine to cool down. Fortunately on the second occasion they had broken down on the outskirts of a village and had been able to top up the header tank. Sasha had also bought five eggs which he'd cracked and emptied into the radiator in the belief the egg white would find the leak and seal it. Katya still didn't know whether or not the remedy had worked; some forty minutes after leaving the village, they'd had a blow-out and lost at least another fifteen minutes changing the wheel.

With the night closing in rapidly, Sasha had persuaded her to let him do the driving, while she navigated, which was no joke when you were somewhere in the middle of a huge forest of fir trees and all you had was a small-scale map. It didn't help either when it was pitch-dark and there were no distinguishing landmarks she could use as reference points. And to cap it all, the alternator was on the blink and the main beams were about as effective as a couple of glow-worms.

'How much further to the Tver' highway?' Sasha asked.

'No more than ten minutes,' Katya told him. The truth was she hadn't the faintest idea how long it would take them.

'Does the map show this dirt road crossing the railway?'

Katya opened her handbag, took out a pocket flashlight and trained it on the map. They had crossed the main St Petersburg-to-Moscow line back at Novo Osery, where they had stopped for a bite to eat, and they wouldn't meet another railtrack before Tver'. Yet approximately one hundred metres ahead a red light was flashing intermittently.

At fifty metres she could see there were two vehicles drawn up at staggered intervals on opposite sides of the track to form a road block. Any driver going through it would be forced to slow right down in order to negotiate what amounted to a tight S-bend. As they drew even nearer, the feeble main beams on the Skoda picked out a police car and a grey-coloured van. A split second before a powerful spotlight was trained on the windscreen which practically blinded her, Katya saw the road block was manned by a group of civilians armed with pump-action shotguns, Kalashnikov AK-47s and Uzi sub-machine-guns.

In that same instant Sasha realised they were driving into a carefully prepared ambush. Mouthing a stream of obscenities, he put the wheel hard over to the right to aim the Skoda at a fire-break between the fir trees, and floored the accelerator. As they left the dirt road they came under a hail of small-arms fire.

The noise was incredible. Everybody was screaming — Sasha, Raya Oskinova, Katya and Vladislav Kochelev. Round after round punched through the car, shattering both windows on the offside as well as the rear. Sasha lost the top of his head, which resulted in a fountain of blood and brain tissue hitting Katya in the face. Then the Skoda smashed into a tree and came to a dead stop.

Two things saved Katya: the seat belt and her presence of mind. The seat belt might have bruised her chest and stomach but it undoubtedly saved her life. Although winded, she instinctively released the belt, opened the door on her side and tumbled out of the car. Nursing her injured stomach, she started running. Behind her, Katya could hear Kochelev begging for his life, trying to convince the gunmen he had no intention of going into the witness box to testify against Pavel Trilisser. Somebody laughed, evidently amused by the incongruity of it all; moments later Kochelev's silence was permanently secured by a prolonged burst of fire from a sub-machine-gun.

Katya blundered on, running blind in the dark. She tripped over an exposed root, crashed through a clump of bushes and fell headlong into a large pool of stagnant water. She came up spluttering, thought about remaining submerged while the gunmen searched the immediate area, then rejected the idea because she had disturbed the algae covering the pool and the hunters would know she was in there. Katya clambered out, started jogging again, then fell down exhausted after covering less than forty metres.

Flashlights bobbed and danced about like fireflies, the hunters calling out to one another as they searched for her. Both of her parents had been lifelong members of the Communist Party and Katya had been an atheist for as long as she could remember. But at ten past nine that night she embraced Christianity with all the fervour of a convert who knows her life is in grave danger, and she prayed to God they wouldn't find her.

The voices came closer and Katya heard one

of the men shout in triumph that she was hiding in the pool. And if the subsequent cacophony was anything to go by at least five gunmen must have lined up on the bank to empty their magazines into the water. The echoes from the gunfire died away to nothing and in the silence which followed, she thought she could hear them moving back towards the dirt road. Presently there was a hollow whoomph as they set fire to the Skoda. Then one after the other the drivers of the police car and the grey van started their engines, shifted into gear and drove away.

7

George Elphinstone was in his third year, as Head of Station, Moscow, although there were times when it seemed as if he had been holding the appointment since the year dot. His first and only love was the Middle East, where he had spent the greater part of his career. He had cut his teeth in Jordan and had subsequently honed his skills in Syria, and the Lebanon, which had been the most hazardous assignment to date. Immediately prior to 1992, when he had attended the two-year Russian language course run by the combined services at Beaconsfield, Elphinstone had been the Deputy Head of Station, Cairo, a city, which despite the squalor, had fascinated him more than Moscow ever would.

Hazelwood's predecessor had given Elphinstone to understand that Moscow was merely a stepping stone to bigger things. Rightly or wrongly, he had taken this to mean that he was in line for the post of Assistant Director, Mid East Department. Then Ms Jill Sheridan had been appointed in his stead barely seven months after he had arrived in Moscow and he had had to revise his original assumption to next but one in line. That illusion had lasted until the beginning of June when Jill Sheridan had been confirmed in the appointment of Deputy DG and Winston Reid from the FCO had been brought in to run the Mid East Department.

It was now blindingly apparent to Elphinstone that his superiors considered he had reached his ceiling and would go no further. Although this was hard to take, he had concealed his disappointment behind a mask of indifference. He had, however, lost all enthusiasm for the job and the irregular hours it frequently entailed. When there had been a reason for him to believe he was going places, he hadn't minded working all the hours God made, but it was a different story in the twilight of his career and he resented being called into the office on a Sunday morning.

The man who was responsible for dragging him into the office was Chris Neighbour, a very bright grade II intelligence officer whose only fault was a tendency to allow his youthful enthusiasm to influence his judgement.

Elphinstone drove through the gates of the large, elegant Tsarist villa on the Maurice Thorez Embankment and parked his Rover 600 in the space allocated to the Counsellor, European Union Affairs, the diplomatic cover for Head of Station, Moscow. The SIS cell was on the top floor along the corridor from the Ambassador, Minister and Head of Chancery. From his office Elphinstone had an unrivalled view of the Great Kremlin Palace, the golden onion domes of the Cathedral of the Annunciation and the Ivan the Great bell tower. It was a vista his successor would have little time to appreciate. Work had already started on the new purpose-built Embassy on Sofiyskaya Naberezhnaya at the bend in the Moscow River directly opposite the White House, the Russian parliament building. It would take three years to build and would cost £80 million. If everything went according to plan the move would take place in March 2000, by which time Elphinstone would be enjoying his retirement years in Dartmouth.

Chris Neighbour was waiting for him at the desk manned by one of the embassy's security officers who controlled access to the high-risk area. His exuberance and cheerful good morning grated on Elphinstone and he was barely civil to the younger man.

'So what's this all about?' Elphinstone demanded when they were ensconced in his office.

'I've had a phone call from a woman claiming to be Katya Malinovskaya,' Neighbour told him.

'The name sounds vaguely familiar.'

'Malinovskaya is known to us; she was a rising star in the Criminal Investigation Division before she went freelance.'

'And what does she want from us, Chris?'

'Political asylum,' Neighbour said.

'She'd better have a damn good reason.'

'Her security agency was hired by Major General Gurov, the Chief of Police, to ensure Vladislav Kochelev remained fit to testify against Pavel Trilisser. After two postponements the trial date was set for tomorrow.'

'Was,' Elphinstone intoned.

'Kochelev was killed in an ambush last night.'

Elphinstone sat down behind his desk and waved the younger man to his chair. 'I think you had better give me the whole story according to Katya Malinovskaya,' he said.

'She says Major General Gurov was determined that Trilisser should stand trial but a person or persons unknown had put a hundred-thousand-dollar price tag on Kochelev's head and he had feared his own men might be tempted.'

As evidence of his commitment, Moscow's Chief of Police had provided Katya Malinovskaya with a war chest of twenty thousand US dollars for expenses. Gurov had also undertaken to pass on any information which could affect the wellbeing of the State's star witness. To do this, he had devised a simple method of communication between them.

'He gave Katya the number of his mobile to enable her to phone him every night between seven-thirty and eleven.'

'When presumably he would be at home?' Elphinstone said.

'Yes. Gurov couldn't possibly phone Katya because she kept her mobile switched off until she was ready to ring him.'

'Didn't save her from driving into an ambush, did it?'

'No, it didn't,' Neighbour agreed with some reluctance.

'Does she have any idea who set the ambush?'

'A police car formed part of the roadblock, but the gunmen were definitely Mafiozniki.'

'We shouldn't have anything to do with organised crime.'

'With respect, George, apart from the money

114

the Mafiozniki had nothing to gain by murdering Kochelev but the people who hired them to kill him most certainly did. Katya Malinovskaya looked after Vladislav Kochelev for over five months and I believe her when she says there were no secrets between them.'

In Elphinstone's opinion Chris Neighbour was one of those eager young men who were inclined to be a little blinkered once they got a particular bee in their bonnet. He reminded himself it was Neighbour who had persuaded him to pay a thousand pounds for a dubious snapshot of Pavel Trilisser, taken outside the Park Kultury Metro station.

'Have we heard from London concerning the print we sent them of Pavel Trilisser?' he asked.

'This morning,' Neighbour told him. 'They agreed our identification. I left word with the duty clerks to contact me if they received anything from London over the weekend. That's how I happened to be here when Katya Malinovskaya rang the embassy.'

Elphinstone thought it also explained why Neighbour was so fired up about Katya Malinovskaya and the information she could give them about the ailing President Yeltsin and the power struggle between the Kremlin and the Russian Parliament.

'How much does the lady want?' Using his feet, Elphinstone turned the swivel chair towards the window and gazed at the nine gilded onion domes of the Cathedral of the Annunciation towering above the Kremlin wall. 'There's always a price, Chris,' he added in a low voice.

'She wants to be relocated in England, provided with a fully furnished house of her choosing and given enough start-up money to launch a new business.'

'And how much might that amount to?'

'She thought three hundred thousand would be about right.'

'I imagine she did,' Elphinstone said derisively.

'I'm sure we can beat her down to a more realistic figure, George.' Neighbour glanced at his wristwatch. 'Katya is going to phone me at one p.m., which is just under two hours from now.'

'Tell her we're not interested.'

'If we turn her down she will go to the Americans.'

'You presume.'

'No, I got that from Malinovskaya herself and she wasn't bluffing.'

'So we were and still are her first choice?' Elphinstone snorted. 'If you believe that you'll believe anything.'

'Malinovskaya chose us because she knows Peter Ashton and apparently trusts him.'

Elphinstone swung round in the chair to face the younger man again. 'Ashton, that loose cannon?'

'Well, I don't know about the loose cannon bit, George, but that was the name she mentioned.'

Elphinstone had met Ashton only once but he was the sort of man you didn't forget in a hurry. Known as Hazelwood's Rottweiler, his reputation had preceded him on what must have been his fifth trip to Moscow. Although there had been none of the usual mayhem and bloodshed while he was in town, it hadn't all been sweetness and light. Ashton had been arrested on a trumped-up charge and deported, which would have been pretty straightforward had it not been for the fact that some of Pavel Trilisser's friends had wanted him dead. Instead of putting Ashton on a British Airways flight out of Sheremetyevo, they had sent him to St Petersburg by train where he was supposed to be handed over to the British consular officer. However, the escort had had other ideas, and they had dumped Ashton miles away in the Karelian Peninsula on a bitterly cold February night with the temperature down to minus 9 degrees centigrade, in the confident expectation he would be frozen to death.

'It's now twenty-five minutes to twelve, George.'

'I'm aware of the time,' Elphinstone snapped. 'I'm more interested to hear what our Minister had to say about this development.'

'I haven't informed anybody on the diplomatic side. I thought it would carry more weight coming from you,' Neighbour said, colouring.

'You're right. Where is Katya Malinovskaya now? Somewhere in Moscow?'

'No, she's in Tver'. She wants us to collect her.'

'That's over a hundred miles away.'

'Katya's broke, she has no transport and the Mafiozniki are looking for her.'

'People who are seeking political asylum

117

usually present themselves on the doorstep. It's not our job to go out and collect them.' Elphinstone shook his head. 'I can't see the Ambassador wearing this.'

'Is that what I'm to tell Katya when she calls?' Neighbour asked.

'No, it damned well isn't; use your initiative and stall her.'

★ ★ ★

Hicks opened his eyes, then hurriedly closed them again as the blaze of sunlight through the gap between the curtains half blinded him and immediately reawakened a splitting headache. His mouth felt like the proverbial bottom of a baby's pram — all piss and broken biscuits. From past experience he knew his tongue to be coated with a thick white paste because his lips were gummed up. 'Never again,' he promised himself, repeating a vow he'd broken many times.

It had been the Saturday night to end all Saturday nights, a celebratory gathering of the best five-man team in the tenpin bowling club. The wives, girlfriends and partners had been there to cheer them on as they won the team championship. And everybody had been drinking 7-Up or Coke laced with vodka so that they were all in a very happy mood by the time they arrived at his semi-detached in Sunleigh Road.

He had laid in cans of lager, best bitter and a dozen bottles of assorted wines. As Hicks recollected the proceedings, they had then got down to some serious drinking and before long most of the girls had been pretty much the worse for wear. The partner of one of his best mates had started acting the goat by putting herself about, with the result that Hicks's wife, Lorna, had said her piece and then gone to bed, leaving them to it.

Hicks supposed it must have been almost three o'clock in the morning when he had finally staggered up to bed. He distinctly remembered the Westminster clock chiming twice and that had been a good while before he'd phoned for a minicab to take the last of the travellers home. Lorna would have barred him from the bedroom if she had had her way but the key had gone missing years ago. There had been no kiss and make up; when he had reached for her, Lorna had pinched his left nipple hard enough to make him yelp. That, Hicks had to admit, had dampened his ardour.

He turned over in bed to face Lorna but when he reached out to embrace her, he discovered she was no longer there beside him. If by chance Lorna had gone downstairs to make a pot of tea, he nursed a faint hope she would be forgiving enough to bring him a cup. Suddenly the phone in the hall started ringing and he pulled the bedclothes over his head, hoping to shut out the noise. For a few brief moments it seemed he had been successful; then Lorna yelled the call was for him and would he get down there straight away?

'Tell whoever it is to call back later,' Hicks shouted, and winced from the effort of raising his voice.

'You tell him, he's your workmate. Name's Peters.'

Hicks kicked off the sheet and duvet and sat up on the edge of the bed. Peters: who the hell was Peters?

'Did you hear what I said?' Lorna screamed.

'All right, all right, I'm coming.'

He stood up on legs that felt as though they would give way under him at any moment, and somehow made it to the landing without falling down. Thereafter he held on to the banisters with both hands and went downstairs sideways one step at a time. On reaching the hall, he leaned against the wall for support, picked up the receiver and croaked a hello into the mouthpiece.

'You sound rough,' a familiar voice told him.

'Oh, it's you, Mr Ashton, my wife told me it was somebody called Peters. What can I do for you?'

'That depends on what sort of treatment you've received, Terry.'

'Treatment?' Hicks frowned. 'I'm not with you.'

'That little job you did for me; are the people upstairs making waves about it?'

'No. When I went back to work on Friday, Brian Thomas told me you'd phoned him and he asked for the transmitters I'd found. Said he would square things with the high-priced help and not to worry.'

'We're talking about Jill Sheridan,' Ashton said in a flat voice.

'Yeah. According to Brian, Ms Sheridan was going to brief Special Branch. That's all I know.'

'And you're definitely not in hot water on my account?'

'I would have told you soon enough if I was.'

'I see.' Ashton clucked his tongue as if still undecided. 'Fact is, Terry, I need your help again,' he said presently.

'What is it this time?'

'I believe a homing device has been attached to my car. If I'm right, and there is one, I reckon it's somewhere behind the instrument panel.'

'And you'd like me to remove it?'

'Yes, the sooner the better.'

'OK. Can you find your way to Sunleigh Road, Alperton?'

Ashton didn't think that was a good idea. Although reasonably sure nobody was tagging him now, he wasn't inclined to take any chances, especially when it could mean endangering a colleague.

'Have you got an A to Z of London?' Ashton asked.

'Not on me.'

'OK. I'll meet you on Hendon Wood Lane at the junction with Highwood Hill and Totteridge Common. That's out Mill Hill way, page 13 of the A to Z.'

'Right.'

'Any idea when you might get there?'

Hicks peered at his wristwatch and saw it was twenty-five minutes after nine. He needed to

121

wash, shave, change into street clothes and maybe grab a bite to eat. At the very least he could use a cup of strong black coffee and a couple of aspirins. The North Circular was only half a mile away and from there it shouldn't take him more than fifteen minutes to reach Mill Hill, especially on a Sunday morning when the traffic would be relatively light.

'About forty minutes from now,' Hicks said, giving himself a certain amount of leeway.

'See you then,' Ashton said, and switched off the mobile.

* * *

Neighbour tapped the desk with a pencil like a drummer beating a slow cadence. In five minutes' time Katya Malinovskaya would be on the phone to him and he still didn't know what he was going to say to the woman. Elphinstone expected him to stall her while he and presumably the Ambassador consulted London. Neighbour couldn't see either of them getting a response before Monday, if only because the politicians would have to be apprised of the situation. Furthermore, with a general election less than a year off the Government would be reluctant to initiate any action which would enable the Opposition to make hay with them should things go wrong.

That was understandable; trouble was, Katya Malinovskaya wanted an answer today, not the middle of next week. She had seen Vladislav Kochelev and her two colleagues die in a hail of gunfire and was lucky to be alive. As Katya had pointed out to Neighbour, the star witness for the prosecution might be dead but she had spent the last five months in his company and that was a good enough reason to suppose there was now a price on her head. Even though he had been expecting the call, Neighbour still flinched when the phone rang. Lifting the receiver, he gave the number of his extension and identified himself as the Third Secretary, Consular Affairs, the ghost appointment shown on the Foreign and Commonwealth staff list.

'So what's your answer, Mr Neighbour?' Katya demanded in Russian. 'Are you going to help me or do I go to the Americans?'

'It's not easy . . . ' Neighbour began.

'Yes or no?'

'You must do whatever you think is in your best interest,' Neighbour said carefully. 'Should you decide to approach the Americans, I will of course advise my opposite number in the United States Embassy, and prepare the ground for you, so to speak. However, I have to say I doubt the Americans will take kindly to being threatened either.'

He had tried to sound both polite and diplomatic but it wasn't easy to convey such nuances in the Russian language. The stream of abuse which erupted after a momentary silence told Neighbour he had failed lamentably.

'Listen to me, Katya. Please listen to me,' he said in his most soothing tone of voice.

'Fuck your mother, Englishman. I don't want to hear another word.'

'You want asylum. Yes?'

'Isn't that what I've been telling you all along, you asshole.'

'If that's what you want, you have to come to us; we can't pick you up off the street. Neither will the Americans.'

'I can't do that. I am in Tver'.'

'I know you are,' Neighbour said.

'I have very little money and only the clothes I stand up in.'

She didn't have enough for the train fare to Moscow and if she tried to hitchhike, nobody would give her a lift because she had fallen into a pond of stagnant water and stank to high heaven.

'I am alone,' she continued. 'No one will help me and I am frightened.'

'What about Major General Gurov — '

'He won't help me,' Katya said before Neighbour could finish.

'Have you asked him?'

'Of course I have. I phoned Major General Gurov last night to report what had happened. When I told him Vladislav Kochelev was dead, he put the phone down. When I rang back, he wouldn't take my call.'

Neighbour could tell from the catch in her voice that Katya Malinovskaya was close to breaking down. The man who had provided her with a war chest of money to protect the star witness didn't seem to care now if she ended up in a ditch somewhere with a bullet in the head.

'Give me the number of your mobile telephone,' Neighbour demanded.

'Why?'

124

'So that I can get in touch with you as soon as we've worked something out.'

'I can't afford to wait that long. I will call the Americans while there is still time.'

'What do you mean?' Neighbour asked.

'How long do you suppose it will be before my phone number is erased?' Katya said, and cut him off.

Neighbour slowly replaced the transceiver. In the SIS index of Russian personalities there was a passport-size photograph of Katya Malinovskaya attached to her card, and it wasn't difficult for him to visualise the haunted look on her face. She was alone, frightened and without hope. Although today was the first time they had spoken, he was quite certain her despair was genuine. When Elphinstone walked into his office some five minutes later, Neighbour was trying to raise his opposite number in the United States Embassy with the intention of pleading her cause.

'What's been happening?' Elphinstone asked.

Neighbour hastily put the phone down. 'Just checking with our American friends,' he said, colouring.

'Why? Hasn't Malinovskaya been in touch?'

'Yes she has and I lost her.'

'Could you be a little more specific, Chris?'

Neighbour gave him a verbatim account of the conversation he'd had with Katya Malinovskaya. He also told Elphinstone that in his opinion she would be lucky to survive until nightfall.

'I think you have underestimated her resourcefulness,' Elphinstone said cheerfully.

'Yes? Well, I know I handled it badly and destroyed whatever confidence she had in us. She wouldn't even give me the number of her mobile.'

'Don't worry about it, she'll phone you again soon enough.'

'That will only happen if the Americans turn her down.'

'Chances are they have already done that.' Elphinstone smiled. 'Walk down Arbat Street any time of the day or night and you'll find the US dollar is more attractive than the pound sterling. You can bet she tried the CIA before she came to us.'

'But she talked about Ashton; how he was the only man she could trust.'

'Yes, one has to admit that was a pretty good stratagem.'

It was, Neighbour knew, another way of saying that he had allowed himself to be taken in by Katya Malinovskaya. What really annoyed him was the fact that Elphinstone was undoubtedly right.

★ ★ ★

DS Milburn was in a foul mood. He didn't mind being called out on what should have been his rest day. What had touched a raw nerve was the bollocking he had received from his Detective Chief Inspector because the Durbans had done a bunk. Why his guv'nor should have held him personally responsible for their disappearance was beyond him. The Durbans knew his office,

126

home, and mobile telephone numbers but they hadn't contacted him about a threatening note, nor had they reported an attempted break-in.

Milburn assumed Caswell, the Assistant Chief Constable, had received this information from another force, which would have embarrassed him. As a result, Caswell must have given the DCI in charge of Special Branch a real earwigging and he in turn had taken it out on him. Whatever the chain of events, here he was in Gaia Lane on a Sunday morning, trying to close the stable door after the horses had bolted. With him were Police Constable David Ancram and Janice Barnwell, who were busy making door-to-door enquiries, hoping to find a neighbour who might have heard some sort of disturbance during the small hours of Friday morning while he, Milburn, checked out the six-bedroom house the Durbans had occupied.

Milburn walked round the house but could detect no sign of a forced entry. However, the putty surrounding the window in the back door looked fresh and was still soft to the touch. Donning a pair of protective gloves, he sifted through the dustbin and discovered a substantial amount of broken glass in an old shoe box. Under a large empty carton which had contained orange juice, he also came across a steel arrow belonging to a crossbow.

Special Branch had fitted security locks on all the doors and windows before the Durbans had moved in. In theory, it was possible to make a house as safe as Fort Knox but all the security measures in the world were rendered ineffective

127

if procedures were lax, and it was evident to Milburn that, contrary to instructions, the Durbans had failed to remove the key from the door before going to bed. He took out a spare set of keys, found the one that fitted the lock and let himself into the house.

The kitchen was of no interest to Milburn; moving into the hall he immediately noticed that Polyfilla had been used to plug the hole in the front door which the arrow had made. Upstairs, the empty wardrobe and chests of drawers told him the Durbans had no intention of ever returning to Lichfield.

8

Ashton parked the Volvo 850 in Hendon Wood Lane facing north, one hundred yards from the junction with Highwood Hill and Totteridge Common. He switched on the hazard warning lights, tripped the bonnet release catch under the dashboard, then got out of the car and raised the hood to its full extent. He walked a few yards towards the T-junction and waited on the footpath where Hicks couldn't fail to spot him as he drove up the lane. The raised bonnet and flashing lights indicated that he had broken down; he just hoped some Good Samaritan didn't stop to offer him assistance before the electronic whiz-kid arrived.

Ashton was used to seeing Hicks behind the wheel of the ubiquitous white van, and was caught unawares when the driver of a dark blue Ford Escort tooted the horn, swept past the Volvo and pulled up in front of it. The fact that Hicks was wearing a pair of the darkest sunglasses Ashton had ever seen hadn't made recognition exactly easy.

'I'm feeling a bit under the weather,' Hicks told him. 'We really tied one on last night.'

'You should have told me. I wouldn't have dragged you out here if I'd known that.'

'I'm glad you did; the wife was giving me hell.' Hicks opened the nearside front door and retrieved a Gladstone bag containing an assortment of screwdrivers, pliers, hand drills, and spanners to fit every possible type of nut. 'You reckon this bug is somewhere behind the instrument panel?'

'That's right.'

'Why so?'

'Because I've still got a peeper and I check the underside of the Volvo every day. If anything had been attached to the chassis I would have seen it.'

Hicks sucked his teeth. 'A transmitter is not like a bomb. Some of them are no bigger than a thimble.'

'I was very careful, especially after the opposition left their calling card taped to the facia.'

'Did you check the wheel arches?' Hicks asked, unimpressed.

'Yes.'

'Bound to be a fair amount of muck on the inside of the panel. Putting the Volvo through a car wash every now and again doesn't remove it entirely.'

Hicks opened the Gladstone bag and took out a pair of disposable latex gloves from a cardboard box containing a hundred, and put them on.

'Nothing like copping a good feel, as the actress said to the bishop.'

Hicks started with the rear, nearside wheel arch and worked round the car in a clockwise direction. He could have saved himself a lot of time and effort had he chosen to go the other way because the transmitter was located under the rear offside panel. It was about the size of a one-pound coin but thinner and had been anchored on the inside of the metal archway by its magnetised surface.

'A neat job all round,' Hicks mused with a professional air. 'Hairline aerial wrapped round the circumference, continually transmits a homing signal over a maximum range of a mile, solar-powered battery, good for up to three weeks depending on how many hours of reflected sunlight it soaks up, and above all, ridiculously easy to install.'

'How long would the battery last if the Volvo were kept in a garage?'

'Depends whether the garage has a window or not. The short answer is anything from three to seven days.'

'Ever seen one of these before, Terry?'

'Yes. They're manufactured by Rubic Corporation of Fremont, California for the FBI and CIA.'

'OK. Let's take a look behind the instrument panel.'

'What for? We've found the bug.'

'They might have done a belt and braces job,' Ashton said.

'You're the boss.'

It took Hicks a good two hours to remove the panel and almost half as long again to put it back. There was no second transmitter.

'What now?' Hicks asked.

'You go back to Alperton and I'll make my way to King's Cross and check into a backstreet hotel.'

'Sure there is nothing else I can do for you?'

'I can't think of anything off hand, Terry.'

'Well, you know where to reach me if you do.'

'I can't thank you enough for all you've done for me.'

'Hey, you're welcome any time, Mr Ashton.'

Hicks picked up the Gladstone bag, got into the Ford Escort and drove up the lane to make a three-point turn where there was a gap in the footpath. Ashton followed his example, then turned right into Highwood Hill and made his way to King's Cross via the A41 and A501 trunk routes.

Where the transmitter had been concealed, and the absence of a second homing beacon behind the dashboard, made Ashton see the anonymous note in a different light. Its purpose had been to undermine further their confidence in the new identities they had been given. The opposition didn't know the level of protection they were receiving from Special Branch; what they had aimed to do was to make the Ashtons cut and run.

★ ★ ★

The golf course was only two miles down the road from where Rowan Garfield lived in Churt. He had just pulled into the car park and was about to get out of the Jaguar when his mobile phone rang and Eileen broke the news that his presence was required at head office. They had been married for twenty-two years and he had met Eileen when she had been in charge of the

132

typing pool back in the days before the SIS had moved from the combined premises of 54 Broadway and 21 Queen Anne's Gate to Century House. She had continued in the post until their first child was born in 1977, by which time what Eileen didn't know about communicating sensitive information in veiled speech wasn't worth knowing. Although she hadn't said as much, Garfield guessed Eileen had taken the call from the branch duty officer at Vauxhall Cross on the Mozart crypto-protected phone. It had been the emphasis she put on the word 'required' which convinced Garfield he'd no option but to drive up to London.

His golf partner, who was waiting for him at the first tee, wasn't too pleased when Garfield broke the news, and there were no prizes for guessing that hell was likely to freeze over before they met on the course again. It being Sunday, most of the traffic was heading for the coast, and except for the usual bottleneck at Hindhead, Garfield made pretty good time into London.

Bosnia was top of the list of trouble spots and Garfield had convinced himself that he had been called into the office because everything had gone pear-shaped out there. He was therefore taken aback when the branch duty officer handed him a signal from George Elphinstone, Head of Station, Moscow. It carried a message precedence of Emergency which was only one step down from Flash, and you couldn't go any higher than that. The originator had given the subject matter a security classification of Top

Secret, which was not to be used lightly. Ordinarily Garfield would have said the signal had been overgraded on both counts but not in this instance. Katya Malinovskaya was asking for political asylum and if only half of what George Elphinstone said about her was true, she was the hottest property since Colonel Oleg Penkovsky had been recruited in December 1960, which had happened before Garfield had joined the SIS. The Emergency precedence was also justified because Her Majesty's Ambassador had signalled the Foreign and Commonwealth Office asking for guidance and Head of Station had decided quite rightly that The Firm would wish to have an input.

'Who else knows about this signal?' Garfield asked the duty officer.

'The senior officer on the Russian Desk arrived twenty minutes ago. I also rang Mr Hazelwood because the signal was addressed Personal for the DG.'

'I see. And how long has the Director been in the building?'

'Since nine o'clock. I made two photocopies of the signal on his instructions.'

Hazelwood had been quick off the mark but he was still too late. Moscow was four hours ahead of Greenwich Mean Time and the time when Katya Malinovskaya had said she would phone again had come and gone. Garfield hoped George Elphinstone wasn't being unduly optimistic in maintaining nothing would be lost if they missed her deadline.

'I'd better go upstairs,' Garfield told the duty

officer. 'Please make a note that I've got the original signal.'

Hazelwood was on his second Burma cheroot when Garfield walked into his office and despite the extractor fan a blue haze of tobacco smoke eddied below the ceiling. Dennis Eberhardie, the senior officer on the Russian Desk, was sitting bolt upright in one of the leather armchairs, a millboard balanced on his bony knees. He was an exceptionally tall man and had to lower his head whenever he walked through a doorway. Since Eberhardie was also as thin as a rake he was inevitably nicknamed the human beanpole by his peer group and lesser mortals.

'Make yourself comfortable, Rowan,' Hazelwood said, and waved him to the other armchair. 'Dennis and I have just been discussing this signal from George Elphinstone. We would be interested to hear what you make of it.'

Eberhardie was another Foreign Office man who had recently joined the SIS. A brilliant linguist, fluent in Russian, Ukrainian, French, German and Italian, he had spent the last seven years in New York as one of the UK's permanent representatives at the United Nations. There wasn't much Eberhardie didn't know about Russia's foreign policy, and the last thing Garfield wanted was to be shown up by him.

'There's no doubt Katya Malinovskaya would be a valuable acquisition,' Garfield said carefully.

'We already know that,' Hazelwood growled. 'Question is, how do we play the FCO if they jib at the idea of granting Katya Malinovskaya political asylum as Dennis thinks they will?'

'Why would they do that?' Garfield asked, glancing in Eberhardie's direction.

'Malinovskaya claims to have detailed knowledge of widespread financial jiggery-pokery in the day-to-day operation of the Kremlin's domestic budget. If we take her in, the fear is that President Yeltsin may feel we are trying to bring him down.'

'But that's ridiculous.'

'Nevertheless, I can guarantee the Foreign Office won't touch her with a bargepole,' Eberhardie said with an air of superiority that grated.

'You've read the signal,' Garfield told him heatedly. 'Vladislav Kochelev and two of Malinovskaya's employees were shot to death. What will the FCO do if she manages to reach Moscow in one piece and hammers at the door of our embassy? Will Her Majesty's Ambassador Extraordinary and Plenipotentiary be instructed to turn her away?' Garfield laughed derisively. 'That would do our international reputation the world of good.'

'I agree with you,' Hazelwood told him. 'All the same we have to ask ourselves how we propose to get Katya Malinovskaya out of Russia should she gain admittance to the embassy.'

Garfield was about to suggest she could lie low in the embassy until the Mafiozniki stopped looking for her, then had second thoughts and kept quiet. It would be impossible to hide Katya Malinovskaya from the locally employed staff, and her presence was bound to be reported to the Russian authorities. In that event, the embassy could become her semi-permanent residence.

'Why did Katya Malinovskaya tell Neighbour she knew and trusted Ashton?' Eberhardie asked.

'Why?' Garfield snorted. 'Perhaps because the poor woman thought his name would open a few doors for her.'

'Come on, Rowan, you can do better than that. It's possible she was sending us a coded message.'

'Coded message?' Garfield hadn't the faintest idea what Eberhardie was alluding to.

'Stilson Manufacturing, Rowan.'

Suddenly the penny dropped and everything clicked into place. Stilson Manufacturing was a small company which made industrial tools, dies, in fact all kinds of precision instruments. The firm had had trade links with the former USSR, and the chairman, managing director and sole share holder had been well disposed towards the SIS to the extent that he had been prepared to do his bit for Queen and Country. Three years ago he had provided the requisite cover for an operation directed against the Russian Intelligence Service in which Ashton had had a major role. There had been an almighty foul-up and Stilson Manufacturing had lost several lucrative contracts as a result. This hadn't pleased the chairman, MD and sole shareholder, especially as the amount of compensation the firm had received from the SIS had in no way equated to the loss. The Ashton — Katya Malinovskaya connection was simple enough: he had hired her to protect a bogus sales representative for Stilson

Manufacturing, a job that had called for intruder alarms, and physical and electronic surveillance.

'What friendly businessmen do we have in Moscow at the moment?' Hazelwood asked.

Garfield's mind went blank. Unable to recall a single name he looked hopefully to Dennis Eberhardie and got no help at all. The man seconded from the FCO saw himself as purely a political analyst and was not concerned with such mundane matters as friendly businessmen. Garfield wished to God the duty officer had thought to call in one of the grade II intelligence officers on the Russian Desk who would know just who was currently in Moscow.

'I'm afraid I can't give you an answer off the top of my head, Director,' Garfield admitted reluctantly.

'That's all right, Rowan, there's no immediate hurry. We're not doing anything until Katya Malinovskaya shows up at the embassy.'

'I'm sorry . . .'

Hazelwood leaned forward and crushed the stub of the Burma cheroot he'd been smoking in the cut-down shell case which served as an ashtray.

'There is no need to apologise,' he said. 'I appreciate how overstretched you are.'

The European Department had become the largest when it had merged with the former Eastern Bloc. If that reorganisation wasn't unmanageable enough already, the number of desk officers had been steadily reduced even as Yugoslavia began to fall apart. Garfield had pleaded his case for a deputy to run an East

European subdivision and before the coroner's inquest, rumour had had it that Ashton was the front runner for the job. Garfield had swallowed the rumour hook, line and sinker until he had talked to Jill Sheridan and discovered his colleagues had simply been winding him up. In the light of his remarks, he wondered if Hazelwood had been doing the same thing.

★　★　★

Peachey read the notes he had made in his own brand of speed writing, then told the caller there were no queries and hung up. He was, however, in no hurry to rejoin Ann and Harriet in the sitting room. It had been the busiest weekend Peachey had had since retiring seven months ago, back in December 1995. The phone hadn't stopped ringing from the time he had contacted Victor Hazelwood yesterday evening to warn him that he was sheltering Harriet Ashton and her children. The first man to ring him had been the Deputy Chief Constable of the North Yorkshire Police, who had wanted to know why he had hit the panic button and summoned an armed response vehicle. Lacking a secure means of communication, Peachey had referred him to the Home Office on the assumption that Victor Hazelwood would have alerted the Assistant Under Secretary of State of F6 Division, the warning and monitoring organisation.

Nobody was happy about the unforeseen development, especially the Deputy Chief Constable, whose force, with their limited resources, would again be called on to provide round-the-clock protection. But it had been Ann who had really gone off the deep end. The cottage only had three bedrooms, one of which was painfully small, and it had been bad enough the last time when the bodyguards had taken over two of them. Now that they also had to contend with Harriet, her two-year-old son and baby daughter, the situation was, in Ann's view, simply impossible. In bed last night she had demanded to know how long Harriet and her brood would be staying with them, a question which Peachey was unable to answer. Once the Home Office and the North Yorkshire Police were involved, the decision was not his to make. Ann was well aware of that but she wouldn't accept it and had refused to listen to him. Instead she had accused him of lusting after Harriet.

'I've seen that look in your eye,' Ann had whispered furiously, 'you touch her at every opportunity, a guiding hand under the elbow, the friendly pat on the shoulder, the palm resting on the small of her back. Any time now you'll be fondling her buttocks.'

'I'm not listening to this,' he'd told Ann in a low but angry voice.

'It wouldn't surprise me if Harriet didn't actually encourage you.'

There had been more, lots more, and at the end of it Peachey had lain there in the darkness questioning his attitude towards Harriet. It had been monstrous of Ann to suggest she had led him on, but while the thought of fondling her had revolted him, he had shown a fatherly affection. Fatherly? He had asked himself if he would have been quite so protective of Harriet if she had been a plain-looking girl. It was a question he hadn't wanted to answer last night and still didn't.

Peachey sighed: much as he would like to, he couldn't sit here in the front parlour for ever. Reluctantly, he got to his feet and returned to the sitting room to find Harriet and Edward watching *The Jungle Book*.

'I hope you don't mind, Clifford,' she said. 'I brought the tape with me; it's his favourite video.'

'Of course I don't mind. Where's Ann?'

'She's busy preparing supper for the bodyguards.'

'Oh, right.'

'I seem to be causing you all sorts of problems,' Harriet said quietly. 'It can't be easy for either of you.'

'Nonsense.'

'You couldn't have got much sleep last night, what with Edward waking up at the crack of dawn and disturbing Carolyn.'

'It was only to be expected. Edward had had a long day and he was staying in a strange house. Don't worry about it, Harriet, he'll get used to us in a day or two.'

Peachey squeezed her right shoulder affectionately. Harriet was sitting on the couch while he was standing by the arm and slightly behind her. She glanced at his hand, then looked up at him, a perplexed expression on her face. It was only

141

then that he saw his fingertips were touching the swell of her breast. He could feel the colour suffusing into his face and whipped the offending hand away as if he had received a shock from a live wire.

'I'm sorry,' Peachey muttered. 'I didn't mean to . . . ' He cleared his throat and rapidly changed the subject. 'I've just had a phone call from the Home Office. The Driver and Vehicle Licensing Agency, Swansea, have checked the registration numbers you gave me against their records. Seems the red Ford Sierra plates originally belonged to a Rover 2000 which was written off in a traffic accident twelve months ago.'

'What about the pale green Mazda?' Harriet asked. 'I missed the letter after the three digits.'

'Well, naturally Swansea can't be quite so precise but they are adamant no Mazda was allocated a registration number beginning LKV 533.' He waited for Harriet to make some sort of comment but she remained silent, her face unreadable. Peachey began to wonder if she hadn't grasped the implications and decided to spell them out for her. 'The odds against two vehicles with dodgy number plates being on the same stretch of road are pretty astronomical. They were tracking you, no doubt about it.'

'Are you saying some people didn't believe me, Clifford?'

Peachey liked the 'Clifford' bit; he thought it showed she had accepted that he hadn't intended to grope her. 'The doubt was expressed by the Met's Special Branch. Of course, it's a

142

different story now; nothing like a bit of hard evidence to convince the sceptics. I'm happy to say I wasn't one of them.'

'I never thought you were,' Harriet said.

'Something else you should know. Detective Sergeant Milburn visited your house in Lichfield this morning. He found the steel arrow from the crossbow in your dustbin which I'm afraid put your husband in his bad book.'

'Really? Well, I'm sure Peter will be worried sick about that when he hears.' Her voice was loaded with sarcasm and she clearly didn't give a damn that Ashton had fouled things up for the police.

'I think you should be aware that the intruder who broke into your house is an armed robber not a terrorist.'

'That's the official line, is it, Clifford?'

'It happens to be the truth,' Peachey said coldly. 'In early December last year the landlord of a pub in West Bromwich was shot and wounded in the shoulder by a steel arrow from a crossbow. He had gone downstairs to investigate a disturbance in the bar and blundered into three men who were trying to break into the till. Five months ago, back in mid-February, the same thing happened to the owner of a small travel agency with branches in Newcastle-under-Lyme, Stoke-on-Trent and Stafford. He and his wife came home late one night after dining out to find three intruders in the house, one of them armed with a crossbow. They were wearing balaclavas, which hid their faces except for their eyes, and to make good their escape, the bowman shot the husband in the thigh.'

For the first time ever he was really angry with Harriet. Peachey wanted her to realise that sooner or later the bowman would kill somebody; he wanted her to understand that there was a chance the man might not have been wearing gloves when he'd handled the arrow. Now, thanks to the way Ashton had pulled the arrow from the door, any chance of lifting a latent print from the shaft had gone.

'You're assuming he has got a record.'

'Why else would he have been wearing gloves, Harriet? In their statements both the publican and the businessman have said that the bowman was wearing cotton gloves. You told me Peter made his way downstairs in the dark; the other two put the lights on. That's why they saw things Peter didn't.'

Harriet shrugged. 'What am I supposed to say?' she asked. 'That I'm sorry we messed everything up for the police and made life difficult for them?'

'You don't have to apologise; if anyone is to blame it's Peter.'

'He did it for me, Clifford.'

'You surprise me.'

'Peter told me to phone the police. I didn't because I knew DS Milburn would turn up on the doorstep a few hours later. Then before we knew it, the SIS would be relocating us with yet another identity.'

The rest came disjointedly in staccato phrases as if Harriet was a robot which had been programmed to respond to a given situation.

144

Peachey took everything she was saying with a large pinch of salt. Maybe their cover had been blown as a result of an error made by Roy Kelso or Jill Sheridan but he knew who had planted the idea of going it alone in Harriet's mind. It was Ashton he heard when he listened to her and it was more than he could stomach. He had to say something to open Harriet's eyes to reality.

'So Peter is out there looking for a new bolt-hole, is he?' Peachey asked acidly.

'And the men who forced us to go into hiding. The two go hand in hand, Clifford.' Harriet stood up. 'I'd better go and see if Ann needs a hand,' she said, and left him with Edward.

On the screen Baloo the Bear had Shere Khan the Tiger by the tail. Peachey could empathise with the bear; he couldn't bring himself to let go either.

★   ★   ★

Katya Malinovskaya slept fitfully, her head resting against the window of the second-class compartment on the night train from Tver' to Moscow. The floral dress she was wearing was not a good fit and ordinarily she wouldn't have been seen dead in it. However, like the underwear, the low-heeled shoes and accessories, it hadn't cost her a single kopek. They had originally belonged to an unknown young woman who'd gone swimming with her boyfriend in a tributary of the Volga north of the city, which was apparently a local beauty spot. The woman had left her street clothes neatly

145

folded near a large clump of bushes, behind which she had changed into a one-piece swimming costume. Although there had been a number of families picnicking on the river banks, nobody had seen Katya steal the clothes.

The money for the train fare had been provided by a middle-aged drunk whom Katya had subsequently met in a bar not far from the city centre of Tver'. He had been sitting alone in a corner booth and although the place had been half empty at the time, she had sat down opposite him.

'Mind if I join you?' she had murmured, and pressed a knee against one of his under the table.

He had told her his name was Boris which she hadn't believed for a second, although it was equally questionable whether he'd accept her name was Natasha. Boris had bought her two hundred and fifty grams of pepper vodka, which etiquette demanded she downed in one go. An ambitious attempt by Boris to grope her had been thwarted by the width of the table between them, which had meant he could reach no higher than her knee. A firm believer in the principle of if at first you don't succeed, try again, Boris had signalled the bartender to bring another vodka, then quickly sidled round the table to sit next to Katya, hip to hip. Moments after the drinks had arrived, a hand had come to rest on her right thigh. When she made no attempt to remove it, Boris had begun to scrunch up the dress and rayon slip.

'Not here,' Katya had whispered, clutching his wrist in a grip of iron. 'Somewhere quiet.'

'I know just the place,' Boris had told her.

Somewhere quiet had been a run-down block of flats, the concrete façade of which was crumbling. The interior had been just as bad; both lifts had been out of order, cockroaches lived behind the skirting boards which had come adrift from the walls, the composite tiles on the floor were a mosaic of scuff marks and the whole building had reeked of unwashed bodies. But that hadn't worried Boris; unoccupied apartments on the first and second floors were rented out by the hour and he knew the janitor well from previous visits.

From the moment she had picked him out in the bar, Katya Malinovskaya had never doubted she could overpower Boris with ease. She was the younger by a good twenty years, was twice as fit and had been trained in unarmed combat by the KGB. In addition there wasn't much she didn't know about fighting dirty. As Boris began to raise the dress and slip above her hips, she had moved in close to fondle him, then crushed his testicles hard enough to put him down on the floor. Thereafter she had used her feet to good effect and had gone on kicking Boris until he was barely conscious. She had removed the laces from his shoes and had used one of them to tie his thumbs together behind his back. That done, she had bent his legs at the knee and wedged both feet behind the thumbs so that he was drawn like a bow. A strip torn from her rayon slip had served as a gag to muffle his cries of agony as the boot lace cut into his swelling thumbs.

There had been sixty thousand roubles and a hundred and three US dollars in the money belt Boris had been wearing, which had been more than enough for the fare to Moscow. Katya Malinovskaya had no idea what she was going to do after the train arrived at St Petersburg station. The Mafiozniki would be watching the office she rented at 124 Gorky Street, and the villa on the road to Zagorsk. And it was also likely they would be lying in wait for her outside the British and American Embassies. Her first priority was therefore to find a safe house for the rest of the night. If the worst came to the worst, she could always shack up with one of the hookers who plied their trade in the vicinity of the station.

9

Waking did not come gently; one moment Katya Malinovskaya had been sound asleep, the next she was hyperventilating, unable to breathe properly, her heart racing like a runaway train. Frightened and disorientated, Katya instinctively threw up both arms to ward off her attacker, brushed against a hand, and, grabbing the wrist, twisted it violently. A woman yelped and called her a bitch in a voice she recognised from last night.

The woman sharing the double bed with her was Valeria, an erstwhile physician who had become a prostitute because you could earn more money lying flat on your back than as a doctor at the Sklifosovsky Institute.

'You hurt me,' Valeria complained bitterly.

'It was a misunderstanding,' Katya told her. 'I thought I was being attacked. I didn't know you were one of those restless sleepers who throw their arms about.'

'I didn't ask you to spend the night with me.'

Damned right she hadn't. Katya had met the good doctor at St Petersburg station shortly after the train from Tver had arrived at 02.00 hours. Valeria had been shocked when she had approached her and had wanted Katya to know that she didn't perform with other women. To convince Valeria that that was the last thing she had in mind, Katya had invented a mythical, violent husband from whom she had run away and had nowhere to stay in Moscow.

'Just for tonight,' Katya had pleaded, and the US dollars she had stolen from Boris had clinched it.

The tenement where Valeria rented a one-room apartment was on Yokzal Street between St Petersburg and Yaroslavi, the terminal of the Trans-Siberian.

'You must leave now, Katya,' Valeria told her.

'Why?'

'Because the sun is up and you have no more money.'

'What's that got to do with it?'

'Everything. You paid for one night only.'

Katya looked round the one-room flat. If anything it was even more sordid than the dump where Boris had taken her. The ceiling was the colour of soot, dry rot was attacking the dividing wall, and the door frame was eaten up with woodworm. There was no bathroom, no lavatory, only a sink with a cold water tap. Katya had noticed these defects last night; this morning it was evident the place was infested with cockroaches which lived under the food cupboard and gas cooker in the left-hand corner of the room furthest away from the double bed.

'One night,' Katya echoed. 'You've got to be joking.'

'You go now.'

Katya rolled over on top of the hooker, placed a forearm under her chin and pressed it against her throat, deliberately choking Valeria. 'Now you listen to me, you raddled, clapped-out whore. I'll go when I'm good and ready, not before. In the meantime, do yourself a favour and keep your fucking mouth shut.'

Unable to breathe, Valeria shook her head frantically, then broke into a paroxysm of coughing and spluttering when Katya rolled off her.

'You almost killed me,' she rasped.

'Don't tempt me, I might finish the job.'

Katya was certainly tempted to recover the hundred and three dollars she had given the whore. Hard currency could unlock almost any door in Moscow; without it, her chances of survival were minimal. There was a slush fund of US dollars, pounds sterling, German Deutschmarks and French francs in the office safe at 124 Gorky Street but she couldn't go near the place because the Mafiozniki would be watching the building. And if she gave Valeria the combination of the safe that would be the last she ever saw of the good doctor and the money. The only thing of value immediately to hand was the large gold Rolex which she had bought herself even though it was meant for a man. If she was prepared to let it go for a knock-down price, street traders on the Arbat would give her at least four hundred dollars for the wristwatch.

The money would buy her time but not protection — only the Americans and the British could provide that but neither one was willing to pick her up off the streets. She had to make it to their front door on her own and that ruled out the American Embassy on Novinskiy Bulva? The square block was built like a fortress and was surrounded by high walls; you would need a T-72 tank just to get through the gate.

She badly needed a friend, somebody who could get her into an embassy, British or American, it didn't matter which. But who? She no longer trusted Major General Gurov after what had happened on Saturday night. Moscow's Chief of Police was the only man who'd known where she was going after leaving Torzhok on the Saturday morning. So who could she turn to? No one or was there? What was the name of that English journalist who had interviewed her after she had been stabbed in the back four years ago? Irons? Ireland? Iremonger? Yes, Walter Iremonger; he had a flat somewhere on Petrowski Avenue and he'd met Ashton one time, which could be a definite bonus. She couldn't remember his phone number but she could look that up in the directory or maybe get it from the British consular officer, provided Iremonger was still in Moscow.

Katya refused to contemplate the possibility that Iremonger might have returned to London or been assigned elsewhere. That was negative thinking. Clear in her mind what she was going to do, Katya slipped out of bed and started dressing.

'Does this mean you are now good and ready to go?' Valeria asked in a surly voice.

'It's eight o'clock and people are on their way to work.' Katya snapped her fingers as if she had just remembered something. 'Except for you, of course. I was forgetting you work nights.'

Francesca York was the first name on the list of people Ashton intended to call on. From the Hotel Claremont in King's Cross where he had spent the night, Ashton made his way across town to Hyde Park and garaged the Volvo in the underground car park. Exiting on Broad Walk, he walked to Marble Arch, caught a Central Line train to Notting Hill Gate, then changed on to the Circle and alighted at High Street Kensington. The flat which Francesca shared with another girl was on Derry Street, approximately one hundred and fifty yards from the station. To say she was surprised to see him on her doorstep was an understatement.

'What the hell are you doing here?' she asked in a strangled voice.

'It's better I catch you at home than in the office. Isn't it?'

'It's better you go away and leave me alone.'

'I think you should invite me in,' Ashton said quietly. 'You can tell your flatmate I'm a colleague.'

'She's away on holiday.'

'All the more reason to let me in.'

Francesca stepped aside, allowed Ashton into the hall, then closed the door behind him. 'I don't want to be late at the office,' she said, leading him into the sitting room. 'So make it snappy.'

'Anything to oblige.' Ashton dipped into his jacket pocket and produced the transmitter. 'Seen one of these before?'

'Looks like a pound coin to me.'

'It's a solar-powered homing beacon manufactured specifically for the CIA and FBI by the Rubic Corporation of Fremont, California. This one ended up on my car.'

Francesca gnawed at her bottom lip. 'I've never known the IRA to use a tracking device before,' she said thoughtfully.

'Neither have I,' Ashton said.

When the IRA targeted an individual, a surveillance team kept the victim under observation until they knew where and at what time their quarry would be the most vulnerable. Armed with this information, the hit man would then move in to finish the job.

'I'm wondering if anybody in Northern Ireland has come across a Rubic homing beacon,' Ashton said.

'Meaning you would like me to make some enquiries?'

'It wouldn't do any harm to check with the Royal Ulster Constabulary and 10 Intelligence Company.'

'I think I can manage that,' Francesca said with a faint smile.

'Thanks. For what it's worth I don't believe the Rubic Corporation went into mass production when they were awarded contracts by the CIA and FBI. I can't see the need for a vast quantity of homing beacons. If the IRA has acquired any I'd like to know which brigade has got them.'

'May one ask why?'

'I'm curious to know which murderous lot is

stalking me — the IRA, the Provisional IRA, Continuity IRA, the Real IRA or the Irish National Liberation Army.'

'Anything else?'

'The lady in Lewisham, Kevin's widow — is anybody keeping an eye on her?'

'Special Branch began to take an interest in Sandra Hayes the day you killed her husband. Nobody has stood them down to my knowledge.' Francesca made a great show of consulting her wristwatch. 'I hope that was the last question because time's running on and I'm going to be late as it is.'

Nobody has stood them down to my knowledge: the assurance had been just a little too glib for Ashton's liking. Maybe Sandra Hayes hadn't come to the notice of MI5 and Special Branch before her brother-in-law had been identified as one of the IRA's ace bomb makers, but that didn't mean she was as pure as the driven snow. If she hadn't been an IRA sympathiser prior to the death of her husband, her behaviour at the inquest suggested Sandra Hayes was ready to help the cause in any way she could.

'I'll walk you to the station,' he said.

'Oh, you don't have to do that.'

Ashton smiled. 'Don't look so worried, nobody will see us together. I'm not going your way.'

'There's no answer to that.'

'How soon will you have the information? Two, three days from now?'

'More like a week,' Francesca told him. 'I'll

call you when I have something.'

It didn't need a huge amount of sagacity to realise Francesca had no intention of phoning him. The heated exchange began on the way out when Ashton told her she had better not switch off her mobile because with effect from Thursday, he was going to ring her every night until he got the answers he wanted. The altercation only ceased when they parted company outside the District and Circle Lines underground station in Kensington High Street.

* * *

Walter Iremonger rubbed the aftershave into both palms, then applied the lotion to his face until his cheeks felt as if they were on fire. On 18 December, he would be forty-nine and, much as part of him wanted to deny it, Iremonger had to admit he looked his age. He was also unfit, overweight and had been through the usual mid-life crisis early on when his wife had divorced him in 1979 after they had been married eight years. Back in England he had two daughters, Christine, now twenty-one and in her final year at Loughborough University, and Emma, nineteen, who'd decided higher education was not for her and was doing something in market research. Iremonger had an uncomfortable feeling she was paid to stop people in the street and ask which brand of washing powder they were using and had they thought of trying Brand X.

Apart from a fleeting visit to the UK in 1993 to attend his mother's funeral, Iremonger had had no contact with his daughters during their formative years. After their grandmother's funeral they had told him point-blank it was a little late in the day to assume the mantle of parenthood when they had acquired a perfectly adequate stepfather. Iremonger couldn't blame them; he was an agency man and had been with the Associated Press all his working life. Until the divorce he'd occupied a desk at the London office; it was only after 1979 that he had started to travel further afield.

He had been assigned to Moscow in '92 for three years and had been extending it twelve months at a time. He had until Thursday, 1 August to make up his mind whether to sign on again. The bureau chief and most of his colleagues reckoned it was a foregone conclusion that he would. Well, why not? Moscow was beginning to fit him like a comfortable shoe that had been worn in, his Russian had come on by leaps and bounds and he had no burning ambition to see the rest of the world. The sad thing was that on this, his day off, he could think of nothing better to do than get up an hour later than usual.

Iremonger returned to the bedroom and finished dressing, pulling on a sweatshirt that did nothing to conceal the pot belly he had acquired from overeating and lack of exercise. As he had done many times before he decided that henceforth he would cut out breakfast, starting tomorrow. He was about to enter the kitchen when the telephone in the sitting room hauled him back.

'Hello, 6100,' he said, lifting the receiver.

'Mr Iremonger, I am Katya. I would like to see you.'

A hooker, Iremonger told himself. It wasn't the first time he had been propositioned on the phone, but unlike the others this particular woman was making sure he got the message, speaking slowly in case his command of the Russian language wasn't up to much.

'Listen, save your breath. I already have a girl.'

'But Mr Ashton said you needed me.'

Iremonger blinked, wondering if his ears had deceived him. 'Who did you say?'

'Mr Ashton. You remember him, don't you?'

'Oh, yes, I remember Ashton all right.'

Iremonger had met him only the once but he was the sort of man you weren't likely to forget. Ashton had borrowed the name of the embassy's junior commercial attaché to persuade Iremonger to open the door to him and had then forced his way into the apartment. They'd had a bit of a set-to, Iremonger literally throwing dozens of punches which the younger man had blocked with ease. Ashton hadn't landed a single punch either but then he hadn't needed to; he had known it was merely a question of a few minutes before his adversary ran out of puff and collapsed into an armchair. It had been some months before Iremonger had discovered his real identity.

'You will see me now — yes?' Katya asked.

'Well, I'm rather busy at the moment,'

Iremomnger said, hovering.

'I will give you another name — Elena Andrianova.'

Iremonger had a feeling that if he wasn't careful he could find himself in deep shit. Elena Andrianova had worked for the junior commercial attaché at the British Embassy and had been sacked after admitting to Ashton that she had been passing confidential economic intelligence to the KGB under duress. Her case officer had described in graphic detail what would happen to Vera, her six-year-old daughter, if she refused to cooperate. Acting on instructions from the same case officer two KGB thugs had put her in hospital with four cracked ribs, a dislocated elbow, a fractured pelvis and a broken nose, simply as a punishment for losing her job. The British Embassy hadn't wanted to know; they denied all knowledge of Elena Andrianova and had refused to countenance the idea of finding a niche for her in the British Council office, which had been the inducement Ashton had offered to turn her around. So Ashton had given him the whole story and had used the power of the press to remind the FCO of their responsibilities. Iremonger smiled wryly, recalling that he had almost got himself deported in the process.

'I'm still waiting for an answer,' Katya said.

'Do you know where I live?'

'Yes, Petrowski Avenue.'

'So when can I expect you?' he asked.

'Very soon,' she said, and hung up.

Iremonger put the receiver down. The woman who called herself Katya had been very cagey, as if she suspected his phone was tapped. He was curious to learn where, when and how she had met Ashton.

* * *

The Hammersmith branch of Mitchell and Webb, estate agents, was located in Black's Road off the Broadway. Getting there from High Street Kensington wasn't a problem for Ashton; making an appointment to see Harvey Littlewood was. Since Brian Thomas, Terry Hicks and Francesca York had been warned off, it was a fair bet that by now the estate agent had been asked to report any attempt by Mr Durban to contact him. By the same token it was reasonable to assume Special Branch would not have divulged his real name to Littlewood or the partners of Mitchell and Webb.

After parting company with Francesca York outside the underground station, Ashton had boarded a number 73 bus then walked round Hammersmith, killing time until the secretarial staff of Mitchell and Webb began to arrive at the office. Littlewood's secretary was a formidable brunette of indeterminate age who saw it as her bounden duty to ensure her boss wasn't plagued by time-wasters.

'My name is Ashton,' he told her. 'I have reason to believe Mr Littlewood can put me on to a valuable building plot in Ravenscourt Park.'

The story contained a grain of truth and had paved the way for him to see Mitchell and

Webb's foremost agent and branch manager when he walked into the office at five past nine.

'May I ask who recommended me?' Littlewood enquired.

'Well, you already know his name. It's Patrick Durban.'

'A friend of yours?'

'We are one and the same person,' Ashton said, and saw him eye the telephone on his desk. 'What did they tell you to do, Mr Littlewood? Phone Hammersmith police station?'

'Something like that.'

'I don't mind if you call them after I've left.'

'I'm not that bothered.'

Ashton reached into the breast pocket of his jacket and produced the rogues gallery DS Milburn had given him. 'I expect the police have already shown you a whole portfolio of suspects but I would be grateful if you'd take a look at these mugshots. Do any of them bare a resemblance to Simon and Julie Carmichael?'

'Is there a woman amongst them?' Littlewood asked, looking up with a smile.

'The one who's growing a moustache.'

'Well, I can tell you she is not Julie Carmichael.'

'That doesn't come as a surprise.' Petite, slender, dark shoulder-length hair framing a pert-looking face with the bluest eyes he'd ever encountered was how Littlewood had described her. 'What about the men?'

'No resemblance there.'

'It was worth a try.' Ashton retrieved the Polyfotos and tucked them into the inside pocket

161

of his jacket. 'I'd like you to do one more thing for me.'

'What's that?'

'Tell me everything that happened after Mrs Carmichael told you she could smell gas in the kitchen. I want to know who did what and when, step by step.'

In Littlewood's opinion there wasn't much to tell. Julie Carmichael had said she had smelled gas in the kitchen and her husband had put it down to her vivid imagination. Husband and wife had had a bit of a spat and to make the peace Littlewood had suggested they check it out. It was only when Ashton began to question him that he recalled Julie Carmichael had been the last person to look inside the cupboard where the gas and electricity meters were installed.

'Is that significant?' Littlewood asked.

'It could help us to trace the lady,' Ashton said. 'It's likely Carmichael isn't her real name and I doubt the IRA has too many foot soldiers of her calibre.'

★　★　★

Katya's idea of very soon was somewhat elastic. There was an interval of some thirty-five minutes between the time she had hung up following their telephone conversation to when she pressed the call button to Iremonger's apartment on Petrowski Avenue. Her voice had sounded tinny on the squawk-box and he had refused to trip the electronic lock on the street door and let her into the building until she had repeated the salient facts of their previous conversation. The moment Iremonger saw her face through the spyhole he knew who she was and remembered where they had met before.

'You're Sergeant Katya Malinovskaya,' he said, opening the door to her. 'I interviewed you in hospital three or four years ago. You were one of the officers detailed to protect Elena Andrianova.'

'You have a good memory,' Katya told him.

'Some renegade policeman had knifed you in the back.'

'I need your help, Mr Iremonger.'

'Yeah, well, you'd better come on through,' he said, and ushered her into the sitting room. 'Can I get you a coffee or something stronger?'

'Something stronger would be welcome. Have you any Scotch whisky?'

'Bell's, VAT 69, Johnnie Walker Black Label — take your pick.'

'The Black Label with only a little water.'

Iremonger crouched in front of the drinks cabinet, opened the Johnnie Walker and poured a generous tot into a tall glass, then went into the kitchen to dilute it a little under the cold tap. He thought it wasn't only the whisky that could do with a drop of water; Katya was giving off a sour smell as though she hadn't washed herself for days. The silk dress she was wearing looked cheap and wasn't a good fit, and the plastic uppers of the low-heeled shoes were cracked. Iremonger returned to the sitting room half expecting Katya to touch him for a loan.

163

'Your whisky water,' he said, and handed the glass to her.

'Thanks.'

'So what exactly is it you want from me?'

'I want you to smuggle me into the British Embassy. I won't make the front gate if I try to do it on my own. If you do this for me, I will give you an even bigger story than Elena Andrianova.'

'Who's after you?'

'The Mafiozniki.'

'Oh, no.' Iremonger shook his head vehemently. 'I'm not getting mixed up with that crowd. Neither will the embassy. They won't touch you with a bargepole.'

'You think I'm a criminal?' Katya said furiously.

'Innocent bystanders have been shot down by the Mafiozniki because they were unfortunate enough to be in the wrong place at the wrong time. They blundered into a bank when it was being held up and robbed, or else they were caught in the crossfire when the police raided some Mafiozniki-controlled establishment. People like you who are deliberately targeted by Moscow's criminal fraternity have tried to muscle in on one of their rackets.'

'For a reporter you know very little about the Mafiozniki. They also do contract work: a businessman wants to have a rival eliminated; they do it for a consideration. Sometimes it is more complicated.'

'I bet it is,' Iremonger said acidly.

'Vladislav Kochelev: does the name mean anything to you?'

164

The name sounded familiar but he couldn't place it in context. Then Katya murmured something about the Kremlin domestic budget and suddenly everything clicked.

'The government auditor. Somebody had been milking the fund and he was appointed to look into it. Eventually, Pavel Trilisser was charged with twelve counts of embezzlement. The actual trial date has been put back a couple of times.'

'It will never take place,' Katya said.

'Nobody at the agency ever thought it would. I mean, a trial could be a major embarrassment for President Yeltsin. After all, Trilisser was his special adviser on foreign affairs.'

'There will be no trial, Mr Iremonger, because Vladislav Kochelev was murdered on Saturday night.'

'How do you know? It wasn't featured on any of the TV newscasts yesterday and it wasn't mentioned in the Sunday papers.'

'I was there when it happened. That's how I know, Mr Iremonger.'

He listened to Katya, never once interrupting her as she told him that Moscow's Chief of Police Major General Gurov had hired her to protect the State's star witness because somebody had put up a hundred-thousand-dollar price tag on Kochelev's head and he'd feared his own officers might be tempted. It wasn't necessary for Katya Malinovskaya to point out just how much Kochelev had told her during the five months they had been on the run. But enough of the sceptical newsman still remained

165

for him to want to verify the facts before he accepted her story.

'This ambush you ran into,' Iremonger said, 'how far was it from Tver'?'

'It couldn't have been more than sixteen to twenty kilometres.' A wry smile appeared on her mouth. 'I should know, I walked the whole way.'

'So the incident would have been reported to the Chief of Police, Tver'?'

'Yes. Why do you ask?'

'Well, I'm going to phone Major General Gurov's private office to ask for confirmation.'

'Are you mad?' Katya yelled. 'Do you want to have me killed? Haven't I just told you that he was the only man who knew I was going to Tver' and which route we would be taking? I don't know why Major General Gurov should suddenly have turned against me but the fact remains he did.'

'In other words I have to take everything you have told me on trust?'

'You want confirmation? Then phone the Public Prosecutor's office. Tell him your agency wants you to cover the Pavel Trilisser trial and would they confirm the hearing is scheduled for court number one today, commencing at 11.00 hours.' Katya finished her whisky and held out her empty glass to him, silently asking for another. 'I will be interested to hear what they have to say.'

'So will I.' Iremonger took the glass from her and placed it on top of the bookcase-cum-bureau in the alcove to the right of the window. Lifting the bureau top, he took out his personalised telephone directory, looked up the number he wanted and started dialling. As he did so, Katya Malinovskaya moved up to the window and stood there gazing down at the avenue.

'Do you happen to smoke?' she asked.

It was the last thing Katya ever said. A pane of glass suddenly shattered and a myriad of cracks appeared around the entry hole. Iremonger saw her instinctively turn away from the window and he assumed some vandal had thrown a stone at it. She managed just one step before she went down, both hands pressed against her chest as if she was trying to hold herself together. The circumference of the exit wound in the back was about the size of a tea plate.

A second hole appeared, this time in the adjoining window, and the bullet, striking the wall above the bookcase-cum-bureau at an oblique angle, ricocheted around the room. Iremonger threw himself flat on the floor before the sniper across the street could get off a third shot.

10

Iremonger hugged the floor, convinced the second aimed shot had been meant for him. He had been standing by the telephone, which was positioned on top of the bookcase-cum-bureau in the alcove. If he hadn't turned sideways on to see what was the matter with Katya Malinovskaya, the bullet would have hit him under the left shoulder blade and exited somewhere on the right side of the chest, dependent on what sort of obstruction the round encountered as it tore through his body. The only certain thing was that, like Katya, he would have been dead before he ended up on the carpet.

Obviously the sniper had decided to drop him because the former KGB sergeant had spent a few minutes in his company; it was as simple as that. Katya had asked him to help her because she believed the Mafiozniki were watching the American and British Embassies; it now looked as if they had also been watching the houses on Petrowski Avenue. Or at least numbers 232 to 236, which for the most part were occupied by members of the foreign press corps, TV news reporters and agency men like himself.

Suddenly it occurred to Iremonger that the sniper would want to make sure both of his victims were dead. The electronic lock on the street door wouldn't keep him out. Before glasnost the KGB had entered the building whenever they felt like it, and if the number of burglaries in the neighbourhood during recent months was anything to go by, the criminal fraternity were equally adept at breaking and entering. Iremonger pictured the sniper, back to the wall, climbing the spiral staircase to his apartment on the third floor, and broke into a cold sweat. Whether or not it was simply his imagination working overtime, it would only be prudent to summon help.

The telephone was on the floor near the bookcase-cum-bureau where it had fallen when he had thrown himself flat. The receiver had separated from the cradle and was emitting the normal dialling tone. Keeping his head well down, Iremonger crawled over to the instrument and dialled 02, which automatically raised the police operator. In addition to his name and address, he gave his phone number and then recounted what had happened in a few brief sentences. Out of an innate sense of caution, Iremonger invented a family name for Katya Malinovskaya and made no mention of her involvement with Vladislav Kochelev. Instead, he merely said the victim had been shot by an unknown sniper in the apartment building at 237 Petrowski Avenue on the opposite side of the road to his place. Then he hung up and immediately rang the junior consular officer at the British Embassy followed by the bureau chief of the Associated Press. The way things were, Iremonger didn't relish the prospect of facing Moscow's finest on his own.

The two clocks displayed side by side in an ivory stand had been presented to Elphinstone's great-grandfather by the Maharaja of Patiala in 1884 as a mark of his esteem. In keeping with a long-established family tradition, one showed the time in London while the other reflected that of the host nation. A sixth sense told Elphinstone that Chris Neighbour was hovering in the doorway and was about to announce his presence with a discreet cough. It was the second time the younger man had been to see him that morning and it wasn't difficult to guess what was on his mind. The only guidance the embassy had received from the FCO with regard to Katya Malinovskaya was a brief and unhelpful signal drawing their attention to the relevant paragraph in Regulatory Standing Instructions which dealt with requests for political asylum. As Head of Station, Elphinstone took his lead in such matters from the Ambassador and His Excellency was still waiting to hear how London wanted him to deal with Katya Malinovskaya, a key witness in a major trial with strong political implications.

'You're too early, Chris,' Elphinstone said, looking up from the file he was reading to point at the family heirloom on the desk. 'It's only 10.30 a.m. in London. I doubt we will hear anything before 4 p.m. our time at the earliest.'

'That's not why I'm here, George. I've just learned that Katya Malinovskaya has been murdered.'

170

'Who told you?'

'Walter Iremonger, the AP man. She was shot to death in his apartment on Petrowski Avenue. I'm going there now.'

'I don't think so . . . '

'Iremonger has reported the incident to the police and he doesn't want to face them on his own and I don't blame him. Before she was killed Katya told Walter that Major General Gurov was implicated in the assassination of Vladislav Kochelev.'

'You're not to get involved,' Elphinstone told him firmly.

'I don't see how I can avoid it. Walter asked me to be present when he gave his story to the investigating officers.'

'You're not listening to me,' Elphinstone growled.

'I'll be wearing my other hat, George,' Neighbour said, deliberately choosing to ignore the direct order he had just received from his superior officer. 'According to the embassy's staff list I'm Third Secretary, Consular Affairs and that was who Iremonger believed he was addressing.'

'Iremonger is a reporter; it's more than likely he knows you are with the SIS.'

'Perhaps he does. Maybe Katya Malinovskaya did too when she rang the embassy from Tver' and asked to speak to the consular officer. Who can tell? You can, however, be sure of one thing: if I don't show up, Walter Iremonger and his bureau chief will soon put two and two together.'

Elphinstone had to admit the younger man

171

had a point. Furthermore there was nobody else the Embassy could send in his place. The chief consular officer was in London arranging the funeral of his widowed mother and there was no longer a second secretary. That appointment had been deleted when the post of Consulate General had been established in St Petersburg.

'Do I have permission to go?' Neighbour asked him quietly.

'Yes.' Elphinstone paused, then said, 'Just remember you are supposed to be a diplomat, Chris. Make out you've never heard of Katya Malinovskaya.'

Neighbour smiled. 'Who's she?' he said, and left the office.

* * *

If there was one solicitor Ashton would remember for a long time to come it was Lionel Jebens. He had briefed the barrister who had represented the Hayes family at the inquest and who, in accordance with the instructions he had received from Jebens, had stripped Ashton of his anonymity.

Jebens had first come to the notice of MI5 in 1988 when he had defended five nuclear protesters who had been arrested inside the Cruise missile base at Greenham Common, having cut their way through the perimeter fence. Instead of a custodial sentence, the women had been bound over to keep the peace by a sympathetic magistrate who was rumoured to share their views on nuclear disarmament. In those days Jebens had been employed by the People's Law Centre in Finchley Road. Following the trial of the so-called Greenham Five, he had founded his own law practice with a like-minded solicitor and a legal executive. Their registered office was Candlewick House in Red Lion Yard, a quiet backwater off High Holborn.

Jebens was thirty-seven and the embodiment of Jimmy Porter, the angry young man created by John Osborne, even though he was getting a little long in the tooth for the role. His hate list started with the monarchy and embraced hereditary peers, the Tory Party, landowners, big business, public schools, especially Eton, officers of the armed services, the police, the law lords and all well-heeled members of the legal profession. He was four inches under six feet and was a good twenty pounds overweight, which showed in his plump thighs and round face. Observing him at the inquest, Ashton thought there must have been a time in his youth when Jebens had been passably handsome, but nowadays the ponytail made him look ridiculous. He had got so accustomed to sniping at the Establishment that his features wore a perpetual sneer.

Ashton had been told that Jebens was not the easiest man to get hold of. When he wasn't in court, the solicitor was often out of the office conferring with animal rights activists, hunt saboteurs and the like. Shortly after leaving the estate agents, Ashton had rung the law practice and spoken to the legal executive. He had given a false name and told her he was being harassed

173

by Customs and Excise who had wrongfully accused him of selling contraband goods at his tobacconists and news agency on the Portobello Road. Jebens, he learned, was not in court that morning and would see him at a quarter to twelve.

Red Lion Yard was a narrow pedestrian passageway between High Holborn and Eagle Street. If MI5 was still interested in the solicitor, Ashton thought their foot soldiers in Special Branch would have a hard time keeping him under surveillance. There was nowhere to park a vehicle in High Holborn and anybody loitering in that area would be about as inconspicuous as Telecom Tower. That left Eagle Street, where parking was restricted by double yellow lines. The only suitable place was a similar narrow-fronted three-storey building directly opposite Candlewick House but that was in the process of being renovated.

Ashton tried the front door of Candlewick House, found it wasn't locked and entered the building. A desk positioned across the hallway took up most of the available space. On it was a six-line switchboard and a Pental computer with printer. There was, however, no sign of a receptionist. As he moved further inside, a pressure plate under the carpet rang a bell and a stocky brunette in her early twenties appeared from a small office to his right.

'My name's Ross,' Ashton told her. 'I made an appointment to see Mr Jebens at eleven forty-five. I think it's possible I may have spoken to you?'

174

'You did indeed. My name is Pauline Dando, I'm the legal executive.'

'Nice to meet you,' Ashton murmured.

'Would you like to follow me, Mr Ross?'

She moved towards the staircase on his left, went on up to the next floor and introduced Ashton to Jebens.

The solicitor was not best pleased to see him. 'What the hell are you doing here?' he snarled.

'This is Mr Ross — ' Ms Dando began, and got no further.

'You're wrong, Pauline, his name's Ashton. He's the man who killed Kevin Hayes and got away with it.'

'Oh!' Her lips formed a perfect circle and she fell silent but only for a few minutes. 'Shall I send for the police, Lionel?' she asked in a faint voice.

'Yeah, you do that.' Ashton closed the door behind him and sat down in one of the two fireside armchairs Jebens provided for clients. 'Then you can listen to your boss attempting to persuade Special Branch he isn't involved in a conspiracy to commit murder.'

Jebens wagged a finger at him. 'You repeat that allegation outside these four walls and you will find yourself in very serious trouble.'

'Well, you'd better get ready to sue me because, if I don't get some answers, that will be your only means of redress.'

'You're bluffing.'

'Try me,' Ashton said.

'Do you want me to call the police?' Ms Dando sounded even more uncertain than she

175

had the first time she had asked.

There was a longish pause before Jebens answered her question and then all he did was shake his head.

'I think you are very wise,' Ashton observed. 'After all, there are things we need to talk about.'

'Do you want me to stay, Lionel?'

'No, that won't be necessary,' Jebens told her. 'This had better be good,' he added, scowling at Ashton after she had left the office.

'You won't be wasting your time. This is your chance to prove you didn't give my new address to the IRA.'

'Don't be stupid, I don't know anybody in the IRA.'

'That's your defence, is it?' Ashton said coldly.

Before the coroner's inquest, Francesca York had told him what MI5 knew about the solicitor. Among other high-profile cases, Jebens had instructed the barrister who had defended Martin Barry, a twenty-four-year-old Irishman from Newcastle, County Down, who was employed as a barman at the Dunmow Flitch Pub in Cricklewood. Barry had been pulled up for exceeding the speed limit in a built up area. Because active service units of the Provisional IRA were engaged in a bombing campaign directed against mainland Britain, his vehicle had been routinely searched. The boot had contained a Kalashnikov AK-47 assault rifle and two 30-round box magazines.

At his trial Barry had claimed that the vehicle belonged to his cousin, who had asked him to sell it at a car auction. The cousin had returned to Northern Ireland the day the motoring offence had been committed and in the absence of any forensic evidence linking the Kalashnikov to Barry, the jury had believed him when he had sworn he'd had no idea there was a rifle in the boot.

'You're forgetting Martin Barry,' Ashton reminded Jebens.

'I didn't know he was in the IRA until he was shot by the army.'

Three months after being acquitted at the Old Bailey, Martin Barry and seven other gunmen had set out to attack the police station at Dungannon. Forewarned of their intention, the army had laid an ambush and in the subsequent shoot-out, Barry and four other IRA gunmen had been killed.

'Let's say I believe you. Who asked you to represent Barry?'

'He approached me himself, said I had a reputation for defending the underdog and knew I would do right by him.'

'What about Kevin Hayes?' Ashton asked.

'I had a phone call from West Belfast.'

'Yeah? How did you know it wasn't a hoax?'

'The man said I would find an envelope containing five hundred pounds on the doormat when I came home that night.'

'This was a retainer?'

'Sort of. I called it evidence of good faith.'

'So you took instructions?'

'Yes.'

'How?'

Jebens sneered. 'I had the phone number of

the Sinn Fein representative in West Belfast.'

'Was this the same man who sent you the five hundred?'

'His voice was similar.'

Ashton counted slowly up to ten and told himself to cool it but he had already taken all he was going to from the solicitor. 'Now you listen to me, you little shit,' he said in a voice as chilling as the wind off the Polar ice cap, 'this Sinn Feiner has got a name and you know it.'

'Are you threatening me?'

'Is that what you believe?'

Jebens looked away, gazing at the window as if seeking inspiration from the building opposite Candlewick House. 'His name is Foley,' Jebens said presently, 'George Foley. I have a feeling he isn't Sinn Fein.'

It was, Ashton recognised, the closest the solicitor would come to admitting he knew Foley was a Provo gunman.

'You want to write down his telephone number for me, Lionel?'

'Do I have any choice?'

'Not a lot,' Ashton said grimly. 'And don't go all clever on me by making up a false one.'

The perpetual sneer on Jebens' face was fleetingly replaced by a sickly smile. Reaching out, he plucked a small sheet of headed notepaper from the holder on his desk, then produced a Biro and wrote out the number, bearing down so hard on the ballpoint it almost went through the paper.

'Here, take it and get out of my office,' Jebens

said, thrusting the slip of crested notepaper at him.

'Simon Carmichael — ' Ashton said, unmoved — 'does his name ring any bells with you?'

'Not in a million years.'

'How about Julie Carmichael — petite, slender, dark, shoulder-length hair framing a pert-looking face with the bluest eyes you've ever seen?'

'The same applies.'

'Well, I guess that's it for now.' Ashton got to his feet and moved towards the door, then suddenly turned about as though some last-minute thought had occurred to him. 'This George Foley,' he said, 'do you think he was the man who was given my new address?'

'I wouldn't know,' Jebens said coolly. 'Perhaps you should ask your friends.'

★ ★ ★

Two police officers were already on the scene by the time Neighbour arrived at 236 Petrowski Avenue, so too was the bureau chief of AP. All three men were engaged in a shouting match, with Iremonger very much on the sideline. The reason for the hullabaloo was the determination of Moscow's finest to arrest Iremonger and take him into custody for questioning. When Neighbour attempted to explain who he was and produced his diplomatic credentials, the burlier of the two policemen snatched the document from his hand and hurled it across the room.

Undeterred, Neighbour walked over to the

telephone, lifted the receiver and rang police headquarters. When the operator answered, he informed her that he was calling on behalf of His Excellency the British Ambassador and wished to speak to Major General Gurov or his deputy in order to avert a major diplomatic incident. Less than a minute into his conversation with the Chief of Police, Moscow's finest were eager to make amends, especially after Neighbour handed the phone over to the senior of the two and told him the Major General wished to have a word. Thereafter both officers were entirely compliant. In practice this meant everything was on hold until detectives of the Criminal Investigation Division arrived.

'I reckon we've got no more than five minutes,' Neighbour said quietly after distancing Iremonger and the bureau chief from the two Russians. 'First thing we have to do is work on your story, Walter.'

'What are you suggesting? That I should tell the police a pack of lies?'

'No, I'm just hoping those two over there don't know the victim is Katya Malinovskaya.'

'I didn't tell them who she was.'

'Neither did I,' the bureau chief said.

'OK, so far as you are concerned, Walter, she is a complete stranger. You didn't see her arrive, and you don't know how she got into the building. You heard her pounding on the door to your apartment, screaming for someone to help her and you opened the door to see who it was. Before you could stop her, she had pushed you aside and run into the living room. She was hysterical and you tried to calm her down.'

'At least that's true,' Iremonger said quietly. 'I gave her a drink.'

'Fine. All she told you was that the Mafiozniki were determined to kill her but wouldn't say why. Instead, she went over to the window, looked up and down the avenue . . . '

'And was promptly killed by a sniper from somewhere inside the apartment building across the street,' Iremonger finished.

'Right. You can put a little flesh on the story but don't overdo it and don't volunteer any information.'

'Don't worry, that's the last thing I'll do.'

Neighbour turned to the bureau chief and told him nobody could guarantee Iremonger's safety if he remained in Moscow. Even in police custody, the Mafiozniki would eventually get to him.

'So what do you propose we do?' the bureau chief asked.

'I want you to slip away before other police officers arrive, and start booking flights with British Airways, commencing with the one departing at 17.55 hours this evening. Make the reservations in the name of William Price.'

'Why?'

'If the police release Walter into my care, they are sure to retain his passport as part of the surety, but don't worry, I'll issue him with another.' Neighbour smiled. 'I'm not a third consular officer for nothing.'

'I guess you aren't but it may well cost you your job.'

'That's preferable to Walter losing his life.'

'You won't hear me deny it. How do I get the plane ticket to you?'

'I'll phone you and set up a rendezvous,' Neighbour told him. 'Now get moving.'

Lieutenant Arkadi Leonidovich Olenev, two detectives, a medical examiner, a police photographer, three technicians from the forensic science laboratory and a covey of uniformed officers arrived just two minutes after the AP bureau chief had left the apartment. His departure had not gone unnoticed by Moscow's finest, and the first thing Lieutenant Olenev wanted from Neighbour was an explanation for his absence. The fact that the bureau chief had arrived on the scene after the event and was therefore not a material witness did not impress the lieutenant, who accused Neighbour of obstructing the police. From there on Neighbour knew he would have to do a lot of grovelling before Olenev would agree to release Iremonger into his care.

★ ★ ★

Francesca York listened to the cassette a second time, then walked the recording next door and asked Richard Neagle if he could spare her a few minutes.

'Is it important?' Neagle asked without looking up from the document he was studying.

'I think so.'

'Very well, two minutes it is.'

With considerable difficulty Francesca kept a

tight smile on her face. For reasons she didn't begin to understand, Richard appeared to have taken against her in the last few months. Sometimes it seemed to Francesca that he deliberately went out of his way to humiliate her. However, she was damned if she would give him the satisfaction of knowing how successful he had been.

'I have just heard from the painters and decorators in Red Lion Yard,' Francesca said, and placed the cassette on Neagle's desk. 'The quality is not very good because they had to play the tape down the telephone line so that I could record it.'

'What's the content?'

'Jebens had a visitor at eleven forty-five this morning, a man calling himself Ross. Turned out it was Peter Ashton.'

'I see. When can we expect to receive the original?'

'Shortly after five when the painters and decorators knock off work for the day.'

'Then I think I will wait for the original.'

Francesca picked up the cassette. 'Whatever pleases you,' she said through gritted teeth, and turned about to leave.

'I would still like you to relate the gist of their conversation, Fran.'

Neagle gave her a warm, intimate smile as she turned about to face him again. 'I only want to hear the original recording to make sure I catch every inflection. Their respective tone of voice might be illuminating.'

As of that moment there was nothing

Francesca York would not have done for him.

'Of course. I should have guessed that.'

'You're being too hard on yourself, Fran. I should have told you what was in my mind. Anyway, please go ahead.'

'OK. Well, Pauline Dando, the legal executive, was present to begin with and she asked Jebens if she should send for the police when Ashton refused to leave his office. Jebens didn't want her to do this and in the end it was Ms Dando who left the office. Ashton wanted to know who had instructed Jebens to find a barrister to represent the Hayes family at the coroner's inquest. After a lot of argy-bargy Jebens said it was a man called George Foley who was a Sinn Fein representative in West Belfast. A little later on Jebens hinted that George Foley was IRA.'

'Do we know of him?' Neagle asked.

'No. I've signalled 10 Int. Company in Northern Ireland to see if Foley has come to their notice.'

'Good girl.' Neagle waved a hand inviting her to continue.

'Ashton then threw a couple of names at him — Simon and Julie Carmichael — only for Jebens to claim he had never heard of them. For what it's worth I don't think he was lying.'

'I've always valued your opinion, Fran.'

Substitute occasionally for always and there would be a grain of truth in the assertion but it was still nice to hear him say it.

'Anything else?' Neagle asked.

'Well, just as Ashton was about to leave, he asked Jebens if he thought Foley was the man who'd been given his new address.'

'And?'

'Jebens suggested he should ask his friends. Why do you suppose he said that?'

'The man is a born mischief-maker, he was just trying to stir things up. Take my word for it.'

Nine times out of ten Francesca would have done so without a quibble. On this occasion, however, she was not convinced.

11

Splinter groups like the Continuity IRA were not without friends and sympathisers in the Provos who were prepared to assist them with material help. It had been a sympathetic quartermaster in the Provisional IRA who had furnished George Foley with a list of safe houses in the outer suburbs of London as far apart as Sutton, Blackheath and Bexley south of the river to Greenford, East Barnet and Chingford north of the Thames. The same man had also donated a fighting fund amounting to four thousand pounds in twenties and fifties which Foley carried in a money belt around his waist. Finally, the High Command's Chief of Intelligence had given him the names of half a dozen part-time foot soldiers in the West Midlands.

Foley's contact in London was Lionel Jebens. He had never met the solicitor and had only seen an out-of-focus photograph of him in the newspapers at the time of the coroner's inquest. Chances were he could pass Jebens in the street and not recognise him. They communicated by telephone, had done so ever since he had called Jebens from West Belfast and engaged him to ensure the Hayes family were represented at the inquest.

It had been Jebens who'd given him the green light to visit Sandra Hayes when he had first arrived in England four weeks ago. Before Foley left Northern Ireland, Barry Hayes had given him a wad of money to deliver to his widowed sister-in-law and it had been vital to make sure the police weren't keeping an eye on Sandra Hayes. Money hadn't been the only thing Foley had delivered to the widow and while he had enjoyed spending the odd weekend in her company, you could have too much of a good thing. Too many visits and your face gets known by the neighbours, and he didn't want her kids being questioned by some nosy parker. Yesterday morning he'd moved out to a safe house in Greenford, just off the Ruislip Road in Hampton Close. By then he was aware that his foot soldiers in the West Midlands had managed to lose Ashton. How he was going to discover Ashton's present whereabouts was a problem Foley was still trying to come to grips with when his mobile suddenly interrupted his train of thought.

'It's me, Lionel,' Jebens said when he answered.

'Yeah? What do you want?'

'Ashton's been to see me; he left the office about fifteen minutes ago.'

'And?'

Jebens cleared his throat. 'You're not exactly a stranger to him, George. In fact he seems to know an awful lot about you. Ashton said you were the man in West Belfast who'd engaged me to represent the Hayes family — '

'Where are you calling from?' Foley demanded, cutting him short.

'A pay phone in High Holborn. I thought I'd

better warn you straight away in case he decides to call on Sandra Hayes.'

'Did you give him my mobile number while you were at it?'

'What?' Jebens sounded as if he couldn't believe his ears, which only went to prove that the theatre had lost a consummate actor when he'd decided to become a solicitor.

'I said did you give him — '

'I heard you the first time,' Jebens said angrily.

'OK, you've warned me,' Foley said, and switched off the mobile.

Jebens was only one of five people who could put a name to him. It was inconceivable that the quartermaster of his old battalion in West Belfast would have betrayed him; the same applied to the IRA's Chief of Intelligence. Sandra Hayes didn't have a motive, to his knowledge — besides which, Special Branch would have picked him up long ago had she been the stoolie. As for Barry Hayes, he would sooner cut out his own tongue before turning informer. That left Lionel Jebens and if it was a question of saving his skin, the solicitor would probably shop his own grandmother.

The question which exercised Foley was how much damage Jebens could do to him should he make a deal with the police. Since they had never met, Jebens couldn't describe him and the solicitor knew next to nothing about his background. To Jebens he was merely a name; there might be a Sinn Fein representative in West Belfast called Foley but they weren't even distantly related.

No, the solicitor wasn't a threat. Sandra Hayes, however, was in another league. She could describe him down to the strawberry birthmark on his left hip which a tattooist had made even more disfiguring when he had tried to disguise it. Foley knew he had also been a touch indiscreet at times when in bed with Sandra and there were things he'd told her about himself which he now wished he hadn't. The police might well question her, goaded into it by Ashton, but they would get nothing from Sandra unless they had something on her which would stand up in court. If they could put Sandra away, even for as little as three months, it would be enough to make her sing like a canary. There was nothing she wouldn't do for her kids and the thought of them being taken into care while she was doing time would be all the spur she needed to become a snitch.

Foley told himself to think positively. At least Ashton had come out of hiding and nobody was covering his back. What he had to do was find a suitable killing ground and then lure Ashton into it. He couldn't do that on his own but the only potential helpers immediately available were Sandra Hayes and Lionel Jebens. Their greatest asset, so far as Foley was concerned, was the fact that they were both known to Ashton.

★　★　★

In the convening order the coroner conducting the inquest had been required to ascertain the

189

circumstances in which Kevin Hayes of Sandrock Road, Lewisham had sustained fatal injuries. Only the house number had been omitted but that wasn't an insoluble problem for Ashton. After leaving the solicitor's office in Red Lion Yard, he made his way to Cannon Street station and caught a stopping train to Lewisham. He wanted either the public library or the council offices, neither of which was shown on his copy of the London A to Z.

There were two means of obtaining the house number; from the electoral roll, a copy of which would be available in the public library, or the council tax office. As a result of laziness or because of an innate sense of caution Kevin Hayes may not have completed the form for electoral registration but there was no way he could avoid paying the community charge. However, Ashton knew he would need a pretty good reason before the council tax officials would allow him to see the rating bands applicable to houses situated in Sandrock Road. On balance, Ashton thought it best to try the public library first. He stopped three people to ask the way, two of whom claimed to be strangers; the third was able to point him in the right direction. After that discovering the house number was child's play.

That morning he had asked Francesca York if Special Branch was still keeping an eye on Kevin's widow and she had told him nobody had stood them down to her knowledge, a somewhat indefinite answer, to his way of thinking. Ashton went to another section of the library and pulled out the appropriate BT directory that covered the Lewisham area and listed all the local estate agents. He then called them one by one from a pay phone in the High Street to say he'd heard the tenants of a rented, furnished house in Sandrock Road were about to move out and was the property on their books? As he had anticipated none of the estate agents knew of such a property.

Whenever it was necessary to watch a house and its occupants, Special Branch and the Intelligence services followed the same procedures. The first step was to recce the area and choose a number of potential observation posts in descending order of merit. The occupants of those properties would then be discreetly vetted to gauge their attitudes and ascertain if they were trustworthy. After narrowing the field to a first and second choice, the preferred family would be visited by a senior officer who explained the situation and asked for their assistance. If they agreed, at least two Special Branch officers would move in with them, becoming part of the family while they watched the suspect house. It was how they would have kept Sandra Hayes under surveillance.

The trick was to find out if they were still doing so. The upwardly mobile bright young people networked with bulging Filofaxes; Ashton, on the other hand, kept a few useful phone numbers in the back of a pocket diary. Leaving the call box, he picked a quiet-looking spot off the street map and made his way to the Ravensbourne. Down by the river, he then took out his mobile phone and rang Commander Anderson, Head of Operations, Special Branch.

'My name's Roy Kelso,' he said when Anderson picked up the phone. 'We haven't met and I've got to be pretty discreet because, at the moment, I don't have access to a Mozart, if you follow me?'

'I do,' Anderson told him.

'OK.' He gave Anderson his number. 'I mostly deal with Richard Neagle or Francesca York but right now I can't raise either of them.'

'What is it you want from me, Mr Kelso?'

'Well, I'm in Sandrock Road,' Ashton said, 'and I do hope we are still looking after the nice widow residing in 104 because a particularly nasty individual called George Foley has just forced his way into her house. If you have anybody in the vicinity, now might be a good time to send them round. Otherwise I will have to do the best I can on my own.'

'I'll alert the divisional station in Catford. Meantime you'd better stay where you are, Mr Kelso.'

'Will do.'

Ashton switched off the phone and walked towards the railway station. Without saying so Anderson had confirmed his hunch that Special Branch no longer had Sandra Hayes under surveillance. The lady, however, was about to receive an unpleasant surprise.

★ ★ ★

Ever since Monday, 13 May, when Lionel Jebens had been placed under physical and electronic surveillance, Francesca York had rarely left the MI5 building in Gower Street before six-thirty. That the starting date of the operation was only sixteen days prior to the Kevin Hayes inquest was purely coincidental. Had it not been for the financial constraints imposed by the Treasury on all government departments, MI5 would have moved against the solicitor when he took on the Martin Barry case. The on, off, on again nature of the Provisional IRA's ceasefire and the need to keep track of the mushrooming terrorist fringe groups had loosened the purse strings. By a fortuitous stroke of luck the dilapidated property opposite Candlewick House had come on the market at the same time.

With commendable speed agents acting on behalf of MI5 had acquired the building on a short-term lease. In consideration for what in the London borough of Holborn had amounted to a peppercorn rent, the agents had agreed to renovate the property, an arrangement which had suited the Security Service down to the ground. The painters and decorators were semi-skilled do-it-yourself enthusiasts drawn from the ranks of MI5 and Special Branch. At eight o'clock in the morning and five-thirty in the late afternoon, a closed van entered the pedestrianised Red Lion Yard to deliver and collect the workers.

Each shift kept a hand-written ops log which was subsequently double enveloped and mailed by the watch commander to The Secretary, Box

500, the coded address for the Central Registry of MI5. In addition the watch commanders were required to report in person to Francesca York when they came off duty.

The current watch commander of the day shift was known to all and sundry as Barney. He was forty-one, a detective sergeant in Special Branch, and was often described as a thoroughly amiable and totally laid back character. Amiable he might be but on duty Barney was needle sharp and nobody messed with him. Francesca York couldn't understand why his wife had divorced him five years ago.

'Good to see you, Barney,' Francesca told him when he tapped on her door. 'Come on in. What have you got for me?'

'A quality recording of the conversation between Ashton and Jebens,' he said, and placed the cassette on her desk.

'It's that good?'

'You would think you were in the room with them.'

'What do you make of Jebens?' she asked. 'You know, from the tone of his voice?'

'Well, beneath all the bluster you could tell he had the wind up. I've never met Ashton but I wouldn't want to get on the wrong side of him.'

'Jebens came back at him before he left,' Francesca pointed out diffidently.

'You mean when he suggested Ashton should ask his friends if Foley was the man who had been given his new address?' Barney wrinkled his nose. 'I reckon Jebens was hoping to needle him.'

Francesca mulled it over. Although Richard

194

Neagle hadn't listened to the first recording, he had said much the same thing.

'Didn't work, though, did it?' Barney continued, 'I mean, Ashton didn't rise to the bait.'

Francesca thought it was one way of interpreting Ashton's silence. However, she was inclined to believe it owed more to the fact that the solicitor had given voice to what Ashton had already suspected. Her reasoning had a lot to do with the Rubic homing beacon Ashton had shown her first thing that morning.

'Tell me something, Barney, amongst all the electronic gadgetry Special Branch has, do you hold any solar-powered homing beacons?'

'No. But if we needed to track a vehicle from a distance, we'd borrow one from you people. Not that we need one for Jebens; he doesn't have a car.'

'Yes. I should have remembered.'

'It's not like you to forget.'

'We all have our off days,' Francesca said hastily before he thought to ask her why the sudden interest in homing beacons.

Barney snapped his fingers. 'Seems I'm also having one of those forgetful days. Five minutes after Ashton left Candlewick House, Jebens emerged and walked down the yard to High Holborn. He was in a hell of a hurry and looked pretty agitated to me when I focused the binoculars on him.'

'Did you have someone follow him?' Francesca asked.

'Not immediately. The man was on edge and expecting trouble in one form or another. If we

195

had diverted from our daily routine he would have spotted us for sure.'

'What daily routine?'

'At twelve-fifty every working day, Jebens leaves his office, walks down the yard to High Holborn and returns ten minutes later with a sandwich in a greaseproof paper bag which he's bought from Ley's Delicatessen. I send one of the painters to the same deli either just before or just after Jebens. Every watch commander does the same.'

'I didn't know that.'

'Well, you do now, Fran. It's got so our guys exchange a friendly nod with Jebens and sometimes he'll ask how the work is going.'

'Oh my God, he'll have made him.'

Barney shook his head. 'We ring the changes, send a different guy every day. The point is our man Jebens broke his routine today. Instead of finding him in Ley's Delicatessen, he was spotted leaving a BT phone booth further down the street. That's something he's never done since Special Branch has been watching him.'

'Shit. Shit. Shit,' Francesca said wearily. 'He knows his phone is bugged.'

'I'm not convinced. His partner is away sunning himself on the beach at Torremolinos and the secretary bird is doing the same thing at some resort in Turkey. That leaves Ms Pauline Dando, the acceptable face of the law practice. We know from what Ashton said that she is temporarily running the switchboard. I'm betting Jebens made his call from a pay phone because he didn't want to risk Ms Dando listening to his conversation.'

'Maybe,' Francesca said in a voice full of doubt.

'You're not going to pull the plug on this operation on the strength of a hunch, are you?'

'It's not up to me, Barney.'

'Well, for what it's worth, tell the man my advice is to let it run and see what happens.'

The man faced with making the decision was Richard Neagle. It didn't altogether surprise Francesca York when he opted for the policy of wait and see. Neagle, however, was not thinking clearly. As Francesca rapidly learned he had just concluded an acrimonious conversation with Commander Anderson, Head of Operations, Special Branch.

'Ashton is now calling himself Roy Kelso,' Neagle grated. 'He set the bloody police on to Sandra Hayes, implied she was harbouring a dangerous IRA gunman called Foley. Somehow he managed to convince Anderson that normally he only dealt with me or you but had been unable to raise either of us.'

'That's Ashton for you, Richard. You always said he was a loose cannon.'

★ ★ ★

The four-bedroom house in Bisham Gardens overlooking Waterlow Park at the top of Highgate Hill had been part of the settlement when Jill Sheridan had divorced Henry Clayburn fifteen months after they had married. In return for not claiming maintenance from her ex she had also acquired his top-of-the-range Porsche 928 GTS. The house had cost Henry Clayburn four hundred thousand. Unlike the sports car, which had depreciated alarmingly in the last thirty-one months, Urquhart estimated the property would now fetch close on three-quarters of a million.

The house was called Freemantle, the significance of which Urquhart still hadn't discovered even though he and Jill had been lovers for the past nine months. In that time he had come to regard Freemantle as his second home though in practice for every night he passed under Jill's roof he spent three at his miserable bachelor flat in Finchley. Now that he had left Rosalind and filed for divorce, it seemed to Urquhart that Jill was trying to keep him at arm's length. He had telephoned her about seven o'clock yesterday evening on his return from Belfast, and had expected Jill to welcome him with open arms, only to be told she was sickening for something and had been in bed all day. Urquhart had wanted to believe her but he had a nagging suspicion Jill was putting it on.

Fortunately yesterday's rebuff was now history; shortly after three o'clock Jill had rung him at the FCO to suggest they had dinner at her place. She had also let it be known she would be home by six and would be happy to see him any time after that. At exactly five minutes after the appointed hour Urquhart parked his second-hand Rover 400 in her driveway and rang the bell. He could not have asked for a more loving welcome when she opened the door to him. In full view of any of her neighbours who might be watching Jill flung her arms around his neck and pressed herself against him.

'There, that should give them something to think about,' Jill said when she finally released him.

'Well, I don't know about the neighbours,' Urquhart said in a strained voice, 'but I certainly enjoyed it.'

'So did I, Robin.'

The jug of Pimm's she had made for them would never be his favourite tipple but in his present state of euphoria even dental mouth wash would have tasted like nectar.

'So how were things in Belfast?' Jill asked, curling up on the settee beside him, legs tucked under her rump, a familiar posture that never failed to excite him.

'Bloody, perfectly bloody: all we did was talk about talks. I spent the whole of Thursday, Friday, Saturday and Sunday morning in Stormont sitting across the table from a baby-faced sanctimonious politician with mean, piggy eyes whom I knew to be a bloody gunman. To my certain knowledge the little bastard has shot at least two policemen in the back.'

'Which political party was this animal representing?'

'Let's say the Orange Order certainly hadn't been invited to the talks.'

'That's no surprise,' Jill said contemptuously. 'We all know the Ulster Unionists are not the people the Government is hell bent on appeasing.'

'I wouldn't repeat that accusation outside

these four walls if I were you, Jill. It wouldn't do your career a lot of good; appeasement is a dirty word.'

'You could fool me, Robin.'

'Me too,' Urquhart admitted, 'especially when I listened to what Sinn Fein wanted from us if the Provos were to maintain their ceasefire. The army confined to barracks, troop levels to be reduced, all vehicle checkpoints to be withdrawn. In fact, a cessation of all counter-intelligence operations. And not only in Northern Ireland — the same demands apply to mainland Britain, if you ever did.'

'That might be a little difficult to observe,' Jill told him laconically.

'I don't see why it should be.'

'Ashton is on the prowl. This morning he went to see Lionel Jebens, the solicitor who acted for the Hayes family. According to Richard Neagle, who telephoned me this afternoon, it seems Jebens disclosed the name of the Sinn Feiner who hired him.'

Urquhart found himself listening to Jill with growing disquiet because there was more, much more, and all of it was bad news. The new identities which had been so laboriously constructed for the Ashtons were now in ruins, they had been tracked by a team using the most sophisticated homing beacon and Harriet had taken refuge with the Peacheys. Finally, Ashton had bounced the police into raiding the Hayes household.

'And you know what?' Jill continued. 'It was Harriet who urged Ashton to cut loose.'

Urquhart set his glass down on the low table in front of them. 'What is Victor doing about him?' he asked.

'Nothing. As a matter of fact I think he's quite happy for Ashton to go on the rampage.'

'Evidently your suggestion didn't work.'

'What suggestion?'

'To give him a knighthood in order to secure his co-operation.'

'Did your honours and awards man phone him with the good news like he was supposed to?'

'Of course he did.' Urquhart frowned. 'Somebody ought to remind Victor Hazelwood the knighthood is dependent on his good behaviour.'

'Well, don't look at me, Robin. Officially I don't know about the proposed honour.'

'I'm not suggesting you should do it.'

'Good. I'm in enough trouble as it is,' Jill said, and got to her feet.

'What are you talking about?'

'I vetted the new identities we provided for the Ashtons. In fact, I did most of the detailed work. It's therefore largely my fault that they were blown away in no time.'

'Has anybody said so or implied as much?'

'Not yet but they soon will.'

'Not if I have anything to do with it.' Urquhart reached out and grasped Jill by the hand as she attempted to pass in front of him. 'Where are you off to?' he asked.

'The kitchen. Apparently it's where I belong.'

'I don't think so.'

Jill didn't exactly resist when he drew her down on to his lap.

★ ★ ★

The day had started early for Rowan Garfield. He had been shaving when the duty officer of the European Department had telephoned to inform him that Head of Station, Moscow, had sent another Emergency Top Secret signal concerning Katya Malinovskaya, this time to report her death. Breakfast had gone by the board, he had driven to Hazlemere, left the Jaguar in the station car park and caught the next train to London.

A second communication had been waiting for him when he had arrived at Vauxhall Cross. This one had been originated by the Ambassador and was prefaced 'For attention SOSFA', the official abbreviation for Secretary of State for Foreign Affairs. It had simply stated that a Mr Walter Iremonger, a UK national residing in Moscow, was helping police with their enquiries into a fatal shooting, and had been accompanied to the central police station by the Third Secretary, Consular Affairs. Since Chris Neighbour had been involved in his capacity as the Third Secretary, the signal had been copied automatically to the SIS. Garfield had therefore concluded that Katya Malinovskaya had been killed when in Iremonger's company, an opinion Hazelwood hadn't questioned when he had raised the matter during morning prayers.

The two signals from Moscow had been

202

dispatched at 10.51 and 11.37 local time, which was four hours ahead of London. After an interval of seven hours nineteen minutes the FCO had received another signal which they had repeated to Vauxhall Cross. SOSFA had been informed that detectives of the Criminal Investigation Division were satisfied with the statement Mr Walter Iremonger had given and had inferred that he would be called as a witness for the prosecution should the murderer be apprehended. Meantime, Iremonger should not leave Moscow without first informing the appropriate authorities.

'They've got Iremonger's damned passport,' Hazelwood had growled when he'd shown the signal to him.

And that had been the start of yet another mini conference involving Victor, Jill Sheridan, Dennis Eberhardie and himself, all of them trying to second-guess what was really happening in Moscow. At the end of a lengthy discussion they had agreed Iremonger would be at risk unless he was given adequate protection by the Russian authorities. They had also concluded that in addition to the usual watchkeeper, a grade II intelligence officer from the Russian Desk should be on immediate call.

Unfortunately for Dennis Eberhardie, his only grade II intelligence officer had taken a fortnight off to spend time with his young family. But despite the fact that Eberhardie lived in Victoria, less than half an hour from the office, Garfield had still felt compelled to stay on long after everybody else had gone home. He had telephoned Eileen to warn her he would be late and had promised faithfully he would leave the office at seven come what may. Ten minutes after the self-imposed deadline, he reluctantly began to clear his desk and lock the files away. The telephone rang just as he was about to reverse the hanging card on his door from 'Occupied' to 'Vacant' for the benefit of the security guards. Answering it, he found he had Nancy Wilkins of Central Registry on the line.

'Sorry to trouble you, sir,' she said, 'but I've just received a weird message from my opposite number at the FCO. It doesn't make sense to any of the watchkeepers and I wondered if you could solve the mystery?'

'You'd better tell me what it is first.'

'It's a low-grade priority signal from Moscow classified Restricted. The text reads: 'Package is on British Airways Flight 875 arriving Heathrow at 22.35 hours. Please arrange collection. Price of item to follow under special cover.''

'Did your opposite number give you the date/time group of the message?'

'Yeah. It's 22 July 96, 1805 hours, Zulu. I guess that means it was sent on the twenty-second of July 1996 at five minutes past six this evening Greenwich Mean Time?'

'You're learning fast,' Garfield observed drily. 'Now tell your friend at the FCO the message has been received and understood.'

Garfield put the phone down, then rang Amberley Lodge to warn the administrative officer of the SIS training school that two guests requiring long-stay accommodation would be

204

arriving shortly after midnight. His next step was to put one of the duty drivers at five minutes' notice to move with effect from 21.00 hours. Finally he rang Dennis Eberhardie at home and told him his presence was required a.s.a.p.

Allowing for the different time zones the signal from Moscow had been originated one hour after Flight BA875 had cleared Russian air space. The package was clearly Walter Iremonger; the bit about the price of the item suggested the AP correspondent had been issued with a new passport and was probably travelling under the name of Price.

12

The office cleaners had already departed and the day staff were beginning to arrive when Nancy Wilkins left Vauxhall Cross at eight o'clock, having spent the past twenty-four hours on duty in the Central Registry. Setting off at a brisk pace towards the underground station, Nancy unzipped her shoulder bag, took out the mobile and rang Ashton. Brian Thomas, Head of Security Vetting and Technical Services, had given her the number of Ashton's mobile phone on Friday morning and had instructed her to contact him at the earliest opportunity. Even before Nancy had spoken to Ashton that same evening, she'd had a pretty shrewd idea of what he wanted from her and hadn't been disappointed.

'It's me, Nancy,' she said when Ashton answered. 'I think I may have something for you, but it depends on how you interpret the facts — '

'Tell me something, Nancy,' he said quietly, interrupting her. 'Did this involve gaining access to Codeword material?'

The alarm bells started ringing in her head. Generally speaking, any individual who had been cleared by positive vetting enjoyed constant access to Top Secret. There were, however, additional security caveats. Officers who needed to see the transcripts of intercepts captured by Government Communications Headquarters had to be specially indoctrinated, which included a written undertaking by the person concerned that he or she would not visit specified countries for a period of five years after being removed from the GCHQ approved list. Nancy was also aware that, before allowing access to satellite intelligence, the RAF demanded a certificate in writing from Brian Thomas to the effect that there was nothing whatever in the candidate's security file which even hinted at an undesirable character trait. Codeword material was the ultimate defence against a breach of security. If your name wasn't on the select list, there was no way you could access the document, no matter what security clearance you might have.

'Are you still there, Nancy?'

'Yes.' Her voice sounded strained; clearing her throat, Nancy tried again. 'Yes, I'm here,' she said in a louder tone.

'Well then, did you gain access to Codeword material relating to me and Harriet?'

'Not exactly.'

'That means you did.'

It had been said of Ashton that people would go the last mile for him without being asked to do so and even when instinct told them it wasn't in their interest. In her case, he had told her point-blank to back off and leave well alone the moment she discovered access to his new identity was subject to Codeword procedures. And what had been her response? She had gone ahead and done it anyway.

'It's all rather complicated,' she said eventually.

'Too complicated to discuss over the phone?' Ashton suggested.

'In my opinion it is.'

'So where shall we meet?'

'I'm on my way home. Do you know where Market Lane is in Burnt Oak?'

'You've got me there.'

Nancy hesitated, thought about giving him directions to her place, then had a better idea.

'We'll meet in the entrance hall of Burnt Oak station. Whoever arrives first waits for the other. OK?'

'Yes.'

'I should be there in about fifty minutes from now.' Nancy paused, then added, 'Problem is I have to change to the Northern at Warren Street and you know what that line is like.'

'No, but I have a feeling I am about to find out,' Ashton said.

'You can bet on it,' Nancy told him cheerfully, then switched off her mobile and walked into Vauxhall underground station to catch a northbound train.

★ ★ ★

There were days when morning prayers were something of an ordeal for Rowan Garfield. Not only was his European Department the largest and most unwieldy organisation in the SIS, it also had more than its fair share of potential trouble spots. He wished somebody in the

208

Treasury would explain to him how he was supposed to keep on top of the job with an establishment which had been cut to the bone. Naturally a man like Hazelwood, who enjoyed the reputation of being a 'thruster', wasn't the least bit interested in his difficulties. Victor simply expected him to have all the facts at his fingertips, as well as the answers to any questions which might suddenly occur to him.

This morning the number-one topic for Hazelwood was certain to be Walter Iremonger. Garfield had done everything possible to prepare himself for what was bound to be a lengthy interrogation. Yesterday evening he had stayed on at the office to brief Dennis Eberhardie and had then caught a semi-fast train to Hazlemere, finally arriving home to a disgruntled Eileen at five minutes to nine. Although used to the unsocial hours which the job frequently entailed she had become even more disgruntled on learning he would be leaving for Amberley Lodge as soon as they had eaten.

Except for the satisfaction of knowing that nobody could possibly accuse him of being a nine-to-five man, visiting the training school had proved a waste of time and effort for Garfield. Iremonger had had an exhausting and harrowing day. A woman he scarcely knew had been shot dead in his Moscow apartment, he had been questioned by the Russian police for hours on end and then whisked out of the country under an assumed name. He had faced another interrogation after clearing Customs and Excise at Heathrow, Eberhardie firing one question after another at him all the way to Petersfield. Stressed out and dog-tired into the bargain, Iremonger had told Garfield bluntly that he had nothing more to tell the SIS and was damned well going to bed.

Short of dragging the AP correspondent out of bed at an unearthly hour in the morning, which really would have put his back up, Garfield had had no choice but to leave any further debriefing to Dennis Eberhardie. A faint hope that the intelligence officer might have something for him before morning prayers began had been dashed when he had arrived at Vauxhall Cross. With so little information at hand, he had intended to pad things out by giving a résumé of events in Moscow up to close of play last night. Unfortunately, Hazelwood took it upon himself to do this.

'You've stolen most of my thunder, Director,' Garfield said with a tight smile when Hazelwood invited him to say what he had learned from Walter Iremonger.

'Really? I find that hard to believe, Rowan. After all, you're the only person here who has spoken to Mr Iremonger. What did he tell you?'

'Not a lot. He claims Katya Malinovskaya was shot roughly ten minutes after he'd let her into his apartment. During that time she promised Iremonger that if he would smuggle her into the grounds of the British Embassy in the boot of his car, she would give him an even bigger story than Elena Andrianova.' Garfield looked round the table. Everybody was nodding sagely with the exception of Winston Reid, who had joined the SIS too recently to have heard of her. 'Andrianova was a locally employed civilian who worked for the junior commercial attaché,' he explained for Reid's benefit. 'She was a single mother and the KGB had described in graphic detail what would happen to her six-year-old daughter and aged parents if she didn't co-operate. Ashton discovered she was passing economic information to the Sovs when he was carrying out a routine check of the embassy's security. He was in charge of the Security Vetting and Technical Services in those days.'

'Can we move on?' Hazelwood said impatiently.

Garfield managed another thin smile. Well, of course he could move on and if time was so bloody precious he could wrap up the whole business in a couple of sentences. The fact was Katya Malinovskaya had told Iremonger no more than they had already learned from Head of Station, Moscow.

'And that's it?' Hazelwood said as if unable to believe his ears.

'Iremonger did say she had a thing about Major General Gurov, and was adamant that he had betrayed her for the simple reason that he was the only person who'd known which route she was taking to Tver'. She couldn't explain why Gurov should have switched sides after supporting her for close on five months. The allegation didn't make sense to Iremonger. He said the General couldn't have been more helpful after Neighbour rang him to complain about the treatment the AP correspondent was

211

receiving at the hands of the two policemen who had responded to the 02 emergency call.'

Jill Sheridan looked pensive. 'Is it possible Iremonger is not being entirely frank with us?' she asked. 'After all, Katya Malinovskaya did promise to give him a major scoop.'

'I don't think so,' Garfield told her firmly even though the possibility hadn't occurred to him.

'If Iremonger disclosed everything to us he could suffer financially. By that I mean we could go to a judge and obtain an injunction banning publication citing the Official Secrets Acts.' Jill smiled. 'I'm just putting myself in his shoes. It's the way he might see it.'

'Quite so, and don't think we shan't make that point when we meet with Iremonger later this morning.'

'I have a question,' Reid said. 'Why did Katya Malinovskaya go to Iremonger with her story?'

'He's interviewed her once before,' Garfield said. 'She had to remind him, of course. And they had both known Ashton.'

'He was a good intelligence officer?' Reid enquired.

'No better than Dennis Eberhardie, if as shrewd.'

'He got results,' Hazelwood growled. 'Whether Dennis can remains to be seen.'

Garfield felt obliged to defend his subordinate and was about to take issue with Hazelwood when Jill weighed in to describe Ashton as a loose cannon who did more harm than good. For the Director and his deputy to disagree publicly was unheard of and Garfield listened spellbound. Usually he had little time for Ashton but it rapidly became evident that the former desk officer had done something which had resulted in Ms Sheridan getting rapped over the knuckles. That this should have happened to this overly ambitious, utterly ruthless smarty-pants with friends in high places was, Garfield reckoned, a thought to be savoured.

★ ★ ★

Ashton had been used to seeing Nancy Wilkins wearing some outrageous outfit in leather, suede or denim. During the last seven weeks, however, there had been a transformation. Gone were the tight-fitting toreador trousers that looked as if the seams would split if ever she had to bend down to pick up something off the floor. The wet look and the micro mini, which Jill Sheridan in a moment of crudity had once described as a pussy pelmet, had also been dropped. Currently in favour was a pale blue linen skirt with a modest hemline and matching jacket with elbow-length sleeves worn over a white, silk jersey blouse. There was no golden chain around her ankle, no heavy metal bracelets around her wrist and no Doc Martens on her feet. In fact, Ashton wouldn't have recognised Nancy if she hadn't accosted him when he appeared in the booking hall.

'I like the outfit,' he said.

'You mean I look different.'

'There's no denying that. Who or what prompted the change?'

'Personal choice,' she said, and moved out onto the pavement. 'We have to cross the road and go up the hill a bit.'

Market Lane looped off Watling Street, rejoining the thoroughfare just short of the crossroads at the top of the hill. The only thing which distinguished the semi-detached where Nancy lived from the other houses was a small ornamental pond with a solar powered fountain in the front garden.

'My dad's pride and joy,' Nancy informed him.

'You're living at home?'

'Until I get enough money together for a place of my own.' Nancy produced a bunch of keys, unlocked the front door and nudged it open with a knee.

'I'm going to make myself a cup of coffee,' she said. 'Can I get you one too?'

'Please.'

'OK. The sitting room's the second door on your right.'

'Hadn't I better say hello to your parents first?'

'They've gone to work. Black or white?'

'What?'

'Your coffee,' Nancy explained.

'Oh. White please, no sugar.'

Ashton wandered into the sitting room. French windows opened onto a well-kept garden lawn, free of buttercups, dandelions, clover and daisies. The flowerbeds were laid out with military precision, dwarf bedding dahlias in the front, hybrid tea roses in the centre and in the rear rank, stately gladioli were just beginning to bloom. Each row was dressed off by the right like so many guardsmen on parade. Cupressus planted close together formed a tall hedgerow, enclosing the garden on all three sides.

'Admiring the garden?' Nancy asked, passing him a mug of coffee.

'Yes, it's quite something.'

'The way your security file was shuffled around was quite something too. Mr Durban was created by a committee run by Jill Sheridan.'

'How do you know this?'

'The Chief Archivist neglected to destroy the bin card.'

A bin card was used to record the movement of a file after it left the archives. The Deputy DG had ruled that Ashton's security file should be held in the Central Registry as opposed to the Security Vetting and Technical Services Division. The Chief Archivist had made out a bin card for the file and had immediately recorded that the document had gone to the Deputy DG. Jill had kept the file for two days and had then marked it up for the attention of Ken Maynard, the officer in charge of the Pay Section. The file had reached him via the Central Registry where the Chief Archivist had noted the onward movement on the bin card. If Jill had walked the document straight to the Pay Section, thereby bypassing the Central Registry, the system would have broken down.

'From the Pay Section it was sent to Roy Kelso and thence to Brian Thomas,' Nancy continued. 'On each occasion it was consigned

215

to the relevant addressee via the Deputy DG and Central Registry.'

'How long did Maynard keep the file?'

'He turned it round the same day.'

'And Roy Kelso?'

'He kept it longer than most, Mr Ashton — five working days with a weekend in between.'

Nancy had only seen the bin card and couldn't tell him what instructions the various addresses had been given. However, it was easy enough for Ashton to draw his own conclusions. Ken Maynard would have arranged banking facilities for the Durbans with the head office of Lloyd's Bank PLC, which undoubtedly included the transfer of current and deposit accounts to the local branch at Lichfield. Kelso would have dealt with the purchase of the house in Gaia Lane and arranged with the Post Office to intercept and redirect all mail addressed to 84 Rylett Close to The Secretary, Box 850. Brian Thomas would have had the more demanding task of providing the requisite documents to support the legends Jill Sheridan had compiled for Harriet and himself. These would have included birth and marriage certificates for the Durbans and a certified copy of an entry pursuant to the Birth and Registration Act 1953 in respect of Edward. In addition, death certificates were required for both sets of fictional parents. Everything had had to be completed within a matter of days and copies of the various documents lodged with the Office of Population Censuses and Surveys, St Catherine's House.

'The codeword 'Phantom' made its first appearance one week before the coroner's inquest,' Nancy told him. 'Meantime, your security file and Mrs Ashton's were going back and forth between the Deputy DG and Brian Thomas. According to the entries on the bin card, your files were still with Ms Sheridan on Tuesday, the sixteenth of July, the day before your old house in Rylett Close was torched. In fact, she had returned them both to Brian Thomas on Monday the eighth. Apparently that wasn't the first time Ms Sheridan had returned the file in person. She'd also collected them on at least two previous occasions.'

'How do you know?'

'I showed the bin card to Brian Thomas and asked him if he could shed any light on the present whereabouts of the files. He nearly blew a gasket, said our Deputy DG couldn't have made a better job of sabotaging the tracking system if she had put her mind to it.'

Ashton shook his head in disbelief. Where in-house security procedures were concerned, Jill had always done everything by the book. She wouldn't have flouted the rules without some ulterior motive.

'The Durban identities were prepared under the codename 'Phantom'.' Nancy twisted her mouth in a lopsided smile. 'And before you ask me how I found that out, I was the duty watchkeeper in Central Registry last night.'

'You opened Quayle's safe,' Ashton said in a hollow voice.

'His wasn't the only safe I needed to open,'

217

Nancy told him cheerfully.

Quayle was the Chief Archivist, the custodian of Codeword material, and the only man who knew the combination which opened the safe. Although most of the junior clerical officers would disagree, Quayle was only human; he fell sick or went on vacation. The world, however, did not stop revolving in his absence and situations could arise when it was necessary to open his safe. The combination to Quayle's safe was contained in a sealed envelope which the Deputy Chief Archivist held in his safe along with the combination to various other ones.

'As you know the duty watchkeeper has the combination to that particular safe.'

'There's more than one clerk on night duty,' Ashton observed.

'Yes indeed. Fortunately he has a weak bladder. I did my safe cracking whenever he was out of the room.'

It had been a race against time for Nancy. She'd had to open the safe containing the sealed envelope, extract the slip of paper on which the combination had been written, open Quayle's safe and then go through the codeword registers until she found the right one.

'Obviously I had to close one safe before opening the other so that I would have a chance to put things back before my colleague with the weak bladder walked in on me.'

Nancy had needed three bites of the cherry to complete the task. Discovering the register for the Durban file hadn't been as difficult as she had anticipated. The reference for Ashton's security file was JPS, the initials of the officer who had originally vetted him, followed by 134, the running total of the number of individuals he had interviewed. All Quayle had done when allocating a codeword and reference number for the Durban file was add an oblique stroke followed by a capital A. The Top Secret register for Phantom was therefore JPS 134/A.

'The sealed envelope was my biggest problem,' Nancy said.

Finding another small brown envelope had been easy enough; Nancy had a packet of them in the top drawer of her desk. She also had a red star-shaped label which had to be gummed across the flap. The really difficult part had been the forging of Quayle's signature across the red star.

'I think I finally got it right.'

'Oh my God.' Ashton closed his eyes briefly. 'Why on earth did you go so far out on a limb for me? That's the last thing I wanted.'

'I didn't like the way the people on the top floor dumped on you. Anyway, I got away with it.'

'I surely hope so.'

'Phantom is lodged in the Deputy DG's safe,' Nancy said, changing the subject abruptly. 'However, the names of those officers permitted access to the Durban file are listed inside the register held by Mr Quayle.'

'Let me guess,' Ashton said. 'Hazelwood, Sheridan, Kelso, and, of course, the Chief Archivist.'

'You've left two names out,' Nancy informed

219

him. 'Robin Urquhart of the FCO and Richard Neagle at MI5.'

★　★　★

The atmosphere in the Peachey household was becoming more and more fraught and, while Ann hadn't said anything, Harriet had the distinct feeling that she had outstayed her welcome. Ever since Clifford had accidentally touched her breast he had danced around her like a cat on hot bricks, pressing himself against the wall to avoid any possible contact whenever they were obliged to pass one another in the narrow hallway. Unfortunately, the only thing Clifford succeeded in doing was to confirm his wife's suspicion that there was something going on between them.

His odd behaviour rubbed off on Harriet and made her question their past relationship. Had all those many kindnesses Clifford had shown her in the past and his fatherly attitude been symptomatic of something more carnal? She remembered those early days in five when she had been assigned to K2 after spending eighteen months on the Armed Forces Desk in Bolton Street. Back in those days Clifford had been the leading light of K1, the so-called Kremlin watchers, and she'd had a lot to do with him because part of her job had been to monitor the activities of possible subversives.

One way or another Harriet had spent a fair amount of time in Clifford's office and nearly always when they had been comparing notes, they had sat side by side at his desk, the very experienced senior intelligence officer and the still wet-behind-the-ears probationer. Looking back now, Harriet thought it incredible that she hadn't questioned why she had been singled out for such preferential treatment. Although he had never attempted to fondle her, there was no denying Clifford was very possessive and he had been absurdly jealous of Ashton even before they were married. How many times had he inferred that Peter was not for her? Too many to count, was the short answer.

Things just couldn't go on the way they were. They were living on top of one another, the two Special Branch detectives were getting under everybody's feet and, to make matters worse, Ann was politely declining her every offer of help in the kitchen. In desperation Harriet had volunteered to do some weeding in the garden. She was on her hands and knees busily replanting the polygonum and saxifrages in the herbaceous border, which Edward had uprooted in his eagerness to help, when Ann called from the kitchen to tell her she was wanted on the phone. Taking Edward with her before he did any more damage, Harriet went through to the study and picked up the transceiver.

'Hello, Harry,' a familiar voice said, using her childhood nickname. 'It's me, Richard.'

'Richard,' she repeated, dumbfounded. 'How did you know I was staying here?'

'Peter rang on Saturday evening and gave me the number.' Her brother cleared his throat. 'There's no easy way to tell you this, Harry . . . '

221

'Tell me what?'

'Pa died early this morning.'

Harriet listened in silence to what her brother was saying, unable really to take it all in. It seemed Alzheimer's had lowered Pa's resistance and he had picked up some bug which had rapidly turned to pneumonia. Richard had called the doctor in on Sunday afternoon when he had been taken ill and there would be no post mortem to establish the cause of death, which was a blessing. Richard had been in touch with the undertakers and the usual notices would appear in *The Times* and *Telegraph* — family flowers only, donations to Imperial Cancer Research.

'Subject to confirmation, the funeral will take place at two o'clock this Friday at St Swithin's church.' Richard paused, then said awkwardly, 'Will you be able to attend, Harry?'

'I'm leaving now.'

'What?'

'I'm coming home.'

'Is that wise?'

'My mind's made up, Richard.'

'We're a bit pushed for space, old girl,' he said lamely.

'That's OK. We'll stay in Ferris Drive. We should be there by six. Perhaps you would warn Pa's housekeeper.'

'If you're sure . . . '

'I'm positive,' she said, and put the phone down.

For some time afterwards, Harriet sat there wondering why the tears didn't come, why there wasn't a lump in her throat.

13

In one respect Walter Iremonger was unique. He was the first and likely to be the only unauthorised civilian who had been admitted to Amberley Lodge and stayed the night. Had the training school not been between courses, Garfield wouldn't have known what to do with the AP correspondent. There had been insufficient time to arrange accommodation for Iremonger in a safe house within the Greater London area and he had dismissed the idea of finding a hotel room for him. The training school was a cost-effective alternative, especially as the security was as effective as any safe house. Guard dogs and their armed handlers patrolled the grounds at night, backed up by an infrared anti-intruder fence. The lodge itself was protected by floodlights, CCTV cameras and an alarm system linked to F Division of the Surrey Constabulary.

However, as good as the security arrangements were, the sooner alternative accommodation was found for Iremonger the better it would be for all concerned. Garfield had had no difficulty in persuading himself that it wouldn't be long before the AP correspondent started to bellyache about the restrictions which would have to be placed on his freedom of movement while he was staying at the SIS training school. Garfield also accepted Jill Sheridan's argument that the longer

Iremonger stayed at Amberley Lodge, the more good copy he was mentally filing away.

How to get the most out of the man in the shortest possible time was a problem Garfield had been considering on the train journey to Hazlemere. He was still no nearer to a solution when he turned into the drive leading to Amberley Lodge, having picked up the Jaguar from the station car park. Dennis Eberhardie was waiting for him on the doorstep as he drew up outside the lodge; from the Gallic shrug and the way he spread his hands, palms uppermost, it was evident to Garfield that the senior intelligence officer on the Russian Desk had learned nothing new.

'What have you done with our friend?' Garfield asked on alighting from the Jaguar.

'I left him in the library with a cup of coffee.'

'I take it that Iremonger still hasn't told you anything you didn't already know?'

'I get the impression you believe he is holding out on us,' Eberhardie suggested.

'Your crystal ball is a little clouded, Dennis. As it happens, I have an open mind.'

'Well, I'm damned sure I haven't. I'm convinced Iremonger has been absolutely straight with us. Let's face it, we wouldn't have known Katya Malinovskaya had promised to give him a major scoop if he hadn't told us.'

'He could have been boxing clever,' Garfield said, and was conscious of sounding paranoiac.

'Katya Malinovskaya didn't have time to do more than whet his appetite. She was shot dead minutes after he had let her into his apartment.'

'We've only his word for that, Dennis. And don't forget, the sniper did fire twice. He wouldn't have had a go at Iremonger unless he'd reason to believe Katya Malinovskaya had told him everything she knew.'

'It was probably an opportunity shot. The gunman had just put Malinovskaya down when Iremonger obligingly presented himself in the window.'

'That's a little too convenient for my liking.'

'Have it your way then,' Eberhardie said curtly.

'I'm just playing devil's advocate, Dennis.' Garfield smiled unconvincingly. 'As I said earlier, I've an open mind.'

'Then listen to Iremonger.'

'That's what I intend to do.'

Garfield stepped past his subordinate and went inside the house. Amberley Lodge was the sort of Georgian residence he would like to own if he had the money. An incurable romantic when it came to lifestyle, he could picture himself and Eileen standing in the oak-panelled hall, waiting to greet their guests on New Year's Eve, a log fire burning in the huge open grate. Reality returned when he opened the first door on his right and walked into the library.

Garfield knew very little about the AP man other than he would be forty-nine on 18 December, had two daughters and was divorced. He had never seen a photograph of Iremonger, but since there weren't too many years between them, he'd imagined the press reporter would be pretty much like himself and look younger than his age. To his surprise, Iremonger was overweight, unfit and probably had to resort to a puffer on occasions, judging by his nicotine-stained fingers.

'Good morning, Walter,' Garfield said cheerfully. 'I hope you slept well?'

'I did, and before you go any further, I've nothing more to say on the subject of Katya Malinovskaya. So you can forget any questions which may have occurred since last night.'

'Actually I was going to ask where you were thinking of going when you leave here. Is there anyone you could stay with?'

Iremonger was dumbfounded; his mouth fell open and he blinked several times as though he had been winded by a vicious punch in the solar plexus. Eberhardie looked equally stunned and froze in the act of adding a dash of milk to the coffee he had just poured himself.

'I have a sister living in Pwllheli,' Iremonger said, recovering. 'I dare say she could put me up for a few days — and there's a bachelor cousin in Edinburgh. Of course, I would have to find out what plans the bureau has in mind for me first. That could mean staying in London for a day or two.'

'I imagine it would.'

Iremonger started blinking again. 'You don't think the Mafiozniki pose a threat?'

'Not in this country,' Garfield said airily. 'They were hired to kill Katya Malinovskaya and Vladislav Kochelev.'

'The sniper tried to kill me too.'

'He was merely being overzealous; the

Mafiozniki don't do freebies. Besides, they don't have the intelligence capability to target you in England.'

'Major General Gurov is ex-KGB.'

'So is half the Russian Government.'

'Katya believed he'd betrayed her.'

'And I recall you saying Gurov couldn't have been more helpful after Mr Neighbour spoke to him.'

If ever a face could betray what a man was thinking it was Iremonger's. He had drawn in his bottom lip and was nibbling at one corner with his teeth.

'The police were very quick to respond to the emergency call. It was as if they had a patrol car in the neighbourhood waiting for somebody to report the incident.'

Garfield was tempted to ask Iremonger why he hadn't mentioned this during any of the earlier interviews but managed to restrain himself. From experience he knew that long after the event a person sometimes did recall an incident which had been buried deep in the subconscious. If he had indulged in a sarcastic rejoinder, Iremonger might well have clammed up and who knows what other undisclosed revelations might have been buried for good.

'I realise that must sound pretty contradictory in view of what I said earlier.'

'Not at all.' Garfield assured him. 'I think both you and Katya Malinovskaya were right about Major General Gurov. I believe he did betray her, possibly because the people who were determined that Pavel Trilisser should not stand trial for embezzlement learned that he was helping Katya to stay one step ahead of the Mafiozniki. I also believe Gurov washed his hands of the whole business when he learned she had survived the ambush.'

After Katya had severed all contact with him the Mafiozniki hadn't needed Moscow's Chief of Police. They had plenty of other senior officers on their payroll who were prepared to put Katya Malinovskaya on the Most Wanted List and deploy the necessary resources to track her down. They had covered every likely bolt-hole; what they hadn't foreseen was the possibility of a major diplomatic incident as a consequence of their actions.

'But Gurov did,' Garfield continued. 'That's why he was so quick to intervene after Chris Neighbour phoned him. And for once Gurov and the supporters of Pavel Trilisser saw eye to eye.'

'You're guessing,' Iremonger said.

'It's not an unreasonable deduction. What I can't explain is why Pavel Trilisser was released from house arrest back in March. I wondered if you had heard anything.'

'I thought you people never believed anything you read in the newspapers?'

Garfield laughed, feigning amusement. 'I can't think what gave you that idea. Sometimes even the wildest rumours may contain a grain of truth, and very occasionally it can point to an area previously neglected by your Intelligence-gathering resources.'

'Well, if you're in the market for rumours,

Trilisser is said to have a brain tumour. The story goes he was released from house arrest to attend the Raisa Gorbachev Clinic for tests.'

Nevertheless, Trilisser had not enjoyed complete freedom of movement. He had attended the clinic under escort and it was assumed he must have given his minders the slip when he had been photographed outside the Park Kultury Metro station. One source maintained Trilisser had sneaked out of the clinic to meet his mistress, twenty-four-year-old Masha Voronova, the wife of General Nikolay Voronov, Commander of Russian Airborne Forces. Another source had told Iremonger that Trilisser's current mistress was the ballerina Anna Berezhkova, and that his minders were present but out of camera shot when the lovers had met. Yet a third source had pooh-poohed the allegation on the grounds that Berezhkova was a lesbian with a string of girlfriends.

'However, all my sources agree the brain tumour is inoperable. It's also widely believed Trilisser will not be alive to see in the New Year.'

'And where do these sources think Pavel Trilisser is now?'

'Yalta, St Petersburg, Archangel, Murmansk — anywhere in fact but Moscow.'

An inoperable brain tumour: Garfield wondered if it was fact or fiction. Either way, would the alleged fatal condition have formed part of the defence had the trial taken place? Deep in thought, he did not hear a member of staff enter the library and paid little attention to the murmur of conversation in the background.

'Rowan,' Eberhardie said in a loud voice.

'Yes? What is it?'

'You're wanted on the telephone — Commandant's office.'

'Could you take the call, Dennis?'

'Afraid not. It's personal, the Director has asked for you.'

There was only the one Mozart secure-speech facility at Amberley Lodge. This was located in the Commandant's office, which meant the retired Intelligence Corps lieutenant colonel in charge of the training school had to get up and leave whenever someone like Garfield was called to the phone.

'I'm afraid this is not your day, Rowan,' Hazelwood told him when he picked up the transceiver. 'You are going to lose Dennis Eberhardie. He's off to Moscow.'

'Oh? Why is that?' Garfield asked, his voice tight with anger.

'Chris Neighbour has been declared *persona non grata* by the Russian Government. He will be on British Airways flight BA871 departing Sheremetyevo airport tomorrow at 09.40 hours local time. He will, of course, be assigned to the Russian Desk, which means you will have to reshuffle the pack.'

A straight swap between Eberhardie and Neighbour was out of the question. Despite his time in Moscow, Neighbour lacked the necessary experience to take over the Russian Desk. The present number two would have to be moved up a peg, even though he wasn't really up to the job yet. But what of it? The musical chairs was already one big cock-up because Eberhardie was far too senior to be a third secretary, consular affairs. Still, that was Hazelwood's problem to sort out, not his.

'How long will Dennis need to hand over his post?' Hazelwood asked.

'Three days minimum.'

'All right, you can have the rest of today, tomorrow and Thursday. I'll leave you to break the good news to Dennis.'

It was only after Garfield hung up that he remembered Eberhardie's grade II intelligence officer had taken a fortnight off to spend time with his young family.

* * *

Francesca York was about to read the signal from 10 Int. Company a second time when her phone rang. Without taking her eyes off the text, she reached out with her right hand and lifted the receiver.

In her pseudo-upper-class voice, she said, '5947.'

'You want to tell me what Five was doing with my security file?' Ashton demanded without any kind of preamble.

The assertion brought Francesca up with a jolt and made her hesitate. Richard Neagle had given her strict instructions to hang up the moment Ashton identified himself. But things were no longer so clear-cut as they had been and she couldn't bring herself to put the phone down.

'Say that again, Peter.'

'You people helped to provide new identities for Harriet and me. I know that to do this you were given access to Codeword material. Now I'd like an explanation. Think you could give me one?'

'You're asking the wrong person. I'm not on any Codeword list and I haven't seen Harriet's security file or yours.'

'I'm not looking for an excuse. Why do you think Five was consulted?'

'I guess because we are responsible for providing intelligence to combat terrorist activity in the UK. In a nutshell, we could have been asked to assess the potential threat from the IRA in whatever area it was they proposed to relocate you and Harriet.'

She didn't think it prudent to point out that while the SIS might be adept at squirrelling away a defector, protecting one of their own from an internal threat was a novel experience for them. It was, however, permissible to remind Ashton that traditionally the Security Service maintained a much closer liaison with Special Branch than the SIS did.

'It would have been our job to make sure the police provided adequate protection for you and your family.'

'Well, thank you, Fran. For the record our protection consisted of two brief visits by a Detective Sergeant Milburn. The first time I saw him was last Wednesday, the day 84 Rylett Close was virtually destroyed by fire. The second occasion was the following day after it had been established the gas explosion had been triggered by an incendiary bomb.'

'What can I say? Perhaps my superiors thought — '

'You mean Richard Neagle,' Ashton said interrupting her.

'OK. Maybe Richard decided there was no way the Provos could discover your new address. Maybe he concluded a police presence would only arouse the curiosity of your new neighbours, which could have had damaging repercussions — '

'Let me tell you something,' Ashton said, cutting her short a second time. 'Somebody who had access to Harriet's security file obtained the name and address of her brother and passed the details to the Provisional IRA.'

'Now, steady on,' Francesca said angrily. 'You've no right — '

'One Monday morning in late May, a workman claiming to be employed by the East Midlands Electricity called at Richard Egan's house in Lincoln and planted two bugs. Now what have you got to say?'

Francesca closed her eyes and recalled word for word the way Jebens had responded when Ashton had asked him if George Foley was the man who'd been given his new address. 'I wouldn't know,' Jebens had said coolly. 'Perhaps you should ask your friends.'

'Do I take your silence to mean 'no comment'?'

'Don't go putting words into my mouth.'

'I'll try to be less contentious. Have you heard anything from Northern Ireland concerning the

233

Rubic homing beacon?'

'Not yet. Anyway, you gave me until Thursday.'

She didn't need to wait for an answer from 10 Int. Company. Barney had already told her that if Special Branch should ever need a solar-powered homing beacon they would borrow one from the Security Service.

'You're right,' Ashton told her, 'I'm pressurising you and I've no call to do that.'

'Don't go, Peter.' Francesca looked at the signal from Northern Ireland again. 'You may be interested to know that George Foley is related to Barry Hayes, also known as Brian Aherne. They are cousins but the Security Forces have nothing definite on Foley. In '80 he was linked to a sectarian massacre at Dromore but the source was later discredited.'

'Is he the Sinn Fein representative in West Belfast?'

'No, that's a different Foley.'

'Well, thank you, Fran. You've been very helpful and I can guess just how difficult that must have been for you. I'm not going to ask how you knew I was interested in George Foley.'

'That's all right, I wouldn't have told you anyway,' Francesca said, and hung up.

Foley hadn't been the only name in the signal she had sent to 10 Int. Company. She had also included Simon and Julie Carmichael, and the response from Northern Ireland now struck her as distinctly chilling. It read: 'No knowledge of the Carmichaels. Suggest they may be English sympathisers.'

★　★　★

In theory nobody could see Victor Hazelwood or converse with him on the telephone without first going through his PA. However, not everybody observed this procedure. If a green light was on above the communicating door, Jill Sheridan simply walked on through without waiting for the PA to introduce her. The other offender was Roy Kelso, who could not forget that he had been an assistant director when Hazelwood had been a grade I desk officer. It was his custom to enter the DG's office from the corridor whenever the door had been left open.

Since nobody would dream of using the Mozart secure-speech facility to ring the Director, the PA filtered all incoming and internal calls made on the BT network with one notable exception. Although the number of times Alice Hazelwood had telephoned her husband could be counted on the fingers of one hand, she had no intention of going through a third party.

To circumvent the PA she had given Hazelwood a mobile phone. This was kept on his desk between the ornately carved cigar box, one of a pair Hazelwood had purchased during a field trip to India, and the cut-down brass shell case which served as an ashtray.

From the moment news of Chris Neighbour's expulsion from Moscow had broken, the Mozart and BT telephones hadn't stopped ringing. For the mobile suddenly to come to life after so many weeks of total silence fooled Hazelwood

235

into answering the other two phones before picking it up.

'Yes, Alice,' he said tersely, 'what can I do for you?'

'It's the other way round. Clifford would like you to ring him, he said it was urgent.'

'When did you speak to him?'

'A few minutes ago. Do you have his phone number?'

'I think so but just hang on a minute while I make sure.' Hazelwood opened his personal directory at the letter P and saw that he had in fact crossed out the old number for Belmont Court, Cheyne Walk and had inserted the one for Peachey's new address in Helmsley. 'I'm more efficient than I thought,' he told Alice.

'I'll leave you to it then,' she said and terminated the call.

Hazelwood reached for the land line, lifted the receiver and obtained an outside line, then tapped out 01439 followed by the subscriber's number. He did not have long to wait for an answer.

'I'm glad you called,' Peachey said before he even had time to ask how Ann was keeping. 'We're very worried about Harriet. I'm afraid she's had some very distressing news. Her father died early this morning. Apparently the funeral will take place at two o'clock this coming Friday.'

Hazelwood sensed what was coming before Peachey told him that Harriet had already departed for Lincoln, taking the children with her. He had done his best to persuade her to stay on until the Thursday morning but she had refused to listen to him.

'Does Peter know what's happened?' Hazelwood asked.

'Not yet. From what she said I believe Harriet intends to keep the news to herself.'

'Leave it to me. I understand what you are saying, Clifford.'

'She may think it's for the best.'

'I'm sure she does, but I don't.'

'Harriet wants the funeral to be a quiet, family affair.'

Hazelwood said he was going to do his best to ensure it was, thanked Clifford Peachey for alerting him to the danger and hung up. Ashton was the prime target and unless he was present at the funeral Harriet and the children were unlikely to be afforded anything like the same degree of protection by Special Branch. Before apprising MI5 of the situation, it was vital to contact Ashton. To do this he needed to ascertain the number of the mobile phone Roy Kelso had provided for 'Mr Durban'.

* * *

Estonia was not one of the world's hot spots. If you were a career diplomat or were looking to make a name for yourself in the CIA, a posting to Tallinn could mean one of two things. Either you were just starting out and needed to cut your teeth in a not-too-testing appointment, or you were on the last lap and some anonymous grey suit had decided your last foreign assignment should be stress-free.

237

A graduate of Iowa State where he had majored in German, Carl Bucholtz was thirty-one and had put in eight years with the Central Intelligence Agency. Although in the élite Directorate of Operations, he was pretty sure that if he wasn't on the last lap, the Deputy Director was none too impressed with him. When he looked back on his relatively short career, Bucholtz couldn't help feeling that he had been dogged by bad luck. His initial training had been directed towards the Iran Desk and he was to have been posted to the CIA's 'Tefran' base in Frankfurt which directed all field operations inside the Islamic Republic. Unfortunately, repeated warnings that the CIA's radio communications with their agents in Iran were not secure had been ignored, with the result that the entire intelligence-gathering network had been destroyed. Although Bucholtz was still at Langley when this had happened, he had somehow become tainted by association.

In 1990 he had been a member of the CIA team which had been sent to Berlin to wade through the records of the Stasi. Much to everybody's dismay they'd learned that well over seventy per cent of the agents the CIA had recruited had in fact been working for the East German Intelligence Service. On the Roman principle of executing the messenger bearing bad tidings, Bucholtz reckoned the discovery had done little to enhance his reputation.

The Berlin interlude had been followed by a further three years at Langley with the Defector Resettlement Centre. Six months ago, he had been posted to Tallinn as Assistant to the Chief of Station. So far as the Estonians were concerned he was the Consular Officer. Both appointments bored him stiff and he was about to leave the office earlier than usual that afternoon in late July when he was informed by the Chief Archivist that a former professor of Political Studies at Moscow University wished to see him on a matter of some importance.

'Did he say who he was?' Bucholtz asked.

'Yeah, Ivan Gulag.' The Chief Archivist grinned. 'I think it was meant to be a joke, though he looks ravaged enough to have been in a gulag.'

'What are you saying?'

'I think maybe you should see him.'

The man the Chief Archivist showed into his office was a couple of inches short of six feet and looked as if he was on a starvation diet. His cheeks had fallen in, there wasn't a spare ounce of flesh on his body and he was wearing a blue pinstripe that was at least one size too big for him. At some stage during his illness he had obviously lost his hair but this was now growing back and the scalp was partially covered with grey bristles. He also had remarkably blue eyes.

'Good evening, Mr Bucholtz,' he said in passable English. 'My name is Pavel Trilisser and I am going to make you famous.'

14

The transmission from Tallinn had been intercepted by the army's 252 Communications and Security Group, a GCHQ signals unit stationed at Camphill barracks near Ashby Parva in Leicestershire. Although classified Top Secret, the message had been encrypted with a fairly low-grade cipher which was far from being a hundred per cent secure. It had taken the duty watch commander of the night shift less than five minutes to identify both the originator and the recipient. After decoding the opening sentence, he had immediately faxed the whole signal to GCHQ Cheltenham, using the dedicated crypto-protected line.

Similar dedicated lines existed between Cheltenham, MI5, the SIS, Defence Intelligence and the Cabinet Office. When decoded, copies of the transmission were faxed to the other intelligence agencies. The copy addressed to the SIS was received at Vauxhall Cross in time to be photocopied and distributed to heads of departments before morning prayers.

'The clear text in front of you was transmitted by a friendly intelligence agency.' Hazelwood looked round the table. 'Since we did not acquire it legitimately, the usual procedures will apply.'

'Usual?' Reid queried as if shocked to learn that eavesdropping on a friendly power was almost a routine occurrence.

'It means you hand your copy to me when you leave the conference room, no notes will be made, subordinates are not to be briefed and the matter will not be discussed outside this room. These instructions will no longer apply after the information is released by the CIA, which it will be in due course.' Hazelwood smiled. 'Happy now, Winston?' he asked.

'Oh, definitely,' Reid said.

'Good. The first question is do we believe the defector is Pavel Trilisser from the description given by the Chief of Station?'

'I do,' Garfield said when it became obvious that nobody else was prepared to put their hand up. 'I know the CIA's man in Estonia says Trilisser looks ravaged but there is a story going the rounds in Moscow that he has a brain tumour which might account for his appearance. But for me, the clincher is the description of his eyes. Everybody who has met him has used expressions like 'cobalt blue', 'dazzling', 'burns with the intensity of an oxyacetylene torch'. The man's eyes are unique, something that no impostor could fake. The business about a joint Anglo-American operation involving Ashton and Reindekker and their subsequent incarceration in Moscow's Lefortovo Prison for seventy-eight days are facts that could have been fed to an impostor.'

It was the longest dissertation Garfield had given at morning prayers for a long time. Hazelwood had been responsible for that: the way he had kept nodding his head in agreement had encouraged him to continue.

'So now we have to ask ourselves why did Trilisser choose to defect at this particular moment in time?' Hazelwood paused, then said, 'Any suggestions, Rowan?'

'Whatever I said would be pure speculation.'

'We'd still like to hear your thoughts.'

Unless it was definitely a one-horse race, Garfield was the sort of man who invariably hedged his bets. It was possible Trilisser didn't know the principal witness for the prosecution was dead and had decided to skip the country ahead of the trial date. Then again, maybe he had been told the trial would still go ahead, the prosecution having received permission to submit in evidence the report compiled by Vladislav Kochelev prior to his death. Perhaps the former Deputy Head of the Foreign Intelligence Service did have a brain tumour and was prepared to go to any lengths to obtain the best possible medical treatment for his condition. Or even more unlikely, Trilisser was running from the General Commanding Airborne Forces who had only just learned that he was having an affair with his wife and was determined to have him assassinated. Finally, Trilisser could be an unwilling cat's-paw in some major intelligence operation.

Garfield took note of the sceptical expression on Jill Sheridan's face and sought to bury his own suggestion. 'Of all the possible theories, I have to say that is the least likely.'

'I don't think we should rule anything out at this stage,' Hazelwood said. 'Instead we should look at the various flash-points around the world and assess which ones Russian Intelligence might consider were ripe for exploitation.'

With Russian troops forming part of the peace-keeping force in Bosnia, Garfield couldn't see how the Kremlin would benefit if Russian Intelligence engineered a full-scale civil war in Kosovo. Likewise, Henry Orchard of the Asian Department couldn't see any profit for them in aggravating the long-running dispute between India and Pakistan over Kashmir. For Roger Benton, the Communist régime in North Korea was the biggest threat to peace and stability in the Pacific Basin. The country was still officially at war with South Korea and was believed to have nuclear weapons. It certainly had the missile capability to deliver a strike at ranges in excess of five hundred miles. If the North was persuaded to launch a strike against its neighbour south of the 38th Parallel, the United States would immediately deliver a counterstrike which would be something no sane Russian wanted.

'The Middle East is Washington's oyster,' Reid said quietly. 'Destroy America's influence and Russia takes over the role of peacemaker for the region, which means the Kremlin is in a position to control over eighty per cent of the world's oil reserves.'

'What about President Yeltsin?' Hazelwood asked. 'Would he back such a policy?'

'No. 'It's the kind of dangerous undertaking which would appeal to the faction who want to remove him from power. Broadly speaking these are the unrepentant hard-line Communists who have no time for the market economy and are determined to put the clock back. In other words, the resurrection of the former USSR under a different name but with the needs of the armed forces given precedence as before.'

'And how is American influence in the Middle East to be destroyed, Winston?'

'I imagine Israel will be the crucible. Perhaps it will begin with some major terrorist incident?'

A man who had been accused of raiding the Kremlin's domestic budget had walked into the United States Embassy in Tallinn and suddenly the whole Middle East was about to go up in flames? Garfield thought it pretty far-fetched but he could tell Victor had got the bit between his teeth and could guess what was coming. Consequently he wasn't surprised when Hazelwood told him the Russian Desk was required to trawl their records with a view to identifying the Communist hardliners opposed to Yeltsin. It was also no surprise when Winston Reid was requested to produce an assessment of such terrorist groups as Hezbollah, al-Fatah, and the Popular Front for the Liberation of Palestine. It was, however, a surprise when Hazelwood asked him to remain behind as the other heads of departments filed out of the conference room at the end of morning prayers. It was an even greater surprise when Hazelwood wanted to know how many foot soldiers they could mobilise in Tallinn.

'To do what?' Garfield asked, playing for time.

'To watch the American Embassy, the

residence of the CIA's Chief of Station, and the international airport.'

'Not nearly enough, that's the short answer. We have two intelligence officers on the embassy staff and I can't remember the last time we ran a surveillance operation in Estonia.'

'Are you telling me that our people haven't recruited a single agent?' Hazelwood said in a dangerously quiet voice.

'Of course I'm not. We have the usual collection of place men in the civil service and amongst the business community but I wouldn't like to put any of them on the street.'

They weren't trained for the job and would be spotted immediately. Garfield also feared that if they used a local inquiry agency, the hired help might sell them out to the CIA.

'Why not brief the Estonian Intelligence Service?'

'To spy on the Americans?' Garfield said incredulously.

'Trilisser is a Russian and a former KGB officer; that's two reasons why the Estonians won't be averse to keeping an eye on him while he is in their country. At any rate, I want our people in Tallinn to sound them out.'

'Right.'

'And with or without the help of the Estonians they are to monitor the activities of their opposite numbers in the CIA.'

Three years ago that would have been a relatively simple task. In 1993 the British Embassy had occupied the second floor at number 20 Kentmanni, sandwiched between the youth hostel office above and the United States Embassy below. Things had moved on since then and the British Embassy had been relocated at Wismari 6, approximately half a mile away, which made the task virtually impossible. However, before he could point this out, Hazelwood had changed tack and was emphasising how essential it was to interview Chris Neighbour as soon as he reported for duty at Vauxhall Cross.

'Let's see if he can't throw some light on Trilisser.'

'That's in hand,' Garfield assured him. 'I've arranged for Neighbour to be met at Heathrow and brought straight here.'

'Good. How about Dennis Eberhardie, has he started the handover yet?'

'Yes.' Garfield mentally crossed his fingers and hoped that was true. Eberhardie's assistant hadn't been very happy when he had telephoned him yesterday afternoon at the guesthouse in Dawlish where he was on holiday with his family. Provided everything had gone to plan, his wife should have driven him into Exeter in time to catch the evening train to London. The only worrying thing was that he'd failed to put in an appearance before morning prayers, though this was not unusual.

'Nearly forgot.' Hazelwood snapped his fingers. 'Moscow has been informed that Dennis Eberhardie is slated to be the next Consul General in St Petersburg and is merely joining the embassy for the time being in order to get a feel for the country. Dennis is far too senior to be a third secretary and we had to come up with some explanation. I doubt if the subterfuge will fool the Russians but they won't make a five-star production out of it. When all is said and done it's simply a matter of two countries trying to save face.'

'Is Dennis really going to be the new Consul General in St Petersburg?'

'Oh, he'll do the full tour — no question.'

'But the present incumbent is in the diplomatic service.'

'Indeed he is. I'm afraid you are going to be short-handed.'

Life, Garfield decided, was getting shittier by the minute. As a result of being short-handed he personally would have to interview Neighbour and identify the Communist hard-liners opposed to President Yeltsin. All this while running the European Department at the same time.

* * *

Lionel Jebens left the house he rented in Priory Avenue and walked to Walthamstow Central on the Victoria Line. The *Daily Mail* was more to his taste than any of the broadsheets, but Simon had rung him at home last night to suggest he might care to buy *The Times* or the *Telegraph* if he really wanted to keep abreast of the news. Like George Foley, Simon was just a name on the telephone. They hadn't met and were never likely to but when Simon made a suggestion Jebens didn't ignore it.

He knew that somewhere between the front

and back pages of the newspaper he would find it. Then suddenly on page 26, among all the announcements, a name leaped at him from the second column under the subheading of Deaths.

EGAN Frederick, suddenly at home on 23 July. Much loved father of Richard and Harriet, grandfather to Miles, George, Melissa, Edward and Carolyn. Funeral Service at 2 p.m. on Friday 26 July at St Swithin's church, Lincoln. Family flowers only please. Donations to Imperial Cancer Research c/o J. W. Marsley and Sons, Lincoln.

Egan, Harriet Egan, wife of Peter Ashton; Jebens recalled the details which Simon, the unknown face, had posted to him before the coroner's inquest. He wondered if Ashton would attend his father-in-law's funeral. If he were in his shoes and was aware that somebody was stalking him, he wouldn't go within a hundred miles of Lincoln. But that was beside the point; the problem he faced was what to do with the information he'd been given. He asked himself how Simon could have known last night that the notice of Egan's death and the date of the funeral service would appear in today's *Telegraph*. Simon had to be very close to the family and, judging by the other stuff the postman had delivered to his house in Priory Avenue, the man had known them a long time. Yet he had no hesitation in betraying the Egans to the IRA. Of course, Ashton was the target and he wasn't really family. Jebens had met others like Simon who were able to compartmentalise their actions in this way and never lose a wink of sleep in the process.

Close to the family but unsuspected by them and not known to the police — that was Simon. The same could not be said of himself; the police had had their beady eyes on him ever since he had represented the Greenham Five in 1988. So did he want to draw Foley's attention to the notice in the *Daily Telegraph* or did he keep the information to himself? He was still undecided when the train drew into Oxford Circus and he switched to the Central Line, catching an eastbound to Hainault.

There was a chance Foley didn't read either *The Times* or the *Daily Telegraph* and would never hear about the funeral. It was obvious to Jebens that had Simon known how to contact the gunman from West Belfast, he would have telephoned and put him wise. As a lawyer he also knew that if he did what was expected of him, he could be an accessory to murder, assuming Foley shot and killed his intended victim. Of course, Foley would have to be apprehended first and turn snitch, which was something no IRA man did in a hurry.

There was no denying it, Ashton was one big pain in the arse. He had demonstrated that yesterday afternoon when he had set the police on to Sandra Hayes, who had ended up in Paddington Green. In response to a frantic telephone call, he had sent Pauline Dando, the legal executive, to represent her, knowing that under the Prevention of Terrorism Act the police could detain Sandra Hayes for up to seventy-two hours without wheeling her up in front of a magistrate. If nothing else, he'd figured Ms Dando could at least make sure the Hayes children were taken into care.

The more Jebens thought about him the greater threat Ashton became. Alighting from the train at Holborn, he turned left outside the station and called Foley from a pay phone. He merely drew his attention to the death notice in the *Daily Telegraph* and left him to draw his own conclusion. It was the way Jebens chose to absolve himself of all responsibility.

★ ★ ★

Jill Sheridan opened the communicating door, saw the green light was showing above the one opposite and walked on through to see Victor Hazelwood before his PA could alert him. Victor had his back to her and was looking up river in the direction of Chelsea Bridge when she walked into the office. It wasn't until he swung round in the leather upholstered swivel chair and put a finger to his lips that Jill realised he was listening to somebody on the secure link. She hand-signalled him, asking him if she should leave and come back later and got a headshake in return.

'That was GCHQ,' Hazelwood said after he had put the phone down. 'Langley has replied to the signal from their Chief of Station, Tallinn. It appears they are sending a valuer to look at the goods on offer. At a guess, I'd say Pavel Trilisser will be cooling his heels in Estonia for two, maybe three more days before he is moved Stateside. Obviously the CIA wants to know what they're getting for their money.' Hazelwood pursed his lips. 'That should give Rowan a better chance to get something organised over there — men on the ground, that sort of thing.'

'Rowan has got a lot on his plate at the moment.'

There was an amused smile on Victor's lips and it wasn't difficult to deduce what had provoked it. Even Jill thought her words had sounded perfunctory.

'Indeed he has.' Hazelwood reached for the cigar box, flipped the lid open and helped himself to a Burma cheroot. 'I dare say Rowan could do with having Ashton on the team.'

This time his amusement extended to his voice and she knew Victor was deliberately winding her up. Pretending to be equally amused, Jill sat down in the nearest armchair and crossed one leg over the other.

'Actually I wanted to have a word with you about Peter,' she said. 'I know Roy Kelso can be very tiresome but he tells me Hicks has been sent up to Lincoln again, apparently without his prior knowledge.'

'My fault,' Hazelwood said, and lit the cheroot with a match. 'I must have given Brian Thomas the impression Roy had been told.'

'But I thought Hicks had already been over the Egans' house?'

'That was the place in Church Road; this is the residence in Ferris Drive where Harriet's

251

father lived. His son wouldn't allow Hicks to look the house over when he was up that way last Thursday. Said it would only upset the old man who had Alzheimer's.'

'None of this makes any sense to me.' Jill frowned. 'Am I missing something?'

'Old man Egan died in the early hours of yesterday morning.'

That was one item of news Jill had not heard; there were others. Harriet had left the Peacheys and was now in Lincoln and would be staying at 11 Ferris Drive until after the funeral. She hadn't told Ashton that her father was dead and according to Peachey she had no intention of doing so. Victor, however, had contacted Ashton and broken the news.

'After I'd told Peter what had happened, he rang his brother-in-law, then got back to me.' Hazelwood contemplated the tip of his cheroot, attempted to flick the ash into the cut-down shell case and missed completely. Fortunately most of the debris fell on the large blotting pad. 'Harriet doesn't want him to attend the funeral.'

'You surprise me. I didn't think she was that resilient. Is their marriage on the rocks?'

'No. Harriet is afraid the IRA will spot the notice and will be waiting for him either at the church or the graveside. You see, she was too late to stop the announcement appearing in the *Times* and *Daily Telegraph* this morning. However, Ashton will be joining her as soon as Hicks gives the house in Ferris Drive a clean bill of health.'

'Is that wise, Victor?'

252

'It's the only way of ensuring the family is afforded adequate protection by Special Branch.'

'They will be there in sufficient numbers to deter the IRA?'

'I should never have allowed Ashton to be subpoenaed by that bloody coroner.'

'You had no choice, Victor.'

She did not think it necessary to remind him that Ashton had thrown Kevin Hayes out of the top-floor window of number 5 Depot Close, a derelict house in the back streets of King's Cross. Hayes had been armed with a .22 calibre target pistol and had turned it on Ashton, who had grabbed him by the wrist and raised his arm aloft a split second before he squeezed the trigger. Despite Hayeses obvious connection with the IRA through his brother, and the fact that the body of a murdered MI5 informer had been hidden in a cupboard, there had been a widespread feeling among politicians and senior civil servants that Ashton had used excessive force. Before the truce there might have been an internal enquiry but things were different now. Around Whitehall it had been felt the Government should demonstrate its impartiality to both Dublin and Washington. The Hayes inquest had been one way of doing this and Victor had been powerless to prevent it.

'I should never have allowed Peter to be identified in open court.'

'There was never any chance of that, Victor.'

The police had taken Ashton to 76 King's Cross Road, one of the divisional stations in N District, where he had made a full statement.

Crime reporters had a tout in every district of the Met, a police officer who, in consideration of a back-hander, would tip them off whenever there had been a major incident. Ashton's name and address had been known to all and sundry before he signed his statement.

'You're probably right.' Hazelwood shuffled the papers on his desk and used them to sweep the ash from the blotting pad. 'But naming Ashton in court is one thing, blowing his new cover is an altogether different kettle of fish. Somebody leaked the details to the IRA when the file was doing the rounds. It could have been one of our people, somebody in Five or even the FCO. Since you led the team which produced the legend you are the ideal person to conduct the investigation.'

What Hazelwood wanted from her were the names of everybody who'd handled the file. In compiling the list she was to bear in mind that the Top Secret register was not necessarily an accurate record. Sometimes a file could travel by hand of an officer without the knowledge of the custodian.

'I want Ashton back in the fold, Jill.'

'I'm sorry.'

'When they interrogate Trilisser the CIA won't invite us to the party unless we have something to contribute. That's why I need Ashton. He's the ace up my sleeve.'

Jill was about to ask why the Americans should rate him as highly as Victor obviously did, then thought better of it. Ashton was the only man in either Intelligence service who had met Trilisser

254

head on more than once in both Moscow and Warsaw.

'He'll know when the Russian is lying,' Hazelwood said, as if this hadn't already occurred to her.

'I know that, Victor; the fact is all his security clearances were withdrawn the day he left us to go into hiding.'

'They can be restored at the drop of a hat.'

'I don't think that would go down well in Whitehall, Victor. It could even jeopardise your — '

'My what?' Hazelwood said sharply. 'My career? I'm already at the top of my particular tree.' His eyes narrowed. 'Or do you know something you shouldn't?'

'Me? You are joking, aren't you, Victor?' Jill said in a nervous voice which betrayed her.

★ ★ ★

It seemed Wednesday was going to be one of those rare occasions when Francesca York left the office before 6.30 p.m. On this particular evening Barney, the current watch commander, reported in at five minutes to six and presented her with one of the shortest ops logs she had seen in weeks.

'Been a quiet day at Candlewick House,' Barney said when Francesca looked up after reading the log. 'Jebens was late into work this morning, didn't show up until five minutes to ten.'

'Any idea why he changed his routine?'

Barney shook his head. 'Our foot soldiers lost him at Walthamstow Central. Jebens dropped into the newsagent's to get his morning paper the way he always does, except he went for the *Daily Telegraph* instead of the *Daily Mail*. Anyway, as luck would have it there was a train waiting at the platform which he managed to catch just as the doors were closing. The foot soldiers didn't — end of story.'

'Was it deliberate?'

'Not from what their watch commander told me.'

There were two details watching the lawyer: the painters and decorators of Red Lion Yard who kept Candlewick House under surveillance, and the foot soldiers who shadowed Jebens to and from work. Each detail had their own watch commander.

'Jebens was on his ownsome today,' Barney continued. 'Ms Dando was over at Paddington Green trying to spring Sandra Hayes, so Jebens — '

Francesca heard a faint tap, and waved a hand at the detective sergeant to silence him. 'Yes, Donald,' she said briskly, 'what can I do for you?'

Barney looked over his shoulder. Donald was about five feet seven, had dark hair cut short, and was blessed with a narrow face with slate-grey eyes and thin lips. He was in shirtsleeves and was carrying a millboard in his right hand.

'Oh, I'm sorry,' Donald said, and started to back out of the room. 'I thought you'd gone home.'

'No need to apologise,' Francesca told him cheerfully. 'Come back in five minutes.' She waited until he had closed the door, then said, 'You were saying, Barney?'

'Only that Jebens had all the incoming calls routed to him.' Barney cleared his throat. 'Who was that just now?'

'Donald Simon, he's one of the clerks in our section. He's doing the usual security check to make sure nothing has been left out that should have been locked away. Why do you ask?'

'I was just wondering how much he heard,' Barney said.

15

The redhead who met George Foley off the London train at Newark-on-Trent that evening was petite, slender and remarkably attractive. Had she been wearing a wig of shoulder-length dark hair and contact lenses which had transformed the hazel pupils to a deep blue, Harvey Littlewood, the estate agent, would have immediately recognised her as Julie Carmichael. However, to the British Medical Association and her peer group at the Kirkby in Ashfield Medical Centre she was Doctor C. J. Pearce.

Born in Manchester on 27 March 1968 and the only child of middle-aged parents, she had been christened Cara Juliana. Cara, which in Irish meant 'friend', had been in honour of her father's side of the family while Juliana had been her mother's choice based purely on a whim. Disliking both names, she had dropped Cara and foreshortened Juliana to Julie. She was not related to the man who had called himself Simon Carmichael and had had no contact with him since the firebombing of 84 Rylett Close.

Much respected by the other members of the practice, Julie was seen as a caring physician by the National Health patients, not one of whom had ever dreamed of asking to be re-registered with some other doctor. There were, however, a significant number who wanted to be looked after by Dr Pearce. Little was known of Julie's private life, since she lived in the village of Upton, some fifteen miles from the medical centre. Colleagues who had been invited to dinner at her cottage came away lauding her culinary expertise. She was known to be a member of the tennis club at nearby Southwell, though she was rarely seen on court. First and foremost she was a keen biker and the proud owner of a ten-year-old Harley-Davidson, which was only marginally older than the Citroën 2CV she used as a runabout.

Unlike the man known to her as Simon Carmichael, George Foley was no stranger. Julie had met him in 1989 when she had gone on holiday to Southern Ireland during the long vac at the end of her second year at St Hilda's. That chance encounter in a Dublin bar had been the start of a relationship which had led her to embrace 'the Cause' and take up arms against her fellow compatriots. However, the more active she and Foley became in the armed struggle, the less frequently they saw each other. In fact when Foley alighted from the train at Newark-on-Trent it was the first time they had met in sixteen months. Polite but distant with him on the platform, Julie made her feelings known when they were in the 2CV heading towards Upton on the A617.

'Don't ever phone me at the surgery again,' she said angrily. 'It's too risky.'

'It was an emergency,' Foley told her. 'Anyway, what are you complaining about? I rang your mobile number.'

'I was with a patient.'

'Like I said, it was an emergency.' Foley took out a packet of Silk Cut, lit two cigarettes and passed one to Julie. 'They're burying Ashton's father-in-law the day after tomorrow, two o'clock St Swithin's church, Lincoln. He's bound to attend the funeral.'

'You wish.'

'I'd stake my life on it.'

'You probably will. If Ashton does attend the service, half the Lincolnshire Constabulary will be out on the street.'

'We'll take a run up to Lincoln tomorrow and look at the route from the church to the graveyard.'

'We?' Julie said. 'What makes you think I am coming with you?'

'We'll leave after surgery. There will be time enough; it stays light up to nine-thirty.'

'You're crazy.' Julie opened the ashtray, removed the cigarette from her lips and stubbed it out. 'What the hell was I doing with that cigarette? I don't smoke.'

'Friday will be different. You'll have to arrange for somebody to cover you.'

'Yeah? What reason do I give my colleagues? That I need time off because I'm going to help a friend kill somebody?'

'You'll be taken ill around eleven-thirty — sweating, running a temperature, maybe vomiting.'

'Just like that,' Julie said acidly.

'You're a doctor, you can fake it.'

A conversation that was already surreal became even more so as Julie tried to reason with him and Foley continued to act as if he was stone deaf. He seemed to think she could come and go pretty much as she pleased. A week ago she had spent two days in London but her colleagues at the medical centre had been prepared for her absence well in advance. 'A hen party for an old friend from college days', she had told them and they had accepted it without question, been happy for her to have the time off. 'No need to hurry back', one of them had told her but a lot of eyebrows would be raised if she took this Friday off without notice. And as for faking an illness, that was just too damned risky. What if one of her colleagues decided to call at the cottage to see how she was faring and discovered she wasn't at home?

'I can't do it, George. I'd never get away with it.'

'Don't tell me you're getting cold feet?' The familiar ready smile was still there on his lips but it was beginning to look a little strained.

'No, it's simply a matter of common sense. When you rang me at the medical centre you talked about biking and I knew what you had in mind.'

'Is that a fact? Well, suppose you tell me what I'm planning to do because I would really like to know.'

What Foley had in mind was damned nearly standard operational procedure with the IRA but, what the hell, she would tell him any way. If the intended victim was in a car driving through a crowded city street a motorbike was the ideal machine for the hit. It was the job of the rider to

261

bring the gunman on the pillion abreast of the target and then get the hell out of it, weaving through the traffic. You could take a bike where a vehicle couldn't go, down narrow alleyways and along pedestrian walkways.

'That's not how we will be doing it.' Foley wound the window down, and flipped the lighted cigarette into the gutter. 'The bike will be the getaway vehicle but you won't be riding it. Matter of fact you will be the other side of town when I squeeze the trigger.'

'Doing what?'

'Waiting for me in the 2CV. I will have dumped the bike before I join you.'

'You're talking about a Harley-Davidson,' she said impatiently.

'So?'

'Well, it's hardly your common or garden Yamaha; there are not that many of them on the road round these parts. Neighbours in the village, colleagues at the medical centre and some of the patients know that I own one.'

'No worries. You're going to phone the police and tell them it's been stolen.'

Foley had an answer for every contingency but in her opinion all her solutions involved an unacceptable degree of risk and she didn't hesitate to say so. As a result, the smile which had already faded disappeared altogether in a flash of temper.

'That's the trouble with you fucking Anglos,' he snarled. 'All your fine talk about reuniting Ireland by force of arms vanishes the moment you're ordered into the firing line.'

'I'm not an Anglo,' she told him vehemently. 'The only Irish connection in the family was my great-grandfather who came to this country in 1841, four years before the potato famine. He married an English girl, as did each successive male issue down the years. I may have distant relatives somewhere in America and Australia but I've never heard of them.'

In taking up arms Julie wanted him to know she hadn't been indoctrinated from childhood with rebel songs and IRA mythology. Even though it wasn't true she wanted him to think nobody had persuaded her to embrace the Cause, that it was something she had done entirely of her own volition.

'I was out of order,' Foley told her contritely.

'And another thing, the bombing in Rylett Close was not the first time I've been in the firing line as well you know.'

On her last visit to Dublin sixteen months ago, Foley had collected her from the boarding house where she was staying. He had taken her to an isolated farmhouse somewhere between Louth and Dundalk where she had operated on a member of the Provos who had been badly wounded in a firefight with the RUC.

'I'm under a lot of pressure,' Foley said quietly. 'If I don't get Ashton I could find myself in serious trouble. Will you help me, Julie?'

'Of course I will,' she assured him without hesitation.

She dropped down a gear, signalled a right turn, then shifted into second and drove into the garage in front of the cottage. She had no recollection of turning off the A617 into the Southwell Road.

★ ★ ★

Ashton spotted Francesca York in the rear-view mirror the moment she turned into Derry Street. Her body language, head bowed, eyes focused on the pavement immediately ahead told him she'd had a bad day. To get to the flat she shared with another girl, Francesca would have to walk past the Volvo. As she drew level with the Ford Fiesta two cars back, Ashton got out and closed the door loudly enough to attract her attention. Too many neighbours had been keeping an eye on him since he had arrived half an hour ago and he didn't want to risk spooking her.

'Hi, Fran,' he said in a normal tone of voice.

'I've had a lousy day,' she told him. 'Please don't make it even worse.'

'All I want is a few minutes of your time.'

'I've heard that one before.'

'Well, it happens to be true.' Ashton aimed the remote control transmitter at the Volvo and pressed the button to lock all four doors and activate the alarm. 'I'm driving up to Lincoln this evening.'

'I heard you were planning to attend Mr Egan's funeral,' Francesca said, and walked on.

'Who told you? Richard Neagle?'

'Yes. K has been bending his ear all day. Apparently your former colleagues are determined Special Branch will give you maximum protection.'

K was the official designation for the Director General of the Security Service and dated back to the days before World War I when Captain Vernon Kell of the South Staffordshire Regiment had been charged with forming the Secret Bureau, the forerunner of MI5. Either Victor Hazelwood or Jill Sheridan must have lobbied K. Ashton liked to think it had been his former mentor.

Francesca tried the front door and discovered that the last person to enter the building had locked it. Moving to her right, she punched out the entry code on the electric key pad, got a low buzzing noise in return and opened the street door. One of the residents had sorted the mail and she collected a postcard from St Tropez from her pigeonhole before leading Ashton up to the flat she occupied on the first landing.

'I'll give you ten minutes,' she said, 'then I'm going to take a shower. Meantime I'm having a drink, how about you?'

'What have you got?'

'I know there are a couple of tots left in the bottle of Grant's whisky.'

Francesca crouched in front of the sideboard in the living room and opened the left-hand cupboard. 'My flatmate has a bottle of sherry she brought back from Cyprus last year plus a smidgen of vermouth and a can of Carling Black Label.'

'I'll have the lager if that's OK?'

'I don't see why not.' Francesca passed him the can and a tall glass, then fixed herself a small

265

whisky with a splash of soda. 'So why are you here?' she asked.

'I think you may have a mole. The life history of Mr and Mrs Durban was an open book almost from the moment the legend was conceived.'

'And we are to blame for the leak, are we?'

'Five had the files more frequently and held on to them longer than any other outsider.'

'What about the SIS? The files are permanently in their custody.'

'By outsiders I meant the Foreign and Commonwealth Office as well as Five.'

'Oh, I get it,' Francesca said angrily, 'everybody in the SIS is squeaky clean.'

In her shoes Ashton knew he would have reacted just as angrily. When some outsider criticised your organisation you instinctively closed ranks and defended its reputation tooth and nail, no matter what private misgivings you might have. But that didn't mean you ignored the allegations and swept everything under the carpet, hoping the problem would vanish.

'You're wrong,' Ashton told her. 'We are not complacent, which is why an internal investigation is already under way.'

'How can you possibly know that when you are *persona non grata* with the SIS?'

'I've still got friends on the inside,' Ashton said, and left it at that.

'If I'm wrong, so are you,' Francesca said in a more reasonable voice. 'Richard Neagle is the only person who has had access to the Durban files. You may not care for him but he has done more to combat terrorism than anyone else I know.'

'I'm not talking about Richard or any other senior officer. I'm referring to the paper keepers.'

The archivist or chief clerk who could be suborned was of far greater value to a hostile intelligence service than a sympathetic desk officer. The archivist was the custodian of all Secret and Top Secret files belonging to the section to which he was assigned, and the one person who had unfettered access, whose name never appeared on a transit docket. He or she could be caught if they were careless and drew attention to themselves by indulging in a lifestyle that was not commensurate with their salary. Photocopying the material or capturing it on microfilm was all very well but doing the business after normal office hours was decidedly risky and damned nearly suicidal at any other time. The archivist who could walk out of the building carrying the information in his head was a diamond to be treasured.

'There are no bad apples among our clerks,' Francesca said. 'Apart from being cleared for constant access to Top Secret, they have also been screened.'

'You mean Irish screening?'

'Yes.'

'Well, we both know Irish screening is a long way from being foolproof. OK, you can pull the birth certificate of the subject and the next of kin but if they don't reveal an Irish connection, you have nothing to get your teeth into. All you have is what the subject has seen fit to tell you.'

All the clerks who worked for Richard Neagle and Francesca York would have been subject to Irish screening. In addition to providing details of their parents and, where applicable, their spouse and in-laws, they were required to disclose the names and addresses of all Irish friends living in Eire and Northern Ireland. In completing the requisite form they were also asked to show any holidays spent in Ireland with dates and locations, and to list any acquaintances and friendships they may have made during such vacations. The consolidated lists were then sent to 10 Int. Company in Northern Ireland, who checked to see if any of the names were connected in some way with the Provisional IRA or the Ulster Freedom Fighters. should there be a terrorist connection, then no matter how tenuous the link might be, the individual concerned was moved sideways into a different section which was not involved with Northern Ireland.

'There never has been a leak from our section,' Francesca told him firmly, 'or even a hint of one.'

'Your support staff has never changed?'

'Well, of course there have been changes of personnel — people get promoted, retire or decide to change jobs.'

'So when was the last time you had a change of personnel?'

'The beginning of March this year.' Francesca finished her whisky and set the glass down on the low table by her chair. 'Not that it's any business of yours,' she added.

'You're right, how you vet your people is no concern of mine.' Ashton smiled. 'It's just that when you are being stalked, you tend to get a little twitchy. You keep looking over your shoulder, wondering who you can trust.'

'I can understand that.'

Ashton wondered if she did. He had to make her see that negative information could make a man look good on paper.

'Whenever a person needs to be cleared by positive vetting, MI5 is the first agency to be consulted. Right?'

'Yes. We check to see if the applicant and the immediate next of kin have ever been members of a proscribed organisation like the Communist Party of Great Britain or the fascist British Union Movement.'

'And after you have given the subject a clean bill of health, the parents subsequently split up and one of them shacks up with a member of the Revolutionary Socialist Workers Party. That sort of situation is not unknown, is it?'

'It happens occasionally,' Francesca said, and looked pensive as if she had a particular person in mind.

'The same thing can happen with Irish screening with one slight difference of course.'

'Such as?'

'The subject is likely to have deliberately withheld the information.'

Ashton finished his lager, got to his feet and left the glass and empty can on the mantelpiece above the fireplace which was now occupied by a convector heater.

'Time I was going,' he said.

'About that homing beacon manufactured by the Rubic Corporation,' Francesca said. 'The RUC and 10 Int. Company say they have never come across them in Northern Ireland.'

'Well, thanks for trying, anyway.'

'Apparently we have been in the habit of supplying them to Special Branch whenever they had need of one.'

'Any idea how many you've got?'

'In January last year ten were purchased for trial and evaluation purposes; this evening the storeman could only account for seven when I checked.'

Ashton frowned. 'Would I be right in thinking you don't know when the others went missing?'

'The homing beacons are merely stamped with a lot and batch designation. There is no room for an individual registration number.' Francesca picked up her empty glass, went over to the sideboard and managed to squeeze one last tot from the bottle of whisky. 'And before you ask, that means they weren't kept with the controlled stores,' she said, her back still towards him.

'I guess it also means the beacons weren't subject to the usual periodic check by a duty officer?'

'You guess right.' Francesca turned about to face him. 'Richard didn't like it but he finally agreed there should be an internal inquiry.'

'Now I know why you've had a lousy day.' Ashton produced his pocket diary, wrote down a phone number, then ripped out the page and gave it to Francesca.

'Whose number is this?' she asked.

'George Foley's,' Ashton told her. 'I persuaded Lionel Jebens to give it to me.'

★ ★ ★

Richard Neagle was no stranger to Paddington Green. As a divisional police station in D District, which covered part of the London Borough of Westminster, Paddington Green had much in common with a fortress. It was the place where terrorists of every nationality and political persuasion were held while they were being interrogated. Sandra Hayes had already spent twenty-eight hours in custody by the time Neagle arrived to question her. Other than ensuring Sandra Hayes was not subjected to sleep deprivation, Ms Pauline Dando wouldn't have been able to do much for her client. However, Neagle was sure the legal executive would have pointed out to Mrs Hayes that, under the Prevention of Terrorism Act, the police could only detain her for another forty-four hours before they were required to bring her before a stipendiary magistrate. There was not the slightest chance the police would seek to detain Sandra on what little evidence they had. It was therefore his job to convince both Mrs Hayes and Ms Dando that this was exactly what they intended to do. The interview did not get off to a good start.

'The time is now ten past eight,' Pauline Dando informed him coldly. 'With the exception of thirty-minute breaks for lunch, afternoon tea and supper, Mrs Hayes has been interrogated for eleven and a half hours. I will give you until nine o'clock, after which I will advise her not to — '

'This won't take long,' Neagle said, cutting her short.

Completely taken aback, Ms Dando gaped at him for some moments before slowly recovering her composure. 'I'll hold you to that,' she said in a hollow voice.

'I'm sure you will. As it happens I'm here to inform Mrs Hayes that she will be appearing at the North Westminster Magistrates' Court in Marylebone tomorrow morning.' Pauline Dando and her client had contrived to look bored and indifferent but now he had their complete attention. 'We've been talking to some of your neighbours in Sandrock Road,' Neagle continued cheerfully. 'It's amazing how interested they are in the coming and going of your lodger, Sandra. Of course they couldn't put a name to him but from their descriptions it's obviously George Foley.'

The police had talked to her neighbours but the rest was pure conjecture. Then Sandra Hayes made the biggest mistake of her life.

'Never heard of him,' she said.

'You surprise me,' Neagle drawled. 'He is a cousin of your late husband.'

He went through the rest of the family tree, describing in detail the murders committed by Sandra's brother-in-law, Barry Hayes, when he had been a member of the West Belfast battalion of the IRA. Then he spelled out what sort of case could be made against Sandra, which put the fear of God into her and rocked Ms Dando to her heels.

'You could be looking at two, possibly three years' imprisonment but it doesn't have to be like that.'

'Are you offering my client immunity from prosecution?' Ms Dando asked before Sandra could say anything.

'Yes, provided she is willing to help us.'

'I think we would like that on record.'

'Certainly.' Neagle switched on the VCR and faced the camera, his image appearing on the small TV screen mounted high up on the wall. 'My name is Richard Neagle,' he said. 'I'm with the Crown Prosecution Service. For the record Mrs Hayes, I am prepared to offer you immunity from prosecution in return for your co-operation.'

'What do you want to know?'

'I'd like an up-to-date description of George Foley, especially any distinguishing features.'

'He's got a strawberry birthmark on his left hip. Some tattoo artist tried to do something about it and made a right mess of the job.'

Somehow Neagle managed to keep a straight face. 'Well, that's hardly visible,' he said. 'Tell you what, Sandra, I'll get a photofit technician and you can help him make a picture of Foley.'

16

Ashton woke up about ten minutes after first light when the sun was above the horizon and playing on the window. He turned over on to his right side in an effort to drift back to sleep only to find it eluded him. Wide awake, he kicked the duvet off and got out of bed, then walked over to the window and opened the curtains. He remembered Harriet once telling him that of all the rooms in the house, this had been Frederick Egan's favourite, especially in summer. Whenever there was a match he would come up here to watch the cricket played against the backdrop of Lincoln Cathedral.

His other love had been the garden which had been his pride and joy before Alzheimer's had begun to destroy him. Now the flowerbeds were choked with weeds while the roses, which needed dead-heading, were being slowly strangled with bindweed. It needn't have been in such a neglected state had he agreed to employ a gardener for a couple of afternoons a week but every time the family had suggested this, Frederick Egan had flown into an ungovernable rage. If Harriet's sister-in-law had her way, a jobbing gardener would arrive on Saturday to tidy the place up before 11 Ferris Drive was put on the market.

Ashton heard one of the Special Branch officers open the kitchen door and immediately stepped back from the window. There were two of them in the house and both were insistent that he shouldn't go near the window. 'You'll be giving them a hell of a target to aim at,' they had told him separately at different times. He had no quarrel with their assessment but a sniper wasn't exactly spoiled for choice. The ground was as flat as a billiard table and the only cover was the six-feet-high wooden fence at the bottom of the garden.

To take a bead on him the sniper would need to drill a loophole in the fence with a big enough diameter to accommodate the blade foresight of a rifle. The job would have to be done under cover of darkness and of necessity, the sniper would be obliged to lie up in the fire position overnight. It would be a highly risky business; he might be discovered by a man out walking his dog in the evening or be seen from one of the neighbouring houses. But the officers of Special Branch weren't taking any chances. Observing the same routine as yesterday's shift, the detective sergeant in charge was checking the garden fence to make sure no woodpecker had been chipping away at it during the night.

The current shift would be relieved at 08.00 hours, which meant good old Steve and Russell, who'd been in the house when he had arrived late on Wednesday, would be back on duty again. Ashton had driven up to Lincoln a full day earlier than necessary because Harriet had always been plagued with guilty feelings about her father and he had wanted to be there for her. In practice all his good intentions had counted for nothing. Once MI5 and the SIS learned he was planning to attend the funeral service, they had become the decision makers. He was the sole target and in the interests of security, Special Branch had moved Harriet and the children from 11 Ferris Drive to her brother's house in Church Lane.

The arrangement had been effected before Ashton had arrived and he had been discouraged from going round there to see Harriet. However, Terry Hicks had left a note informing him that he had spring-cleaned the house, something he hadn't been allowed to do when Frederick Egan had been alive. If nothing else it meant Ashton had been able to speak to Harriet on the phone without locking himself in the bathroom and turning on all the taps.

He had spent all of yesterday cooped up indoors, a restriction which was going to be repeated today until they left for the funeral service at St Swithin's just over half a mile away. What happened after that had been a matter for debate; the Assistant Chief Constable (Operations) had said unequivocally that he didn't want Ashton to accompany the hearse to the cemetery. The area was too exposed and Ashton wouldn't be the only person at risk when the family and friends were gathered at the graveside for the interment. But in the end they had reached a compromise: instead of being part of the funeral cortège, Ashton and the Special Branch officers would hang back and watch the actual interment from a distance.

Ashton stripped off, went into the *en suite*

bathroom, and stood under a cold shower to freshen up before shaving. With no reason to hurry, he did everything at a snail's pace. Even so, it was only ten minutes to seven when he went downstairs to breakfast. There was over an hour to go before the shifts changed, then another six to kill until it was time to leave for the church. With every minute seeming more like five it was going to be a long day.

★ ★ ★

Foley covered the kitchen table with yesterday's newspaper, then unzipped the canvas holdall at his feet and took out a carton of fifty 9mm rounds. Using one of the small kitchen knives in the drawer, he slit the binding tape around the lid and fished out a round. There was, he thought, nothing like a spot of nitroglycerine mixed with nitroguanidine to make a person feel off colour. To get at the mixture he had to separate the bullet from the cartridge case, which was easier said than done.

He couldn't cut through the case because the friction might ignite the propellant and, in the worst case, he would end up with a bullet ricocheting off all four walls. Leaving the kitchen table, Foley went into the utility room and returned with a pair of pliers and a small screwdriver which Julie kept in a cupboard above the washing machine. The pliers in his left hand served as a vice to hold the case steady while he attempted to prise the bullet loose with a small screwdriver. It was a slow and occasionally painful business but after puncturing his thumb and index finger when the screwdriver slipped he eventually managed to loosen the bullet. From then on it was more or less plain sailing. With the aid of the pliers he separated the bullet from the casing and tipped out the propellant onto a strip of clingfilm which he twisted up to make a sachet. He had just finished tidying up when Julie Pearce walked into the kitchen.

'What can I get you?' Foley asked.

'Nothing. I don't want any breakfast.'

'Are you sure?'

'Well, maybe a glass of orange juice. You'll find a carton in the fridge.'

'I'm going to have a cup of coffee.'

'Fine.' Julie smiled nervously. 'Why are you staring at me?' she asked.

'You look pale.'

'I'm supposed to. God knows, I used enough face powder.'

'It's very realistic,' Foley told her. 'What excuse will you give them at the medical centre?'

'A bad period.'

'Do you have them? I mean would your colleagues be surprised to hear you say that?'

'No.'

'Ever given into it before and gone home?'

'I can't recall doing so.'

'Well, that's not a problem, girl.' Foley poured a glass of orange juice and gave it to her with the sachet of propellant. 'This will add a little realism, make you sweat and feel nauseous. But watch how much you take.' He smiled. 'We don't want any of your colleagues calling at the house to see how you are.'

'I know what to do,' Julie said in a voice that verged on the brittle side. It was, Foley thought, a bad omen. Yesterday evening when they had gone to Lincoln she had been as tense as an overwound spring. Correction: her nervous disposition had started on Wednesday evening when they had arrived at the cottage in Upton and she had been worried stiff one of her neighbours would see them go indoors and tongues would start wagging. Her naked fear had manifested itself again after breakfast yesterday when Julie had told him not to answer the phone, not to go to the door, not to show himself. And she had become even more agitated when he'd told her to go into Nottingham and buy him a crash-helmet during her lunch break. But jumpy or not she had done what he'd asked, that was the main thing.

'Just remember you've only got a forty-minute window,' Julie said.

'There's nothing wrong with my memory, girl.'

The woman next door was a partner in a firm of chartered accountants in Mansfield and left for the office promptly at ten to nine every day. Her husband was some hot shot in Lloyds and was away in London all week, returning home on Friday evening. Julie Pearce had a cleaning woman who came in on Tuesdays and Fridays at nine-thirty. The cottage was on the outskirts of Upton and except for the property across the road, it was out of sight from the rest of the village. Provided he left the cottage after the chartered accountant had departed and before the cleaner arrived, the risk of being seen was minimal. Foley had lost count of the number of times Julie had told him that when they were in bed last night.

'I'll be going then,' Julie said.

'OK. I'll see you later.'

'Yes.'

Never had so much doubt been expressed in a single word.

'Don't look so worried,' Foley called out to her as she went into the hall. 'Everything is going to be all right.'

She mumbled something in return but Foley didn't catch it and then the front door closed behind her before he could ask her what she had just said. Presently Foley heard the distinctive whirl of the starter motor on the Citroën 2CV followed by the even more distinctive note of the 602cc engine as it fired into life. He waited until she had moved off, then lifted the canvas holdall onto the kitchen table and took out a 9mm Mini-Uzi sub-machine-gun which he had collected from an arms cache in Wembley, courtesy of the quartermaster of his old IRA battalion in West Belfast.

The only weapon Foley had used in combat was the .50/12.7mm calibre long-range sniper rifle but the Uzi was ideal for this particular operation. With the butt folded back against the magazine housing and barrel, the sub-machine-gun was a compact fourteen and a quarter inches in length and weighed a shade under six pounds when empty. Making sure each bullet was seated properly, he loaded the magazine with thirty-two rounds and inserted it into the pistol grip, then cocked the weapon and put the change lever on safe.

Foley went upstairs, packed his washing kit, towel, underpants, socks and two spare shirts into the now empty canvas holdall which he then hid under the standing wardrobe before returning to the kitchen. He hoped Julie wouldn't forget to bring the holdall with her when she set off for the rendezvous in Lincoln.

At eleven minutes past nine, Foley rode out of the village heading towards Newark-on-Trent, the Uzi sub-machine-gun in the right pannier on the Harley-Davidson. Nobody saw him leave and he reached the junction with the A617 before encountering another vehicle.

* * *

The signal from 10 Int Company carried an Op Immediate precedence, was classified Secret and was addressed 'Personal for York'. The date time group was 260015 Zulu July which in plain English meant it had been dispatched that morning fifteen minutes after midnight Greenwich Mean Time. Francesca saw it for the first time when the Chief Archivist walked it into her office shortly after she arrived at a quarter to ten. She was not in the best of moods, having been stuck in the tunnel midway between Notting Hill Gate and Queensway on the Central Line after a passenger had thrown herself in front of a train at Lancaster Gate two stops further on. Her temper didn't improve when she took note of the signals precedence.

'Op Immediate.' Francesca looked up from the signal. 'Why wasn't I informed when this message was received?'

'Donald sought the advice of the duty officer and was told the signal could wait until this morning.' The Chief Archivist leaned forward and pointed to the top of the message form. 'Those are his initials,' he added.

'I see. Which Donald are we talking about?'

'Donald Simon, he was on duty last night. Personally I think in his shoes I would have done the same thing.'

'On reflection, so would I,' Francesca said.

'I gather the duty officer thought it was just 10 Int Company trying to justify themselves.'

The text could certainly be read that way. The subject was George Foley and there was a reference to a previous signal in which 10 Int Company had informed her that the Security Forces had nothing definite on him. They had also stated that the source who had linked him to a sectarian massacre at Dronmore in '88 had been discredited. But now they had come up with a new source, one that had been graded A1 and you couldn't get a higher rating than that. It meant the source was thoroughly reliable and the information was probably accurate.

'Has Mr Neagle seen this?' Francesca asked.

'Not yet.' The Chief Archivist moved towards the door. 'Nobody is with him at the moment,' he added.

Francesca thanked him for the tip, picked up the signal again, then left, locking the door behind her. Neagle was on the phone when she looked in on him but he beckoned to her to come inside and pointed to a utility ladder-back chair.

'This will interest you, Richard,' she said, placing the signal on his desk after he had put the phone down. 'I think somebody pretty high up in the Provos must have shopped Foley.'

It was the most detailed biography of a terrorist Francesca had ever seen. 10 Int. Company had been given the date and place of his birth in County Monaghan and the reason why he had moved to West Belfast, which had a lot to do with his cousin, Barry Hayes, and the promise of easy pickings. According to the source, Foley had been a fund-raiser, which meant he persuaded bookmakers, publicans and owners of drinking dens in his area to pass the hat round for the IRA every Friday night. Unlike some other fund-raisers, he hadn't pressurised his shopkeepers into taking out an all-risks insurance policy.

'The RUC didn't know Foley when he was in Belfast,' Neagle said, looking up.

'Well, he wasn't greedy, Richard, so none of the traders he tapped passed his name on to the police. He didn't leach off the Social Security either, which would explain why the local authorities had no record of him.'

Foley had quietly gone about his business winning the trust of the Provo commander in West Belfast. From fund-raising he had graduated to weapons mule and then on up to targeting. In '88 he had attended a weapon training course south of the border where his skill at arms and prowess as a marksman had been duly noted. It had therefore been only a question of time before he became a sniper operating cross-border into South Armagh.

'I have a feeling 10 Int Company have had all they will get from this source,' Francesca said.

'Oh, yes.'

It was hard to tell what Neagle was thinking from his somewhat negative response. The only way to find out was to press on.

'Foley left the Provos and joined Continuity IRA,' Francesca continued. 'There is a clear inference in the text that he wasn't the only disaffected member of the West Belfast battalion. Evidently the commanding officer felt he had to do something to stop the rot. That's why Foley was shopped. It could be the start of a major upheaval.'

'It won't come to that.' Neagle picked up the signal and gave it back to her. 'Get a signal off to 10 Int. Company asking them if their source can provide a photograph of Foley. All we've got at the moment is a photofit likeness.'

'Anything else?'

'Yes. The duty clerk . . . ' Neagle snapped his fingers, trying to recall the name.

'Donald Simon,' Francesca said.

'That's the man. He was told to dispatch copies of the photofit to Special Branch and Immigration for distribution to all ferry terminals and airports. Please make sure that's in hand.' Neagle pushed his chair back and stood up. 'Meantime I will be with the legal branch trying to see if there is some way we can pull Mrs Hayes in for further questioning without getting our fingers burned.'

'About the photofits,' Francesca said, accompanying him to the door, 'are we sending any to the Lincolnshire Constabulary?'

'But of course. I made it clear they were the number-one priority.'

★ ★ ★

Despite the lack of manpower Head of Station, Tallinn, had come up trumps. True, his foot soldiers had been unable to identify the man from Langley among all the arrivals on commercial flights from Copenhagen, Stockholm, and Helsinki, but that was of no consequence. What pleased Hazelwood was the fact that they had made Pavel Trilisser when he had boarded a chartered Learjet bound for Frankfurt late yesterday afternoon. The Russian had been accompanied by Carl Bucholtz, the CIA's Assistant Chief of Station in Estonia, whose face was known to the foot soldiers. Since only three passengers had boarded the Learjet they had concluded he must be the man from Langley and had photographed him for the record.

Rowan Garfield had given him the good news at morning prayers. The Head of the European Department had also informed Hazelwood that the photographs his foot soldiers had taken were in the diplomatic bag and could be expected to reach Vauxhall Cross by mid-afternoon. Hazelwood, however, was not prepared to wait; the report from Tallinn would enable him to pretend that the information had not come to hand because GCHQ had been listening to the CIA's network. Whether or not Walter Maryck believed him was immaterial; the pretence would save his and Walter's face.

Walter Maryck had been appointed Chief of the CIA's London station in 1991 when Hazelwood had then been the newly appointed Assistant Director in charge of the Eastern Bloc Department, as it had been known in those days. Now aged forty-nine he was by any standard a handsome man who, as it happened, was also married to an extremely attractive woman. To make them the perfect nuclear family they had a thirteen-year-old son and a daughter of twelve.

Neither Walter nor his wife, Debra, cared for designer clothes which were supposed to make some kind of statement about the wearer. Instead he affected a style of dress which gladdened the hearts of every tailor in Savile Row, while Debra bought most of her clothes from Burberry and Aquascutum. They were, in fact, the sort of people you would expect to appear in such quintessentially English publications as the *Field, Country Life*, and *Harpers & Queen*. As a result Walter's enemies in the CIA frequently accused him of being too pro British, a charge so removed from the truth as to be laughable.

As Hazelwood could testify, whenever there had been a possible conflict of interest there had been no doubting Walter's allegiance. He was quite simply a patriot first, last and always.

Maryck had enlisted in the army straight from college and had completed two tours of duty in Vietnam with the Green Berets, winning a Distinguished Service Cross and Silver Star in the process. With the end of the Vietnam War a sideways move into the CIA's East Asia Division had been a logical progression. In 1982 he had joined the European Circuit.

As he listened to the number ringing out, Hazelwood could picture Walter in his office on the second floor of the embassy in the ultra-high-security area. Although spacious, the room had no outlook whatsoever, a legacy dating back to the late seventies when CIA chiefs throughout Europe were being targeted by such diverse terrorist organisations as Black September, the Japanese Red Army faction, and the Popular Front for the Liberation of Palestine. Nothing much had changed in the last twenty years; nowadays it was the Iranians, Iraqis and Hezbollah that people like Walter Maryck had to look out for.

The phone stopped ringing and a familiar voice said, '8473.'

'Hello, Walter,' Hazelwood said, 'it's me, Victor. How are you doing?'

'Fine, just fine. And you?'

'Couldn't be better.'

'I'm glad to hear it. Is this business or social, Victor?'

'It would be wise to switch the crypto on.'

'Let's do it then.'

A moment later both men confirmed they had a green light which meant the secure-speech facility was operating.

'An interesting thing happened in Tallinn yesterday,' Hazelwood said cheerfully. 'One of our chaps was stooging around the international airport when he happened to see that nice Mr Bucholtz of yours boarding a Learjet to Frankfurt and who should be with him but Pavel Trilisser.'

'That's news to me. No offence, Victor, but I'll need to check the story with Langley. It could be your guys were mistaken.'

'It's possible. Fortunately, they took a number of photographs which will arrive this afternoon. So why don't you drop round for a drink between six and six-thirty and have a look at them? Bring Debra with you.'

'I'm afraid this evening is out of the question, we're going to the theatre.'

'Another time then.' Hazelwood moved his diary closer to the phone so that Maryck should hear him turning the pages. 'How about you and Debra having dinner with us a week on Wednesday?'

'August seventh?'

'Yes.'

'Looks OK to me,' Maryck said. 'Can I confirm it after I've spoken to Debra?'

'By all means.'

'OK, Victor, we've done the social bit, now let's get down to business.'

'It's just a suggestion. The fact is we both know Trilisser has been our implacable enemy for donkey's years. That he should suddenly defect to the CIA strikes me as wildly improbable.'

'I don't agree. Trilisser has been misappropriating government funds — '

'The charges were dropped before he walked into your embassy.'

'All right,' Maryck said wearily, 'give me the sales pitch.'

'I'd like to have one of our people sitting in on the interrogation. Purely as an observer, of course. The man I have in mind knows Pavel Trilisser better than any one else on either side of the pond. He could tell you at a glance whether or not Trilisser was lying.'

'You're talking about Ashton.'

'Indeed I am.'

'Well, I guess there is one thing you can say for Ashton, life is never dull when he is around. And yes, that does mean I will talk to Langley.'

★ ★ ★

Ashton went upstairs into the bedroom, sat down in front of the dressing table, which had been left undisturbed since Margaret Egan had committed suicide, and tapped out his brother-in-law's phone number on his mobile phone. If Russell and Steve of Special Branch had been given half a chance they would have had him sitting on the bathroom floor, the one place in the house where nobody could see him.

'Hi,' Ashton said when Richard answered the phone, 'it's me, Peter.'

289

'You'll be wanting Harriet,' Egan said, and put the phone down with a clatter.

The seconds ticked by while Ashton waited for her to come to the phone. Somewhere in the house a radio was playing and nearer at hand he could hear a murmur of unintelligible conversation. The transceiver picked up the sound of footsteps in the hall, then Harriet came on the line.

'How are things?' Ashton asked.

'A little hectic, you know how it is — a house full of children, a couple of minders, everybody getting on top of one another. And you?'

'One long card school.' Ashton paused, tried to think of a tactful way of putting the next bit and found inspiration was lacking. 'About the church service,' he said. 'I don't know if you have been told this but I can't sit with the family. In fact Special Branch reckon we should be divorced from the rest of the congregation. They are worried that my presence might endanger people and they've got a point.'

'Yes they have,' Harriet said in a voice devoid of expression.

'I can't be at your side during the interment either. I have to watch from outside the cemetery gates.'

'So I have been told,' she said in the same flat voice.

'And if Richard should be inviting people back to the house, I can't be there.'

'You won't be missing much.'

'Was I wrong to come? I mean I'm not being much help to you, am I?'

290

'You're in the same city, that's what counts.'

'I love you,' Ashton said

'I should hope so, otherwise it would be a little one-sided. Look, I have to go. It's time for Carolyn's feed and I can hear her crying. Call me again after the funeral. OK?'

'You bet.'

Ashton terminated the link, then on impulse he pressed out the number of the mobile Jebens had given him. He had tried it three times in the past forty-eight hours without getting a ringing tone and fully expected to draw yet another blank. Instead, to his amazement, a woman answered.

'Is George there?' he asked.

'Who?'

'George Foley.'

'You have the wrong number,' the woman said, and gave a brittle laugh.

'I don't think so, Mrs Hayes.'

'How many times do you need telling that you have the wrong number?'

The woman sounded more frightened than angry.

17

Julie Pearce checked to make sure the road was clear behind before she pulled out from the layby near Kirklington on the A617 to Newark. Her hands were still shaking, she also felt sick and her body was clammy all over, symptoms that had more to do with the phone call she had just received than the revolting nitroglycerine powder Folcy had given her.

Until her mobile had rung everything had gone pretty much like clockwork. On her arrival at the medical centre one of the receptionists had remarked how pale she looked and had asked if she was feeling under the weather. 'It's that time of the month', Julie had told the receptionist and had immediately secured her sympathy. She had said the same thing to the nurse, adding that her period was worse than usual in the confident expectation that it wouldn't be long before her colleagues learned she was feeling very off colour and ought to be sent home.

Her confident assumption had been fully justified; shortly after ten o'clock the senior member of the practice had caught her between patients to suggest she called it a day. Julie had thanked him and had said she might take advantage of his kind offer if she was still feeling groggy in an hour or so. The fact was she couldn't afford to arrive home before her daily left at noon. In staying on until eleven-fifty she had earned herself a few Brownie points with the other members of the practice. She had also taken steps to ensure no one would feel compelled to drop by the cottage by emphasising that all she needed to put her right were a few hours in bed.

Julie had answered her mobile thinking it was George Foley checking to make sure she was on her way back to Upton. Then a stranger had asked if George was there and she couldn't think how the man had obtained the number of her mobile. A faint hope that he had misdialled and was enquiring about a different George had been blown away seconds later when he had made it clear it was Foley he wanted. The one crumb of comfort had been the fact that the man had thought he was talking to Sandra Hayes.

It suddenly dawned on her that George had picked up the wrong mobile phone from the pair they had left on top of the chest of drawers last night. He hadn't noticed and neither had she. There were two other, more disturbing conclusions to be drawn from the brief conversation with the stranger: first, he wasn't on their side, and secondly, an informer had given him the number of George's mobile.

Julie left the A617 shortly before the Y junction with the road to Southwell and turned into a narrow, unclassified lane. It was a short cut which entered the village the far side of her next-door neighbour. She used it regularly going to and from the medical centre and knew all the hazards like the back of her hand, especially the one where the lane joined the Southwell Road.

Today, however, Julie had other things on her mind and made a left turn on to the Southwell Road without first looking to make sure it was safe to do so. A horn blared, tyres screamed in protest and a Ford Sierra fishtailed abreast of the Citroën 2CV. At first Julie braked instinctively but her cottage was only a few yards up the road and suddenly it was a safe haven she just had to reach.

The driver of the Sierra was leaning across the passenger's seat screaming abuse at her as he lowered the nearside window. Ignoring him, she drove on, edged towards the crown of the road, then made a sharp left-hand turn and ran up onto the garage front. When she got out of the car the driver was on the pavement calling her every name under the sun. He looked to be in his mid-to late twenties, was in shirtsleeves, the top button undone, the tie loosened. He was roughly a couple of inches under six feet and flabby with it from a round face that was beginning to show a double chin to a stomach that suggested beer was his staple diet.

'Stupid fucking whore,' he bellowed at the top of his voice, 'shagging is the only thing you're good for.'

'Get off my drive,' Julie said in a voice that betrayed her fear.

'Are you talking to me, bitch,' he snarled, and advanced towards her.

'Yes I am.' Julie reached into her shoulder bag, took out the mobile and erected the aerial. 'If you won't leave me alone I'm going to call the police.'

In what was a battle of wills Julie knew she was going to lose. Then suddenly the man who gardened for her neighbour across the road intervened.

'Is this man bothering you, Dr Pearce?' he asked.

He was almost twice the driver's age but that was the only advantage the younger man had. There wasn't an ounce of spare flesh on his body and he was well muscled. The way he was hefting a pair of garden shears in his right hand like a club sent yet another message.

'Fuck you, Doctor,' the driver said, and walked back to his Ford Sierra.

'I can't thank you enough, Henry,' Jill said to the gardener as the younger man drove off. 'I don't know what I would have done without you.'

'Are you going to be all right, Doctor?' he asked anxiously.

'I'll be fine, Henry. Just fine.'

Somehow Julie let herself into the cottage, somehow she made it to the kitchen on legs which threatened to buckle under her. Everything had started to go wrong from the moment she had answered the phone and she was no longer capable of thinking straight. For the first time in her life Julie Pearce was physically sick with fear.

★ ★ ★

The phone was ringing when Francesca York unlocked the door to her office. Anxious to answer it before the caller lost patience and hung up, she scuttled towards the desk, leaned across it and lifted the receiver. '5947,' she said in her natural voice, forgetting the elocution lessons for the moment.

'Hello, Fran.'

'Ashton?'

'Got it in one.'

'What do you want this time?' she sighed.

'Have you tried that phone number I gave you the other day?'

'Once. It doesn't ring out.'

'It does now. I've just had an interesting conversation and it wasn't with George Foley. A woman answered the phone.'

'Was it Sandra Hayes?' Francesca asked.

'No, I don't think so. This lady didn't have a London accent.'

'So where does that leave us?'

'Well, she sounded very rattled and I think if you play it right we might discover who she is.'

'If *I* play it right,' Francesca said.

'I want you to phone that number right now and pretend you are Sandra Hayes. I'm betting the lady is not too far away from Lincoln. Work that into your conversation and she might jump through the hoop.'

'OK.'

'Have you still got Foley's number?'

'Of course I have.'

'You can reach me on this number.'

He gave her the Lincoln number and Francesca repeated it, scribbling it on the topmost file in the pending tray.

'You've got it,' Ashton said, and hung up.

Francesca did the same, then walked round the desk and sat down. From her handbag she took out a pocket diary and checked the number she had written down on one of the blank pages at the back. Then she lifted the receiver, pressed 9 to obtain an outside line and punched out the number of Foley's mobile.

★ ★ ★

There was, Julie thought, nothing like a large tot of whisky to stiffen the backbone and restore one's confidence. True, she was still highly strung but at least her limbs were no longer trembling. Twelve-forty by the kitchen clock: another two hours and ten minutes to go before Foley made the hit. She needed to get her head together and decide what was best for her, what she was going to do.

The mobile trilled and made Julie flinch. Her pulse started racing again and she couldn't breathe properly. She tried to ignore the strident summons, hoping the caller would give up but the mind-numbing sound went on and on. Finally convinced that this time it had to be Foley, she answered.

A woman said, 'About bloody time. Put George on.'

'Who is this?' Julie asked in a strained voice.

'My name's Sandra Hayes, who the hell are you?'

'That's none of your business.'

'I'm making it my business. You've got George

Foley's mobile and he's supposed to be in Lincoln.'

Julie cried out, broke the connection, then ran upstairs with the cellnet and buried it under the dirty clothes in the linen basket. First there had been a phone call from a man who'd wanted to know if he was speaking to Sandra Hayes, then there had been the altercation with the driver of the Ford Sierra and now there had been this menacing call from a woman claiming to be Sandra Hayes who knew Foley was going to be in Lincoln. In a daze, Julie sat down on the bathroom chair and hugged herself as she began to rock backwards and forwards. She was at the end of her tether and couldn't take any more.

★ ★ ★

Ashton heard the phone ringing in the hall and ran downstairs to answer it. There were three phones in the house, one in the hall, another in Egan's study and the third in the sitting room where Steve and Russell, the two Special Branch officers, were ensconsed. Although he told them it was almost certainly a colleague returning his earlier call, the telephone in the study had stopped ringing by the time he reached it.

'I'm here, Fran,' he said.

'So who was I speaking to just now?'

'Me — Russell. I'm one of the guys looking after your friend.'

'I think he should listen in, Fran,' Ashton said before she could tell Russell to get off the line. 'It will save a lot of time if he does.'

'Fine. I'm afraid I missed out with Foley's lady friend, whoever she is. I had her really going at one time and I swear the lady was about to give me her name but then I overdid it and she switched off her mobile.'

'At what point did you overdo it, Fran?'

'When I told her she had Foley's mobile and he was supposed to be in Lincoln. Of course I was just guessing but I heard her cry out and then the line went dead. I think she is one frightened lady.'

'I'm sure she is,' Ashton said. 'That's why I'd like you to ring the number again.'

'I already have and it's not ringing out.'

'Well, keep trying, Fran. She may switch it on again. If she does and you get through, promise her immunity from prosecution in return for her co-operation. If nothing else try to get her name and address.'

'I'll do the best I can.'

'I know you will. If you have any luck, call me back on this number. I'll be here until one-forty-five when we leave for the church.' Ashton paused, then said, 'Have you got any questions or points to make, Russell?'

'No, neither has Steve.'

'Don't go for a moment,' Fran said. 'I've asked the Met to fax photofit likenesses of Foley to the Chief Constable of the Lincolnshire Constabulary. Have you received a copy yet?'

'No, but don't worry about it,' Ashton said. 'Russell will call Police Headquarters in Deepdale Lane here in Lincoln.'

Julie waited for the electric kettle to switch itself off, then poured the boiling water over the tea bag in the mug, leaving just enough room for a dash of milk. She eyed the bottle of whisky, which was still on the kitchen table where she had left it before running upstairs in a blind panic. Another tot would do her the world of good but she wasn't used to drinking in the middle of the day — nor at any other time for that matter. She needed to have her wits about her and although there was nothing like a generous measure of Bell's to steady one's nerve, it could leave a person befuddled.

She had already concluded that some informer had betrayed the number of Foley's mobile, now she had to decide whether George was hopelessly compromised to the point where he posed a threat to her. The Security Forces obviously knew a great deal about him, worse still he had signalled his intentions and they were prepared. Foley was using Continuity IRA to settle a family vendetta against Ashton and there could be serious repercussions if George was successful and the British Government decided his action was a clear breach of the ceasefire. Sinn Fein wouldn't like it and the Provisional IRA might take it upon themselves to make an example of Foley and everybody who had assisted him.

However, the question uppermost in Julie's mind was of a more personal nature. If arrested by the police, would Foley betray her? It was a point of honour with the IRA not to recognise the British courts, and betraying a comrade in order to secure a lenient sentence was regarded as a heinous crime. Thinking it through Julie came to the conclusion that Foley would abide by the code. But Foley didn't have to open his mouth. If he was arrested while the Harley-Davidson was still in his possession, it wouldn't be long before the police were knocking at her door.

Next question: in view of what had happened so far today what were Foley's chances of success? The short answer was fifty-fifty and that wasn't good enough. He had told her to report the theft of her motorbike but she wasn't expected to do that until she had picked Foley up in the Citroën 2CV and delivered him to Newark-on-Trent.

It wasn't going to work, not after the altercation with the driver of the Ford Sierra. Henry, the gardener, had come to her aid, something he was unlikely to forget in a hurry. He had noticed how upset she had been and he would think her behaviour was very odd if he saw her leaving the cottage in the car shortly afterwards. It was the sort of thing that would stick in anybody's mind. The only way out of the mess lay in persuading Foley to call off the operation, at least for the time being.

Julie finished the mug of tea, then got up from the kitchen table and went into the sitting room to use the telephone. Lifting the receiver, she punched out the number of her own mobile and almost screamed in frustration when she couldn't even get a ringing tone.

Julie stared at her Omega wristwatch, unable to believe only eight minutes had elapsed since the woman who'd claimed to be Sandra Hayes had phoned her. All the same, time was running on and there was a limit to how long she could afford to wait before taking steps to protect herself. Foley had said he would make one last call at 13.00 hours to make sure there was no last-minute hitch. It would, she reasoned, do no harm to wait another twelve minutes.

Julie went upstairs, took out her jewel case and removed the half-hoop of diamonds, the sapphire and diamond brooch and the emerald dress ring she had inherited from her mother. With some reluctance she placed the items on top of the lavatory cistern where they would be handy to flush down the toilet if push came to shove. Knowing she would need to retain Foley's mobile, she retrieved it from the linen basket and returned to the sitting room. There was still the holdall he had left under the free-standing wardrobe but that would have to wait until much later. At three minutes past one she tried her own mobile number again with the same negative results. She then dialled 999 and asked for the police.

'My name is Dr Julie Pearce,' she told the woman police officer on duty in the incident room. 'My address is Rose Cottage, Upton near Southwell. I wish to report the theft of my expensive motorbike, a black Harley-Davidson, registration number AUZ 613 C.'

'When did you discover it was missing, Doctor?'

'Five minutes ago. The man who stole it is George Foley, who was staying with me.'

The woman police officer wondered if perhaps Mr Foley had merely borrowed the machine without asking her permission. Such things did happen from time to time.

'Not in this case,' Julie said coldly. 'He stole a quantity of valuable jewellery. He also tried to poison me.'

★ ★ ★

Ashton had often wondered how many terrorists had been apprehended because a member of the Security Forces or the general public or an informer had recognised the wanted man from a photofit likeness. Those relating to Mr George Foley, which had been delivered to 11 Ferris Drive, showed a youngish handsome-looking man with a round, somewhat plump face and a mouth that seemed to be hovering on a smile. He was said to be six feet one and weighed approximately one hundred and seventy pounds. The only thing which distinguished Foley from other tall, apparently good-humoured men was a strawberry birthmark on his left hip, which was hardly the most useful piece of information in the world, unless they managed to catch Foley with his trousers down. Ashton reckoned he could literally bump into Foley and not recognise him.

The curriculum vitae which appeared below

the photofit had provoked a whole spate of phone calls to his house. It was one thing to speculate that Foley would aim to kill from a distance, quite another to learn he was an accomplished sniper who had already put three soldiers in the ground. Even as Ashton studied the photofit for the umpteenth time, Steve was out in the hall getting yet another lot of last-minute instructions. However, this time round whatever instructions the Detective Chief Inspector in charge of Special Branch had for them were commendably brief.

'So what's new?' Ashton asked when Steve returned to the sitting room.

'There's been a change of plan, Mr Ashton.'

'Good.'

'Of course, our guv'nor would be much happier if you decided not to attend the funeral.'

'No chance,' Ashton said.

'That's what I told him. Anyway, the Assistant Chief Constable has got the uniforms checking all the hotels, guesthouses and bed-and-breakfasts overlooking the route from the church to the cemetery. Any guest who has booked in since the announcement appeared in Wednesday's *Times* and *Telegraph* will have his room searched.'

'That's good thinking.'

'But?'

'What?'

'There's always a 'but' with you,' Steve told him.

'OK. Foley made his reputation as a sniper

and it's right to take cognisance of that but there are a number of points we should keep in mind. In Northern Ireland he had plenty of time to plan each operation, he had the active support of a lot of people in South Armagh, and he enjoyed a safe haven in Southern Ireland. In this instance he's had just two days' warning, the population isn't friendly and there is no safe refuge this side of the Irish Sea. What I'm saying is we shouldn't rule out other possibilities.'

'Like a car bomb detonated by remote control?' Russell suggested.

'That's one method.'

'Measures are already in hand to combat that particular threat, Mr Ashton.'

'There's also the hit-and-run technique for which you need two people and a motorbike. We know Foley has got an accomplice, though something must have gone very wrong because the lady in question sounded badly rattled to Francesca York and me.'

'That's some crystal ball you've got,' Russell said.

'I'll tell you something else. I've got a hunch the mystery lady doesn't live here in Lincoln, or even in the county.'

'So where are you going with this?'

'Well, I'm just wondering if the Nottingham-shire Constabulary has been asked to keep you people informed of any unusual occurrences.'

'I hate to seem negative,' Russell said, 'but what do you mean by unusual occurrences?'

'It's not easy to define.' Ashton shrugged. 'Anything to do with a stolen motorbike.'

'You'd be spoiled for choice there,' Steve observed.

'Narrow it down then. Tell them we are only interested in those that have been stolen today.'

'I don't know,' Russell said doubtfully.

'And where the thief has been named,' Ashton finished.

There was a longish pause, then Russell said he thought their guv'nor would go for that.

★ ★ ★

The sun on his face woke Foley up. Feeling stiff, he got to his feet and stretched both arms above his head, flexing the shoulder muscles to loosen up. Curious to know how long he had been asleep, Foley glanced at his wristwatch and saw it was only ten past eleven. In just under two hours from now he would call Julie to make sure she was all set and to remind her not to forget his canvas holdall. From Upton he'd taken the A617 towards Mansfield and had turned off into Sherwood Forest just beyond the junction with the A614. With four and a half hours to kill before making his way to Lincoln, the forest was an ideal place to spend time. He'd gone in deep, found a spot off the beaten track and stretched out.

Foley lit a cigarette, hunkered down again and stretched out his legs, his back resting against a tree trunk. Waiting was the worst part of any operation because time seemed to stand still like it was doing now, except that the second hand on his wristwatch had stopped moving. Jesus H.

Christ: Foley threw his cigarette away, scrambled to his feet and took out his mobile. He punched out 123 and a man with a very precise but faint voice informed him that 'At the third stroke, the time sponsored by Accurist will be one twenty-nine and fifteen seconds.'

It was only when Foley tapped out the number of Julie's mobile and got an engaged tone that he realised he had picked up the wrong phone. Pulse racing, he rang his own mobile number and could barely hear Julie when she answered. He thought of calling her on the BT line but of course she would be on her way to Lincoln by now. There weren't enough four-letter words in the English Language to express his feelings because it was equally obvious to him that the stupid bitch hadn't recharged the batteries on her mobile.

'Where are you now?' he asked slowly in a loud voice in a desperate attempt to communicate.

Foley thought Julie said she was going to Lincoln but her voice kept breaking up and he couldn't be sure. He did, however, learn that she had left the medical centre at eleven-forty which in the end was good enough for him. Wasting no further time, Foley left the forest and headed north to Ollerton, intending to approach Lincoln from the west.

18

Julie switched off the mobile and left it on the low table in front of the settee. She had told Foley she wasn't going to Lincoln and it wasn't her fault the transmission had kept breaking up, which could mean he had misunderstood what she had said to him. In fact poor communications had made it impossible for her to persuade him to cancel the operation for the time being. Foley said he would call her at 13.00 hours to see if there was any last-minute hitch. When that time had come and gone, she assumed he had met with an accident. She'd therefore had no alternative but to inform the police that her motorbike had been stolen.

Her conscience thus salved, Julie was at ease with herself until the door bell rang and she answered the door to find two women on the step, one in plain-clothes, the other in uniform. Julie knew the police would want a statement from her at some time but the woman in civilian clothes was a detective sergeant, which was unnerving. Her mind in a whirl, Julie didn't catch their names and was slow to react when the detective wondered if they might come inside. At the second time of asking the penny finally dropped and she led the police officers into the sitting room.

'Don't tell me you've recovered my motorbike already?' Julie said in a show of bravado.

The detective sergeant gave her a thin smile. 'I only wish we had, Doctor. The fact is we need to ask you some questions concerning George Foley. For instance, how long have you known him, Julie?'

The sudden and unexpected use of her first name was like a slap in the face. No friendliness was intended. The sergeant was deliberately treating her like some wretched little schoolgirl who had been caught shoplifting.

'Don't be impertinent, Sergeant.'

'You're mistaken, Julie. I was merely trying to make things easier for you because, believe me, you are in serious trouble.'

'My motorbike has been stolen and I'm in serious trouble?'

'George Foley is wanted for murder. He's a member of Continuity IRA; before that he was with the Provos. He is a terrorist, has been for years.'

'I didn't know that,' Julie protested.

'Oh dear, that's what they all say, Julie. Now, how long have you known Foley and where did you first meet him?'

Telling the police a pack of lies would be a dangerous game; what she had to do was to stretch the truth a little and hope to learn something in return.

'I met him in 1989 some time during mid-September. I was holidaying in Ireland with two girl friends from college and we were sampling the night life of Dublin. We were in a bar on Lord Edward Street and Foley introduced himself and started chatting us up.'

'All three of you?'

'To begin with.' Julie avoided the sergeant's gaze. 'Then he concentrated on me.'

'And that was the start of a beautiful friendship, was it?'

'We were mutually attracted,' Julie conceded.

'OK, that was almost seven years ago. How many times have you seen him since then?'

Julie hesitated. The truth was every time she went to Ireland on holiday, which was roughly once a year. In practice this meant she might see him on three maybe four occasions during the fortnight she was over there. She had spent under thirty days in his company in eight years and yet, in reporting the theft of her motorbike, she had admitted Foley had been staying with her. The police would make a meal out of that. On the other hand, if she inflated the number of times they had been together, this butch-looking detective sergeant would ask her about his friends. Had she met any of them? What were their names? Where did they live? One question after another delivered at machine-gun speed.

'How many times, Julie? Ten? Twenty? Thirty? Forty? Fifty?'

'I don't know, I didn't keep account of them.'

'Give me a guesstimate then.'

'Somewhere between thirty and forty times.'

'Always in Ireland?'

Julie sensed trouble and tried to avert it. 'We spent a long weekend in Amsterdam in 1991.'

She had but not George. Foley had once told her that if you had to lie your way out of trouble, your story should at least contain a grain of truth.

'But never in this country,' the detective sergeant said as though accusing her of some unspecified crime.

'Not until now.'

'So when did he arrive, Julie?'

'Wednesday evening.'

'I meant in this country.'

'Oh, well, that would have been last Saturday, a week ago tomorrow.'

Where was he staying before he came to Upton? How long was Foley planning to stay in England? What was the purpose of his visit? It didn't take Julie long to realise that it wouldn't have mattered what day or date she had picked. The police knew more about Foley's movements than he had seen fit to tell her and there never had been any way of avoiding the barrage of intimidating questions which had followed the guesstimate.

'Tell me about Sandra Hayes, Julie.'

'I've never heard of the woman.'

'Don't be silly, of course you have.'

'That's it,' Julie snapped. 'I'm not saying another word unless my solicitor is present.'

'Fine. Tell him to meet us at Police Headquarters, Sherwood Lodge, Arnold.'

'What?'

'You're under arrest, Doctor Pearce,' the detective sergeant told her with evident satisfaction. 'We can have you under the Prevention of Terrorism Act.'

Foley rode past the Eastgate Hotel for the second time, then headed out of town on the road to Skegness. There was no sign of the Citroën 2CV in the hotel car park and Julie Pearce was long overdue. There were, he thought, only two possible reasons for her absence: either she had been involved in a traffic accident or, as was more likely, she had chickened out at the last minute. There was, however, one part of the plan Julie would adhere to: she would undoubtedly phone the police to report the theft of her motorbike. It was also safe to assume she would do this a lot earlier than he had allowed for.

He came to a roundabout and circled back to Lincoln on Wragby Road. His first priority was to ditch the Harley-Davidson and acquire another set of wheels. He went down the hill past Potter Gate into Lindum Road then Broadgate and on across the River Witham looking for a pay and display car park. He found one on the edge of town near St Mark's Shopping Centre. He drove round the parking area, spotted a dark blue Transit and squeezed the motorbike into the gap between the van and a Range Rover. The metered ticket displayed on the inside of the windscreen was still good for two and a half hours. Foley checked to make sure no one else was about, then undid the side pannier and took out the Uzi sub-machine-gun. He removed the magazine, cleared the round in the breach and then hammered the folded butt against the side window until he had made a hole big enough to get his hand through. Raising the catch to unlock the door, he slid it open and tossed the crash helmet into the back of the van before placing the Uzi on the adjoining seat while he hot-wired the ignition.

When it came to stealing a vehicle, Foley believed the quicker you were the more chance you had of getting away with it. Finesse was not an option in broad daylight in a high-risk area like a car park. In a more secluded place, he would have loaded the Harley-Davidson into the van and dumped it at the first convenient location away from Lincoln. In the present circumstances, the best he could do was to hide the bike between two vehicles situated as far as possible from the Transit. When he drove off, less than four minutes had elapsed from the time he had entered the car park.

With no one to help him see it through, Foley knew it was only sensible to call the operation off but life was never that simple. Continuity IRA had invested a lot of hard-earned money in the operation and if he walked away from it, they would expect him to account for every last penny, which would be a mite difficult. He'd always been a gambling man and a lot of the cash had gone on the horses with nothing to show for it. That would not go down well with his mad-arsed cousin, Barry Hayes, or the one-time quartermaster of the West Belfast battalion. At the very least he could expect to have both elbows shattered and his kneecaps shot to hell.

On the other hand, if he killed a senior intelligence officer like Ashton and got clean away, he would be a hero for ever and a day, and nobody would give a damn where the money had gone. As he picked up the outer ring road, Foley assessed the risks in going through with the plan. He started with Julie and quickly came to the conclusion that even if she had a mind to, she couldn't tell the police exactly when, where and how he intended to make the hit. All Julie knew of the operation was the part she was expected to play. Looking at it in another way, Julie might have done him a big favour. Thanks to her the police would be looking out for a Harley-Davidson. If they did find it in the car park, they couldn't initially connect it with the dark blue Transit.

It would be a different story when the van driver returned, but the ticket didn't expire until 16.55 hours, and even if the man returned half an hour earlier, he would still have plenty of time in hand. In theory he could take out Ashton and reach the outskirts of Birmingham before the theft was reported. There were people in the Midlands who would see him right; maybe they weren't too clever when it came to tracking a vehicle but they would provide a sanctuary for him.

Foley made a bargain with himself. There was, he decided, no harm in taking a look at the ambush position; if Special Branch or the Anti-Terrorist Squad were in evidence, he would immediately abort the operation and think about the likely consequences later.

They had sung 'Guide me, O Thou great Redeemer', and Richard Egan had read Chapter 10, verses 1 to 10 from the Gospel according to St John, and now some lifelong friend of Frederick Egan, whose name Ashton hadn't caught, was on his feet to give the address. From where he was sitting in the aisle on the south side of the nave, he could just see Harriet in the front row with her sister-in-law, Lucy, to her left and a statuesque woman of indeterminate age on her right. Ashton thought it was probably the aunt he'd never met who had been unable to attend their wedding. In fact the first three rows were taken up by members of the extended family, many of whom, like Richard Egan's in-laws, were complete strangers to Ashton. So were the rest of the mourners whom he assumed were friends, business acquaintances and neighbours of the deceased. There were no young children in the congregation; they had been left behind in the care of Frederick's former housekeeper.

Seated between the two Special Branch officers at the back of the church, Ashton felt he was an interloper at a private gathering because there was so much Harriet hadn't told him about her family which he was now hearing from the lips of a stranger. He hadn't known there had been a third sibling, a baby girl who would have been aged forty-two now had she not died in infancy.

And in all the time he had known his

father-in-law, Frederick Egan had never mentioned he had been in the navy during the war and had served in the North Atlantic, the Mediterranean and Indian Ocean. For some reason Ashton had assumed Egan had been in a reserved occupation.

The address ended, they sang 'The Lord's my Shepherd'. Halfway through the first verse, Russell's mobile trebled loud enough to be heard above the organ. He turned the volume right down and tiptoed out of the church, trying to make as little noise as possible. When he returned a few minutes later, prayers were being said for the departed.

'You must be psychic,' he whispered to Ashton. 'A Doctor Julie Pearce, of Rose Cottage, Upton near Southwell, rang the Nottinghamshire force to report her motorbike, a black Harley-Davidson, had been stolen. Said the thief was a Mr George Foley who had been staying with her.'

'What time did they receive the call?' Ashton murmured.

'Shortly after 13.00 hours, some fifty-odd minutes before we asked Nottingham to keep us informed.'

Russell looked embarrassed. Valuable time had been lost because in the light of what they had then known, somebody had evidently doubted the wisdom of contacting the Nottingham Constabulary. Nearly an hour had elapsed before that certain somebody had finally changed his mind. Ashton just hoped nobody was going to pay for his indecision.

'Who else has been given this information?' he asked.

'Every officer in Lincoln. Don't you worry,' Russell told him, 'we'll find the bastard soon enough.'

Russell, of course, was an incurable optimist as Ashton had learned in the short time they had been acquainted.

★ ★ ★

In the event Julie Pearce was conveyed to Arnold Police Station instead of Sherwood Lodge. She had immediately assumed this was a ploy to give her solicitor the run-around while she was subjected to police harassment, and had threatened to report the detective sergeant to her MP. That nobody had attempted to interview Julie until her legal representative arrived she attributed to the fact that the police had realised she could make a lot of trouble for them. She also regarded it as a significant victory when the Detective Chief Inspector in charge of Special Branch replaced the woman police sergeant.

Unlike his junior colleague, the DCI didn't attempt to intimidate her. Having checked the voice level on the video, he had identified himself, issued the statutory caution and had then proceeded to interview her in a friendly manner. He had asked her much the same questions as the detective sergeant had and she had told him no more than she had to. Native caution told her that he had to be a lot sharper than his relaxed approach suggested but it wasn't easy to remain vigilant when he appeared to accept everything she said.

Thirty minutes into the interview, a plain-clothes officer tapped on the door, apologised to the DCI for interrupting him and asked if he could have a quick word. The interview was suspended at 14.37 hours and reopened at 14.43 hours. When he returned the DCI was carrying a canvas holdall.

'This was found under the standing wardrobe in your bedroom,' he said, and tipped the contents onto the table. 'As you will observe, it contains a washing bag with razor and shaving soap, a towel, two pairs of men's Y-fronts, a pair of clean socks and two shirts, one of which is ready for the laundry.'

'I trust you had a search warrant,' Julie said, and caught a withering look from her solicitor.

'We made sure of that. Of course, the officers didn't have a key to the house but, fortunately, the gardener who works for one of your neighbours, a man called Harry — '

'Henry,' Julie said, automatically correcting him.

'Yes, Henry. Well, he was good enough to tell us where we could find the lady who cleans for you and she does have a key.' He smiled. 'Funny thing is, she was just as surprised as we were to find that holdall under the wardrobe. She knew you had a man staying with you because he wiped his razor on one of your face towels, and apparently you only shave your legs once a week.'

'Before you ask, Chief Inspector, I don't know

318

why he left the holdall under the wardrobe.'

'Really? Your domestic help thought he might be trying to protect your reputation.'

'I've already told you I've no idea why Foley put the damned bag where he did,' Julie said heatedly. 'He was still in bed when I left the cottage.'

'The thing which interests me, Doctor, is how Foley proposed to collect his kit. Surely he didn't expect to return to the cottage if, as you claim, he'd stolen your motorbike?'

'I'm not a mind reader, Chief Inspector.'

'I understand you've been feeling a little under the weather today.'

Julie blinked, taken aback by the sudden digression. The police had obviously been talking to her colleagues at the medical centre and she would need to be on her guard.

'Yes. Apparently I looked as white as a sheet or so my colleagues told me. Anyway, I was persuaded bed was the best place for me.'

'You left the medical centre shortly before noon?'

'That's correct.' Julie glanced at her solicitor, hoping he would object to the way the interview was being conducted. He could at least ask if the state of her health was relevant.

'And you rang the police at three minutes past one to report the theft of your motorbike?'

'Yes.'

'How did you know it had been stolen, Doctor?'

'I just happened to notice it wasn't in the garage.'

'That's funny. Henry told us the garage doors were closed when you parked your car on the front.'

Julie found it difficult to breathe properly, her heart was pounding and just when she needed to come up with a plausible explanation her brain was unable to function constructively. The DCI had no such problem.

'Correct me if I'm wrong, Doctor,' he said, almost purring like a cat, 'but I expect you decided to have a look in the garage after you discovered Foley had left?'

'Why ask if you already know the answer?' she snapped, and then mentally kicked herself for being so antagonistic towards the man who was holding all the cards.

'We'll take a short break, Doctor. Give you a chance to discuss matters with your solicitor.'

Short was the operative word. Returning to the interview room barely three minutes later, the DCI somewhat dramatically placed a bullet together with an empty cartridge case on the table.

'These two items were found in the wastebin of your kitchen,' he told her. 'The sniffer dogs also discovered a minute quantity of the propellant.'

It was the moment Julie Pearce really began to hate Foley. How could a man who had been the best sniper in the Provos have been so damned careless?

'The staff nurse at the medical centre told us you were having a particularly bad menstrual period. Personally I don't believe it's that time of the month for you.'

'How would you know?' Julie said wearily.

'I don't but a medical examination would settle it.'

'Go to hell.'

'I'd feel the same in your situation, Doctor, but my advice to you is to help yourself by helping us.'

'Don't think I wouldn't like to but Foley didn't confide in me.'

It transpired this was not an insuperable difficulty. The Security Forces were prepared to go easy on her in return for names and addresses of all the people she had met through George Foley. It was, of course, an offer she could ill afford to decline.

★ ★ ★

They had sung the last hymn and the pallbearers were moving slowly and with great dignity along the nave from the chancel towards the west door. The family followed close behind, Richard and Lucy in the lead, followed by Harriet in the company of a stranger. As she came abreast of him, Ashton caught her eye and she gave him a wan smile. It angered him that Richard should treat his sister in such a cavalier fashion. When Margaret Egan, faced with terminal cancer, had committed suicide it had been Harriet who had supported Frederick at the inquest and had ensured he was cared for afterwards. And when Alzheimer's had changed the personality of their father, who was it who had interviewed and hired every replacement housekeeper even though Richard and Lucy were then living in the same city?

'Another fifteen minutes and then we move,' Russell said as the last of the mourners filed out of the church.

Ashton wasn't sure whether or not the observation had been addressed to him but nodded sagely just the same.

'We've got several things in our favour,' Russell continued, as if seeing it as his duty to boost Ashton's confidence. 'Foley will be looking for a Volvo 850, not a Ford Mondeo. We've got his description and we have the registration of the motorbike he's riding — '

'Foley will have acquired a different set of wheels by now,' Ashton said, interrupting him.

'You've been looking into your crystal ball again,' Steve told him, and cupped a hand over his mouth to stifle a yawn, before continuing, 'Maybe you can explain why the family chose to hold the funeral service at St Swithin's instead of All Saints' church, which is a damned sight closer to the cemetery?'

Ashton couldn't. Early in 1993 the Egans had had invitations printed for the forthcoming marriage of their daughter Harriet at All Saints' church on Saturday 18 December. The wedding hadn't taken place on that date; instead Ashton and Harriet had tied the knot in a registry office two months earlier in late October. He wondered if that had led to a spat with the vicar.

'You'll have to ask my brother-in-law,' Ashton

said. 'He made all the arrangements.'

'Time to go,' Russell said. 'I will lead, you will follow close on my heels, Peter, with Steve on your right.'

They walked out into the bright sunlight. Russell opened the rearside door of the Mondeo and shielded Ashton with his body as he got into the back. Then he took a couple of paces to his right and slipped in beside the driver, leaving Steve to walk round the back of the Ford Mondeo to join Ashton. Moments after the police driver had pulled away from the kerb, it was evident Special Branch had little regard for the maxim that the shortest distance between two fixed points was a straight line. If they had been conducting a guided tour of the city, they could not have chosen a more circuitous route.

'Evasion tactics,' Russell announced presently. 'If Foley is lying up in an ambush position somewhere between the church and the cemetery, he is going to be a disappointed man. Right, Peter?'

'I guess.'

'You don't agree?'

'Well, I think he will be waiting for us at the cemetery.'

'There are two cemeteries in town, one off Newport Road, the other at the bottom of Barratts Close.'

'I imagine he will have carried out a recce yesterday evening,' Ashton said. 'The workmen would have finished digging the grave in Newport Cemetery by then.'

'And what if there is also an interment at Barretts Close?'

'Foley knows the time of Egan's funeral service. With that as a guide I reckon he can make a pretty fair guess when the cortège will arrive at Newport Cemetery.'

Although Ashton couldn't see his face, he sensed Russell was not best pleased with him. As if determined to have the last word, the Special Branch officer told him he was presenting too big a target and would he mind lowering his head and shoulders.

'We're almost there,' Russell said unnecessarily as they turned left at the junction of Rasen Lane with Newport Road.

★ ★ ★

Foley was parked outside the university college four hundred yards up the road from the entrance to Newport Cemetery. He had seen the funeral cortège arrive a good ten minutes ago and thought he had recognised Harriet Ashton in the limousine following the hearse. He had assumed that if Ashton did attend the funeral, he would arrive separately with a police escort, but there was still no sign of him. No sign of police presence either, but they were probably at the graveside looking outwards. The fact was he couldn't afford to hang around for much longer outside the college without attracting unwelcome attention. He was about to move off when he saw a Ford Mondeo emerge from a side road and turn left to head north on Newport Road. Suddenly the offside indicator on the Mondeo started winking and the driver pulled across the road to stop just beyond the entrance to the cemetery. And for Foley the waiting was over.

19

Without taking his eyes off the car in front, Foley surreptitiously removed the denim jacket which was covering the Uzi on the passenger seat and dropped it onto the floor. The Ford Mondeo was parked on the wrong side of the road, the driver next to the kerb. The Transit window was already down on Foley's side to conceal the hole he'd made when breaking into it; now he needed to do the same with the nearside one otherwise the whole thing would disintegrate when he opened fire. The nearside window lowered, he reached under the dashboard, bypassed the ignition switch and started the engine. He shifted into gear, tripped the offside indicator and looked into the door mirror to make sure the road behind was clear before pulling away from the kerb.

'Take it steadily,' he muttered to himself. 'Don't go down the road like a bat out of hell, that will only alert them.' Sound advice but hard to observe when the man sitting up front with the driver was already getting out of the car. Steering the vehicle with one hand, Foley went through the gearbox into top, then picked up the 9mm Uzi with his left hand. Without looking at the weapon, he moved the change lever from safe to automatic and curled the index finger around the trigger. He planned to rip off the 32-round magazine in one long burst as he passed the

Ford Mondeo. Then roughly two hundred and fifty yards beyond the car he would make a sharp right turn into Rasen Lane and make his way round the back of Lincoln Castle.

Russell had opened the rear door and was standing in the road a yard from the vehicle, ready to shield Ashton with his body when he got out of the car. Steve had already alighted and was on the pavement, his back to the cemetery.

It was Ashton who first sensed danger when he saw a dark blue Transit bearing down on them. 'Take cover,' he roared. 'Dark blue van twelve o'clock, range fifty yards.' Still inside the car, Ashton twisted round so that his head was pointing towards the pavement where Steve was standing and wedged his body in the well between the seats, his stomach pressing against the transmission tunnel.

Russell lacked the instinct for self-preservation. There was just enough time for him to get behind the boot, throw himself flat and get his head and shoulders under the chassis. Instead he played the hero, closed the rear door with his heel and snatched the 9mm Heckler and Koch self-loading pistol from the holster on his left hip. He moved the safety up to fire and pulled the slide back to chamber a round. He brought the pistol up in a doubled-handed grasp and bent his knees as if he was about to perch himself on a bar stool.

Foley opened fire a split second before he was abreast of the Ford Mondeo, his left hand fully extended like a signpost, the butt still folded. Instead of taking a deliberate aim, the best sniper the Provos had in South Armagh simply hosed the vehicle from radiator to fuel tank. Empty cartridge cases spewed out of the Uzi, striking the windscreen and facia. As he swept past the Ford he saw the officer who had been riding up front go down.

Nose pressed into the haircord carpet on the floor, Ashton couldn't see a damned thing. Moreover, out in the open the noise made by a prolonged burst of gunfire was significantly reduced but he did hear the rapid clunk, clunk, clunk of round after round tearing through the metal bodywork. He also heard the driver grunt as the two windows nearest the blue Transit exploded.

Steve crouched below the rear wing and aimed to bob up when he judged the Transit to be fractionally beyond the Ford Mondeo. If all went well he would be outside Foley's arc of fire, yet still be in a position to get off an oblique shot at the IRA man. While unable to see the target, he would have a pretty good idea of the area to aim at in order to hit the upper part of the body. The one thing nobody could allow for was pure bad luck. As he was about to bob up, a bullet ripped through the car and shattered his right elbow before penetrating the rib cage. He went down onto his knees and, almost in slow motion, began to topple forward onto his face. A natural left-hander, he still retained a grip on the 9mm semi-automatic pistol even though the whole of the right side of his body felt as if it were on fire. Left arm raised, he got off two unaimed shots in the direction of the Transit before his face met the pavement.

For a few brief moments everything seemed to be going Foley's way, then a million-to-one shot smashed through his wrist at an oblique angle and broke up on the pistol grip. The impact knocked the 9mm Uzi sub-machine-gun from his grasp and he bellowed in pain. Foley reared back in the seat and in a state of shock he unintentionally floored the accelerator. Rasen Lane was under fifty yards away on the right and even if he'd had the use of both hands he was going much too fast to make the turn. He stamped on the brakes while at the same time trying to put on a hard right lock with one hand. He shaved across the front of a Nissan that was about to turn left into Newport Road and was still doing over thirty when the nearside front wheel struck the kerb and burst the tyre. Foley had dispensed with the seat belt to give himself greater freedom of movement when he opened fire on Ashton and the bodyguards. As the vehicle mounted the pavement at speed, he was thrown forward over the wheel and cracked his head against the windscreen, then the van overturned and he blacked out.

Ashton reached up, opened the door and crawled out onto the pavement. A few feet away Steve was lying face down, his head turned towards the kerb. He was bleeding profusely from the elbow and rib cage and in obvious pain but conscious enough to tell Ashton to see to the other two first. The driver had unclipped his seat belt and would have fallen out of the car when

Ashton opened the door if he hadn't propped him up with his free hand. The man was alive but in danger of drowning in his own blood. He had been shot through the face, the bullet shattering the lower jaw in two places and chipping the back teeth down to the gums at the entry and exit wounds, as well as destroying a large portion of the tongue.

After clearing the airway as best he could, Ashton propped the driver up, then leaned across him and grabbed the mike just as an outstation identifying itself as Walkman One came up on the air to report the sound of gunfire.

'Reference last transmission,' Ashton said, cutting in, 'shooting occurred on Newport Road outside cemetery gates. Three officers are down, all of them seriously wounded and in need of urgent resuscitation. Over.'

A prim voice said, 'Unknown station, Roger that, assistance will arrive your location in figures zero five minutes.'

Ashton dropped the mike and moved swiftly round the car to see how Russell was bearing up. The Special Branch Officer was sitting bolt upright, his back resting against the car, legs splayed apart, head lowered as if to inspect the bullet wounds in his chest. No matter how swiftly the ambulances might arrive, Ashton could see at a glance that Russell was beyond help. A good man had been killed and two others seriously wounded because he had been determined to attend his father-in-law's funeral. A small voice in Ashton's head insisted he had not done this out of respect for Frederick Egan or concern for Harriet but in the hope of drawing Foley out into the open.

A car pulled up on the opposite side of the road and the driver called to him.

'Are you all right?' the man asked. 'Do you need any help?'

'Thanks all the same but an ambulance and paramedics should be here any minute.'

'Well, if you're sure,' the driver said doubtfully.

'I am,' Ashton told him.

'That idiot in the blue van almost had me too when he turned into Rasen Lane. I think he may have had a blowout.' The driver cocked his head as if to hear better. 'Sounds like an ambulance coming this way,' he said, and drove off.

The Heckler and Koch pistol was lying where Russell had dropped it, just out of reach from his outstretched fingers. Ashton picked it up and started running towards Rasen Lane. There was nothing he could do for the other two officers but it was just possible that Foley was now legging it on foot.

* * *

Nothing looked right to Foley from where he was and it was some moments before he realised the van was lying on its side. He was in a semifoetal position on the floor, one foot trapped under the clutch pedal, the left arm pinned under him, the injured hand thrust under the driver's seat. Foley had no idea how long he had been unconscious and there was no point in trying to work it out because he could hear a siren not too far away, and it was vital to get the hell out of the area while there was still time. He would hold up a motorist, preferably a woman because they were usually more compliant in a hostage situation and she wouldn't try to play for time when he told her she was going to do the driving. Soon as he found somewhere quiet he would bundle her into the boot and drive on to Birmingham before abandoning the car in a back street. Somewhere along the way he would have to do something about his wounded hand, which was dripping blood all over the place.

Foley extracted his foot from under the clutch pedal, then twisted round and picked up the sub-machine-gun, which had become wedged between the seats. He crawled past the gear lever to get at the nearside door which was above his head. The window was already down and he squeezed through the gap, the top of his head nearly lifting off when he put too much weight on the injured hand as he levered himself out of the vehicle.

He landed awkwardly, and stumbled forward, the Uzi in his right hand. When he straightened up it was definitely Christmas in July because there, no more than ten feet away from him, was this woman driver who had stopped her car and got out to see if anybody had been hurt. Then the woman driver saw the sub-machine-gun and immediately ran back to her Ford Escort. Raising the Uzi aloft, Foley squeezed off a short burst of three or four rounds and yelled at her to stand still or else he would blow her goddamned head off.

Ashton heard the burst of gunfire just before he turned into Rasen Lane. Rounding the corner he saw Foley bundling a woman into a three-door Ford Escort and start to edge his way round to the nearside door while threatening her with the Uzi. Ashton waited until the hostage was no longer in his line of fire before he acted and told Foley to freeze. He knew Foley would never put his gun down and had taken up the first pressure on the trigger but, even so, the IRA man beat him to it, opening fire as he turned about to face Ashton. It was the old hosepipe action of putting down suppressive fire while getting into position to engage the target. At close quarters it should have worked but the sub-machine-gun ceased firing after two or three rounds, either because the magazine was empty or there was a stoppage in the breech. Ashton wasn't interested in the probable cause.

'Tough shit,' he yelled, and hit Foley four times in the chest within a perfect one-inch group.

Moments later the first patrol car arrived on the scene.

* * *

Roy Kelso would never have described himself as a clock-watcher but he did aim to leave the office before five o'clock on a Friday evening and invariably did. He knew this was not likely to be the case this Friday when Ms Sheridan walked into his cubbyhole of an office on the top floor at a quarter to five, when he was in the process of clearing his desk. Eight days ago on her instructions he had frozen the next instalment of Ashton's severance pay which normally would have been paid into his account with Lloyds Bank, Lichfield this very Friday. Without explaining why, she ordered him to release the payment forthwith and refused to listen to him when he tried to point out that the Bank was unlikely to inform the appropriate branch before Monday.

Barely two minutes after Ms Sheridan stalked out of his office, Victor's PA called to inform Kelso he was requested to attend a special meeting of heads of departments at 18.15 hours. In government circles 'requested' meant required, a subtlety his wife, Muriel, could never grasp. She also found it difficult to understand why he couldn't say when he might be home, a failing in her eyes which earned him a piece of her mind. Following the altercation with Muriel, he spent the next eighty minutes trying to discover what the meeting was about and was still none the wiser when he walked into the conference room.

Enlightenment came in a few brief sentences from Hazelwood when he described what had happened in Lincoln that afternoon. By the time Victor finished the account of the shooting, Kelso fancied he knew what had prompted Ms Sheridan to cancel the financial sanction she had imposed.

'Those are the facts,' Hazelwood told them,

'now we come to the story the general public will be given. George Foley was an up-and-coming drugs baron in the East Midlands. Acting on information received, the police staked out the Newport Road cemetery where Foley was expected to collect a delivery of heroin with a street value in excess of a million sterling.'

Listening to the revised version of the truth, Kelso had to admire the way every fact had been inverted. Foley had dumped the motorbike he was supposed to arrive on and had stolen a van because he must have suspected he had been shopped. He had parked outside the college from where he could observe the cemetery and had obviously spotted the police presence. Instead of simply driving away, he had panicked and machine-gunned the three police officers in their unmarked car as he drove past.

'Three?' Garfield echoed. 'What about Ashton?'

'He wasn't there, Rowan.'

'So who shot Foley at point-blank range and killed him?'

'One of the plain-clothes officers who was observing the drop from inside the cemetery,' Hazelwood said blandly. 'He pursued Foley on foot and caught up with him after the van overturned.'

'Will the story hold up?' Benton asked.

'MI5 is confident it will, and they are handling the situation.'

'That's all very well but some of the mourners must have seen what really happened.'

'I understand the grave is in the top left-hand corner of the cemetery, some considerable way from the entrance. All they heard was a distant rattle of gunfire.'

'This Julie Pearce could torpedo the story,' Orchard said hesitantly.

Jill Sheridan shook her head. 'It wouldn't be in her interest to do so. The deal is she will plead guilty to a charge of trafficking in drugs and will receive a suspended prison sentence because Foley would still be in business but for the information she gave the police. The IRA certainly won't put their hands up and admit a botched operation because they don't want to be accused of violating the truce.'

'Is this supposition, Jill?'

'No, Bill, it's an established fact. The FCO has a hot line to the IRA's governing council in Dublin.'

And Robin Urquhart has been using it, Kelso thought. That's why you are so well informed.

'Are the police happy to support this story?' Orchard enquired, and there was no mistaking what he really meant.

'Richard Neagle says they are. Only the officers of Special Branch were aware that Foley was a member of Continuity IRA; the uniforms were merely told he was wanted for murder and was probably armed.'

'And now they will be told that Foley was trafficking in drugs?'

'You may depend on it,' Jill said tersely.

Hazelwood asked if there were any more questions, then looked round the table and got a series of headshakes in return. After wishing everybody a pleasant weekend, the meeting broke up. Halfway to the door, Kelso learned that he and Garfield were required to stay behind. Jill Sheridan stayed too. Never one to beat about the bush, Hazelwood informed them that all being well, the CIA would invite Ashton to be present when they debriefed Pavel Trilisser. What he wanted from Garfield was all the latest material on the one-time special adviser to President Yeltsin. The reports were to be placed in a separate dossier for Ashton's perusal.

'We're certainly not letting this stuff out of the building, are we?' Garfield asked, horrified.

'No. We have a reading room, Ashton can use that.'

'Right.' Garfield cleared his throat. 'Any idea when we are likely to see Ashton, Victor?'

Hazelwood told him Monday, Tuesday at the latest, then before he knew it, Kelso was given a list of things to do which looked as long as his arm. Among the more important tasks, he was required to produce new passports for Peter and Harriet in their proper names in double-quick time. In equally quick order he was to close up the house in Gaia Lane, put into store any household items belonging to the Ashtons and sell the property.

'The place belongs to the Home Office,' Kelso said. 'We leased it from them.'

'Then you had better find out what they want to cancel the lease and beat them down to the lowest possible figure.'

'I'll do my best, Victor.'

'I'm sure you will,' Hazelwood said before he

could slip in a proviso. 'The Ashtons will need temporary accomodation — somewhere pleasant, quiet but not too far off the beaten track.'

'How temporary is temporary?'

'A month at the outside.'

'You're asking a lot,' Kelso protested.

'Starting the day after tomorrow,' Hazelwood continued relentlessly.

'Impossible. We'll never get anything at such short notice.'

'I think I might be able to help,' Jill said quietly. 'My parents have a holiday home at Bosham which they won't be using again until the beginning of September.'

'Bosham,' Hazelwood repeated blankly.

'It's on the coast a few miles west of Chichester.'

'Sounds eminently suitable. Could you check with your parents that they are happy to let the Ashtons have it?'

'I'll ring them now,' Jill said, and left the conference room.

She returned a few minutes later with their OK but as Kelso knew from bitter experience, life was never that simple. Everything now depended on Harriet, who might not be happy with the arrangement if she knew who owned the property. There was, Kelso realised, not the slightest chance of him leaving Vauxhall Cross before that particular problem had been resolved.

★ ★ ★

338

Francesca York practically ran all the way from Gower Street to the underground station at Tottenham Court Road. Friday, 26 July had begun quietly enough, then shortly after one-thirty the pace had suddenly hotted up when Special Branch had called Richard Neagle with the news that the Nottingham Constabulary had arrested a Dr Julie Pearce under the Prevention of Terrorism Act. When the SIS had first drawn their attention to the notice concerning the funeral of Frederick Egan, which had appeared in *The Times* and the *Daily Telegraph*, neither she nor Richard Neagle had seriously entertained the notion that Continuity IRA might see it as an opportunity to kill Ashton. However, as a matter of pure routine, Ashton had been afforded police protection.

The pace had become more and more frenetic with each successive report they received. Long before the firefight in the area of Newport Road, Richard Neagle had started work on two different accounts of the incident which the public relations officers of the Nottingham Constabulary and the Lincolnshire Police could give to the press. One was based on the possibility that Continuity IRA had succeeded in assassinating Ashton, while the other envisaged that he had survived the attempt. The IRA was not mentioned in either version; in the blink of an eye a hitherto unknown Provo sniper had become a drugs baron. In Francesca's opinion the really clever part was the fact that Section 'A' was actively engaged in waging war against the international drugs cartels and Richard had been able to make use of their intelligence data for authenticity.

Francesca ran into the underground station and rode the escalator down to the Central Line in time to catch a west-bound train to Ealing Broadway. What she was about to do could land her in serious trouble if her assumption was shown to be false. She had a pretty nasty feeling that, had she consulted Richard Neagle, he would have warned her off but he had been too busy to see her. It had been Ashton who had planted the idea in her head with his theory that a 'paper keeper' with unlimited access would be a prize acquisition by a hostile intelligence service, but that was no excuse for what she had done. Once Harvey Littlewood had agreed to stay at his office, she had phoned Barney, the detective sergeant in charge of the surveillance team covering Candlewick House, and had told him to leave his report with the chief clerk. Then she had walked out of the office carrying a number of classified ID documents in her handbag, which, of course, was a gross breach of security.

At Notting Hill Gate she changed to the District Line. High Street Kensington, Earls Court, West Kensington, Barons Court; the enormity of what she was doing became more and more evident with every stop down the line. By the time Francesca alighted from the train at Hammersmith nervous tension had reduced her to a quivering jelly. Her every instinct was to turn tail and run but somehow she made it to the branch office of Mitchell and Webb in Blacks Road.

'It's very good of you to wait for me, Mr Littlewood,' she told the estate agent, 'and I promise not to detain you a moment longer than necessary.'

'Please don't hurry on my account,' Littlewood said. 'My wife and I have nothing planned for this evening.'

Francesca nodded, opened her handbag, and took out four plastic identity cards, which were otherwise blank except for the name of the holder and a passport-size photograph.

'Well, I wonder if you would mind looking at these,' she said and passed the cards one by one across the desk to Littlewood.

It was the fourth and last card which drew a low whistle from the estate agent.

'That's Simon Carmichael,' he said, 'but it seems his real name is Donald Simon.' Littlewood smiled. 'One of yours, is he?'

There was no way Francesca was going to answer that question.

20

There was no red carpet treatment for Ashton when he walked into Vauxhall Cross on Monday morning. Instead he was stopped by a Ministry of Defence police officer who was new to the job and didn't know him from Adam. He couldn't find Ashton's name on the list of approved visitors furnished by the Administrative Wing and wouldn't believe Ashton was there at the behest of the DG, who had phoned him on Friday evening. The only reason he wasn't escorted to the door was due to the timely intervention of the formidable Edith Sly, who happened to be in charge of the reception desk that morning. One phone call to the people on the top floor and a very pink-faced PA arrived to collect Ashton.

Hazelwood was looking pleased with himself, as if, having ignored the advice of his broker, he had made a small killing on the stock market.

'Good to see you again, Peter,' he said, and waved Ashton to a chair. 'How is Harriet?'

'She's fine.'

'Happy about the house?'

Hazelwood was tiptoeing round the issue. He really wanted to know how Harriet had reacted when told the property at Bosham belonged to Jill Sheridan's parents.

'She would like to buy the house if we could afford it and the Sheridans were willing to sell.'

It was the unadulterated truth. Harriet had fallen in love with the house at first sight and if Hazelwood was surprised to hear him say that, his astonishment was nothing compared to Ashton's. He had expected all kinds of objections when he had told her about the offer on Friday evening after Victor had telephoned him.

'Good.' Hazelwood opened the cigar box on his desk and took out a Burma cheroot. 'Good, very good,' he repeated.

'I thought you'd be pleased.'

'Then there's no problem about flying to Washington tomorrow morning?'

'You are taking too much for granted,' Ashton told him. 'Thursday is the earliest — '

'That's not acceptable. We're losing a day as it is. In four hours from now, the Friends will start to interrogate Pavel Trilisser and we'll be at a disadvantage.'

'Not for long. The Friends will video the interrogation from start to finish and the end result will be better than any polygraph. The camera will capture every response and if Trilisser so much as blinks an eye, I can freeze-frame his reaction and look at it again and again.'

'Wednesday then,' Hazelwood said, as if they were making a deal.

'How long do you see the interrogation lasting?'

'Three weeks.' Hazelwood struck a match and finally lit the cheroot. 'A month at the outside,' he added.

It was on record that in the 1960s the CIA had spent months on end questioning relatively minor KGB defectors like Anatoli Golitsyn and Yuri Nosenko.

In Nosenko's case a very hostile interrogation had lasted four years but there had been strong reasons for believing he was a plant whose mission was to protect a highly placed source within the CIA, codenamed Sasha. However, compared with Pavel Trilisser both men were virtually nonentities.

'I think you are being unduly optimistic,' Ashton said, and left it at that.

'Do I take it you are prepared to leave the day after tomorrow?'

'What's in it for me, Victor? Am I simply a contract player or am I back on the team?'

'You're being reinstated,' Hazelwood said, and flicked ash into the brass shell case.

'In what capacity?'

'As Head of Station, Washington DC.'

Ashton blinked. 'Would you mind saying that again?' he asked, unable to believe his ears.

'The Deputy's post is already vacant.'

'Suddenly I've been demoted to Deputy Head of Station.'

'Look on it as a stepping stone to greater things,' Hazelwood said, unruffled. 'Miles Delacombe is due to be relieved on the fifteenth of November.'

Miles Delacombe had been running the show in Washington for as long as Ashton could remember. He was said to have a safe pair of hands, which meant he had never been known to commit a *faux pas*. It also meant that Miles Delacombe had rarely contributed anything of real value to the SIS.

'Due to be relieved,' Ashton said thoughtfully. 'Nothing is definite then?'

'Delacombe would like yet another year in the post but he won't get it.'

Ashton couldn't see why not when he recalled how highly Delacombe was regarded by the Ambassador. Hazelwood could huff and puff until he was blue in the face but when push came to shove, it was the Foreign and Commonwealth. Office which had the last word on staffing the embassy. There was one other factor which Hazelwood hadn't taken into account: Delacombe would never accept Ashton as his number two and his objection would be supported by the Ambassador. Hell, the Ambassador was the least of their problems; if there was one Englishman the FBI and the US Treasury's Secret Service didn't want to become reacquainted with in a hurry, it was Ashton.

'What about the State Department, Victor? Will they welcome me as a long-term guest in the US of A?'

'You've lost me,' Hazelwood said, his face blank.

'Twenty-one months ago the FBI and the Secret Service were all in favour of hanging me up by the balls. I wasn't too popular with the Richmond Police Department either.'

The local police remembered him as the man who had torched a two-million-dollar property on Nine Mile Road outside Richmond, Virginia, and destroyed three automobiles, the most expensive of which had still belonged to a finance company. He had also been responsible, directly or indirectly, for three fatalities.

'That's all water under the bridge now,' Hazelwood told him airily.

'Not as far as Miles Delacombe is concerned. As I recall he made it clear that he never wanted to see me on his patch again. According to him, the State Department had made its displeasure known to the Ambassador on what they regarded as an unwarranted and unacceptable interference in the internal affairs of the United States.'

'Forget Delacombe, he'll bend with the wind.'

'Well, let's hope it's blowing my way.'

'The State Department won't blacklist you,' Hazelwood continued remorselessly. 'Their attitude changed dramatically once the Secretary of State was made aware of the true facts. Three of our intelligence officers had been murdered at the safe house outside Naburn. When we started to look for their killers we weren't to know how it would end. The Friends accepted that.'

'I'm pleased to hear it,' Ashton said laconically.

'So what about it, Peter? Shall I tell the Friends at Langley to expect you on Wednesday?'

'I'm not going to pick a fight over twenty-four hours but I want an open-ended return ticket.'

'Tell Roy Kelso to fix it.'

'It might be better coming from you.'

Hazelwood crushed the cheroot in the brass shell case, wasting more than half the cigar. 'I'll give you a chit,' he said acidly.

'And I'll give it three weeks, until the twenty-first of August,' Ashton told him quietly. 'Then I'm coming home.'

'You're doing what?'

'Coming home. Jill's parents want their house back at the beginning of September, which means we have to move out and find somewhere else to live. I'm not landing Harriet with that job.'

'I assume Harriet would be happy to join you in Washington?'

'I can practically guarantee it.'

'Well then, what's your problem, Peter? Roy Kelso can provide all the assistance Harriet needs to pack up and leave.'

Hazelwood was just being Hazelwood, confident in his ability to make things happen and get what he wanted. It had been his hallmark right from the time when he had been the grade I intelligence officer in charge of the Russian Desk, but he had made a lot of enemies in Whitehall on the way up the ladder. Ashton had heard on the grapevine that it had only been with the greatest reluctance that Victor had been confirmed in the appointment of Director General by the Permanent Under Secretary of State at the FCO. Victor would undoubtedly do the best he could for him but chances were, he would be labouring in vain.

'Are you satisfied with the arrangement?' Hazelwood asked in a tone which suggested he had been expecting to receive some sign of approval from Ashton.

'Sounds OK to me,' Ashton told him in a

noncommittal voice.

'Good. You'll find Chris Neighbour waiting in the PA's office. He'll take you down to the reading room we've set aside.'

'There is just one thing more, Victor. If I'm really back in the fold, could someone please inform MI5 a.s.a.p.?'

'Yes, of course. Do you have some unfinished business with them?'

'Yeah. I want to know if they have any news on the present whereabouts of Barry Hayes.'

* * *

Francesca York had taken up smoking again. She had resumed the habit on Saturday morning when the full enormity of what she had done in showing Harvey Littlewood four identity cards had really sunk in. Francesca had lost count of the number of times over the weekend she had lifted the receiver to call Richard Neagle at his home, only to funk it at the last moment. There was, however, no dodging the issue on Monday morning; Donald Simon was actively supporting Continuity IRA and could not be allowed to remain in place no matter what harm it might do to her career. Barely five minutes after Richard Neagle had arrived at the Gower Street headquarters she had walked into his office and told him the whole story.

Although Vesuvius hadn't erupted, Neagle had given her a dressing-down the like of which she had never received before. As far as he was concerned, in taking four confidential documents out of the building and showing them to an unauthorised person, she had committed a gross breach of security. Stupid, reckless, irresponsible, immature, naïve were just a few of the adjectives he had used before sending her away to consider her position, which was another way of saying she should submit her resignation. Until Neagle had said he would deal with Donald Simon, Francesca had begun to wonder if the clerical officer hadn't been working under his direction. Then common sense had prevailed and she had dismissed the thought as ridiculous.

Francesca looked at the packet of Benson and Hedges Silk Cut on her desk. She had picked a fine time to start smoking again when it had been banned in the workplace for health and safety reasons. There were even no smoking signs on every door in the ladies room; anybody who wanted a quick drag had to go outside and use the courtyard behind the building, or hang on for a lunch break. She glanced at her wristwatch, saw that it was almost eleven-thirty and told herself she could hold out for another ninety minutes.

Knowing time would pass a lot quicker if she got on with her work, Francesca plucked a file from the stack the chief clerk had put in the in-tray earlier that morning. Then the telephone rang, breaking what, for her, had been a long and stressful silence. Lifting the receiver she gave the number of her extension.

'My office now, please,' Neagle said, and hung up before Francesca could reply. There was no welcoming smile from Richard when she entered his office. A presentiment that she was about to experience a continuation of their earlier and largely one-sided conversation was proved false when he suddenly announced that Ashton had had all his security clearances restored.

'You mean I don't have to hang up should he call me?'

'Has he called you?'

'Only the once and that was the day the ban was imposed,' Francesca said, colouring.

'What did he want?'

'I don't know. I put the phone down as soon as Ashton identified himself.'

It was a blatant lie but Francesca wasn't about to give him yet another reason for demanding her resignation.

'You did the right thing.'

'If you say so.'

'I'm referring to Donald Simon,' Neagle told her. 'Of course you should have asked Special Branch to provide an artist or a photofit expert with the requisite security clearance. You could then have shown the finished likeness to Harvey Littlewood and there would have been no necessity to borrow those four duplicate identity cards.'

'I'm sorry.'

'Well, let's hope you've learned your lesson.'

Francesca didn't know what to say. At the very least she had expected to receive a severe official reprimand in writing which would have been lodged in her personal file for ever and a day. Now it seemed she had been reprieved.

'Donald Simon was arrested at nine-thirty this morning and taken to Paddington Green police station, where he was put in a line-up and immediately picked out by Harvey Littlewood.'

'What did he have to say for himself?' Francesca asked.

'Quite a lot. Simon denied going anywhere near Rylett Close on the seventeenth of July, the day he didn't come into the office. He also claimed it was obviously a case of mistaken identity and demanded to see his solicitor.'

'Not Lionel Jebens.'

'No. Even if Simon knew him, he's too smart for that.' Neagle picked up the plastic ruler on the desk and flexed it between his hands. 'Simon is going to be a tough nut to crack.'

'I don't understand.'

'The fire started just over two hours after he and this woman called Julie Carmichael left 84 Rylett Close.'

'If nothing else, surely the police can charge him with arson?'

'Forensic can't tie him to the fire. All we've got is circumstantial evidence. Since the kitchen was largely destroyed by the initial explosion, a clever lawyer will argue that somebody else broke into the house and put the bomb in place after he had left. There's one other problem. The description which Littlewood originally gave to the police is not a good resemblance. Matter of fact he reckons he wouldn't have been able to make such a positive ID if he hadn't seen Simon's identity card. One thing he won't do is to testify on oath that he picked Simon out from the photofit. That could make life difficult for the prosecution.'

Francesca knew what he meant. If Littlewood insisted on sticking to the absolute truth, the defence would claim the witness had been primed and his evidence would be ruled inadmissible.

'Whatever happens we will end up with egg on our faces,' Neagle said gloomily.

The newspapers would have a field day. Francesca could see the banner headlines now — 'IRA MOLE INSIDE MI5', 'MI5 AN OPEN DOOR FOR IRA,' 'WHAT PRICE SECURITY NOW?' 'SPY CATCHERS CAUGHT NAPPING'.

'We're not about to let him go, are we, Richard?'

Neagle shrugged. 'We can hold him for the normal three days. If we can't break him before then or come up with fresh evidence, we don't have much choice. We'll fire him, of course.'

'I should hope so.'

'Little bastard will probably sue us for wrongful dismissal.'

Fresh evidence? Francesca sucked in her bottom lip and nibbled at it. 'Dr Julie Pearce,' she said presently. 'From the description we've got from Nottinghamshire Constabulary she could be the mysterious Julie Carmichael.'

'Except the good doctor has red hair and hazel-coloured eyes.'

'What if she was wearing a wig and contact lenses?'

'Where is this leading, Fran?'

'Suppose we kitted Julie up, gave her a wig of dark, shoulder-length hair and contact lenses in the right shade of blue, then put her in a line-up? I bet Littlewood would pick her out before you could blink.'

'And her lawyer would claim she had been made up to resemble Julie Carmichael.'

'It won't come to that, Richard. From what I hear, Julie Pearce is one frightened rabbit who has been only too eager to tell the police what she knows about the late George Foley. Soon as Littlewood taps her on the shoulder she will blow the whistle on Simon. Then we can really go to town on him.'

There was a lengthy silence while Neagle mulled it over, then a pleased smile appeared on his face. 'You're a clever girl, Fran,' he said. 'Leave it with me, I'll arrange for Pearce to be conveyed to London under escort.'

Francesca had hoped she might be given the job but that was only a minor disappointment. The important thing was the knowledge that no official action would be taken against her for the breach of security she had committed. The feel-good factor was short-lived; it rapidly vanished and was replaced by a panic attack when she discovered that contrary to standing orders she had left the office wide open and failed to lock the files away before going to see Richard Neagle. If the building security officer had been on the prowl, she could definitely have waved her career goodbye.

★   ★   ★

353

The quality of the coffee dispensed by the vending machines in Vauxhall Cross had not improved one iota during Ashton's absence. The liquid could still pass for tea and lacked any kind of aroma. However, the polystyrene cup of coffee had been provided by Chris Neighbour and Ashton reckoned it would have seemed churlish to leave it untouched while he perused the file on Pavel Trilisser which the Russian Desk had put together for his benefit.

Prior to Gorbachev's rise to power little had been known about Pavel Trilisser other than the fact that at one time he had been the youngest Deputy Head of the KGB's First Chief Directorate. Thereafter unsubstantiated accounts of his involvement in the attempted coups against Gorbachev in '91 and Yeltsin in '93 had been rife. Analysts on both shores of the Atlantic couldn't understand how he had survived when it had been patently obvious that he had only changed sides at the last minute. When he had been the grade I intelligence officer in charge of the Russian Desk, Rowan Garfield had written a paper, discussing the possibility that Trilisser had been an *agent provocateur*. He had returned to the theme in '93 after Vice President Rutskoi had attempted to overthrow Boris Yeltsin. Ashton hadn't seen either paper before and while he didn't subscribe to the hypothesis he thought it conceivable the former KGB General had somehow convinced Yeltsin this was the case. If true, it would explain why Yeltsin had appointed him to be his special advisor on foreign affairs.

For the past two years little had been heard of Pavel Trilisser. Nobody knew precisely when he had been sacked from the post and why, mainly because it had proved impossible to determine what advice he'd given Yeltsin while in the Kremlin. In January Head of Station, Moscow had learned that he was under house arrest and would shortly be tried for embezzling twelve million dollars from the Kremlin domestic budget. Two months later it appeared Trilisser was no longer under house arrest even though he had been indicted. In the absence of any worthwhile information the analysts had been reduced to pure speculation. The fact that Trilisser had subsequently defected after Vladislov Kochelev, the government auditor and key witness, had been murdered had proved equally inexplicable. Of all the rumours floating around Moscow, Trilisser's defection to obtain the best possible medical treatment for a brain tumour had been the most widespread.

The Americans had been aware of the rumour long before he had presented himself at their embassy in Tallinn six days ago. By now, Ashton believed, they would have had the results of the brain scan they would surely have given him. Closing the file, Ashton walked it down the corridor to Chris Neighbour.

'All finished, Peter?' Neighbour asked, looking up as Ashton entered his office.

'Well, let's say I've read the file from cover to cover. Doesn't make me any the wiser, though. All my instincts tell me he has got to be up to something but just what is beyond me.'

'Mr Reid has an interesting theory,' Neighbour said diffidently.

Ashton nodded. Winston Reid, the new Assistant Director in charge of the Mid East Department, had already been to see him and had indicated what he thought might be the purpose behind Trilisser's defection. Shortly after Reid had departed, Jill Sheridan had sought Ashton out to rubbish everything her successor had told him.

'Do you mind if I use your phone?' Ashton said, changing the subject. 'There's no Mozart facility in the reading room.'

'Be my guest. I'll give you some space.'

'You don't have to leave,' Ashton told him.

He lifted the receiver, rang Gower Street and managed to catch Francesca York before she went out to buy herself a sandwich for lunch.

'What can I do for you?' she asked after they had switched to secure.

'Eleven days ago I asked you if Barry Hayes was back in this country and you told me he wasn't.'

'I'm not likely to forget that particular conversation in a hurry.'

'Well, now I'd like to know where he is.'

'Southern Ireland,' Francesca told him promptly. 'I asked 10 Int Company for an update forty-eight hours later.'

'Do we have a more precise location?'

'El Paso.'

El Paso was the nickname for the border town

of Dundalk, the IRA's favourite watering hole and safe haven.

'How good is the source?'

'Charlie three,' Fran said.

That meant the source was fairly reliable and the information was possibly true.

'Can we ask the Garda for a definite sighting? I don't see how Dublin could object if they are serious about turning a truce into a peace process.'

'You could be right, Peter, but I can't do anything at my level.'

'That's understood. I'll channel the request through our Director General.'

'You don't have to worry about Barry Hayes any more,' Francesca announced suddenly. 'He'll never find you again.'

'How do you know?'

'Trust me, I know what I'm talking about,' Francesca said, and put the phone down.

★ ★ ★

The Irish pub in Chicago was just round the corner from the Palmer House Hilton on East Monroe Street. At twelve noon Eastern Standard Time, the American Barry Hayes knew as Daley the Bagman joined him in the booth nearest the entrance.

'You catch CNN this morning?' he asked.

Hayes shook his head. 'I never watch CNN.'

'They were doing a feature on the drugs problem facing the Brits. Seems there was a shoot-out in Lincoln on Friday, and a drugs

357

baron called George Foley got himself shot to death. Would this be the same guy we've been bankrolling?'

'You know it is, otherwise you wouldn't be here. But I tell you this, George never handled the stuff.'

Daley reached inside his jacket, took out a white envelope and pushed it across the table at Hayes. 'We're expecting the Feebies to come down on us fund-raisers . . . '

'Feebies?'

'FBI. Washington is trying to broker a deal between the Nationalists and the Ulster Unionists and they want to appear even-handed.'

'Are you dumping me?'

'No way. We just want you to cover your tracks for a while. There's a lot of Irish in this city to attract the Feebies.'

'Where do you expect me to go?' Hayes demanded.

'Louisville, Kentucky. You're expected. The man has arranged a bar-tending job for you at Mickey's near the Seelbeach Hotel. There's plenty of money in that envelope for the air fare and expenses.'

Hayes reached across the table and grabbed Daley by the wrist as he was about to get up. 'Listen to me,' he said angrily, 'I've already lost a brother and it was my cousin who was shot to death.'

'Yeah, we appreciate that and you'll be the first to know if we hear anything. Now, let go of my wrist and back off while you can still walk away.'

21

The man appointed to look after Ashton while he was on detached duty in the States was Carl Bucholtz, the Assistant Chief of Station, Tallinn, to whom Pavel Trilisser had surrendered himself. The American had met Ashton at Dulles International when he had arrived on British Airways flight BA217 on Wednesday afternoon, and had waltzed him through Immigration. He had then relieved Ashton of his baggage and handed it to a driver with instructions to deliver the suitcase to 252 Cameron Mills Road.

Located in the centre of Alexandria, roughly seven and a half miles from the White House, 252 Cameron Mills Road was a neo-colonial house which the CIA had purchased in the early sixties before real estate prices in the neighbourhood had gone through the roof. It was used to accommodate up to five official visitors such as Ashton, and was more than adequately staffed with a live-in cook, house-keeper, valet, general handyman and a daily cleaner. As the sole guest, Ashton had only to appear outside his room for a member of staff to ask if there was anything they could do for him.

Ashton had anticipated that the rest of Wednesday would be spent meeting people and getting to know his way around Langley. He could not have been more wrong. The only people Ashton had met that first afternoon had been members of the household staff. According to the programme which Bucholtz had left in his room, Wednesday had been deliberately blocked out to enable him to settle in.

The following morning more time had been set aside for Ashton to touch his forelock to Head of Chancery, and Miles Delacombe, the SIS Head of Station in Washington, who had calmly informed him he was about to be extended in post for a further twelve months. At eleven-thirty Ashton had been picked up from the embassy and conveyed to Langley where he had been welcomed by the Deputy Director for Operations. The welcome had also included a lecture on the organisation of the department and the role of its component parts, which embraced HUMINT Requirements, Counter-Terrorism, Military Affairs, Counter-Intelligence and Counter-Narcotics. After lunch in the staff cafeteria, Bucholtz had wheeled him into the office of the Deputy Director for Intelligence and another lecture.

Finally, the day had ended with a presentation by Nathan Zukor, the case officer directing the interrogation of Pavel Trilisser. His team consisted of six first-class interpreters in Russian, two analysts from the Central Eurasian Section, and a roster of liaison officers from the Intelligence Department, which was responsible for providing the President with a daily briefing. Roy Kelso's equivalent in the CIA had provided a team of stenographers and typists with the requisite security clearances whose task was to produce a complete transcript of each session the interrogators had with Pavel Trilisser. As Zukor had pointed out, this enabled the analysts to select what they considered were the most significant passages in the interrogation and then compare the written text with the video cassette recording.

However, although the presentation had been very informative, Ashton had left the agency that evening with no idea where Pavel Trilisser was being held. He had raised the question several times but somehow Nathan Zukor had managed to avoid answering it directly. As a result Ashton had come away with the impression that the case officer was determined to keep him away from the Russian for at least the time being. Why Zukor should want to do this and what he hoped to gain was something Ashton meant to discover a.s.a.p.

Yesterday Ashton had been collected from the British Embassy on Massachusetts Avenue; today Bucholtz picked him up from the house on Cameron Mills Road. On arrival at Langley he was conducted to an office which had been set aside for his use. The furniture was pretty basic — a steel desk, swivel chair, pedestal-mounted TV screen, a video cassette recorder, remote control, and a library cart stacked with ring binder files and cassettes.

'Transcripts of days one to eight inclusive,' Bucholtz said, pointing to the ring binders on the cart. 'Twenty-four volumes in all, same number of cassettes on the bottom shelf.'

'That's going to keep me busy.'

'I guess it is. Can I get you a cup of coffee or something?'

'No thanks.'

'OK, I'll collect you at twelve noon for lunch.'

'Don't go just yet, Carl,' Ashton said. 'There are things I need to know.'

'Yeah? Well, I'll be happy to help you any way I can. But I'm afraid you'll be asking the wrong man if your questions have anything to do with the interrogation. My Russian is only so-so and I'm not on the team. Never have been, never will be.'

Ashton thought he detected a note of bitterness and mentally filed it away. Injured pride was a weakness he could exploit should the need ever arise.

'I'd like to hear what happened in Tallinn. For instance, what did Trilisser say when he walked into your office?'

'He said he was going to make me famous.'

'And he did.' Ashton was prepared to wager few people even in the CIA had heard of Carl Bucholtz before Trilisser came across.

'You could fool me,' Bucholtz said acerbically.

'Did he tell you why he was defecting?'

'He surely did and it was a pack of lies. Trilisser claimed he had a brain tumour and the authorities were doing their level best to ensure it proved fatal by denying him the treatment he needed. First thing we did was send him out of town for the specialists at the John Hopkins Hospital in Baltimore to look him over. They gave the son of a bitch a clean bill of health.'

'Who in the government wanted him dead?'

'A gang of four — the Ministers of Economic Development, Finance, State Security and Foreign Affairs. According to Trilisser, Sholokhov, the Finance Minister and President of the Union Bank of Moscow, was the man who siphoned fifteen million dollars off from the Kremlin domestic budget and set him up for it.'

Pavel Trilisser had had the ear of Yeltsin and had warned the President that his principal ministers were planning to split up the state-owned oil and gas companies and sell them off to the highest bidder. Consequently, the gang of four had been determined to oust him from the Kremlin. 'Nobody here attached much credence to that story even before he was sent to Baltimore,' Bucholtz continued. 'Afterwards I guess they didn't believe a word.'

'You guess? You mean you don't know?'

'Like I said, I'm not on the team.'

Ashton pointed to the library cart. 'But you've read those transcripts and seen the videos.'

'First time I saw them was this morning just before I left to collect you.'

Ashton wanted to ask him why he had been excluded but judged this wasn't the right moment to do so. That question would have to remain in abeyance until he had got to know Bucholtz a lot better.

'Well, thank you, Carl,' he said. 'You've been very helpful.'

'You're welcome. See you at noon.'

'Sure thing.'

Ashton waited until the American had left the office before he removed volume one and the relevant video cassette from the cart. Opening the ring binder he discovered the first session had started after the Russian had been examined at the John Hopkins in Baltimore. Challenged to explain why he had lied about his health, Trilisser had told Zukor that he had believed the CIA would recover him a lot quicker if they thought he was close to death. Ashton inserted the cassette into the VCR and set the tape running. Watching him on the TV screen and listening to the sound of his voice, Trilisser was a damned sight too confident for his liking.

★ ★ ★

Until two o'clock Francesca York had had a warm, elated feeling that all was right in her world. Anxious to save her own skin, Julie Pearce had picked out Donald Simon in a lineup and had made a full statement implicating the clerical officer. He in turn had given Special Branch the telephone number of his contact, which had led the police straight to the house in Priory Road, Walthamstow, rented by Lionel Jebens. As a result, Richard Neagle had complimented her on the initiative she had shown, which was high praise coming from him.

The champagne effect suddenly vanished when she returned from lunch and the chief clerk dropped by her office to place a classified fax on top of the files in her in-tray. The signal had been originated by the Northern Ireland Office and was addressed to the Secretary of State, the Home Office, with a copy to the FCO.

Beneath the text, the DG had written in green ink: 'Irish Section. What is this all about?' Not to be outdone Richard Neagle had penned an even briefer note in red ink. It read: '10 III please speak.' The subject matter concerned the present whereabouts of Barry Hayes.

Five days ago Ashton had asked her for a definite sighting report and she had told him he didn't have to worry about the IRA man any more. According to the latest update from 10 Int. Company Hayes was still in Dundalk where he had been skulking since the beginning of February. She had been led to believe that should he merely have a few jars in his local, 10 Int. Company would hear all about it the following afternoon. Now the Garda were saying he'd last been seen on Friday, 28 June when a man answering his description had boarded an Aer Lingus flight for Chicago. He was thought to be travelling on an American passport under an assumed name.

Francesca looked at the message in red ink again. It was, she thought, not at all friendly. She was used to receiving notes which began with her first name. This one was addressed to the Intelligence Officer, Grade III, which was about as cold and impersonal as you could get. The signal from the Northern Ireland Office had clearly displeased the DG and Neagle appeared to hold her responsible, which was ridiculous because she hadn't done anything wrong. Clutching the signal, Francesca left the office, locked the door behind her and marched in to see Neagle.

'You asked me to speak about this,' she said, and waved the fax at him. 'Before I do, I'd like to know what I'm supposed to have done.'

'I would have thought that was obvious,' Neagle told her icily.

'I didn't signal the Northern Ireland Office, if that's what all this is about. Ashton rang me and asked for a sighting report shortly after you'd told me he had been reinstated. I told him I didn't have the necessary authority and his request would have to be sanctioned at the highest level. Ashton then said he would take the matter up with his DG and that was the last I heard about it.'

'Whoever signalled the Northern Ireland Office did not consult K,' Neagle said.

'Well, don't look at me, Richard. I didn't keep our Director in the dark.'

'The whole thing smacks of Hazelwood; he's never been one to bother with the niceties.' Neagle frowned. 'Or his deputy, Jill Sheridan,' he added. 'I hear she has friends in high places.'

'Am I off the hook now?'

'Did Ashton tell you why he wanted to know the present whereabouts of Barry Hayes?'

'No. But then he didn't have to. He had killed Kevin Hayes in self-defence but elder brother, Barry, wouldn't accept the verdict and sent his cousin George Foley after him. Now Foley is dead and while his death was not attributed to Ashton by the media, Hayes will assume he killed his cousin. Hayes and his family have been waging a vendetta against Ashton for the last four months; he obviously thinks it will continue.'

Their hatred was both fanatical and suicidal — Foley had demonstrated that. Even the most dedicated gunman in the Provisional IRA would have backed off when they saw how well protected Ashton was. But not Foley; he'd gone in there blazing away with an Uzi. That took a special kind of madness.

'I hear what you are saying, Fran, and fortunately Ashton is now in America where he can't do any harm or come to any harm.'

'Do any harm?' Francesca echoed. 'What are you inferring, Richard?'

'You know my opinion of Ashton. He's a loose cannon and ruthless enough to play dirty if he feels threatened. Oh, I'm not saying he would be stupid enough to take out Hayes himself but I fancy he would have no hesitation in passing on his address to a Protestant terrorist group like the Ulster Freedom Fighters.'

'I don't believe I'm hearing this.'

'Don't take it to heart, Fran. I was merely airing a possibility which has been overtaken by events.'

'So what are we doing about this fax?'

'Leave it with me. I'll explain the situation to the Director.'

'You've misunderstood me,' Francesca said in a brittle voice. 'Are we going to pass the information on?'

'It's not our responsibility.'

Francesca didn't know how he could say that. If they had done their job properly they might have discovered that Donald Simon was passing information to the IRA a whole lot sooner. They owed Ashton and she said so loud and clear.

'Look at the signal again,' Neagle told her curtly. 'The FCO is an information addressee. Since they exercise control over the SIS, it's their job to advise Hazelwood, assuming he doesn't already know.'

★ ★ ★

The tapes and transcripts showed that the debriefing of Pavel Trilisser was being conducted on classical lines. Nathan Zukor and his team had begun by asking the Russian a number of questions to which in varying degrees they already knew some of the answers. In theory the technique was a means of assessing the value of the defector. In Trilisser's case this was irrelevant. When Deputy Head of the KGB's First Chief Directorate he'd had unlimited access. Furthermore the subject matter which Zukor had raised in the first two sessions fell into the category of ancient history and there had been no reason for Trilisser to lie. The main interest was to see if he had any reservations about embarrassing his fellow countrymen. The B47 incident showed he had no compunction about that.

In 1954 a B47 returning from a reconnaissance mission over T'bilisi in Georgia was intercepted and shot down over Batum, barely two minutes' flying time before entering Turkish airspace. All five crew members were reported killed. Now, according to the transcript, Trilisser was saying the captain and co-pilot had ejected. Feeding the appropriate cassette into the VCR Ashton ran it fast forward until he located the passage where Nathan Zukor had asked the Russian to repeat his claim.

'I'm afraid the co-pilot didn't survive,' Trilisser said calmly. 'His ejection seat evidently malfunctioned in some way and he sustained fatal head injuries as he exited from the plane. The captain was more fortunate . . . '

'What was his name?' demanded one of the interrogators who was out of camera shot.

'Lieutenant Paul M. Vanderhoyt. I'm afraid I've forgotten his serial number but I do remember his home town was Augusta, Georgia. At least that's what I read in the clipping from the *Augusta Chronicle*, which had been included in his KGB file.'

Ashton pressed the freeze-frame and studied the Russian close up. There was a faint smirk on Trilisser's lips which told Ashton he had enjoyed stamping on the unidentified interrogator. Releasing the freeze-frame, Ashton caught the flash of anger in Zukor's eyes as he glared at his subordinate while asking Trilisser to continue.

'Lieutenant Vanderhoyt landed heavily, breaking his left femur, and he was arrested by border guards of the KGB's Ninth Directorate within an hour or so. He was stripped of everything which would identify him as an officer in the USAF and was flown to Moscow where he was held in the psychiatric wing of Lefortovo Prison. After he was shown the report of his death, which had appeared in the *Augusta Chronicle*, the lieutenant became extremely co-operative. He told us a great deal about the type of radar equipment on the B47 and the defensive capabilities of their electronic countermeasures.' Trilisser broke off, his lips pursed as if considering some unforeseen problem. 'You shouldn't blame Vanderhoyt,' he went on presently. 'He was, after all, trying to save his life.'

'And did he succeed?' Zukor asked venomously.

'Up to a point. After he had been sucked dry, Vanderhoyt was sent to the Cheryabusk labour camp in the Urals where he supposedly committed suicide in November 1979.'

'Supposedly?'

'He was found hanging from one of the rafters in the latrine block, but the strut was over three metres above the ground and he would have needed a step ladder to get up there. There was a women's camp on the other side of the perimeter fence and, at night, there was a lot of movement under the wire in both directions. The guards turned a blind eye on these nocturnal visits and a lot of close relationships were formed as a result. The maintenance of discipline within the camp was largely in the hands of the criminal fraternity. In his report the camp commandant stated it was more than likely Vanderhoyt had taken up with the wrong woman.'

'Meaning what?' Zukor asked.

'He'd stolen the woman belonging to the gangster in charge of the hut and he had decided to make an example of the American. He and his friends cut a strip from the blanket issued to Lieutenant Vanderhoyt and strangled him with it.'

Ashton stopped the tape, rewound it and ejected the cassette. What followed thereafter concerned incidents which had occurred during the Korean War and details of Soviet involvement in Vietnam from 1966 to 1975 which only the Americans could validate. However, when skim-reading the second volume, he had marked up two occurrences of particular interest to the UK which could perhaps be verified from service records. Selecting the related cassette, he loaded it into the VCR and played around with the tape until he found the section where Trilisser had mentioned a Sergeant Thomas Vincent from Hull.

Vincent had been a troop leader in the Recce Squadron of 1st Airborne Division. He had fought in Tunisia and Sicily with the division and had taken part in the seaborne landing at Taranto but his luck had run out at Arnhem where he had been wounded and taken prisoner. Following the amputation of his left hand, Vincent had spent thirteen days in an emergency hospital near the railway station in Arnhem.

On the night of Monday, 9 October 1944 he and 586 wounded prisoners of war had been loaded into wooden box cars for onward transportation to Germany. Shortly before the train crossed the border, Vincent managed to break off several of the rotten planks to make a hole large enough for him to squeeze through and jump off. Within twenty-four hours he had

371

made contact with the Dutch Resistance and had operated with one of their cells until they were betrayed and rounded up five months later.

There had been no prisoner of war camp for Sergeant Vincent; he had been handed over to the Gestapo who had torn out his fingernails in a fruitless attempt to make him betray every resistance fighter he'd met while in hiding. They had finally given up on Vincent and had sent him to Auschwitz-Birkenau, where he had been liberated by the Red Army. Then the NKGB, the forerunner of the KGB, had got their hands on him and sometime in January 1947 he had been executed in the cellars of the Lubyanka.

The way Trilisser told it Vincent's detention and subsequent death had been entirely due to the Nazis' love of documentation. All the papers pertaining to his interrogation had been handed over to the commandant of Auschwitz-Birkenau by the Gestapo, who had uprated Vincent, describing him as a British Secret Service agent trained in guerrilla warfare.

The case of Warrant Officer 'Bill' Gadney, RAF, was slightly different. A navigator bombardier, he had been the only survivor from the crew of a Lancaster bomber shot down over Poznan in 1943. His knowledge of 'OBOE', the most accurate radio bombing system produced by either side during World War II, had made him of special interest to the Luftwaffe. Although rigorously interrogated about OBOE by Luftwaffe Intelligence he had been treated humanely and had ended up in Stalag Luft 38 near Lodz, due west of Warsaw. Following the encirclement and liberation of Warsaw on 17 January 1945, Marshall Zukov's First White Russian Front had threatened Lodz. Three days after the prisoners of Stalag Luft 38 had set off on their long march to the west, they had been overtaken by a column of T-34 tanks belonging to the Fourth (Guards) Tank Army.

The former PoWs had had to wait until the war was over before they could be repatriated. Of the 1,723 prisoners who had set off from the camp, all but 18 returned to the UK. The majority of these eighteen, who had died by the roadside, had been seriously ill in the camp hospital before the march had started. Bill Gadney hadn't been sick. He had been as fit as the next man. He had simply disappeared without trace and the Russians had resolutely denied all knowledge of him. Now, facing the camera square on, Trilisser was saying that Gadney had suffered the same fate as Sergeant Vincent and had been shot when his usefulness had expired.

'You have to realise this was the normal practice when Stalin was alive,' Trilisser said calmly.

'That's one cold-hearted son of a bitch,' Zukor observed as he entered the room.

Ashton switched off the VCR and TV. 'Pavel Trilisser is not my favourite Russian, Mr Zukor.'

'It's Nathan,' the American told him.

'Right.'

'So do you believe what he told us in the first two sessions?'

'Yes I do.'

'Without any reservations?' Zukor asked smiling.

'Well, it wouldn't be me if I didn't have a few, Nathan. I keep reminding myself Trilisser was only eleven years old when the war ended and he hadn't come to our notice before the Moscow Olympics when he was nominally in charge of security at the village. I just don't think Trilisser would have had the time or the inclination to read ancient history when he was making his way up the ladder.'

'So what are you saying, Peter?'

'I think somebody must have spoon-fed him that information just before he defected.'

22

The diplomatic bag from the embassy in Washington arrived shortly after morning prayers had started which, in retrospect, Hazelwood thought was no bad thing. There were two letters for him, one from Ashton, the other from Miles Delacombe, the SIS Head of Station. Both concerned Pavel Trilisser and were politically sensitive. Technically the letters were of interest to Rowan Garfield but even had they arrived in time for the morning conference Hazelwood would have sat on them while he sought a second opinion. He read each letter again, then buzzed Jill Sheridan and asked her if she could spare him a few minutes.

He had felt more at ease with Jill's predecessor and had had no reservations about consulting him, but of course, brilliant interrogator though Clifford Peachey had been, the former MI5 man had not been riven with ambition. Ms Sheridan, however, made no secret of the fact that she was determined to become the first woman to head the SIS. Even though she made him feel uncomfortable, Hazelwood recognised that Jill had a far better brain than Clifford and was equally as shrewd. Political awareness was her greatest asset, thanks principally to Robin Urquhart. But she was not without other well-placed acquaintances who were sometimes indiscreet in her company. For all the years he had spent in Five the machinations of Whitehall had been a closed book to Clifford Peachey whereas Jill knew how the system worked and could find her way round it blindfolded. It was the reason why he wanted Jill to run her eye over both letters and let him know what she thought.

'In writing?' she asked smiling.

'Heaven forbid. Read the one from Peter first; it's succinct and a model of clarity.'

Jill sat down in one of the leather armchairs provided by the Property Services Agency. She was wearing a blue silk dress cut on simple, unfussy lines which Hazelwood realised must have set her back a bob or two but then she could afford it with her more-than-generous divorce settlement in lieu of maintenance.

'I think Peter is right to be suspicious,' Jill said, looking up from the letters. 'I doubt if Trilisser had unlimited access to KGB files while he was Yeltsin's special advisor on foreign affairs. So unless he had made up his mind to defect all those years ago when he was still the number two man in the First Chief Directorate, and started mugging up a few juicy titbits, I think he was spoon-fed those intriguing stories, but don't ask me why.'

'Do you think Peter was right to pass on his doubts to Nathan Zukor?'

'Yes, so long as he did it tactfully. The Americans haven't complained, have they?'

'No. However, Miles Delacombe feels it is only a question of time before they do.'

'I wouldn't pay any attention to what

Delacombe thinks, Victor. Furtherance of Anglo-American relations is his self-imposed mission in life. Miles is such a creep; he doesn't even give Nathan Zukor a chance to complain before he rushes to their defence.'

'What about the Ambassador?'

'Close as Miles likes to think he is to him, I bet you the Ambassador will want to dissociate himself from Delacombe's letter. I mean it's ridiculous of Delacombe to suggest we should recall Peter before he does any more harm. Zukor asked for his opinion of Pavel Trilisser and he expressed his reservations. It's as simple as that.'

'My feelings exactly.' Hazelwood opened the ornate cigar box on his desk and helped himself to a Burma cheroot, noting to his amusement the way Jill wrinkled her nose in disapproval as he lit it.

'Will that be all, Victor?' she asked, and half rose from the leather armchair.

'About Barry Hayes. The Northern Ireland Office were pretty stuffy about our enquiry, don't you think?'

Jill sank back into the chair. 'That's one way of looking at it, Victor. Personally I think they were merely adhering to the proper channels of communication in addressing their reply to our query to the Home Office. If anybody had their noses out of joint it was MI5.'

'You think?'

'I know,' Jill told him firmly. 'I had a roasting from Cavendish, my opposite number, on Friday morning.'

'You didn't say anything to me at the time.'

'No. It didn't seem important. Besides, Cavendish was almost eating out of my hand after I'd given him lunch.'

'Good girl.'

'Well, Cavendish is easy to handle once you get to know him.'

Hazelwood masked a smile. Handle? Manipulate would be a more accurate description.

'Could you persuade Cavendish to advise the FBI that Hayes entered the United States illegally on the twenty-eighth of June? I have, of course, signalled Ashton this morning, warning him about Hayes.'

'You want the FBI to go looking for him?' Jill said in a hollow voice as if unable to believe Hazelwood was serious.

'You don't think much of the idea?'

'No I don't. The information we have from the Garda is much too vague. Hayes is said to have travelled to Chicago on an American passport under an assumed name, which would give the FBI precious little to go on. Furthermore, by no stretch of the imagination could it be argued that Ashton is in danger when the IRA man isn't aware that he is in America and has no way of finding out. There's something else we should bear in mind,' Jill continued. 'Clinton is running for re-election this November and every President has always courted the Irish vote. A man like Barry Hayes could be looked on as a hero over there and the FBI will tread very warily.'

378

'I think you are overstating the Irish factor, Jill.'

'Fine. Let's look at the problem from a different angle. When Delacombe goes, you want Ashton to move into his chair as Head of Station. Correct?'

Jill didn't expect an answer and didn't wait for one. She had thought it wouldn't be necessary to remind Victor that Ashton was not the most popular man in town with an impressive number of law-enforcement agencies. Placing him was going to be difficult enough as it was without advertising the fact that he was an endangered species.

'If we suggest Peter is a moving target, the CIA, the National Security Agency and the Defence Intelligence Agency will have nothing to do with him and he can't function in a vacuum.'

'Has friend Cavendish a reasonably up-to-date photo of Barry Hayes?'

'You've not been listening to me, Victor,' Jill said, exasperated.

'Oh, but I have and I'm going to take your advice. I don't want Cavendish to mention Ashton when he contacts the FBI. All I want is for him to pass on the information we received from the Garda and fax the latest photograph in his possession. Where's the harm in that? I'm not asking for the moon.'

'What is Ashton expecting from the Americans?'

'Nothing.' Hazelwood sifted through his pending tray, found the actioned copy of the signal which the Communications Section had returned to him and passed it to Jill Sheridan. 'I'm sorry,' he said, 'I should have marked this up for your information.'

The signal was prefaced 'PERSONAL FOR ASHTON' and was headed 'Sighting Report'. It read: 'Reference your query. Subject is believed now residing Chicago.'

'I think you will agree there's nothing in the signal to excite either the Ambassador or Delacombe.'

'You're right, there isn't,' Jill said, and returned the signal. 'All the same I believe Cavendish will be extremely reluctant to meet the request.'

It was a matter of international politics. The Government wanted President Clinton to act as an honest broker between Sinn Fein and the Ulster Unionists while winning the backing of the Irish Government. However, the whole initiative would collapse if the President was seen to be biased in favour of the British Government. Listening to Jill as she opined that any request which resulted in the deportation of Barry Hayes would be regarded as prejudiced, Hazelwood wondered if she was simply repeating the pearls of wisdom Urquhart had dropped when they were in bed together.

'Five is under tremendous pressure from the Northern Ireland Office, the Home Office and the FCO not to rock the boat.'

'Look, Jill, instead of sitting here playing will he, won't he, put the request to Cavendish and see what he has to say.'

'And if he turns us down?'

380

'Just remind him who destroyed Ashton's cover and forced him to run,' Hazelwood said grimly.

* * *

You could do a lot of reading over the weekend when you were alone in a city like Washington. Carl Bucholtz had wanted to show Ashton Jamestown and Williamsburg, maybe stay at the Inn, play a round of golf, do a little fishing — something like that. But Ashton had politely declined because he had set himself a deadline and come hell or high water, he was going home on Wednesday, 21 August. So they had settled for dinner on the Friday night at Chez Francoise on Connecticut Avenue North West, and Bucholtz hadn't been the least offended. In fact he had looked relieved, which was understandable because he'd turned up at Chez Francoise with a very attractive brunette in tow.

Saturday and Sunday had been like any other day of the week. A car had collected Ashton from the neo-colonial house on Cameron Mills Road at 8 a.m. and conveyed him to Langley where he'd spent the next ten hours locked away in the small office that had been set aside for his use. He had expected much the same routine this Monday and was surprised to find Nathan Zukor waiting for him outside the house at seven-thirty with a Cadillac De Ville.

'Thought we would give you a crack at Pavel Trilisser today,' he said, and opened the rear nearside door for Ashton.

'You mean as an observer?'

'No, I was planning to turn you loose.' Zukor closed the door on Ashton, walked round the back of the Cadillac and got in beside him, then told the driver to move off. 'It's crunch time for Comrade Pavel. Incidentally, I want you to call him Comrade General when you're face to face. The idea is to make him feel that we know he hasn't changed his goddamned spots. Up to now we've allowed him to set the agenda. Today we're going to talk about the twelve million dollars he is said to have misappropriated from the Kremlin domestic budget. I'll start the session with the primary team, which should lull Trilisser into a false sense of security. Our Russian friend thinks he's got the measure of my people.' A wolfish smile appeared on Zukor's mouth. 'He's going to have a nasty shock when you walk into the interrogation room.'

Ashton had no idea where the interrogation room was. He'd always assumed it was somewhere in the Langley complex but they were travelling in the wrong direction. The driver had taken them on to the Capital Beltway and was heading in an easterly direction. They were in fact crossing the Potomac on the Woodrow Wilson Memorial Bridge. A sign by the roadside indicated that Interchange 38 for the Anacostia Freeway was five hundred feet ahead.

'Where are you holding Trilisser?'

'We moved him on Saturday to a house not too far from Bryantown,' Zukor said.

Ashton smiled. 'I'm none the wiser,' he said.

'We stay on the Beltway until we come to the

interchange for US50 to Annapolis, then we cross the toll section over Chesapeake Bay and we're practically there.'

All told it was roughly forty-five miles from the interchange for Route 50. Zukor had planned on starting the first session at nine but there was a lot of traffic on the Beltway and there was absolutely no chance of them getting there on time. Tomorrow, he promised Ashton, they would start out at seven.

'I'm told you have unrivalled knowledge of this man Trilisser,' Zukor said, abruptly changing the subject.

'Who told you that?'

'It's the line your DG sold our Station Chief in London.'

'Victor's inclined to exaggerate,' Ashton said quietly, 'but, yes, I've crossed swords with Trilisser a few times. It hasn't always been face to face but I never had any doubts concerning who I was up against.'

'So let's see you set out your stall.'

'You want a few examples?'

'More than a few,' Zukor told him. 'And start at the beginning.'

'You'd have to go back to 1990 when the Red Army were pulling out of East Germany. Trilisser was the driving force behind TRIPWIRE, a very special type of minefield that involved the use of Atomic Demolition Munitions. Had the operation not been betrayed by an officer in Military Intelligence the ADMs would have been buried at irregular intervals across the whole of the Eastern Zone. In the event of hostilities the nuclear mines would be command-detonated by satellite. The aim was to create maximum fallout, each mine throwing a load of contaminated spoil over a wide area that would emit a lethal dose of four hundred rads an hour.'

A year later, at the height of the Serbo-Croat-Bosnia Herzegovina conflict he was master-minding ways and means of circumventing the oil embargo imposed on Serbia by the UN. He had also tap danced out of a tight corner after initially siding with the hard-line Communists who had tried their best to oust Gorbachev.

'This is all very well,' Zukor said, 'but what you're telling me is already on record. What I would like to know is where did you first meet him face to face?'

'Deep Shelter Four, a nuclear civil defence bunker on the outskirts of Moscow. That was in '93 when we thought we were running an 'insider' who called himself Valentin — '

'We?' Zukor said, interrupting him.

'Ourselves and the CIA. We were paying out good money for information; turned out our informer was Pavel Trilisser and he was using the cash to finance a private army to overthrow Yeltsin. Your guy was called Hal Reindekke.'

'Yeah, I've heard of him. He was killed in a car crash eleven months ago. Got hit head on by a drunk driver on the wrong side of the road.'

'I'm sorry to hear that,' Ashton said.

Zukor shrugged his shoulders. 'These things happen,' he said, and effortlessly resumed where he had left off, wanting chapter and verse on the

384

last occasion Ashton had encountered the Russian.

'Two years ago in Warsaw, the summer of '94. The Mafiozniki had sold a number of 13 omm artillery shells with nuclear warheads to a disparate group of Islamic fundamentalists and we wanted the Russians to do something about it.'

'And did they?'

'Well, it turned out to be a one-off deal but I doubt Trilisser had much to do with the outcome.'

Zukor grunted, leaned back in the seat and closed his eyes as if in deep thought. They had bypassed Annapolis and were in sight of Chesapeake Bay when it dawned on Ashton that Nathan Zukor was asleep.

★　★　★

Hayes came to, the sun playing on his face through a gap in the drawn curtains. He felt like death warmed up, his head splitting, the sour taste of vomit on his tongue. Beside him the blonde girl was snoring. What the hell was her name? Marlene? No, Arlene, that was it, a cute little Southern girl blessed with a ferocious appetite for sex who knew more tricks than your average hooker back home. With her mouth wide open, lipstick smeared and blotchy complexion she didn't much resemble the show-stopper of yesterday evening, but she was still the best thing to have happened to him since coming to Louisville.

Inside a week Hayes had done the tourist bit — Churchill Downs, home of the Kentucky Derby, the sternwheelers on the Ohio River, Cherokee, Seneca and Iroquois Parks. Inside a week the Blue Grass State had lost most of its attraction for him. Tending bar at Mickey's was not his idea of making a living. The hours were long, the pay was nothing to write home about and he couldn't understand what half the clientele were saying. San Francisco was where he wanted to be, he'd heard good things about the city and knew he would feel at home there. It was the place Provos on the run from extradition hearings in Dublin instinctively made for, and just as soon as he had enough for the air fare he would be joining them. At least that had been his intention until yesterday.

Late on Sunday afternoon, Wesley, one of the stable hands at Churchill Downs who lodged at the same rooming house, had asked him if he would like to make up a foursome.

'They're good-looking broads,' Wesley had told him. 'One's a blonde, the other a brunette. Yours is the blonde, her name is Arlene.'

Hayes had taken a lot of persuading. The only blind date he'd ever been out with had been a real dog. To his delight Arlene didn't belong in that category. She was fairly tall, had shoulder-length hair, and a size 36 bust which didn't need a bra to support it, a flat stomach, child-bearing hips, a well-shaped, firm butt and legs that were definitely worth a second glance.

Arlene was also very friendly; Hayes had discovered that at a roadside diner when he'd sat next to her in a corner booth. He had tentatively pressed his leg against hers and instead of moving her limb out of the way, she had done the same only a lot firmer. By the time they'd finished eating, his right hand had been resting comfortably on her left thigh. After dining they had returned to the city and had taken in two, maybe three, bars, including one down by the river where things had got a lot more intimate in the dim lighting on a dance floor little bigger than a tablecloth. Even with the mother and father of a hangover, Hayes found himself getting a hard on as he recalled how she had rubbed herself against him when he had run his hands up and down Arlene's spine before swooping to cup her buttocks briefly.

'Oh Jesus,' he groaned aloud, and rolled over onto his back.

'Whaaa?' Arlene mumbled in a sleepy voice.

'Nothing.'

A hand found its way into his boxer shorts, the fingers curling round his member. 'Doesn't feel like nothing to me,' she said, and began to arouse him still further.

Some men he knew of fantasised about having it off with an oversexed woman who couldn't get enough of it but Arlene was the first genuine nymphomaniac he'd met. She had been all over him when they'd left the riverside bar, and Wesley's girl hadn't been exactly frigid. He seemed to recall it was she who had suggested they find somewhere nice and quiet. They had crossed the river and headed north on Interstate 65 and between thirty and forty minutes later had checked into the Baytree, a rundown motel in the middle of nowhere. Because they'd arrived a few minutes after midnight without any luggage, the manager had refused to accept Wesley's credit card and they'd had to pay cash in advance, which had cleaned Hayes out.

'My, oh my, you are getting impatient,' Arlene giggled. 'Guess I'll have to do something about that. Huh?'

Teeth gritted, Hayes sucked in his stomach and made a supreme effort to delay the inevitable orgasm as she first straddled, then mounted him. He failed lamentably to hold himself back and climaxed in seconds.

'Goddamit,' Arlene yelled at him. 'What the hell's the matter with you?'

Hayes pushed her off, rolled out of bed and went into the bathroom. He ran the cold water tap, rinsed his face and looked at his reflection in the mirror above the wash basin. 'You look rough,' he told himself, then froze.

The muffler on Wesley's '89 Plymouth Acclaim was blowing and there was no mistaking the deep-throated snarl of its 2.5 litre engine. He ran back through the bedroom, out into the hall and wrenched the door open in time to see the dark blue Chrysler turn right in front of the manager's office. Wearing nothing but his boxer shorts, Hayes tore after the car, screaming abuse at Wesley and the brunette sitting next to him. He caught one last glimpse of the car as Wesley made a right on Interstate 65 and headed back to Louisville.

No money, no transport, nine o'clock in the

morning and no idea how he was going to get to work on time. Hayes ran back to the cabin, told Arlene to get off her backside and put some fucking clothes on. He dressed on the run, pulling on a pair of socks, not caring that they were inside out. He stepped into a pair of Levi's while shoving his feet into brown loafers. He zipped up the pants before tucking in the shirt tail and was still buttoning up the shirt as he jogged towards the manager's office where more trouble was waiting for him than he could possibly handle.

The night manager was bleeding profusely from a nasty-looking gash above the right eye, a wound inflicted by a Coca-Cola can which Wesley's girlfriend had hurled at him when he'd caught them trying to break into his cash drawer. They had managed to make their getaway but everything was against Hayes doing the same. The night manager had recovered sufficiently to arm himself with a 12-gauge repeating shotgun and was quite prepared to blow Hayes in two if he so much as blinked an eyelid.

In response to the night manager's 911 call, two officers from the highway patrol arrived fifteen minutes later. From then on things went from bad to worse. It transpired that Arlene wouldn't be seventeen until 25 November and he had transported a minor across the state line for the purpose of having sex with her, which he learned was a federal crime. He would automatically be charged with statutory rape and was probably looking at fifteen to twenty in a federal penitentiary.

As if he had a built in alarm clock Nathan Zukor woke as they turned onto a narrow track which led to the safe house just outside Bryantown. Except for the chimney breast the house, including the roof tiles, was made of timber. The green shutters and white exterior looked as though they could do with a fresh lick of paint but the salt air from Chesapeake Bay undoubtedly had weathered the paint more quickly than if the house had been sited elsewhere. Going by the number of air-conditioning units he could see from the outside, Ashton reckoned there were five rooms upstairs at the front and one less downstairs. The whole two-acre plot was enclosed by a post-and-rail fence that wouldn't keep a dog out. There were no security guards in evidence and no electronic sentinels that Ashton could see. It seemed to him that too much reliance was being placed on the signboard by the entrance which indicated the house belonged to the Marine Ecology Research Establishment.

'What do you think of the place, Peter?' Zukor asked.

'Back home estate agents would describe it as a desirable property ideally suited as a small hotel.'

The interior presented a very different picture. The boiler room and basement had been converted into a cell, interrogation room and a recording centre. The cell was furnished on Spartan lines — a single folding flat steel bed, horsehair mattress, three blankets, a canvas chair and a table of sorts. The toilet was an Elsan hidden by a curtain, the washing facilities consisted of a bowl and pitcher of water. There were no windows anywhere. The interrogation room was only marginally less intimidating. The recording centre, however, was comfortably furnished, more spacious and, amongst other items, was equipped with a two-way mirror.

'We're going for the carrot and stick routine,' Zukor informed him. 'Any time we get the impression that Trilisser is playing games with us he ends up in the cell. Right now it's pretty cool in there but we can raise the temperature until it becomes damn nearly unbearable.'

'Throw in a little sensory deprivation and it should remind Trilisser of times past,' Ashton said drily.

Zukor gave him a funny sideways look, then announced it was time they got started, and led Ashton back to the recording centre, where a stenographer, sound engineer and a cameraman were waiting. A few minutes later in response to a summons over the intercom, the primary interrogation team and Pavel Trilisser appeared in the interrogation room and sat down round a small oval table.

The team leader said, 'Let's talk about twelve million dollars you stole from the Kremlin domestic budget.'

'Only twelve?' Trilisser shook his head as if perplexed. 'Some people in Moscow claim it was fifteen million.'

'We'll stick with twelve, Comrade General.'

'Whatever pleases you.' Trilisser looked into

the two-way mirror and waggled his fingers as if to say hello.

'He can't see us,' Zukor said angrily.

'You're right,' Ashton told him quietly, 'but he knows he is being watched.'

23

The primary interrogation team was getting nowhere with Pavel Trillisser. For over two hours now they had questioned him with the utmost hostility without affecting his composure in the slightest. He had readily conceded that there had been a shortfall of at least twelve million dollars in the Kremlin domestic budget and had agreed there was an account in his name with the Trust and Fidelity Bank of the Grand Bahamas. Furthermore, he had volunteered the information that Vladislav Kochelev, the government auditor, had produced a bank statement showing his deposit account to be 2,091,000 dollars in credit as at Monday, 1 January.

The account had been opened by the Mafiozniki, probably at the instigation of General of the Airborne Forces Nikolay Voronov, who had been determined to undermine Trilisser's standing with President Yeltsin.

It was an allegation Trilisser made time and time again, much to the open disbelief of his interrogators.

'Understand this,' he said, gazing at the two-way mirror, 'if you cannot accept this explanation you will not believe anything I tell you and it is pointless to continue.'

'Did you hear that?' Zukor demanded. 'The nerve of the guy.'

'He's a cool one, all right,' Ashton said.

'Yeah? Well, I guess it's time we rattled his cage. How good is your Russian these days? I mean how long is it since you were on the Russian Desk?'

'Four years, but I've kept my language skills up to speed. I made a point of reading a Russian newspaper or magazine every day.'

That routine had been broken when he and Harriet had been relocated in Lichfield with a new identity. He had discontinued the practice on the advice of MI5. 'You'll only draw attention to yourself,' Neagle had warned. 'It's a small cathedral city and word would soon get around if you order a Russian periodical from the local newsagent.' However, it wasn't necessary for Zukor to know that especially when he was as fluent as anyone on the primary team. In any case the American was now in full spate, telling him exactly how he intended to play it.

'I'll go ahead and make the switch. Soon as you see the primary team leave, you make your entrance and bring the house down.'

'And then what?'

'You carry the ball and I back your play.'

'Right.'

'Good. Let's do it then.'

Zukor left the recording centre and walked down the false passageway that had been constructed when the boiler room and basement had been converted. A few moments later he appeared in the adjoining room and told his people to take a break.

'That doesn't include you, Comrade General,' he added as Trilisser started to get up. 'There's somebody I'd like you to meet.'

'And who might that be?'

'Me,' Ashton said, and walked into the room.

Two years ago in Warsaw when Ashton had accosted him on the steps of the Opera House, Trilisser had visibly flinched; this time round he didn't even bat an eyelid.

'Ah, the redoubtable Mr Ashton. Do I take it you are back in favour with The Firm?' Trilisser twisted round to face Nathan Zukor. 'Are you aware that our friend here was once put out to grass by the SIS? He was considered a security risk by his own service so they shunted him off to the Security Vetting and Technical Services Division where he couldn't do much harm. His people thought he had become a little too friendly with one of our lieutenant colonels in the Military Intelligence.'

Zukor didn't like what he was hearing. He was doing his best to appear unfazed but the steely glint in his eyes betrayed him. It also warned Ashton he would have a lot of explaining to do when Trilisser wasn't present.

'Nice try, Comrade General,' Ashton said.

'Try? What are you saying?'

'When outnumbered turn your enemies on one another. It's the oldest trick in the book. Now tell us how you are going to make Carl Bucholtz famous?'

'That was just to get his attention. It is the Director of the CIA who will become famous, Mr Ashton, because he will give President Clinton the day, date and exact time of Yeltsin's death.'

'And when might that be?' he asked.

'You wouldn't believe me if I told you.'

'Now there's an age-old excuse.'

'No, I was stating a simple truth. Your inquisitors virtually laughed in my face when I tried to explain what had really happened to the twelve million dollars. If they've already made up their minds about that minor issue I would be battering my head against a brick wall if I attempted to tell you why Boris Yeltsin will be murdered.'

'You think you're the only person banging his head?' Zukor snarled. 'Jesus Christ, all we've been getting from you is a load of malarky. What we want is a few verifiable facts.'

'You carry the ball and I'll back your play.' Famous last words from Zukor.

'Can we start again from the beginning?' Ashton suggested quietly, and captured the attention of both men. 'For instance, who was responsible for the Kremlin domestic budget?'

'I was,' Trilisser said. 'At least I was required to authorise any expenditure in excess of fifty thousand dollars. However, any such authorisation also had to be countersigned by the Secretary of the Inner Cabinet.'

'How many withdrawals were made to account for the missing twelve million?'

'Seventeen, all for varying amounts ranging from 107,000 to 1.86 million dollars. This was done to make it appear that I had tried to disguise the fraud. Had the money been taken in equal amounts the withdrawals would have caught the eye of even the most incompetent auditor.'

'You didn't sign those withdrawals blind, did you?'

'I didn't sign any of them.'

'Any idea who did?'

'The KGB wasn't short of forgers in my day.' Trilisser smiled. 'I doubt they have all been made redundant since then.'

'Leaving aside the deposit with the Trust and Fidelity Bank, where did the rest of the twelve million go?'

'I'm alleged to have speculated on futures and the like. But I don't have to tell you the kind of people who can afford a seat on the Russian Commodities and Raw Materials Exchange, do I?'

Ashton shook his head. When the exchange had been set up on the old Central Post Office a seat had cost 60,000 roubles. Eighteen months later they had been changing hands at 4.4 million, which at the rate of exchange then being offered amounted to 44,000 pounds, or 67,761 dollars. It wasn't too long before all trading on the exchange was conducted in US dollars. According to the commercial attaché at the British Embassy, seats were now changing hands at a cool three-quarters of a million. Not surprisingly most brokers were fronting for the Mafiozniki.

'Certificates were produced to show that I had invested unwisely and had lost over nine million dollars.'

'And all this was done at the instigation of

General of the Airborne Forces Nikolay Voronov?'

'Yes.'

'Why?'

'In the spring of '95 Voronov approached me with a grandiose plan to restore the prestige of the armed forces and bring all the independent states back into the fold. I told him Yeltsin would never countenance such a harebrained policy and Voronov said he appreciated that and the President would have to go.'

Trilisser had been left in no doubt that the word 'go' had been a euphemism for liquidated. He had come to this conclusion because more than once Yeltsin had demonstrated he could really rally the masses to his side with his powers of oratory and therefore he had to be silenced. Consequently Trilisser had told Voronov he was implacably opposed to the idea and had warned the Deputy Minister for Defence he would report him if he took the matter any further.

'The withdrawals from the domestic budget started a fortnight after my conversation with Voronov.'

'Why the sudden loyalty to President Yeltsin?'

'I admit that in '93 I was prepared to overthrow Yeltsin by force of arms; then I realised that the majority of combat units in Moscow Military District would remain loyal to the President.'

'So you switched sides?'

'You know I did, Mr Ashton. And before you ask I did order the execution of my second in command, Vaseli Petrovich Urzhumov and for your information he was also the Head of the Counter-Intelligence Department of the Russian Intelligence Service.'

'Would I be right in thinking Urzhumov was the man who advised you which units would remain loyal to Boris Yeltsin?'

'You would indeed. Despite knowing the odds were stacked against us, Urzhumov had been implacable in his resolve to proceed with the operation to seize the TV stations, the police headquarters and the offices of the major newspapers no matter what the cost.'

Trilisser maintained if he hadn't acted first, his second in command would have killed him. He wanted both men to know he was, above all else, a patriot.

'I was against Gorbachev initially because for all his fine talk he destroyed the economy. Before he came to power everybody had a job and the rouble was worth one pound sterling; after he took over we had unemployment on a horrendous scale, the rouble went through the floor and pensioners were reduced to begging on the streets of Moscow. I changed sides because I soon realised the ministers organising the coup were a bunch of clowns and the whole business would be an unmitigated disaster. I also had a high regard for Boris Yeltsin and believed he would get the people out on the streets demonstrating against the old regime. Finally I could not see today's soldiers firing on their fellow Russians.'

'What has General of the Airborne Forces Voronov got against President Yeltsin?'

'Everything. As President he has failed to solve the economic ills which beset the country.'

But more significantly the General held Yeltsin entirely responsible for the low morale and breakdown of discipline in the armed forces. The soldiers, seamen and airmen hadn't been paid for months, and officers as well as enlisted men were reduced to selling items of equipment to put food on the table for their families. Routine checks and maintenance were not being carried out on military aircraft, vehicles were being cannibalised for spare parts and the Northern Fleet was a shadow of its former self.

'Half the Delta class nuclear-powered ballistic missile submarines and all but one of the Oscar Cruise missile subs have had to be decommissioned for lack of money. Murmansk is full of rusting hulks leaking radioactive waste. Does that answer your question, Mr Ashton?'

'Yes.'

'Good.' Trilisser pushed his shirtcuff back and looked pointedly at his wristwatch before turning to Zukor. 'It's gone three o'clock,' he said. 'What happened to lunch?'

'We're going to take it right now, Comrade General.'

Ashton thought it was an odd time to call a halt when Trilisser was just beginning to open up but it was Nathan's party and he was calling the play. After leaving Trilisser to his own devices, Zukor stopped by the recording centre to brief the leader of the back-up team, who had been observing and listening to the interrogation next door, then led Ashton to the dining room upstairs.

'The choice is limited but the food is good,' he said, and chose a table by the window. 'So is the view.'

'Looks idyllic,' Ashton said.

'That's Eastern Bay you can see over there.'

'Right.'

'Something bothering you, Peter?'

'I was just wondering why Pavel Trilisser wasn't surprised to see me. Two years ago when I accosted him in Warsaw he practically jumped out of his skin.'

'Yeah? Well, I guess he's aware of your reputation and had mentally prepared himself for a possible encounter.'

'My reputation?'

'You are supposed to know Pavel Trilisser better than anyone else,' Zukor told him enigmatically.

★ ★ ★

The Old Chophouse restaurant was on the corner of Exmouth Market and Rosoman Street in Clerkenwell, which was a little off the beaten track for Robin Urquhart. He had booked the table for 8 p.m. to give himself enough time to go home and change into something less formal before meeting Jill Sheridan for dinner. Life had suddenly become more complicated since last Thursday when his solicitor had informed him that Rosalind was cross-petitioning for divorce on the grounds of his adultery with Mrs Jill Clayburn and others. For a mere eighteen months Clayburn had been Jill's married name; once divorced she had reverted to Sheridan. Had Rosalind known this Urquhart was sure she would have instructed her solicitor accordingly when cross-petitioning. The fact that she had also accused him of committing acts of adultery with other women suggested Roz had possibly hired a private investigator to dig the dirt on him. He and Jill had always been discreet; now they were becoming positively secretive. This evening he had left his poky flat in West Hampstead and caught a Jubilee Line train to Baker Street where he had alighted. Exiting from the station he had hailed a passing taxi and told the cab driver to drop him off at the Lansdowne. Five minutes after arriving at the club he left and caught another cab in Berkeley Square. It was all ridiculously cloak and dagger but Jill was determined to defend her reputation, even though they had frequently shared the same bed.

Urquhart arrived at the Old Chophouse five minutes before the appointed time and was shown to a table at the back of the crowded restaurant near the kitchen. It was a woman's prerogative to be late and for all her talk about the equality of the sexes punctuality was an unfamiliar word with Jill. She finally arrived at eight-fifteen just as Urquhart was about to order a second gin and tonic. She was wearing a sleeveless dark blue silk dress and open-toed sandals and looked marvellous.

'I haven't kept you waiting, have I?' she asked.

'Absolutely not,' he lied. 'What'll you have to drink?'

'A glass of white wine with the meal would be nice.'

'No aperitif?'

'I drove here,' she said, and flashed him a smile before consulting the menu. 'I fancy lobster thermidor,' she murmured presently.

Urquhart told the hovering waiter he would have the same and ordered a bottle of Chablis to go with it.

For some time now, in fact ever since he had filed for divorce, Urquhart had had a worrisome feeling that Jill was doing her level best to distance herself from him. He wanted to challenge Jill about their relationship and hear her deny anything was wrong but lacked the nerve to do so. At the back of his mind was the ugly thought that she knew there was nothing he could do to ease her into Hazelwood's chair when he retired, and Jill had decided he was of no further use to her.

'We had a cable from the Ambassador in Washington this afternoon concerning Ashton,' he said, avoiding the personal issue.

'I bet Delacombe was behind it,' Jill said contemptuously.

'Well, yes, as a matter of fact he was.'

'Let me guess, he's unhappy about having Peter as his number two. Right?'

'So is the Ambassador.'

'Only because that creep Delacombe put him up to it.'

'Ashton comes with a reputation,' Urquhart said patiently.

'If you mean he's not a lap dog, Robin, then yes, he does have an attitude. Also you should bear in mind that Delacombe wants yet another twelve months' extension in post and will do anything to get it.'

'And you should bear in mind that this country got off on the wrong foot with President Clinton. We had too many people who were too eager to see Bush re-elected and were busy trying to dig up something the Republican Party could use to dish the dirt on Clinton. Everybody has worked hard since then to restore the special relationship, particularly Miles Delacombe.'

'Oh, spare me that drivel,' Jill said, raising her voice sufficiently for the people at the next table to hear.

'Not so loud,' Urquhart murmured.

'Then stop making me angry and understand this: Delacombe will go at his appointed time and Peter will be the next Head of Station.'

'I don't think so. Mark my words, Jill, Clinton will win this election by a landslide and will be in the White House for another four years. That's why the FCO will veto Ashton's appointment.'

'You don't know Victor Hazelwood. He won't take any notice of the FCO. He wants Peter in Washington and that's all there is to it.'

'You won't hear Victor shouting the odds. We're gradually bringing him to heel and I'm not referring to the offer of a knighthood.'

'Rubbish.'

'You're closing your eyes to the facts, Jill. If

you don't believe me, look at all the diplomats who have been seconded to the SIS this year.'

'Peter deserves this break.'

Urquhart blinked. There was no mistaking the passion and intensity in her voice. 'My God, you are still in love with him, aren't you?'

'Don't be so bloody stupid,' Jill said, and stood up.

'Where are you going?'

'Home.'

Urquhart leaned across the table and seized her wrists. 'Please don't leave,' he murmured.

'Let go of me.'

Her voice wasn't loud but it carried and diners at the nearest table stopped talking. Like a ripple on a pond after a stone had been cast into the water, the silence spread outwards. Urquhart was suddenly aware that all eyes were on him as Jill stalked out of the restaurant. At that moment he wished the ground would open up and swallow him.

★ ★ ★

As Ashton recalled their conversation over lunch, he was sure in his own mind that Zukor had told him he would get another crack at Pavel Trilisser before the day was over, but either he had been mistaken or the American had changed his mind. They had spent the whole afternoon listening to the back-up team in action. The line they were taking was entirely different from what had gone before. They had wanted to know where Trilisser had been born, whether he had

405

any siblings, what his parents had done to earn their livelihood and so on. Then towards the evening Zukor had suggested they allowed the others to get on with the job while they went for a stroll round the yard. They had almost reached the shore before the American let him know what was on his mind.

'What did you make of Trilisser this morning?' he asked out of the blue. 'How much of what he told you did you believe?'

'Something approaching fifty per cent,' Ashton said. 'To the best of my knowledge today was the first time he's ever admitted siding with the hard-line Communists against Gorbachev, then with the Nationalists against Yeltsin. His reasons for changing sides were, however, bogus. The plain fact is he could see the people he was backing were going to lose and he didn't want to go down with them.'

'What about the business with his second in command in '93? I mean the guy admitted having Urzhumov executed.'

'He had to put his hand up,' Ashton said tersely. 'I was present when Urzhumov was murdered. I was damned lucky to come out of it alive.'

Zukor halted at the edge of the shore and stood there gazing out across the bay, hands thrust deep into the pockets of his slacks. 'You know what bothers me, Peter?' he said presently. 'Why is it I had to learn the SIS had put you out to grass from Pavel Trilisser?'

'That's a question you should address to your Director. Walter Maryck, your Station Chief in

London, is aware of my background.'

'Walter Maryck!' Zukor snorted. 'He's been in London so long now he and his wife are more Brit than the Brits. He needs to remember which country pays his goddamned salary.'

Ashton knew there was no substance to the allegation. Hazelwood had told him many times that nobody he'd met looked after his country's interests with the same vigour as Maryck did. Telling Zukor that wouldn't alter his opinion of Maryck and might even reinforce it.

'Is there anything else I should know about you?' Zukor asked.

'I spent seventy-eight days in solitary confinement at Moscow's Lefortovo Prison.'

'I'm not a happy man.'

'Neither am I,' Ashton told him. 'If you feel I'm a security risk then say so and I'm out of here. Waiting for me back home there's a lady any man would die for, a two-year-old son and a baby daughter. So go ahead and mark my cards, you'll be doing me a favour.'

Zukor didn't take him up on the offer. Next thing Ashton knew he was talking about finding him accommodation in Annapolis to save time going to and fro.

24

Routine administration problems and career appointments were never raised at morning prayers. These subjects were dealt with separately on a one-to-one basis between the Director or Deputy DG and the department head concerned, who was invariably Roy Kelso. Whenever possible Hazelwood preferred to leave the resolution of domestic issues to Jill Sheridan. On this occasion she needed to consult Hazelwood first before dealing with what she regarded as a small housekeeping problem.

'I wouldn't normally bother you with this,' she told Hazelwood, 'but the issue first raised its ugly head when I was dining with Robin Urquhart on Monday evening. For some reason he informed me the FCO had just received a cable from their man in Washington . . . '

'Concerning Peter Ashton,' Hazelwood said, finishing the sentence for her.

'Then you already know the Permanent Under Secretary of State and Head of the Diplomatic Service is going to veto his appointment?'

'Veto? That word hasn't been used in my presence.'

The Joint Intelligence Committee comprising the chiefs of the SIS, MI5, GCHQ Cheltenham and the Defence Intelligence Staff met under the chairmanship of the Cabinet secretary every Tuesday morning. After the meeting was over, the chairman had taken Hazelwood aside to express his disquiet concerning the future employment of Ashton.

'I was merely invited to think again.'

'That's as good as a veto,' Jill told him.

'Did Robin actually say the PUS was going to put the chop on it?'

'Not in so many words but who else can it have been? Knowing Robin as I do, he wouldn't make such a statement unless he had it on good authority.'

'I'll take your word for it.'

'So are you going to think again, Victor?'

'I already have. I told the Cabinet Secretary I wasn't prepared to change my mind. Delacombe has to go. He may be very good on the cocktail circuit but that is not what he is there for.'

A Head of Station needed to have his ear to the ground to know what was going on, a rule of thumb which applied in equal measure when the host country was a friendly power. If it hadn't been for 252 Communications and Security Group up in Leicestershire several weeks could have elapsed before they learned of Trilisser's defection.

'I went on to say why Ashton was the best man for the job and he didn't make any objections.'

'I'd still be careful if I were you,' Jill said.

Hazelwood eyed her thoughtfully. Jill wasn't in the habit of offering advice gratuitously. 'You'd better tell me what other dire warnings Robin uttered.'

'You're not going to like it.'

'I promise I won't shoot the messenger.'

'Well, OK. I told Robin that you wouldn't take any notice of a FCO veto and he said I wouldn't hear you shouting the odds because they were gradually bringing you to heel. In evidence of this contention he invited me to look at the number of diplomats who have been seconded to the SIS in the last year.'

There had been only two. The FCO man who had been with them the longest was Dennis Eberhardie, the brilliant linguist who, for a brief period, had been in charge of the Russian Desk. He had come to them from New York where he had been one of the UK's permanent representatives at the United Nations. The most recent arrival was Winston Reid, who didn't strike Hazelwood as the sort of man who would try to hobble him.

'Eberhardie is out of the reckoning,' Hazelwood said, voicing his thoughts. 'He's in Moscow.'

'One less to keep your eye on,' Jill observed.

'So what's the small housekeeping problem?'

'The CIA has moved Ashton into a rather upmarket B & B in Annapolis to cut down the amount of time he would spend travelling from Alexandria to the interrogation centre.'

'Seems only sensible.'

'The room rate, which includes a full American breakfast, is a hundred and twenty-five pounds per diem.'

'I presume that's not unreasonable?'

'Delacombe thinks it is; wants Roy Kelso to reimburse his contingency fund if he foots the bill. Same applies to the claims for substance allowance which Ashton is bound to submit.'

'Delacombe pays,' Hazelwood growled, 'and he doesn't get reimbursed. Ask Roy Kelso to get a signal off to that effect.'

'Right.'

'Incidentally, when did Ashton move into the B & B?'

'Tuesday afternoon. Apparently Delacombe only heard about the move yesterday and fired off a commercial cable.'

'Are we talking Cable and Wireless?'

'I'm afraid so. However, Miles didn't mention Ashton by name and the cable was graded confidential, though in the commercial world this doesn't afford the same degree of security protection as we know it. The cable was addressed to EXPO London, PO Box 936.'

The head office of EXPO London was on the second floor of 188 Dover Street off Piccadilly. It was a front organisation for the SIS which had rendered valuable service during the Cold War. Basically EXPO London existed to provide administrative support for those businessmen who traded in the more hazardous regions of the world and were prepared to do their bit for Queen and Country.

Administrative support ranged from financial assistance, including the provision of displays for trade fairs, to circumventing export restrictions imposed by the Department of Trade and Industry. These days EXPO was a shadow of its former self and was only concerned with supporting those firms which traded in the Middle East, Asia, and the Pacific Basin.

However, despite the reduced activity, there was no reason to suppose cables addressed to the Dover Street box number were not routinely captured by the Russian Signal Intercept Service. How much attention was paid to them was anybody's guess but Hazelwood had a nasty suspicion that in this instance, the country of origin coupled with Trilisser's alleged defection might well make the Russians sit up and take notice.

'Why the hell did Delacombe send a cable instead of using the diplomatic bag?'

'Perhaps he wanted to raise the issue with Roy Kelso as soon as possible and was reluctant to send it over the crypt-protected satellite link?' Jill shrugged. 'Who knows, Victor.'

'Have you got any more good news for me?' Hazelwood asked wearily.

'I've had to submit a change-of-circumstance report to Brian Thomas.'

'What another?' The question was out of his mouth before he knew it. Jill had submitted one when she had separated from Henry Clayburn and petitioned for divorce.

'Yes, another,' Jill said testily. 'Rosalind Urquhart has cross-petitioned on the grounds of Robin's adultery and has cited me as the co-respondent. And before you ask, there is no chance of an amicable settlement. Rosalind is motivated by revenge and has hired a private investigator to dig up the dirt on us. It's going to be a very messy business.'

Jill expected to see her picture in all the newspapers and Rosalind would undoubtedly

412

corner the market in sympathy. There would probably be photographs of the house in Bisham Gardens and the press would rake over the rumours concerning Henry Clayburn, her ex.

'So you see it's pretty bloody.' Jill got to her feet and moved towards the communicating door. 'If I lose my security clearances I'll have to resign, won't I?'

'It may not come to that.'

'Let's hope you're right,' she said despondently.

But they both knew that even if she retained her security vetting status, Jill could forget about being the first woman to head the SIS. For the first time ever Hazelwood almost felt sorry for her.

* * *

Ashton left the B & B on Duke of Gloucester Street, collected the rented Ford Probe from the parking garage and made his way across town to pick up Route 50. Thirty-five minutes later he arrived at the interrogation centre near Bryantown to find Nathan Zukor waiting for him under the porch.

'You've got Trilisser all to yourself this morning,' the American told him as he got out of the car. 'What's more, the primary team has softened him up for you.'

By softened up Zukor meant Trilisser had been questioned right through the night until 6 a.m. He had then been allowed to rest for exactly one hour before they'd hauled him out of bed. When breakfast was served to him Trilisser had vented his anger by hurling the tray and everything on it at the duty watchman.

'Naturally, he's now under restraint.'

'You mean he's handcuffed?'

'He surely is. Also he's wearing irons.'

'I bet he's a happy man,' Ashton said.

'You disapprove?' Zukor asked.

'It's your show.'

'Damn right it is and I tell you this, from here on Trilisser knows what will happen to him if he persists in feeding us with total crap. Kept insisting that General of the Airborne Forces Nikolay Voronov is an incompetent drunk, which doesn't gel with Trilisser's earlier claim that he is the man who got the Mafiozniki to open an account in his name with the Trust and Fidelity Bank. Then he tells us it's Sholokhov, the Finance Minister and President of the Union Bank of Moscow who siphoned off the money.'

'So what angle would you like me to cover, Nathan?'

'Take him through his story . . . ' Zukor broke off as a helicopter flew low overhead. 'Heading for the Naval Experimental Station south of Browns Woods,' he mused as the noise abated. 'Anyway, I'd like to hear what Trilisser has got to say for himself from the time he was placed under house arrest. OK?'

'Yes. I'll get started, shall I?'

'No time like the present, Peter,' Zukor said breezily.

Trilisser looked unkempt. When he'd hurled the breakfast tray at the duty watchman he'd somehow managed to spill most of the coffee pot down his shirt front. His wrists were locked into handcuffs which were attached to a broad leather belt around his waist. His legs were effectively hobbled by a short length of chain between the irons fastened around the ankles. Unable to walk properly Trilisser shuffled into the interview room. In a cold angry voice, he informed Ashton he was not prepared to answer any question until the handcuffs and leg irons were removed. Furthermore he insisted on changing into a clean shirt.

'You can make all the demands you like,' Ashton said, 'but the Americans won't take any notice of me unless I can give them a few hard facts instead of all this garbage you've been dishing up. So let's start with the date you were put under house arrest back in February.'

Trilisser told him to go to hell and said over and over for ninety minutes that unless the restraints were removed Ashton could go fuck himself. He also invited him to sodomise his father, mother and, of course, Harriet, his whore of a wife who could probably bend over and touch her toes better than anyone else in England. Then suddenly Trilisser changed his tune.

'February the fifth,' he said.

'What?'

'The day I was placed under house arrest, Monday the fifth.'

'Which means Vladislav Kochelev must have finished his audit before that?'

'Obviously.'

'And the trial date was originally set for Wednesday the twenty-seventh of March?'

'Correct.'

'We've got a photograph of you taken outside the Park Kultury Metro station the day before the trial was scheduled to begin. Would you like to explain why you were released from house arrest and under whose authority?'

'You are, of course, alluding to the date shown on the *International Herald Tribune*?'

'Are you saying the newspaper wasn't available on the twenty-sixth?'

'Yes. The *International Herald Tribune* is always a day old when it goes on sale in Moscow.' Trilisser smiled. 'You've no need to look so worried, Mr Ashton. The trial had already been rescheduled for July the twenty-second and I was still under house arrest. I was, in fact, released by Major General Gurov in his capacity as Moscow's Chief of Police.'

What followed was even more fantastic. On Gurov's instructions he had positioned himself by the newspaper kiosk outside the Metro station where he had been photographed by a police officer. Copies of the photo had then been sent to Sholokhov, Nikolay Voronov and the Ministers of Economic Development, State Security, and Foreign Affairs.

'It was Gurov's way of letting them know their plan was going to come unstuck.'

'The negative and one copy was sold to our Head of Station for a thousand pounds.'

'Clearly the police officer who took the photos is a budding entrepreneur. Or maybe he was simply acting on behalf of Major General Gurov?'

'Let's try another name. Have you heard of Katya Malinovskaya?'

Trilisser wagged an admonishing finger at Ashton. 'No more questions,' he said, 'not until these restrictions are removed and I've changed my shirt.'

'I don't think you've earned that privilege, Comrade General.'

'Then you will get nothing more from me.'

'That's too bad,' Ashton said, and left him to think it over.

Zukor was in a buoyant mood when Ashton walked into the recording centre and was loud in his praise for the way he'd handled Trilisser. 'You were definitely in control,' Zukor told him.

'Not all the time, Nathan. I fixed the date Trilisser was photographed outside the Metro station from the *International Herald Tribune*, which was a mistake he was quick to exploit.'

'But he also pointed out the date was immaterial as the trial had already been rescheduled for late July. Correct?'

'Yes. Trilisser was being honest up to a point because he wanted me to believe the big lie when he pitched it.'

'And has he?'

'Not yet, but he has told a few small ones.'

'Such as?'

'Gurov didn't release him from house arrest. For over twenty weeks he paid Katya Malinovskaya to keep the star witness for the prosecution alive. There are things I want to ask

Trilisser about the ambush in which Kochelev was killed. And about Gurov, especially why he suddenly abandoned Katya Malinovskaya.'

'I'm afraid these questions will have to wait, Peter.'

Zukor, it transpired, had other priorities. The Intelligence Liaison Officer responsible for briefing the White House had intimated that what the President wanted was the lowdown on the Voronov plan for the reunification of Georgia, Kazakhstan, the Baltic States and the Ukraine with Russia, and exactly how the conspirators proposed to oust Boris Yeltsin from power.

'Once we've got the big picture, you can sharpen your claws on Trilisser again.'

'And in the meantime?' Ashton asked.

'You revert to being an observer,' Zukor told him blandly.

* * *

It had been a quiet weekend. The Asian, Pacific Basin and the Rest of the World departments had nothing of significance to report, and try as he might to conjure up something of substance, Rowan Garfield of the European Department had to admit the situation in Bosnia, though grave, hadn't altered since Friday. The only man who had anything to impart was Winston Reid, the newly appointed Head of the Mid East Department.

'We have an eye-witness report that Ilya Sholokhov arrived in Tunis on Friday — '

'This is the same Sholokhov who is Finance Minister and President of the Union Bank?' Garfield asked, interrupting him.

'Yes. He was in Jedda the day before and was scheduled to visit Oman, Kuwait and the United Arab Emirates in what is seen as a fund-raising tour of the Organisation of Petroleum Exporting Countries. Tunisia, of course, is not a member of OPEC. Yassir Arafat was also in Tunis at the time and we have it on good authority he met Sholokhov briefly before the latter departed for Sousse, approximately sixty miles south-southeast of Tunis.'

'To do what?' Hazelwood demanded.

'Well, that is where our source is not a hundred per cent reliable. But for what it's worth, our informant claims the Finance Minister met Talib bin Kaliffa, one of the leading lights of Hezbollah.'

Hazelwood considered the possible implications for a moment or so, then asked Jill and Reid to stay behind before dismissing the others. As the last man out of the conference room closed the door after him, he began to ask Reid for chapter and verse.

'Just how good is your information? I mean to what extent can we take it as gospel?'

'Sholokhov definitely arrived in Tunis on Friday afternoon and had an audience with the President of Tunisia at which Arafat was present. We know he departed for Sousse on Saturday morning with a police escort because our Second Secretary, who is Head of Station, followed his vehicle at a discreet distance.'

Reid was pretty sure Talib bin Kaliffa was in Sousse at the time because GCHQ had picked up a CIA tracking report. That Sholokhov had met the terrorist leader was pure speculation.

'Both men were in the right place at the right time.' Reid smiled apologetically. 'That's all one can say.'

'I think we ought to advise Ashton of these developments,' Hazelwood said, and looked at the other two as if seeking their agreement.

'What for?' Jill asked.

'Because the Middle East is Washington's oyster. Destroy America's influence and Russia takes over as the peacemaker for the region. Right, Winston?'

Reid nodded. 'I also indicated that the Kremlin might be in a position to control over eighty per cent of the world's oil reserves.'

'And in answer to my question, you said, in effect, that a major terrorist incident might eventually lead to the destruction of American influence.'

'I'll get a signal off to Ashton.'

'Good.' Hazelwood pushed back his chair and stood up. 'Tell him further details will arrive in the diplomatic bag.'

* * *

The diplomatic bag which was of special interest to the senior intelligence officer, arrived on Aeroflot flight 6631 on Monday, 12 August and was delivered by the foreign service courier to the Russian Embassy on 16th Street at 15.01

hours. The package addressed to the SIO was roughly the size of an A4 envelope and contained five glossy black-and-white photographs of the same man and woman in various attitudes. The pictures had been taken six years ago from the roof of the Hotel Polkovskaya which overlooked Victory Square in what was then the city of Leningrad.

The woman was Lydia Petrovskaya, divorced wife of air force colonel Sergei Vasilevich Kutuzov. Their daughter was Galina Kutuzova, a Starshii lieutenant in the Glavno Razvedyvatel-noe Upravlenie, the military intelligence arm of the Red Army. A close confidante of the Commander of 6 Guards Tank Army, she had defected and gone over to the Americans knowing far too much about TRIPWIRE, the nuclear minefield to be laid in East Germany before the Red Army withdrew.

The man had approached the monument in Victory Square from Moskovskiy Prospekt and walked past the statues of a steel worker and Red Army man before descending to the open ampitheatre where Lydia Petrovskaya was waiting for him. The next three exposures had been taken as they slowly walked on past the bronze figures of Leningrad's defenders — the aviator in goggles and leather coat, the sailor from the Baltic Fleet waving a PPSh sub-machine-gun above his head, the factory guards and the women who had dug the anti-tank ditches around the city. The fifth and last photo had caught them when they were right out in the open opposite the Hotel Polkovskaya. In accordance with the instructions she had received Lydia Petrovskaya had removed the man's sunglasses which concealed a black eye and then stepped back a pace as if to inspect the damage. The man was in his early thirties, was 1.81 metres tall, and weighed approximately 77 kilos. He had dark hair and blue-grey eyes. His name was Peter Ashton.

The SIO could have done with a more up-to-date likeness but that would have meant approaching the head of the Special Investigation Department whose loyalty to President Yeltsin was paramount. In any event he believed Ashton's features wouldn't have changed much six years on. He placed all five photos in a white envelope and enclosed a brief note asking the recipient to confirm that this was the man currently residing at the B & B on Duke of Gloucester Street. In answering the query the recipient was instructed to follow established procedures when contacting the SIO. After addressing the envelope to V. J. Jacob, School of Creative Writing, care of Box 1310, Baltimore Md, he sent for his personal secretary to dispatch the letter by the Express Delivery Company.

25

At the height of the Cold War the KGB's chief of station would appear on the embassy staff list as the ambassador's chauffeur or as the holder of some other minor post. To maintain this deception the officer concerned would actually perform the duties required of the incumbent. It was therefore not unusual for an ambassador to be chauffeured around the town by a man who was in fact his superior officer. In the intelligence world little had changed with the coming of Gorbachev and Yeltsin. In the Washington diplomatic list the SIO appeared as the second secretary (cultural exchange) while the embassy security officer who lived in the same apartment house on Connecticut Avenue, masqueraded as a third secretary (consular affairs). Both men were obsessive about personal security. Every morning, before he even released the central locking on the Chevrolet Cavalier, the SIO inspected the car to see if any of the strands of cotton he'd placed externally from the frame across the door sill had been disturbed. If any had been dislodged he immediately sent for the Embassy Security Officer who then swept the interior of the Chevrolet to make sure it hadn't been bugged during the night. The SIO was equally careful with his digital mobile which he kept on his person at all times, except when attending an official social function. On these occasions he locked the phone in the office safe. So far as A T & T was concerned, the mobile belonged to Mrs Nechiporenko, wife of the First Secretary (Commerce) to whom the phone bill was sent.

That morning the phone rang just as the SIO was leaving the underground garage. When he answered it, the caller identified himself as V. J. Jacob, School of Creative Writing.

'I thought you'd like to know I've just received the photographs,' he told him. 'They arrived by Express Delivery a few minutes ago.'

'I was hoping you'd get them last night V. J.'

'Well, you can rest easy, I've had a quick look at them and they fit the bill.'

'No ifs and buts?'

'Never had any use for them.'

'So when are you planning to deal with the problem?'

'Today — unless the pattern changes.'

The SIO didn't care for the provision but only a fool would rule out the unexpected and he said as much to Jacob before he signed off. If the two men didn't take their usual afternoon stroll along the shore, Jacob and the removal man would have to look for an alternative location.

Jacob was an old hand and wouldn't be fazed by a last-minute hitch. He was an illegal who had spent the last eighteen years in America living a lie. The removal man was also KGB-trained but he was a native-born American and these days his loyalty couldn't be taken for granted. If there was an unforeseen problem he might suddenly develop cold feet. It was also a fact that he hadn't done a 'wet job' since 1984 and the SIO

424

wondered if his marksmanship had deteriorated in the meantime. The SIO dismissed this disturbing thought from his mind and concentrated on driving through rush-hour traffic to the Russian Embassy.

* * *

A pattern of sorts had been established. Every morning after a hurried breakfast Ashton left the B & B at six-fifty-five, collected the Ford from the parking garage and reported to Nathan Zukor thirty-five minutes later. On arrival he was allocated a two-hour head-to-head slot with Pavel Trilisser at some time in the morning or afternoon. The one period that had become constant over the last four days was Trilisser's insistence on a fifteen-minute break at four o'clock in order to stretch his legs. He had also asked for Ashton to keep him company, a request which Zukor had originally granted to satisfy his own curiosity. Ashton had tried to point out that they were allowing themselves to be manipulated but Nathan had become less and less inclined to listen to him. The reason was simple enough; from the first day onwards Trilisser had fed Ashton with some piece of information which complemented the story he was giving the primary and back-up teams.

It was a different story when they were head to head in the interrogation room. It had taken Ashton over an hour to get Trilisser to admit he'd even heard of Katya Malinovskaya. 'I'm not familiar with the name,' he'd said, even though with the coming of perestroika she had been chosen to represent the more acceptable face of the KGB's Second Chief Directorate. It was only after Ashton had pointed out that Katya Malinovskaya's photograph had appeared in the Western press that Trilisser had snapped his fingers and blithely stated he now recalled the name. He could not, however, even begin to guess why Major General Gurov had suddenly abandoned her. 'You should put that question to Moscow's Chief of Police,' he'd said over and over again.

Ashton turned into the narrow track which led to the safe house, swept on past the signboards which indicated the property belonged to the Marine Ecology Research Establishment and parked the Ford Probe in the space that had been allocated to him. As usual Nathan Zukor was waiting for him under the porch. Today, instead of a friendly smile from the American, he met with a frosty reception.

'You want to tell me why I have to learn about Barry Hayes from the FBI?' he asked in a voice harsh with suppressed fury.

'Because I didn't know Five were going to alert the FBI that Hayes was in Chicago.'

'That's not good enough. I should have been told that you had been targeted by the IRA. Your presence here poses an unacceptable threat to all of us.'

'In the first place we are talking about Continuity IRA, a breakaway faction which is opposed to the truce and is therefore not exactly top of the pops with Sinn Fein and the Provos.

Secondly, Barry Hayes was the leader of an exceptionally small cell and was pursuing a vendetta against me because I had killed his younger brother in self-defence. He sent his cousin, George Foley, to finish the job he couldn't do and got him killed in the process. Barry Hayes is a runner; he fled Northern Ireland when things got too hot for him, then high-tailed it out of London in the nick of time, only to find that Eire was equally inhospitable. Barry Hayes doesn't know I'm in America and even if he did, he won't come after me again.'

'You're right, he won't. Hayes is under arrest for statutory rape. He was already in custody when the FBI caught up with him.' Zukor plucked an envelope from his shirt pocket and gave it to Ashton. 'This arrived for you by the special dispatch service in the early hours this morning.'

Ashton opened the envelope, extracted the signal and read it quickly. 'Sholokhov's been busy,' he said laconically, and gave Zukor the Top Secret message to read.

'Are you proposing to confront Pavel Trilisser with this, Peter?'

'Not immediately, but I'd like to hear what he makes of it.'

'So what's your initial thrust going to be?'

'I want to tackle Trilisser about the ambush and what happened thereafter.'

'A little prejudice is no bad thing,' Zukor observed. 'But you've really got it in for this guy. You haven't accepted a damned thing he's disclosed.'

'That's not true,' Ashton told him wearily. 'I believe a lot of the stuff Trilisser has given us is kosher but he's been turning the facts around to make himself look good. My instincts tell me he is here to throw dust in our eyes.'

'Then you'd better go ahead and prove it. Starting now.'

★ ★ ★

In the intelligence game it was rarely possible to dot every i and cross every t, and the account opened on 26 June in the name of Simon Carmichael with the Grey Street branch of Lloyds Bank, Newcastle upon Tyne was no exception. All the branch manager could tell Special Branch was that the account had been opened with a certified banker's draft for the equivalent of eighteen hundred pounds drawn on the Commertz Bank, Munster, Westphalia. When shown photographs of George Foley and Donald Simon, the branch manager had been adamant that neither bore any resemblance to the Simon Carmichael who had opened the account. Unfortunately he was unable to describe the real account holder other than in the most general terms.

Donald Simon had volunteered the information that he had received a cheque book and gold service card for Simon Carmichael through the post. There had been four counterfoils showing withdrawals made out to cash for amounts varying from twenty-five to sixty pounds. The remaining twenty-one blank cheques had already been signed by Carmichael so that presenting one to Harvey Littlewood as a deposit on 84 Rylett Close had been easy. The whole business had come unstuck because nobody had told Donald Simon there was only eighteen hundred in the account. Unhappily for Richard Neagle, Simon had destroyed the cheque book after he had finished with it and a possible line of inquiry had been lost. No cheque book, no latent prints which might have identified the man who had opened the account.

As Neagle saw it, the really worrying aspect was the certified draft issued by the Commertz Bank in Munster. It had all the hallmarks of a secret fund operated by an active service unit of the IRA based in Europe. If such a unit had gone across to Continuity IRA then they were definitely in trouble. It was the kind of alarming prognosis the politicians and the Home Office didn't want to hear and he decided to keep it to himself until such time as the truce collapsed.

*   *   *

If verbal fencing ever became an Olympic sport Ashton knew who would walk away with the gold. When faced with a difficult question Pavel Trilisser simply parried it and counter-attacked.

'You want to know who ambushed Katya Malinovskaya and her companions? Well, it has to be the Mafiozniki, who else could it have been, Mr Ashton? You ask me who was behind it? That also should have occurred to you. Did I not tell you General of the Airborne Forces Nikolay Voronov got the Mafiozniki to open an account for me with the Trust and Fidelity Bank of the Grand Bahamas? Why do you suppose the Finance Minister detailed Vladislav Kochelev to audit the Kremlin domestic budget? He knew the man was incapable of seeing anything unless it was right under his nose. But the lawyers at the Public Prosecutor's office weren't happy with his findings, that's why the trial was postponed the first time.'

'As I have told you over and over again, Mr Ashton, I do not know why Major General Gurov abandoned Katya Malinovskaya after protecting her for just over five months. Maybe Voronov discovered he was aiding her and threatened to kill his wife and daughter, which persuaded Gurov to tell him everything. I am only guessing you understand?'

'You tell me Sholokhov has been in Saudi Arabia and was scheduled to go on to the United Arab Emirates and Kuwait but diverted to Tunis where he met Arafat. Naturally I believe what you are saying but I'm in no position to comment. I imagine President Yeltsin wanted a large interest-free loan to help the ailing economy and Sholokhov was sent round the member states of OPEC with a begging bowl. It's possible the Saudis informed Sholokhov that they would be more favourably disposed towards his request if the Russian Government was more supportive of the Palestinian cause. I'm sorry, Mr Ashton, but that's the only explanation I can think of.'

It had been the worst session Ashton had had with Pavel Trilisser. He had been outmanoeuvred at every turn and his credibility with Zukor had been further undermined. A nagging suspicion that the American resented his presence had been more or less confirmed for him when Carl Bucholtz had dropped by his B & B on Sunday evening. With a little subtle prompting, Ashton learned that he had been wished on Zukor who was under pressure to deliver a result a.s.a.p.

Although Ashton had had enough of Trilisser for one day, the fifteen-minute stroll along the shore was mandatory and there was no getting out of it. In a grim mood he led the Russian towards the sea.

'I enjoy this time of day,' Trilisser observed. 'And your company.'

'Better make the most of it; I'm going home a week tomorrow.'

'I'm sorry to hear that.'

'I know somebody who won't be.'

'Ah yes, Mr Nathan Zukor.' Trilisser smiled. 'He's a good man but inclined to be a little volatile, wouldn't you say?'

'It's no good, Comrade General, he can't hear you. I'm not wired for sound.'

'I do not understand.'

'Yes you do, you've been playing us off against each other ever since I arrived.'

They were down by the shore now and as usual they turned left and headed in the general direction of the Naval Experimental Station. Two men were fishing from a launch about three hundred feet out and somewhere in the distance

431

to their rear, Ashton could hear the blat blat of a helicopter flying low.

'Always there is a noise,' Trilisser complained, then seized Ashton by his right arm and turned him to face the bay. 'Look up there,' he said, and pointed to the helicopter. 'Why is he flying so low?'

One of the men had stopped fishing and had gone aft to start the outboard, then the other man laid his rod aside as the helmsman made a hundred and eighty degree turn and closed on the beach. Trilisser was still trying to get Ashton to look up at the Bell helicopter and in the same instant Ashton knew he was being set up. It was a game two could play. Wrenching his arm free, he swung Trilisser into the line of fire and threw himself flat.

The helicopter was directly above them, the rotors acting as a noise suppresser so that Ashton never heard the burst of gunfire that put Trilisser face down in the grass in an ever-widening pool of blood. Still hugging the ground he heard the helmsman open the throttle and raised his head in time to see the launch hit some underwater obstacle and somersault into the air. When it landed the impact was such that the launch broke up in pieces and sank. A few seconds later the fuel lying on the surface ignited with a hollow whoomf. Then Zukor and most of the back-up team came running.

'Jesus, oh Jesus,' Zukor yelled. 'They've killed the poor bastard.'

'I don't think they meant to,' Ashton told him.

'What are you saying?'

432

'There are two dead men out there in the water. I think we should recover their bodies, then we might be one step further along the road to discovering who they meant to kill.'

'You haven't changed your mind about Trilisser a bit even now,' Zukor said in what sounded like an accusation.

'No I haven't.'

'Jesus, Ashton, you never give up, do you?'

'No I don't,' Ashton told him. 'It's one of my failings.'

26

Hazelwood read the summary of conclusions which Jill had sidelined in his absence yesterday and then transferred the FBI's interim report to his pending tray. The forty-page document told him little more about the incident at Bryantown than he'd already learned from the cables Ashton had submitted through Head of Station, Washington. Although the two bodies recovered from the sea had been disfigured by extensive burns to the head, trunk and limbs, Forensic had managed to obtain the minimum number of fingerprints from both men to be sure of a positive identification. To date, the Bureau had failed to match them with any they had on file. They had had only marginally better luck with the artist's impression of the two deceased. Ray Wilmot, the helicopter pilot who'd overflown the safe house prior to and on the day of the murder, had come forward and had identified one of the killers as William H. Goldman of 1641 Fort McHenry Avenue, Baltimore Md. Subsequent enquiries had revealed that if there was a William H. Goldman, he wasn't known at that address.

Wilmot had been unable to shed any further light on the mystery man. All he knew was that on Monday, 5 August Goldman had walked into the shack which served as his office out at Rockdale Field northwest of Baltimore, and paid him a five-thousand-dollar retainer in cash. In return for this sum of money he was required to be at Goldman's beck and call up to 11.00 hours every day until further notice. If there had been no word from Goldman by that time, he was free to accept other charters. In addition to the retainer, Wilmot had received a thousand dollars for each flight he had undertaken. In practice this meant he had earned an extra seven thousand dollars. Except for the final day, Goldman had always accompanied him.

'I was given to understand he was a developer on the lookout for prime real estate,' Wilmot had told the FBI agents who were questioning him.

He had also expected the agents to believe that Goldman hadn't taken to the air with him on Tuesday, 13 August because he was meeting his principal backer. Asked to explain what he'd been required to do while this was happening, Wilmot maintained he had been instructed to orbit the Bryantown area keeping the launch under observation. When the meeting had been satisfactorily concluded, Goldman would wave Wilmot on to a pre-selected LZ between Annapolis and Arundel on the bay, where he was to wait for the developer and fly him back to Rockdale Field. He had also wanted the FBI to know he'd had no reason to distrust Goldman until that last fateful afternoon. Finally, Wilmot had waited twenty-four hours before reporting the incident because he had thought nobody would believe his story.

The FBI certainly didn't, neither did Hazel-wood. Although Wilmot had no previous convictions, he was known to have financial problems and the law-enforcement agency saw him as a man who wouldn't ask too many questions if there was a chance of making a fast buck. As far as the Bureau was concerned the Russian Intelligence Service had mounted the operation to assassinate Pavel Trilisser. What puzzled them was how the RIS had learned where he was being held and just who had put them on to Ray Wilmot. The CIA shared their curiosity, so did Hazelwood, but as of that moment he had more pressing matters to attend to. This was Wednesday, 21 August and Ashton was on his way home, his future employment in the aftermath of the Bryantown incident still uncertain.

What Hazelwood had in mind for him was eminently sensible though writing a justification to support an amendment to the establishment was Jill's forte. But right now when he needed her sure touch, she had been summoned to the Foreign and Commonwealth Office across the river to be officially reprimanded by the Head of the Diplomatic Service. He was about to ring his PA again to ask what had happened to Ms Sheridan when she walked into the room after tapping on the communicating door.

'You wanted to see me, Victor?' she said in a listless voice.

'First things first. How did the interview go?' he asked, and waved her to a chair.

Jill shrugged. 'The jury's still out.'

On Tuesday her picture had appeared in all the tabloids. The photographer had caught her outside the house in Bisham Gardens as she was getting out of the Porsche and was showing a lot of eye-catching leg. It had been the opening shot in Rosalind Urquhart's campaign to vilify Jill.

'You'll be all right,' Hazelwood told her. 'Nobody's going to demand your resignation.'

'If you say so.'

'I know so. The press think you are with the FO, which is a good thing. Furthermore, by this time tomorrow you will have won their sympathy vote. The newspapers are about to find out what a bitch Mrs Rosalind Urquhart really is.'

'I doubt if that will save my bacon.'

'Maybe not in itself but you have something much more important going for you. You're an icon, a role model for every woman in the SIS.'

'How do you know, Victor?'

'My PA told me and she's never wrong. Now let's get down to business.' Hazelwood opened the top right-hand drawer of his desk, took out a small-scale map which would not have looked out of place in a child's school atlas and handed it to Jill. 'I'm going to split the European Department in two and give the eastern half to Peter. Rowan is always complaining that his bailiwick is far too big.'

Jill glanced at the map. 'In other words, Peter will be responsible for what used to be the old Soviet Union?' she observed looking up.

'Yes. Naturally he will be moving up a peg or two.'

'To Assistant Director?' Jill asked incredulously.

'I think you'll find the FCO and the Treasury are amenable. All you have to do is write up the justification and it will go through on the nod.'

'So Miles Delacombe gets to stay on in Washington?'

'Well, Peter and Nathan Zukor didn't exactly hit it off and they are certainly at odds over the Trilisser business.'

'Isn't there more to it than that, Victor?'

'What do you mean?'

Jill pointed to the FBI's interim report. 'Peter has admitted that he swung Trilisser into the line of fire. Reading between the lines it seems to me the Americans suspect he may have told the RIS where Trilisser was being held.'

'That's ridiculous.'

'You and I may think so but look at it from their point of view. The CIA is aware that in 1993 Peter spent seventy-eight days in solitary confinement in Moscow's Lefortovo Prison. They may think that while he was incarcerated the Russians turned him around.'

'You seem to forget Hal Reindekke also did time in the Lefortovo.'

'But he is dead,' Jill said calmly. 'That's the difference.'

We do hope that you have enjoyed reading this large print book.

Did you know that all of our titles are available for purchase?

We publish a wide range of high quality large print books including:
Romances, Mysteries, Classics
General Fiction
Non Fiction and Westerns

Special interest titles available in large print are:
The Little Oxford Dictionary
Music Book
Song Book
Hymn Book
Service Book

Also available from us courtesy of Oxford University Press:
Young Readers' Dictionary
(large print edition)
Young Readers' Thesaurus
(large print edition)

For further information or a free brochure, please contact us at:
Ulverscroft Large Print Books Ltd.,
The Green, Bradgate Road, Anstey,
Leicester, LE7 7FU, England.
Tel: (00 44) 0116 236 4325
Fax: (00 44) 0116 234 0205

Other titles in the
Charnwood Library Series:

EATERS OF THE DEAD

Michael Crichton

In A.D. 922 Ibn Fadlan, the representative of
the ruler of Bagdad, City of Peace, crosses
the Caspian Sea and journeys up the valley of
the Volga on a mission to the King of
Saqaliba. Before he arrives, he meets with
Buliwyf, a powerful Viking chieftain who is
summoned by his besieged relatives to the
North. Buliwyf must return to Scandinavia
and save his countrymen and family from the
monsters of the mist . . .